Harvesting Legacy

Harvesting Legacy
A Farm's Journey

Michael S. Hutton-Woodland

Combray House

Cover design by Martha Helen Nelson

Further information:
www.combrayhousebooks.com

ISBN 978-1-958659-19-9

Dedication

This book is dedicated to the small family and collective farmers who know their land, love their land, farm their land, and attune to the elements of earth, air, fire, and water to bring forth food and sustenance for their families, their communities, their animals, and you and me.

This book is dedicated to the plants, trees, rivers and animals—the deer, fox, rabbit, coyote, squirrel, mole, and mice—that coexist with these farms in a natural ecosystem.

We are all related.

CHAPTER 1

Doug Stengel sat on the horns of a dilemma. In fact, he could almost feel those sharp points in his rear end. Fran would have called it a pickle, and shook her head sympathetically. On the one side–big money, and he walks away from the farm; on the other–*much* less money, and he can walk away feeling righteous. He's been a farmer, practicality steeped in his bones, so the big money seemed the obvious way to go. And yet, and yet, something pulled at the back of his mind, *"Don't you want to preserve this land like it's been for 6 generations for your family?"* He wished Fran were still around to talk this over.

The late afternoon sun slipped closer to the snow-covered hills on the far horizon. He gunned the engine of his pick-up and crested the low hill through the mud, coming to a stop at the top with the windshield facing the sun. Tim McGraw's *Gentle and Kin*d played on the radio. The western Massachusetts farmland mirrored this country song, with its admonitions based on rural, simple-life values. Doug surveyed two adjacent pastures, one with last year's old corn stalks poking dejectedly through the melting, dirty snowbanks, the other flat and furrowed with pools of water shimmering in the plowed tracks between the deep brown mud. Doug discerned the subtle lift and roll of the fields themselves. Rows of stones lay just outside the plowed fields, and through the leafless trees along the edge he could make out an old running stone wall in the woods, dating from the 1800s. Doug turned off the engine and sat in the cab of his pickup truck, the windows rolled halfway down, radio on, and surveying these fields. His fields. His feelings somehow encompassed all those years working this land, and music had always provided a soundtrack for his moods, his feelings, and his thinking. Right now Tim McGraw was reminding him, and anyone else listening, to *always* be humble and kind. A line came up, *"Visit grandpa every chance that you can (it won't be wasted time...)."* There were no grandkids anywhere who would be visiting him. That was part of the problem.

A vague disquiet crept over him, but, damn it! He'd done the best he could with his kids, and he didn't fault himself that neither child had decided to have children of their own. Nor did they want anything to do with the farm!

They were grown now; both in their 40s, and each one living his or her life. He wasn't particularly close with either one of them, but he was definitely closer to Audrey. She lived nearby, and they did talk and see each other every once in a while.

Ryan was a different story altogether. He lived in New York, and Doug and Ryan never talked.

Thinking of the two kids always reminded him of Mike. What a shitty deal to lose your oldest to war. Mike had enlisted because that was the kind of kid he'd been - upstanding, honorable. But a life cut short for seemingly no real reason. Mike would have wanted to continue the farm, inheriting it from his dad. Of this Doug was certain.

Doug 's eyes flicked as a red-tail hawk launched from the bare branches high up in a sugar maple on the edge of the field. The hawk climbed upward slightly, only to bank and dive like a rocket into the field. Decisive. After a moment of wrestling in the dirt, something dangled from its talons as it rose and headed back to the tree branch. A quick strike for dinner. Why wasn't he that decisive?

Doug's eyes again swept the land spread before him. You could count on the land. You could stand on it, dig into it, put seeds into it, water it, and crops would come forth. He took a deep breath. He had always come back to the land.

And his community. Wasn't there a time when you knew your neighbors, and relied on them as they did on you? The country music he loved mined that same vein of nostalgia and wistfulness when it sang about back porches, pickup trucks, religion, blue jeans, dirt roads, manual labor. And beer.

Doug, in fact, sipped one at that moment. He enjoyed that one IPA after a long day, and he had driven across his fields near the edge of the river, to take a moment for reflection and solace, and drink a beer. *Just that one*, Fran would say. *Then get your supper.*

He often heard Fran's voice, whispering encouragement to him in the silence of the night. He longed for all the ways a spouse helps you fill your time, and shape your life. How it's two lives together, and two hearts and two minds. How two bodies can intertwine in passion and in grace. She had been his rock and his wings. Life on a farm had been hard, and meaningful, and had been purposeful especially when she was around. When he'd come in dog tired from a day plowing, or haying, she'd help him see the beauty of the family through the love she showered over him. Sometimes it was a warm smile, sometimes a playful joke about how his hair was all awry from his cap or *could he have gotten any dirtier?* Fran had been the best of him, of them. He missed her so much. It had been almost 25 years already that she'd been gone.

A family of deer wandered out from the far hedgerow in the fading light. A doe and two fawns. They slowly moved through the darkening fields and nibbled on whatever little shoots of green were coming up. Doug had witnessed this scene so many times. How the deer knew that the tenderest shoots of grasses and weeds, so delectable for them, would begin to appear at this late winter time; that was a miracle of nature. Reassurance washed over Doug; the knowledge that life does go on. This scene was replayed all across the valley in farm fields near and far. Just as it had for thousands of years before now. His mind wandered, and he gently chuckled at himself; feelings changed minute by minute, didn't they? He sipped his beer.

The setting sun had brought out its fluorescent paint set now, and the western sky held clouds that were bright gold turning to flaming orange. The sky itself was a gentle blue, dark clouds in the foreground a bruised purple. Yes! life had a way of working things through. Even now, in his 80s, as he faced major life changes, he knew fretting about what was coming next was not that productive. He had learned that all that worrying when Fran got sick, and then sicker, had not helped nor changed the outcome. His worry about Ryan and Audrey, back when they were teens, had not changed the outcomes with their lives either. In his mind he referred to those times as his "troubles," because it had been years of squabbling with the kids, Mike dying, then Fran getting sick and then dying, and then the two kids were just gone. Lots of troubles. Doug gritted his teeth, swore, threw the empty beer bottle out the window, and vowed to trust that life would take care of him, the farm, and his kids, and help him through this next chapter. He shook his head and jumped out to fetch the empty bottle so as not to litter.

Hard farming labor wasn't something he could keep doing much longer; the deep aching in his lower back and the stiffness in his hands every morning on awakening spoke to that. His doctor also had him up for a series of tests, he wasn't even sure for what, but clearly something else was brewing inside this old body. He looked down at the letter from the Medical Practice he had dropped on the seat of the truck. Lots of words that said something that he didn't understand except it wasn't good. Pressure. Doug had to make a decision about the farm himself, and it was best to do it sooner rather than later.

Of course, his predicament as a farmer was mirrored throughout the valley, across the state, New England, the country, hell, probably the world. Old farmers looking to pass the baton only to find no one to whom to pass it. Farmers' children had so many more options in their lives; farming held less charm and was damn hard work. He loved the farm, no question, and had since he was a boy with his dad and grandpa jointly running the farm. He had the farm life in his bones, and this land in particular. He had known the hard times and the bounty. He had changed his crops when that seemed the most expedient for the markets. Thirty years ago he had shifted mostly away from tobacco, although he had one field still in that. Despite all the dangers from smoking everyone knew about, apparently the Cuban cigar makers still needed the big Connecticut Valley tobacco leaves for their stogies and they bought up whatever crop was still available. Raising the stinking weed and harvesting it in the old drying barn was something he still enjoyed.

Most of Doug's fellow farmers, and himself too, had gone over to corn and soybeans to ride the produce markets for what crops were most profitable. That might produce some profits in the short term–year by year–but he noticed the farmers were pretty stressed out about costs, and learning about the new crops themselves. Not to mention the way the ag companies come on with the various crop seeds and fertilizers and pest control chemicals. Doug spat out the window with the bitter taste of being beholden to the ag companies for his livelihood.

As the sun slipped down Doug felt the first wisps of breeze coming up. This time of the year it was pretty chilly, and sent a shiver through his frame. He turned on his truck and ran the heater for a few minutes. The dry heat from the vents first fought with, then conquered, the cool air from outside. He didn't close the window of the truck, though, enjoying the fresh smell of farmland. When the cabin of the truck was warm enough he shut the engine off again. The truck rattled to quiet. The music changed.

Doug chuckled as the next song came up. He recognized it right away, since it contained a line he thought referred pretty accurately to himself. The line rippled out: *"I know a guy that's got a lot to lose/He's a pretty nice fellow, kinda confused/He's got muscles in his head aint' never been used."* Miranda Lambert's take on this song was just plain wonderful. She had a gorgeous voice, and lots of swagger. John Prine had written the song, and he could turn a phrase, words dripping with irony and pathos all at once. Doug loved John Prine's songs and singing, and missed him. John had finally been claimed by the damn COVID-19 pandemic. Well, they were on the backside of that hopefully.

He had wondered if this lyric also fit "the Rhinestone Redneck." Wayne Bilodeaux had come here all the way from Atlanta, Georgia, and had set his sights on Doug's farm. He had great plans for development of properties outside the Southeast, and they seemed to come more and more into focus as he visited with Doug on Stengel's Farm. Doug wasn't moonstruck with Wayne, as he guessed many were, but he felt the power of Wayne's personality, as well as his vision. Each time Wayne had come to visit Doug, sometimes unannounced, he had started out with his *aw shucks* humble engagement, and became more and more enthralled with his own vision of what this land, this 300 acres could be. He would walk the fields with Doug, waving his arms wide trying to encompass the whole property in his expansive vision of residences, commerce, and leisure. But Doug sensed there was something more basic, more primal for Wayne in his recurring visits to the farm. Something else was calling to Wayne that perhaps he himself could not name or identify. Doug was curious to know.

There was the other side too. The other horn of that dilemma. In a few days, that fellow from Valley Conservation Land Trust was coming over to have another chat. Ben Miller was an earnest and intense man, dedicated to the idea that with an Agricultural Preservation Restriction grant from the state of Massachusetts, Doug could get money and they would keep his farmland just as it was, *in perpetuity.* Doug wondered about that. He loved the land, the farm. Part of him wanted it to stay just so, but *forever*? Didn't things have to change at some point? What was the purpose of holding on to something just to keep it the same?

Twilight was here, and in the deep indigo sky to the west Doug could make out a bright star–probably a planet, actually. It showed like a crystal in that gathering darkness. Venus, Doug thought. Chasing the sun westward, and still able to reflect light back at earth. Doug thought about chasing light, chasing the sun. It seemed like the whole world was doing that. Chasing something, anyway.

Just then through the gathering dusk Doug could see a small pack of coyotes slinking out of the woods on the right. Moving slowly, they had their sights on the mother deer and her two fawns. As the mother deer raised her head in concern, the coyotes broke out in a run, and fanned out. The deer turned away and started running away, but one of the fawns was not as fast to respond. While the doe zig-zagged away with one of the fawns, the coyotes quickly overcame the other and swarmed over it. It was over in less than a minute.

The sudden intrusion of wild nature brought Doug back from his musings. A metallic taste arose in his throat. He started the truck and, shaking himself off, headed back to the house. Life moved on.

CHAPTER 2

Brodi Saunders watched from her window seat as the ground arose toward the descending plane. Hartford looked gray, wet, and uninviting. The remaining snow piles were dirty brown and black. Everything out to the horizon looked bleak. Having left a sunny 70 degree day in Florida only hours earlier didn't make this dark mess any easier to accept. The juxtaposition of the two climates as bookends of her travels also reflected the polarity of working and being home.

Through the gathering dusk the streets and parking lots below the plane glistened in the steadily falling rain. The car lights and street lights reflected off the soaking pavement and accentuated the 32 degree temperature. Even the bare trees, raising their stark branches to the leaden winter sky, seemed to plead with whatever gods there were in heaven to take them away to Miami. Or Oahu. Enough already with the winter!

Brodi once more scanned the trip report she had been composing on her laptop, wanting to ensure she had all the details of the meetings accurate. All the numbers, timelines, and deliverables had to be precise for the team. Satisfied, she saved the document and snapped close the laptop and put it away in her bag. She couldn't wait to be home.

As Brodi gathered her briefcase and overnight bag, and shrugged into her suit coat, she was plenty tired and ready to get the hour-long drive north over with. She walked through the airport terminal, studying her fellow travelers. Airports were one of the great equalizers in American life. People needed to fly, wanted to fly, and apparently had enough money to buy their tickets, and so you saw all walks of life at the airport. That and the pent-up need to be on the move following the pandemic. Her eye casually glanced over the other road warriors like herself in various stages of shucking their work clothes as best they could. Loosened or removed ties, wrinkled suit coats and pants. Many women in painful high heels. In the terminal some were waiting for their flight home, and slumped in those seemingly-purposefully uncomfortable chairs in the waiting area, while those from her flight strode resolutely to the parking garage, or awaiting rides home, cell phones glued to their ears. She noticed the young parents with a toddler and an infant, perhaps heading to grandma and grandpa's house in Philadelphia, or a late flight to Orlando to visit the theme parks. A family conversed in rapid Spanish she couldn't understand, but clearly mama was not happy with papa relative to something he had done, or not done, while he tried ineffectively to corral their two children, running happily all around the waiting area, laughing. A young troubadour, his long dreadlocks inartfully hidden in a knit Rasta-striped cap, a scrawny beard tracing his chin and jaw, strummed on an acoustic guitar and warbled a Bob Marley tune. His voice yodeled a moderate tenor, and it traced the actual melody of the song. *Could you be Love?* Brodi knew it in its original. The young man, like others, a member of the flip-flop nation. A young woman with the man bobbed her head in rhythm to the music. Brodi smiled and trudged onward to the parking lot shuttle.

Brodi was in her mid-fifties, her short-cropped hair salt and pepper, but mostly salt. There were days she felt distinguished with her gray hair, and days she liked it because she had *earned* her gray hair, and days like today, when if she gave it a thought, she merely accepted it. Getting older. Oh well, I am way past 50, and my body is definitely changing, not the way I'd like it to, a little more weight, a little less firmness in the jawline, wrinkles everywhere. It was disconcerting. The days marched along, and the body changed of its own accord. She knew that she needed to start getting more exercise, and sleeping better. Sometimes she just didn't feel like she had the energy for it. Like tonight. As she climbed into her silver Honda Accord at the long-term car park, she was bone tired. But she sat up straight, and started the car. She texted Marion that she would be home in an hour, turned on NEPM, and listened to the Friday evening jazz show. Tonight it was a tribute to Lockjaw Davis, who would have been 100 years old this month. Brodi enjoyed jazz, as she enjoyed so many musical genres. And NEPM gave her a window into the musicians she loved, as well as those with whom she was unfamiliar. Eddie "Lockjaw" Davis was one of the latter. He had played with the greats of the 50s and 60s: Dizzy Gillespie, Sonny Stitt, Coleman Hawkins, Oscar Peterson. A gravelly tenor saxophone rolled into "Lover Come Back to Me," with Dizzy Gillespie, and it was a long rambling treat, and carried Brodi north to the Massachusetts line and almost to Springfield. She loved the way good musicians could play so seamlessly together, and the music flowed and soared. She had that experience of "coming to," as the song ended. She had been listening to every note it seemed, really following the leads through the song, the riffs, and breaks, but then here was Springfield and she couldn't recall the drive here. Had she crossed the bridge over the Connecticut River? Had she passed the strip mall with the huge Target store? Brodi couldn't honestly remember.

Her thoughts had been like that jazz improvisation, really. Her trip, her success with the manufacturer outside DC, meeting a new potential buyer, running into an old colleague, Joelle, at the airport, which took her mind back to her very brief stint with the health insurance company. You never knew when old acquaintances would show up in your life. Sometimes they brought back reminders of who you were, or what you were doing, or with whom you lived, loved or spent time. Sometimes joyous, sometimes painful. That job had shifted her life, which then ran a straight line to now. With Joelle the meeting had been pleasant. They had shared a few memories, laughed at life's strangeness, the incongruities, the crazies with whom they had to work. They caught up. Joelle was married, had two grown kids, was now a policy wonk with a large health system, and en route home to Atlanta. They both said "Let's stay in touch!" as they parted. Would they?

Finally back in Amherst, Brodi pulled into the driveway of their recently remodeled Cape. She so much enjoyed seeing the lights in the windows, and the comforting warmth she felt in coming home. The house was so beautiful now, and so well proportioned following the renovations of the family room addition and dormers. She felt a huge relief that another trip was finished.

"I'm home!" she called out to Marion, as she walked in from the garage to the kitchen. Edna, their Beagle puppy, came sliding at her feet, barking happily as Brodi set down her suitcase and briefcase.

"Hello, girl! How's mama's special girl?" she bent down and petted the dog's soft head, and Edna barked in joy. The dog made two or three quick turns around, her nails clicking on the kitchen floor tiles. Tail wagging furiously like a checkered flag at the car races. Another bark.

"You're home," said Marion, with a smile as she walked toward her, her arms raised for embrace. They hugged long and hard, and kissed each other gently, then more passionately. The dog danced around their feet, sometimes whining, barking, and bumping them at ankle height.

"I am so glad to be home," said Brodi. "Five days away! It is such a relief to walk through that door. How are you, babe?" She really took in her wife's appearance. Marion was already in her comfy clothes, a bulky lavender sweatshirt above turquoise sweatpants and her fleece house slippers. A mug of mint chamomile tea steamed in her cupped hands.

"I'm good! I am tired, but so happy to see you!" Marion smiled even more broadly, and Brodi could detect the tiredness around her eyes, dark and creased. Marion was shorter than Brodi, 5' 6" to her 5'10", and her naturally stocky figure bespoke her mental toughness. With her wiry, shoulder length salt and pepper hair, and open face, she was still as beautiful to Brodi as when they first met.

"How's your mom?"

Marion's smile faltered slightly, but then returned. "Let me hear about your trip first. How did it go? Did you sign the contract? Was Rhonda pleased?" Marion was an aikido adept at changing the subject, smoothly and effortlessly.

"It was great. Chelsea and her team loved my design! The financial officer was a bit of a pain; but Chelsea kind of talked over him and shut him up."

"You've spoken so highly of Chelsea from your earlier trips. She sounds like an ally!"

"Yea! You know I'm not even convinced that our developmental timeline expansion can be justified, but it's just a projection!"

"It's a long way off isn't it?"

"Yea. Anyway, Chelsea walked me around their plant with the team, showing off all their improvements. It's impressive. They're working to keep the "Made in America" approach going, since the Chinese can get their labor costs down so low. It's nearly impossible to compete, but with the new tax breaks it might work…Anyway, Chelsea said, "Let's move this ahead!" so I called Rhonda to let her know, and she's tickled pink…Oh! and I also floated the idea of the wearable wrist watch for Alzheimer's patients and Chelsea was very keen on that. She wants to drag Ted into our next meeting…" Brodi slowed her patter when she noticed that Marion was losing focus. Her face was slack, her eyes saddened. "Anyway, it was a good trip. So. Tell me about your mom."

Marion gave a tight-lipped smile, more an attempt at a smile. Her eyes rimmed tears, and her voice wavered. "Oh Brodi, I'm glad your trip was a success, but it's really getting worse with Mom, and I'm worried. You remember when we last went up and visited her? She was so lighthearted and chipper. But all that's changed!"

"Like how?"

"Remember we noticed a few times when she seemed forgetful – you know how we all laughed when she put her coffee in the fridge instead of getting out the milk. Well, she called me this morning to tell me that she completely melted a plastic leftover container in the microwave! It actually started to smolder before Mom realized it and shut it off. She said there's melted plastic now all over the inside of the microwave, and she called to ask if it was OK to use it again!" Marion shook her head in disbelief. "My God, Brodi! What if it had caught fire? She'd be dead! Oy, oy, oy!"

Marion started rubbing her forehead as she did when she was upset and struggling to figure out a solution.

"What can we do?" Brodi asked.

"Hug?" Marion's smile was half-smile, half-frown.

When Brodi curled her arms around her, Marion's whole body leaned against her. Brodi stroked her hair and murmured to her. Marion gave a sniff, stiffened, and backed away. She wiped away a tear.

"Thanks. I'm fine. But we have to DO something, Brodi. Sometimes Mom doesn't see anyone else for three or four days. If something happened no one would know! We have to get her to move down here, closer to us. Or she can move in here, into the spare bedroom; that will just become her room. She stays there every time she comes to visit anyway."

Brodi got very quiet, and just listened. Marion's mother was often still sharp as a tack, and pretty active for a woman her age. She had a ton of friends she had known for decades, many of them widows like herself, and they were all pretty interesting folks. Beth was proud of her independence. Since her husband, Jack's, passing four decades ago there was only an endless string of dogs; all of them rescue mutts, all of them neurotic. Fortunately, Beth was currently "between dogs." Brodi's stomach knotted at the thought of Beth moving in with them. The responsibility! The lack of privacy!

Marion continued, "We just can't leave her out there by herself. One of these days it'll be the stovetop that she leaves on, or she'll have forgotten to close the wood stove door when she goes to bed. Or she'll fall on the ice on her front step and no one will find her in time. It's just too dangerous for her on her own!" Marion was talking herself into a decision that Brodi knew from experience she would then begin to put into motion.

Brodi interjected, "What about your brother? Maybe he and Jessica can help? Don't you think they might have some ideas about this?"

Marion snorted. "Danny couldn't handle Mom! And Jessica puts up with her, but she doesn't like her, really. Mom would be miserable there, even though they only live a half hour away. No, Mom's going to come to Amherst. I guess the only question is whether it might need to be a nursing home." Marion sounded resolute. Brodi knew Marion's background - being raised in a rigid, strict household where there was a right way and a wrong way to do things, she had learned to be right, be strong, and anticipate various scenarios. She spoke with confidence and authority. *Sometimes wrong, but never in doubt* was how Brodi thought of the Mason home motto. Tears meant she had crossed that boundary with high stress.

Brodi stood behind Marion who was frowning into her reflection in the kitchen window, the bright and cheery kitchen lights making a halo framing her worn and set expression. Rain spattered against the dark panes, and rivulets cascaded down. Brodi could sense Marion's mind racing already with the planning for moving her mom down here, when that could take place, what needed to be done in the guest bedroom to accommodate her mother living down there, etc. Brodi struggled to catch up.

"Marion, I know you really worry about your mom, and I do too. She's slowing down, and she's not as sharp as she used to be. She forgets things, sure, but do you think it's necessary right now to upend her whole life? Can we go up there and assess the situation first?" Brodi paused, thinking: *What was the right thing to do? What if this was the right time to have Beth move down here? What would their life be like?* "Maybe we should head up there this weekend and check things out? We should talk to her."

Marion shrugged, "OK, let's go. But we'll see exactly what we know we are going to see. We'll go up there Sunday and we can start the conversation with her. But I feel like Mom needs to be here."

Brodi felt a surge of adrenaline, but she didn't say anything. She had been dog-tired coming home, but now she felt wide awake. She felt personally ill-equipped to make the decision, but maybe she was in some denial? Marion had been thinking about this by herself for hours, anticipating Brodi's arrival, and the idea had taken shape, with a good rationale and reason. It had taken on the air of something definite, firm.

Brodi was reminded of how she had felt when her own mother had gotten older and frailer. It had made sense for her to go live with Brodi's older sister, who lived in the same town. Brodi's sister had made the decision but hadn't really talked to Brodi. Brodi still had a vague resentment about that, but also some guilt. Maybe this was similar; have the mother go live with the one who could care for her. Brodi could see that this made sense. And just like that any misgivings she had faded into the wave of acceptance. Decision made, onto the implementation.

Brodi smiled at Marion, nodding her head. "So, can we head to bed, now? I've got to wrap my brain around the visit to Stengel's property tomorrow with Ben, and I'm bushed."

Marion replied, "Sure, but I wish you hadn't scheduled the farm visit for the morning after you returned."

Brodi raised her hands in surrender. "I know, I know. But Ben scheduled the meeting and I have to go along. He's as nervous as a tick in this negotiation with Doug Stengel. I can be a calming influence."

CHAPTER 3

Saturday dawned bright and sunny, with puddles in the backyard amidst the melting snow mounds. Ben Miller reached for the coffee pot as he watched his dogs frolicking outside, first one chasing the other, then at some canine-orchestrated moment, turning and being chased. Lots of snarling, growling and barking accompanied this adagio, but these two were the best of friends. Ben felt tremendous joy as he watched the two of them. Rusty and Frieda were actually brother and sister from the same litter, chocolate lab mixed with something or other. When Ben and the family had gone to get puppies, they had planned on getting one, but Frieda and Rusty had let them know they were inseparable.

"Coffee smells good," Ben's wife, Alice, came up behind him and slid her arms around his waist. She hugged him and looked around his broad shoulder to watch the dogs. She leaned into Ben's back, squeezed him harder, and he cradled her arms with his one free hand.

"How did you sleep?" Ben asked as he turned to face her. He smiled into her sapphire blue eyes, and gently stroked her hair.

"I heard Jeremy come in at some ungodly hour. He was trying to be quiet, but I heard every step on the stairs. It must have been 2:00 or 2:30."

"I didn't hear a thing. I was sleeping soundly all night." Ben took another sip of coffee, and turned to the stove. "Eggs?"

"Yes, perfect." Alice said. "Yeah, you're sleeping like a baby and your snoring keeps the rest of us up! You were restless in your sleep though."

"Yeah, I know you're probably right." He gave the top of his head a quick scratch.

He busied himself reaching into the fridge and pulling out eggs, cheese, mushrooms, peppers, and bread for toast. He found an onion in the cupboard under the counter.

"Remember I'm going out to the Stengel property this morning with Brodi. Just gentling him along in his thinking process," Ben was talking with his back to her. Alice watched the hunch of his shoulders in front of the stove.

"Is that what's been bothering you? Doug Stengel's uncertainty?" She asked.

As a volunteer lawyer on the board, Ben had been the Valley Conservation Land Trust lead on a number of these property negotiations. He had done this for a dozen years, as VLCT acquired properties around the valley to preserve open spaces. Something about this deal had always seemed tentative for some reason.

"Well, it's funny. Doug Stengel's family has owned that land for generations. They were one of the first families –"

"*White* families, Dad." Fifteen-year-old Sophia, entered the kitchen in her pajamas, her earbuds affixed to her ears.

"How can you hear with those things in your ears? Please take those out if you're joining the conversation!" Ben was annoyed, and he scratched the top of his head quickly in the same nervous gesture. "And yes, of course, one of the first *white* families in the valley. Good gracious!"

Alice enveloped a squirming Sophia and kissed her on the cheek. "Morning, Sunshine! How'd you sleep?" Alice smoothed Sophia's long chestnut hair with her hands.

"All good, Mom! Stop fussing!" Sophia kissed her mother, then glided away toward the fridge, gripping the airpods from her iPhone in her hand. She pulled the orange juice from the fridge, along with the seltzer bottle. She poured herself a generous glass of juice and soda, and took a deep drink.

Ben was familiar with this morning banter, and smiled into the egg pan. "You want some omelet, Sophia?"

"Gross," Sophia said, sticking out her tongue. "I'll have toast with peanut butter."

"It's always worth a try," chided Ben. "Anyway, as I was saying, the Stengels have been here since god was little; hard to imagine the Valley without their farm. The Trust, of course, would like to protect it. Stengel contacted VCLT, not the other way around, by the way."

Ben raised the pan and cut the omelet into two halves, and deftly slid them onto two plates. He fished pieces of whole wheat toast from the toaster oven and took the plates over to the breakfast table. He got the peanut butter, and a knife, which he placed in front of Sophia.

"Thanks, Dad." Sophia had by now put the earbuds back into her ears, and she was scanning the news headlines on her iPhone. Sophia had an actual interest in what was happening in the world. Often she knew about events or news before her parents did, the advantage of her tech-nology-mediated information source. Ben and Alice still largely relied on the *Daily Hampshire Recorder* for their first news of the day, such as it was. It was their local paper, which they appreciated, but sometimes what passed for news in the daily columns really caused Ben to chuckle.

"I am going to Zumba class with Elise this morning," Alice said. "You want to come, Sophia?"

"Um, s-u-u-re," Sophia replied. Her eyes were scanning the small screen before her. "Uh, what time?"

"10:30 at the Rec Center. There is a new instructor and she has great music."

"Cool beans. " Sophia's attention drifted back to her phone.

The dog door banged open and the two dogs raced into the kitchen, continuing to snarl and growl at each other, and proceeded to slam in the counter. They were wrestling and tumbling, and they were soaking wet. A smear of muddy brown water trailed across the cabinet.

"Knock it off!" yelled Ben, but the dogs ignored him. Teeth and wet fur flew around the kitchen, and they banged into the breakfast table leg. Coffee and orange juice slopped onto the table, and the hot sauce bottle fell over. "OK you two, back outside!" Ben grabbed their collars and led the dogs out the back door. He slid the dog door into its track to keep them outside.

As he walked back into the kitchen he was wiping his hands on his jeans.

"I think I'll take them with me this morning," Ben said. "They can run around out there, maybe work some of that energy out."

"They'd love that," said Alice.

"I wonder when Jeremy will show his face?" said Ben. "I'd like to see him before I head out. Haven't seen him in days!"

"He'll sleep forever if you don't wake him," replied Alice.

Jeremy and Sophia were completely different. Two years older, Jeremy was disinterested in world affairs (although he did have an opin-ion on almost everything), focused on playing guitar, had an interest in African culture and music, and needed to be pushed by his parents to do seemingly anything. He was happy to play music day and night, and his attention to the instrument was admirable, although at times it got in the way of other things. Like schoolwork, or chores, or a job, or social nice-ties. His acceptance into Oberlin College had been a relief to his parents, because it meant his music might take a more legitimized, serious track. The fact that Oberlin was in Ohio made them a bit wary, after all, it was pretty far away. Jeremy had always seemed most comfortable in Amherst and the Valley.

"Maybe I'll get him up and make him come with me," said Ben. "It would do him good to be outdoors for a while today."

"He'll hate every minute of it. Why torture him? And yourself, by the way," Alice added.

"While he is still at home, I still have hope to get him interested in something other than those six strings," Ben replied.

"Good luck with that," Sophia chimed in. Neither Ben nor Alice had thought she was listening. "Jeremy is like, totally, into his music. He gets respect when he's playing or jamming, and it helps him feel less *different*."

Ben's eyes narrowed at this. He knew Sophia was onto something with this.

She continued. "Have you been listening to the new music he's found? Some African guitarists who are pretty cool. You should listen to Vieux Farka Toure sometime --- really good."

Sophia stuck up for her brother. It wasn't that Sophia's observations were unknown to her parents, since they both were observant and vigilant about Jeremy. It was validating; family ties meant for something.

At that moment, staggered footsteps drummed from the stairs and a loud yawn issued from the hallway. Jeremy appeared at the kitchen doorway, his tousled hair in disarray, and a wrinkled T shirt and skin tight black jeans a good indicator that he had slept in last night's clothes.

"Morning." He scratched his tummy through his T shirt, a hint of brown belly showing in the gap between his shirt and jeans.

"Hey, Jer! Good morning!" Ben wandered over and grabbed his son in a bearhug. "Grrr." He rocked him back and forth a few times before Jeremy broke away.

"Ug, Dad! I just got up. Those fuckin' dogs --- "

"Hey, watch your language, please!" Ben jumped in.

"Sorry. But they are making a racket outside my window. I think they got in the garbage again. It's like the Blue Man Group out there."

OK, I'll get them in and check out the damage." Ben turned and walked over to the back door, which he swung open as he yelled, "Rusty! Frieda! Get in here!"

The two dogs once again came bounding into the kitchen, one atop the other and headed straight for Jeremy. They both leapt up and banged into his chest.

"OOF! Hey get down!" Staggering back, Jeremy circled both dogs with his arms and wrestled them to the ground. "You two want to play, eh? I'll show you!" Jeremy pretended to growl and wrestle with the two dogs, and the noise level rose and they yipped and barked.

"Shh! Jeremy! Too loud!" Alice shouted, amidst a grin.

"Mornin' bro," said Sophia as she ferried her glass and plate past the writhing canine mass on the floor. "How was practice last night?"

"Cool," said Jeremy, amidst the dogs on the floor. "We tried some new songs. Antoine asked me about you, where you were and all."

"He's such a tool," said Sophia, a bit too quickly. "What was he doing there?"

"I think he came over thinking maybe you were going to be there. He was just hanging out, listening to us rehearse. He's like a groupie."

"Gross." Sophia said noncommittally. "He acts like a 12 year old. If he wants to hang out, he can just FaceTime or something."

"I'll let him know." Jeremy was rummaging through the cereal cupboard, in search of some breakfast. "Can I have some coffee?"

"Of course," Alice replied. "That's a fresh pot. Or maybe you want some tea? Your Dad made us an omelet, would you like one?"

"Uh, sure. But you're already done. Are you sure he'll want to make another one? Wait, no. Nevermind. I'll just eat cereal."

"It's OK, Jer. Your dad will be happy to make one for you." Alice put her arm around her son's spare shoulders. He was tall and lanky, and no amount of eating seemed to add mass to his frame. She molded his bony shoulders against her side. "And you could eat more."

She went to the back door, and pulling it open called out, "Chef Benjamin!" She made it sound French. "Monsieur Geramee desiree un omelet!"

"Mom! Your French is atrocious!" Sophia chided and rolled her eyes. "Take a class or something." Alice chuckled.

"Hey, Jer. Can I catch a ride with you to the library this afternoon? I have a huge paper for World Civ and I want to focus. I can't get anything done here."

"Sure." Jeremy replied. Ben had returned to the kitchen, grumbling about the recycling containers the dogs had strewn around the yard, and began washing the skillet in preparation for making Jeremy's eggs.

Jeremy moved aside, and stood next to his sister. Alice studied the two of them, then pulled out her iPhone to take a picture.

"Mom! My hair's not even brushed!"

"Put your arms around each other! Smile!"

Alice admired her two children, and what a contrast they presented. Tall and lanky, Jeremy's dark skin was in sharp contrast to his sister's Celtic rosy complexion.

Alice and Ben thought that Jeremy's birth parents were both from Mali, but the adoption agency hadn't actually met his birth father. His mother had been a young immigrant who was struggling to adjust to the US as a cook in a homeless shelter. Her husband, with whom she had come from Mali, had abandoned her shortly after gaining their citizenship papers, and she had then discovered she was pregnant. At the time, 17 years ago, Alice and Ben had been facing the fact that they couldn't conceive. They decided to adopt a child from another culture. That search had led them to work with the Lutheran Adoption Society, and thus they found Jeremy. They loved him deeply, and as sometimes happens, a year later they found themselves pregnant with Sophia. They tried not to think of Sophia as their miracle baby, but how then do you explain the sudden pregnancy? No matter; they were a happy family of four.

* * *

Ben pulled up in front of Brodi's house, the dogs dancing excitedly in the back of the car. Brodi and Marion emerged from the house almost immediately, and walked down the flagstone path to the car. As Brodi opened the car door, the dogs whined.

"Hey Ben! Hey you two," Brodi said, and threw them dog treats over the backs of the seats. She turned to kiss Marion on the cheek, "See you in a few hours, honey!" She climbed into the passenger seat and buckled in.

" You spoil them, Brodi," said Ben. "Hey Marion! How ya' doin?"

"I'm great," Marion said leaning onto the car, "But I wish you two hadn't scheduled this visit the morning after Brodi got home. I haven't seen her all week!"

Ben nodded. "Sorry, Marion! Appreciate you giving Brodi up so

soon after her arrival. With Doug Stengel I can never tell when he's going to want to talk with us, and for some reason this morning's the morning!"

"Ben, I know we have to get on it," said Brodi as they pulled out
of the driveway. "Marion said there was another piece in the paper.
Those developers from Georgia still have their eyes on it, and the paper
reported that the Town of Hadley was actually considering a hearing
about a proposal for the development."

"Yeah, I read that too. Seems that Stengel is working both sides.
He talks very positively about Valley Conservation Land Trust when
he's with us. He talks about how the land's been in his family for generations, how it's prime farmland, with some extensive woodlands, hab-
itat protection, blah, blah, blah. Then he goes and has a picture of himself walking the land with the Rhinestone Redneck and has it published
in the *Recorder*. I don't get his game."

"Rhinestone Redneck?" Brodi looked confused.

"Well, that's what some folks call him. Seems that his wife has
a penchant for huge diamonds that no one can believe are real, and of
course, he *is* from Georgia. Yes, it's a slam...Anyway, since you're joining the VCLT Board I want to get you involved in our property acquisition process with the biggest parcel that's come along in a decade!"

The car rounded a curve in the country road and opened a vista
across the valley to the far western hills. Both were quiet for a moment
as they took in the beautiful sight. The morning light swung in from
somewhere over their shoulders, glanced off tree trunks, painted the
fence posts golden, and glistened like jewels off the raindrops in the
branches. The distant hills rolled and undulated upward. A red-tailed
hawk drifted above the field, sunlight flashed off its tawny underbelly
against the blue sky.

"Oh my," Brodi said. The raptor moved across the landscape like
a dancer. The moment stretched on, the bird glided over the tops of trees
at the edge of the field, and out of sight.

"Beautiful! But can you imagine this field covered in a parking
lot and a strip mall?" Ben was the first to speak.

"Nope. And I can't imagine what would induce someone whose
family has been one of the first into the valley to want to sell off a huge
remaining farmland to a developer who planned just to pave and build.
Except the cash, of course."

Western Massachusetts could be gloriously vibrant, and each turn in the road revealed another exquisite rural scene as they drove out beyond town. Quaint New England farmhouses with wide front porches and classic red barns dotted the sweeping vistas. Most barns sported a tall silo with a rounded dome. The trees were just showing little red buds on their bare branches, and spring was around the corner. The retreating snow piles were giving way to sodden leaves and bare ground, muddy puddles, and here and there a hint of new green shoots.

"How's Marion doing?" Ben asked.

Brodi wiped her face with her hand.

"Marion's now pretty convinced that she has to move her mother out here. To live with us. The dementia is progressing."

"Whoa," replied Ben. "That's a big step."

"Yeah, Marion and I talked about that last night. Seems her Mom nearly accidentally burned the house down a few days back. It's not like I didn't know it would happen someday, but I didn't think it would be so soon."

"Marion's got to be worried sick about her mom. And she's a quick decision-maker."

"Yea, I know! I always take so long to decide! Anyway, Marion's right. For Beth's own sake she needs to be somewhere with other people."

"Brodi, listen, this will be a life changer for you and Marion. Her Mom's only going to need more care as time goes on. Are you sure *you* are ready for this?"

"Ben, it's Marion's mother. It's not like Marion and I haven't talked about this in the abstract before. But now it's time for action, before Beth hurts herself."

"But you've got a say in this, surely."

"Well, of course," Brodi replied, gazing out the window. "And sometimes when the person you love makes up their mind, you just support them."

Ben turned onto County Bridge Road, and drove between the adjacent fields along to where the road dipped into a wooded gully, emerging on the other side into more open farmland. The County didn't pave all the way through the farmland, which discouraged folks using this road in the winter and mud season. Brodi wondered if the County also secretly hoped that if the land was sold to the developer, then the developer would accept the responsibility to pave the road all the way to the development. An old classic turquoise Chevy pick-up truck was parked alongside the road. Ben parked, and they both got out into the chilly morning. The older man standing there looked at them appraisingly as they walked up. Tools and hardware lying about showed repairs in progress. The dogs bounded out of the rear car door as Ben opened it, and they ran like lightning in the direction of the creek. Ben supposed they could smell it. Doug's hunting dog sprinted after them.

"Morning," Doug stuck out his hand. "Good to see you. Glad you wore your muck boots!"

"Good to see you again, Doug. Taste of spring in the air this morning!" said Ben, while shaking his hand.

"Brodi Saunders," said Brodi, shaking Doug's hand in turn. "I'm new to the Valley Conservation Land Trust Board."

"Pleased to meet you. Glad you both could meet here on the far side of the property. I had to get this gate re-hung." He gestured to the pile of tools. "Shall we walk?" Doug picked up the tools, threw them in the back of his truck, and turned and led them along.

They spent the next three hours walking the vast tracts of Stengel's land. For Brodi's benefit he explained that his family had been in the area from when his great-great-great-something grandfather had moved a wagon north along the Connecticut River valley, finally coming to rest just past the Holyoke Range. Brodi could imagine that as those pioneers breached the mountains, the vastness of the Pioneer Valley flat flood plain would have stretched before them. Of course, it would have been mostly wooded at the time. Happy Valley, indeed.

Doug Stengel was an affable man, with a shock of white hair sticking out from under the bill of his Carhartt cap. The deep crow's feet in sun-reddened cheeks bespoke someone who had spent his days outdoors in the weather. He could easily move the banter from the history to a tidbit about how his grandfather had known when to sell off a particular plot or tract when the price was right. Doug had a breadth of knowledge about local history, politics, and even some gossip that made the stories richer in the telling. Through all of this, neither Brodi nor Ben could tell if Stengel had a preference for preserving the farmland he knew so well from living here his whole life, or whether he'd be happy to sell it off to retire with a handsome largess in his pocket, not caring if a developer devastated the whole expanse for cookie-cutter single family homes, condominiums, and a strip mall right here in the midst of what could be corn or tobacco fields.

"My daddy was the last one to plant tobacco extensively around here. The price of tobacco really plummeted after the Surgeon General's warning came out in the 70s, and so growing it became a whole lot less profitable. You still see a few fields that grow tobacco between here and the Hadley town center; mine's the one off Highway 47 over there." He gestured vaguely off to the west. "This land'll still grow just about anything, though. It's rich, fertile, and it drains well."

They looked across open undulating fields, stretching in each direction, now with a still patchy cover of snow that was trying to figure out if spring was actually coming or not. Rotten brown corn stalks stuck up through the snow, interspersed with the puddles from yesterday's rain. At the end of the field the trees stood with their bare branches outstretched, and beyond that the slate hills to the east in Pelham, and further away, to the west, the Berkshires. Dirty gray clouds moved in from the south, slowly overcoming a blue sky that had bravely lasted most of the morning. The gusts were chilly, and Ben and Brodi had donned knit hats against the cold wind. Another red-tailed hawk glided across the landscape, its eyes earthward as it searched for a field mouse or other rodent to appear, foolishly, against the open fields.

"So, Doug," ventured Ben. "I hear that you've spoken to some developers from out of state who are eager to sign you for some of this land."

"It's just talk," drawled Stengel, ambiguously. "You know, I've gotta stay open about all this. I can't say that I'm not swayed when someone's willing to offer millions for a few hundred acres of land."

Millions? Thought Ben. VCLT couldn't offer that kind of cash. The best they had was close to a million, with an Agricultural Preservation Restriction from the state of Massachusetts covering some additional funds. But no way would that raise VCLT's bid to *millions*.

They continued to walk, sometimes in silence. The three dogs raced ahead down to the river's edge. They strolled down an old tractor track, rutted in snow and ice still, and entered a woodland stretch along the river. The river slid past like a giant undulating snake, the surface shifting and changing as it flowed south. Occasionally a log or branch drifted past, brought down from somewhere upriver. This stretch of the river was still in shadow, the rising sun behind them still below the tree line. It was chilly in the shade, and Ben zipped up his fleece.

Doug continued. "It's hard to know what's the right thing to do. I love this valley, this river, these mountains and hills. Some say it was my great-great-great granddad who first coined the term Happy Valley, although Pioneer Valley was the official name you see nowadays. I wish I could say I was all set on preserving the land for future generations, but I'll admit there is some merit to the idea that what this valley needs is a strong, well-thought-out development that can bring some real tax revenue base into this area.   And this land could be a great start for that."

"Are you actually considering that offer?" Ben shook his head. "Doug, this land is irreplaceable! If it gets developed, it will never come back again. This valley has some of the most beautiful river valley vistas in New England, and a large development could put an end to all that. Brodi and I are hoping you're leaning toward the preservation angle."

"Just hold your horses, Ben. I know you and your eco-chewing, anti-development radicals can't see it, but this area needs some economic tax base or it's going down. We need jobs and we need tax revenue, and the only place we can get that is development," Doug was bemused amidst Ben's growing frustration. "I love this land as much as the next guy, but my kids aren't interested in farming, and this valley's changing. How can we stay connected to the modern world and preserve what we have? It's a tough question."

Just then Doug's cell phone rang.

"Dang," Doug looked at the incoming number. "I'm going to take this. Excuse me."

He turned slightly away from them for privacy. They could still overhear Doug's side of the conversation.

"Hello, Doug Stengel here."......"Oh, hello Wayne, funny you should call right now," He shot them a glance before looking back down. "No, I can talk for a minute, what's up?"..."Yes, a gorgeous day up here"...."Yes, as a matter of fact I am out on the property right now"...."Yes, walking under the big white oak down by the river,"..."She's bringing out her buds, yep"..."I know you had some special feeling about her, like those Live Oaks you have down there, so majestic with the Spanish Moss hanging off them..." Doug gave a small chuckle. Listened. "Well, you'll just have to make a trip back up here to see her, is all."..."So, send me some ideas via email so I can see 'em, and then you can come up to discuss it in person"..."I'll look forward to seeing them, and you"..."Bye." He ended the call and turned.

"That was Wayne Thibodeaux, strangely enough," he smiled briefly. "Where were we?"

Brodi cut in. "Look, Doug, I'm really not well versed in this discussion, but as a lover of the outdoors here, I have to say that there are plenty of other opportunities for developers to find people who are willing to sell their land for the cash, and sit back on the proceeds from some subdivision and strip mall. But you've had the opportunity to love this land your whole life. Your family has worked this land, sweated over it. Probably in seven generations you have a ton of family memories and stories to go with it. If I were you I'd think about what is possible here, and recognize that there are a ton of ways you can preserve this land so that it stays a part of this valley's heritage."

Doug squinted across the river, taking in a pair of crows making their way through the far trees, black against black in the shadows. The raucous calls made it across the river to them. He looked at Ben and Brodi, tugged the bill of his cap, and turned. "Well, I ain't made up my mind just yet."

Ben looked deflated. As Doug started walking back away from the river, Ben raised his index finger about to make a point. Brodi arched her eyebrows and tilted her head. "Maybe not now?" She mouthed.

The walk back was taken with small talk, and everyone could feel the tension. The dogs still roamed the periphery, oblivious to the awkwardness. The dogs ran as fast as they could, equally matched step for step, and then one or another would duck sideways, and the others followed a hair's-breadth behind. At some point, one would launch itself onto the other, and they would go tumbling into the wet grass on the field. Dogs knew how to make quick friends, overlooking differences.

Back at the cars, Brodi stuck out her hand to Doug, and said, "Thanks for showing us this beautiful farm. It was a pleasure to meet you."

Ben then shook Doug's hand. "Doug, you've got a big decision on your hands. There is a lot riding on whichever way you decide, and of course, we'd like you to work with VCLT to preserve this land. Is there anything we can do to help you make the decision?"

"Nope," said Doug. He looked Ben squarely in the eye. "But

gimme a call in a week or so. Gimme some time to think." Just then his phone rang again. Making a face he checked the number then shrugged and answered.

"Hello, Doug Stengel here,"..."Yep, Doc, I was expecting your call..."

Brodi and Ben waved goodbye, got the dogs, tongues out and panting, into the back of the car, and got into their seats. They buckled up, and Ben turned onto the road. He was silent.

Brodi looked over at him. "Ben, Doug's not decided to sell to that developer, but obviously those two are very close, judging by the phone call."

"Sounds like he has made up his mind. He's using the developer's words for why he should sell. Damn, it pisses me off. Money always trumps everything."

"I think there's a good chance he's just testing out how it sounds. He's a shrewd man, and he is using our presence to see how the environmental community is going to react."

"Maybe you're right, but he of all folks should recognize what a treasure that farm is for the valley preservation. He should know this valley sits at a crossroads. We're close enough to Springfield to be the next urban development north along the Connecticut. If we don't stop this now, each next parcel that comes on the market will fall like a leaf off a tree."

Brodi could sense the intensity radiating off Ben about this. She guessed that was why Ben wanted her along, to provide a calm, rational balance to his urgency.

"Look, Ben, you and I have known each other since college. I have always appreciated your earnestness, and your deep sense of passion and integrity. What I have also seen –repeatedly–is your fatalism and your narrow vision. Once you get tracked into a viewpoint, it is nearly impossible to get you out of it. You have to have a little faith."

CHAPTER 4

Later on, Alice and her friend, Elisa, chatted in the front seats, with Sophia, in earphones, in the back. The Honda CRV rolled along the rural town roads toward the rec center in town. Headed to a Zumba class, *El Merengue* by Marshmello played on the stereo.

Elisa rocked back and forth in her seat, miming arm movements along with the infectious beat.

"Bailando sola! What a week!" Elisa said. "I am *so* looking forward to shaking it this morning! I am just going to imagine that I'm booting my manager's butt all the way across the studio. Geez, I can't stand that man sometimes!"

"Elisa, you've hated that man practically since the day you got hired. He's been on your case for one thing or another *for years*. He has never respected your training or your skill as a graphic designer."

"Oh I know, I know." Elisa sighed. "It's just that this month he's taken a few of the others onto some secret project; they even moved their computers into a kind of war room, and he's told them they can't say anything about what they're doing. Like architecture is some kind of secret mission impossible. But then that's leaving the rest of us to cover all the other projects in the office, and he's not getting us any other temporary help. We're at his beck and call. I don't work well under these kinds of conditions at all."

"Well, how long will this last?" Alice asked. "It can't go on forever."

"He's responding to some bid, and the plans are due in 3 weeks, so it'll be that long at least."

"You can make it that long, certainly."

"Maybe. It sucks. Anyway, getting to Zumba will be good for my mental and spiritual health. I really like this new instructor, Audrey. Such good energy!"

Elisa lived alone, and in addition to her architectural design work, she was active in the community. In Amherst it seemed like everyone was active in the community in some way. People were on boards and committees, people volunteered at the shelter, or they stood on the Town Common on Tuesdays at noon chanting for peace. It was great that everyone was so involved, but it seemed like there was more dialogue than productive action. Lots of talk. A joke around town was, "Amherst: where only the "H" is silent!"

Elisa volunteered at the local community-supported agriculture farm, helping in all aspects of planting, harvesting, and storing foods. Often on Saturdays she helped pick foods that were then transported to the elders in the retirement community who couldn't venture out, and who received a reduced-fee membership. Elisa took her therapy dog, Rascal, into the retirement community and assisted living facility, bringing smiles and warmth, and offering her Colombian culture and Spanish language skills to the Latinx seniors there. Many of the seniors had known her since she was a small girl, so she helped them feel connected all around.

Alice admired Elisa for her dedication, and also knew that Elisa's life was immeasurably enriched through these activities. One really didn't give without getting back. As a dental hygienist, she knew the act of giving brought something back to you. What goes around comes around. Elisa's volunteer and community activities were what really motivated her. And Elisa was a driven person. Would she ever feel a sense of satisfaction, a sense of peace? Was it as simple as Zumba being the release she craved, something just for her?

They arrived at the rec center, a nondescript 2 story brick and glass building, 100% functional and 0% attractive, and descended into a mirrored dance studio. A blond wooden floor stretched from wall to wall, under a blinding bank of fluorescent lights. The well-used room held yoga, Pilates, step and other fitness classes at various times. Audrey was there setting up, and you had to admire her style. Having taught jazzercise at one point in her own past, Alice admired how serious an instructor Audrey was. She noticed right away that Audrey strove to be good at the moves, to be inspiring, to lead, but she also wanted her students to have fun. She had a fantastic outfit, fitted electric green sports bra with the word Zumba across the back strap, and blue pants that reached just below the knees, with bright pink tassels on her hips. Her shoes were sleek, science-fiction track shoes, with bright colors and black highlights. Audrey had her hair down today, falling in blond ringlets halfway down her back.

Alice also appreciated that Audrey had taught Zumba at other venues in the Valley, and she attended to "her regulars," as she called them, asking about their health, their families, whatever topic of discussion seemed to rise to the surface before classes. It was a ritual, a rejoining of the tribe. Audrey understood that she and Elisa had been regulars here, even before her tenure, so she had established an easy banter. Alice saw Audrey vibing with Elisa's Latin background and the Zumba music, and sensing the fragility underneath Elisa's sometimes brash comments ("That song was boring. No juice!"). Audrey then often demurring with something easy. ("Oh, I'm sure you'll love the next one!," or "Well, Zumba's just the place to work out those kinks!").

Audrey turned to Sophia and gave her a warm smile.

"Hey Sophia, what's up? It's good to see you again! Ready for another Zumba fitness party?"

Sophia was always a bit self-conscious at first. "I guess," she shrugged her shoulders. Audrey seemed to know young people, and attuned to Sophia's awkwardness. She touched her briefly on the shoulder, smiled, then turned her attention to other students. The room began to fill up with athletically-attired women. Zumba was the latest music-fueled dance fitness craze, stretching from Aerobics in the 80s to now.

Soon, the Latin-inspired beat of Pit Bull's *Fireball* started the room moving. It was an oldie-but-goodie in the Zumba canon, and it always got people moving. Audrey began with simple rhythmic dancing, mostly stepping side to side, and then began encouraging more intricate moves with arms and hips. She always kept a smile on her face, which was at first comforting, encouraging, and then more amazing as the class struggled with their breath and their moves. Alice loved the feeling of her body loosening, rhythmically bouncing, and then feeling her pulse increase. She felt the moment when she connected with the music, and it took her away. In Zumba this was known as "FEJ," *feeling euphoria and joy,* and it was well-known to kick in after a short interval for everyone.

Alice glanced at Sophia, who was really such a natural in this medium. Although Sophia was a little heavy for her frame, she had a grace and athleticism that came across through her dancing. Sophia came to these classes infrequently, but she slipped into all the various dance moves that Audrey used. Alice herself still had trouble when Audrey would shift into a new step, and sometimes she wondered if she weren't dyslexic or something, she was on her left foot when everyone else was on the right foot. *Bailando,* by Enrique Inglesias, came on next, and the samba beat was always a bit tricky for Alice, not that it mattered. She was sweating profusely, but she just wanted to move. She glanced over at Elise, perfectly in synch with the rhythm, the music, and the dance moves. Lots of their friends were jealous of Elise's strength and endurance, not even breathing heavily. As Alice and her friends navigated the passages of menopause, and the inevitable body changes, Elise seemed to retain the vitality of a woman of 30. The music shifted to an African tune, *Mama Africa* by Bracket. Alice appreciated the fact that Audrey's music contained songs she knew. It made the dancing even more fun and exciting, and she could excuse her sometimes off-tempo moves. Audrey caught her eye and she smiled as she led them through a turning hip circle.

By the end of the hour, everyone was exhilarated and sweaty. Many "Whoop!" and "Whoo-hoo!" outbursts had been a testament to the increasing sense of freedom and release of tensions, and everyone was thanking Audrey as they filed out. Audrey looked winded, but pleased. 14 happy and tired women funneled out of the rec center into the wan morning sun. Elisa was immediately upbeat, and cheerful now, her brow running with sweat, and her workout outfit clinging to her back.

"That was wonderful! Best therapy I've ever had. You girls want to head over to Share Coffee for a coffee or tea?"

"That sounds great," replied Alice. "Sophia?"

"Sure. I'll probably go for a bottle of water. I polished mine off about halfway through," she held her refillable bottle out and up-ended it; nothing came out but three drops.

Earbuds back into her ear, Sophia dove back into texting her friends, her thumbs moving expertly over the virtual keyboard on her phone. The electronic bump of the music in her earbuds could be heard by both women as they walked down the street. Alice rolled her eyes.

"I think she's going to kill her hearing with that noise. Can you turn that down?" she said to Sophia. Sophia apparently couldn't hear. Alice bumped her upper arm once, then twice.

"What?" Sophia pulled the earbuds from her ears.

"Turn your music down, honey. You'll go deaf."

"Oh Mom!" Sophia gave an exasperated sigh, but in fact turned her music down.

"Thank you," said Alice, but Sophia either still couldn't hear, or more likely simply ignored her mom.

"Oh that was so wonderful! I hate to say it but Audrey is so much better than the last instructor. She has great moves, and changes them up. It's so good to see everyone dancing! Zumba never gets boring!" Elisa was clearly on a post-dancing high.

"I liked her music too. It's so great to just forget about things for an hour. No thinking," agreed Alice. "Great way to start a Saturday."

"I also want to check out that new *chica* who's teaching at the Athletic Club this coming Wednesday. See what she's got." Elisa forged ahead. "What's Ben up to today?"

Alice sighed. "Oh, he's gone with his friend, Brodi, to visit the Stengel property for the Valley Conservation Land Trust. You know, Ben's on the Board committee putting together the offer for the property, and Brodi is joining the Board soon, so she's learning the ropes of acquiring properties. She has volunteered as a land steward for them," Alice wiped more sweat from her brow.

Elisa commented, "You know, I heard somewhere that Stengel's kids don't care about the farm at all. Now that would never happen in my country, Columbia. Children of farmers are so grateful to have the land and a way to make a living. They cherish their parents, and the farm, and are honored to have that lifestyle."

Alice nodded, "Yes, it is kind of sad. But so many farming families are facing this exact situation. The kids see how hard the work is, and how treacherous. Look at those torrential rains we had last year that wiped out so many farmers' crops. That can make a farm go bankrupt. The kids look at how beaten down their parents are by the work and lifestyle and they walk away. So it opens up a huge question about what the farmer is going to do. Sell it to another farmer, sell it for development, or put it into a trust. It's a hard decision."

"Oh, I read about that in the *Recorder*. That farmer is getting wined and dined by that developer from Georgia. Why would a Georgia developer be up here anyway? Is Doug Stengel going to sell it to them? It's right along the river, beautiful views, long stretches of woodland. Prime farmland. Hundreds of acres. If it goes to a developer it's gone for good." Elise was up to date on the issues, apparently.

Alice nodded. "I know! Since Doug's family has been in the valley for generations, you'd think he'd at least want to keep it as a farm. Sell it to another farmer if his kids don't want it. Or, next best, then work with the land conservancy. Ben represents them, and he thought he had a good connection with Doug, the farmer, but then that article appeared in the paper about the developers. I heard from some other Hadley folks that he has always been someone to stir things up."

Elise mused, "Well, the Valley Land Trust could create a little country park there, with trails down to the river. Like the Silvio Conte reserve. Put in an accessible walking trail. It would be so lovely." The conversation trailed off.

Alice sighed, as they pushed their way into the coffee shop. She couldn't help thinking that people were making too much of this. Surely Doug Stengel would sell to the Land Trust for a fair price, preserving the land his family had farmed for over 150 years. But, *whatever*. Alice was much more concerned about these last few years with her children. Where Jeremy and Sophia were heading in their lives.

Alice unconsciously checked her phone to make sure she didn't have a text from Jeremy. Seeing nothing actually wasn't reassuring. She worked very hard not to show her worry directly to him, and to put on a strong and confident face for herself, her son, and the family. Since Jeremy was adopted, and had joined a white family, Alice had known from the start that his would be an uphill struggle. Of course, she had to confront her own internal prejudices, too, and had learned so much about equity issues. She knew that a young black man in society was going to experience all the endemic racism, all the prejudice, and all the attitudes that society has. Alice remembered a third grade teacher who had implied that Jeremy's challenges with math might be due to his inability to concentrate because he was, of course, *different*. Alice had confronted that teacher right away, and even went straight to the principal to register a complaint. She would never stand for injustice, and she was always going to fight for her son.

As she ordered a cold iced latte, Alice reminded herself that she had just had an hour where she didn't have to worry about Jeremy. Or Ben. Or Sophia. Heaven.

"I love forgetting about everything while we are in that class," Alice commented to Elise. "I don't know if it is the music, or Audrey's positivity, or being with a roomful of other women just shakin' it, but it is like going to church!"

Elise laughed. "That is totally right! The Church of Zumba! It is a religious experience. In fact, I go to church every Sunday and it rarely feels like this!" She chuckled at her own comment.

Alice glanced over at Sophia, sitting at the next table and talking with a friend from school. Alice didn't recognize the other girl, but the two were obviously engaged in their own world. They did the social dance that teens did nowadays, one spoke while looking into her phone, then the other responded, then looked down at her phone. They would momentarily look at one another, then quickly glance away. Then both would look again back at their phones. Sophia seemed a bit more comfortable with the direct social interaction, if Alice could judge; the other young woman seemed glued to her phone, thumbs quickly tapping while she also interacted with Sophia. Alice turned back to Elise.

"I know what you mean. I don't have that same work tension, but it does feel like everyone is more on edge these days. Maybe it's leftover from the deep days of the pandemic. Still, your work sounds like hell right now." Alice touched Elise on the forearm with concern.

"Yeah, thanks. You are right of course. But I have to say that in my office this feels like a new thing. It is really so strange to have this weird secrecy in the office, on top of the pressure of some unknown deadline," Elise reflected. "Usually we're a pretty cohesive group. It feels supportive and friendly. Somehow this new project has injected a level of withholding, like we're all watching our backs. The fact that a few folks are working on this secret project and can't even tell us what it is, it's just so odd."

Alice sipped her latte, and closed her eyes. Then she seemed to come to some resolution. "Well, thank goodness for the weekend, thank goodness for a beautiful early spring day, thank goodness for Zumba, and you, and" – raising her drink – "Thank goodness for coffee!" They both laughed at that, and toasted with coffee cups.

"So, what's on your docket for the rest of this glorious day?" Alice steered the conversational ship to less turbulent waters. They chatted about their open weekend afternoons, perhaps filled with gardening or walking in the woods. Elise was planning to visit an old friend who was housebound during chemotherapy treatments. Alice got up, waved to Sophia that they were heading out, and moved toward the door.

CHAPTER 5

The next day, Brodi and Marion climbed into the Accord with Edna in the backseat, sprightly dancing back and forth across the bench seat from one side window to the other. Edna's pink tongue was out, and she was happily scanning the sides of the car for any signs of something to bark at. Brodi drove, as she usually did whenever she and Marion went anywhere. Brodi enjoyed driving, hands on the wheel, like a pilot in a plane. She knew Marion preferred the opportunity to *not* be driving and assumed the navigator and music maestro role when necessary.

Brodi eased down their street, Orchard View Drive, which wound downhill and emptied onto a busier South East Street. Brodi drove slowly down the slope to South East, the better to see the orchard view. Rounding the last bend about 200 yards up the street, she looked east at a spectacular open spread transecting the valley stretching north and south. The valley dipped down into wide fields, separated by short hedgerows that created a patchwork quilt of chocolate, leather and tawny stubble this time of year. One field even showed the first green sprinkling of new growth. The trees on the far side of the valley a half mile away, were also revealing the beginning signs of spring, a reddening of the branches as the individual buds thickened and sprouted. The evergreens, the pines, hemlocks and larches all glistened dark green amidst the budding deciduous maples, oaks, and beeches. It was a spectacular view, and the rising sun alternately illuminated the landscape and hid behind the clouds wreathing the horizon. The symphonic interplay of white, gray, and almost black cotton-like puffs danced shadows across the fields.

"Beautiful morning," Marion noted. "I wish we were going somewhere fun today. I am so worried what we'll find at Mom's, I can barely stand it! I told her we were coming up today, but who knows if she heard me, or remembers."

Brodi gave a grim smile. She knew that, at times like this, Marion would be a swirl of mixed emotions. Of course, she knew this journey entailed engaging with Beth, Marion's mother, so Marion would be focused on what was needed with her mom. And worried. Brodi's style was to be in the moment, in this space right here, with the woman she loved, on a beautiful early spring morning with the warmth of the car enveloping them as they sipped strong, hot coffee from their aluminum travel mugs. She wasn't projecting ahead to what might happen in an hour when they got there. Brodi's upbringing in a house full of nerdy scientists had taught her to weigh the data as it came in, analyze what you had, and don't speculate on what is unknown. Growing up, any emotional charge or conflict had been suppressed and sublimated into the next appliance to fix, the next lawn equipment to tune up. Brodi had been learning about navigating complex emotional discussions with her wife.

Brodi reached over and gently squeezed Marion's hand, widening her smile with love. Marion looked over at Brodi appreciatively, and she squeezed her hand back. Sometimes not saying anything was the right thing to do.

"Mom's going to fight us tooth and nail about moving down here, so we need to be firm and clear. You need to back me up 100% on this," Marion stated her position..

"Marion, for sure. But don't we want to have a discussion with Beth, first? I mean, don't we want to bring her around to our point of view a bit? I think she has a right to decide what her life looks like…"

"I don't think so, Brodi. Her forgetfulness, and inability to make good decisions are already endangering her. She's very tangential in her thinking. She is not processing clearly and, besides, we have discussed this. Why are you waffling on this now? It's no help to me or to Mom. We decided." Marion sank into an frustrated silence, and looked away out the side window at the fields and trees rolling past. Brodi glanced in the rearview mirror at the dog. Edna was looking anxiously at Marion, and whimpered quietly. She was wagging her tail in hopes that Marion would turn around. Brodi reached gingerly through the space between the front seats and petted Edna quietly.

"Marion, I don't mean to get you upset…"

"But you do! You do! Why can't you stick with a decision we made?" Marion was practically in tears at this point, and the resentment and frustration she was feeling crackled in the air between them.

"I'm sorry, honey," Brodi tried to reassure. "I don't mean to get you upset, but it just seems like we moved into this decision awfully quickly. Look, I'm always slower to come around to things. I am still adjusting to it, really. I feel like you kind of caught me off guard on Friday when I got home…"

"Dammit, Brodi! We have been talking about this for months!

We've talked about having Mom move down for months! Where have you been for all those talks? Were you just humoring me? Did you think I was just playing with the idea of having Mom move down here? I'm dead serious about Mom needing to move here, and NOW..." Marion's statements came rapid fire, and Brodi was silenced. She drove along, keeping her eyes on the road, glancing in the rearview mirror as they climbed up Route 9 heading west.

Brodi did know that Marion was actually scared. Marion had talked often about hating the confusion in her mother's voice, the vagueness. Every time she called her mom it was as if another level of reality had drifted away. Beth often retold stories to Marion of activities that had happened before the previous call. Or even years ago. And then, like the sun appearing behind clouds, Beth would be so clear, and so present, that Marion would ask Brodi if she had imagined the more confused moments. Marion hated the uncertainty of the situation, and she knew she was the one who had to make the decision.

Brodi personally hoped it wasn't just the invasion of their nice coupled life that she minded; she hoped she wasn't that shallow or self-indulgent. She *was* terrified of Beth's decline, as much the mental decline as her physical decline. Beth had been slowing down, getting less active over the years. Her walks were less strenuous, and she went to bed earlier now. Beth would become tired at family gatherings as the conversations or evening activities seemed to be getting started. She would often head to bed around 8:00 now. For Brodi the cognitive decline, and the mental loss was more disconcerting. Beth already might say something out of the blue that didn't make any sense, or didn't have anything to do with the conversation that was going on. It wasn't predictable, and that scared the crap out of Brodi.

The last time Marion and Brodi had been to visit, Beth's brother and Jessica had been there. The four younger people had been talking about the Patriots and the slump they were in since Brady had left the team. Beth couldn't care less about football, and usually spoke disparagingly about it whenever the subject arose. Marion's brother was a big fan, and had tickets to many home games that the Patriots played at Foxboro, and so he could be induced to talk about football at the drop of a hat. The conversation that night had drifted in that direction, when suddenly Beth chimed in.

"Jim and I went over to the Skinner's and had a delicious

meal." She smiled at them all.

They had glanced around at one another uncomfortably. Beth's husband, Jim, had died decades previously, and both of the Skinners, long time friends of theirs, had moved to Arizona to be close to their children a while back.

"Mom, you're just confused. Dad's been gone a long time." Marion had responded gently. "Of course we all still miss him," Marion had hoped to get Beth back into the present reality.

"Oh, he'll be back soon. He's just stepped out for a bit." Beth had responded, smiling and looking off in a vague way.

More uncomfortable silence, broken by a snort of derision from Jessica.

"Off in la-la land again!" She exclaimed. The smile on her face was almost triumphant. Jessica had never hidden her dislike of her mother-in-law.

"Here, Mom," Marion said in a pained way, and stood up, moving over to her mother. "Let's get you to bed." She had helped Beth to her feet, and guided her off to the bedroom.

That whole scene had left Brodi nervous, and afraid. This would be happening more and more often. Beth would sink into some reverie, some moment in the past and there she would be. It was terrifying, really. What if it happened when no one else was around? What might she do? Suppose Beth came to live with them? Would Brodi herself be responsible for her? Would they need to have a home health aide come in? At what point do you say you can't handle it and she needs to move into an assisted care facility? Questions and uncertainty had flooded her mind.

Just like now in the car. Brodi realized she had to break the silence.

"Honey, I love you. But I am scared. I don't know how to relate to Beth when she goes off. Somewhere. Suppose she starts to wander away? What will we do?"

"Brodi, I don't know! I haven't had to deal with this before, either. When it's in the hospital you establish protocols, and you have back up personnel. We'll figure it out. But this is my mother, and I will be damned if she's going to some nursing home or something. She's moving down with us, and we'll deal with it." Marion's own frustration was barely below the surface, and her words came clipped and terse.

Brodi could sense Marion's determination strengthening.

"Look, Marion. I know this is hard. We'll make it through this. Together. I promise. We are both nervous, we're both on edge. We'll meet this together. Just like everything else. Let's try to stay calm, OK?"

Edna had by now climbed onto the console between the front seats. Her tail was wagging ferociously, as she licked first one, and then the other.

Marion turned to the dog, and smiling, scratched her head.

"It's OK, girl. It's OK. Everything's OK." Marion had tears in her eyes. "Even the damn dog is upset." She then smiled, "Oh Brodi, this is all so scary. I hate seeing Mom losing it, drifting away like she is. I feel like she needs to have us step in and protect her. If she has any idea that she's losing it, losing her memory and her cognitive functioning, she must be terrified."

"Of course she is. That's why we're going to help. Hey, and re-member I've been working on this wearable device we can design to help us with Beth's dementia. Like I said the other night, it could be a game-changer in helping Beth with location, medications, schedules…" God help us, thought Brodi. I had no idea we'd need it so soon.

When they arrived in Columbia, Brodi was always impressed with the beauty of this little village. A crossroads with a stop sign on one of the streets actually. The public library building was a solid stone struc-ture, not large, but clearly built to last. The cornerstone was carved Ver-mont granite, with the date 1908 inscribed. The Grange Hall was also from the same era, 1911, and stood opposite across the intersection. No other cars in any direction as Brodi made a left onto Main Street. Quaint Massachusetts homes, some Victorian, some Federal brick style, some Capes, lined the streets. The maple trees moved in next to the roadside; there was no sidewalk on either side, but folks just seemed to drive slowly enough to pass the walkers and joggers at the side of the road.

Brodi and Marion pulled up in front of Beth's simple Cape, gray with brick red accents around the windows and solid oak door. Edna jumped from the car as Brodi opened the back door, and ran to the front door. Beth opened it just as the dog got there.

"Oh, hello there," Beth said, opening the screen and petting Edna as the dog's tail wagged a million miles an hour. Brodi smiled seeing how much the dog loved the old woman.

"Hi Mom," called Marion as they walked to the front door.

"Hello dear," replied Beth. She held open the screen door for them as they came into the house. They all hugged as the dog danced excitedly around them.

A slightly stale and moldy smell permeated the house, and Brodi glanced at Marion. Marion was looking intently at her mother, who was smiling but looking a bit hesitant. "How are you, Mom?"

"Fine, fine," said Beth, and she shuffled back in the direction of the kitchen. "Come in, come in."

Marion noticed that the sink was full of dishes, unwashed. And then she, too, apparently registered the unpleasant odor.

"Mom, what is that smell?"

""Oh that's just a little odor from the bacon I cooked for breakfast, dear. Is it bad? Let me open a window," and she moved to open the window over the kitchen sink. She bumped the pile of dirty dishes and a white ceramic coffee cup toppled off the pile and crashed to the kitchen floor.

"Oh dear!" Beth said and bent to pick up the broken bits.

"Here, let me do that for you," Brodi hurried forward and bent down to retrieve the shards scattered across the floor. Coffee pooled under the base; the cup had been almost full, apparently.

"Oh mom," Marion sounded in distress. "Why are all these dishes in the sink?"

"Oh that's just this morning, dear. Nothing to worry about. I'll get to it."

It was clear that dishes had been piling up for a number of days. The smell came from the leftover food on the plates, and flies were circling both the sink and the garbage can in the corner. Marion looked about hopelessly.

"Oh, Mom! Looks like you need some help here!" Marion's eyes teared up. "Seems like it's getting to be too much to keep up with everything. " She took a deep breath as she continued to survey. Dirty countertops, unswept floor, cobwebs across the cabinets.

"Not at all, Marion. I just haven't washed dishes from breakfast. I would have them done if you hadn't come in just now!" Beth seemed angry now, and defensive. "Your father's gone off to play golf and left me with this mess to clean up...it's always my responsibility! I'll do it!"

Brodi intervened, "Beth, it's OK. Why don't you just sit down here," she steered Beth to a chair by the dining room table, which had 4 or 5 days worth of newspapers, many unread, scattered across it. Crumbs scattered across the table indicated multiple meals.

"Marion, why don't you sit here with your Mom. I'll make us some tea and start in on cleaning some dishes," Brodi looked pointedly at Marion. Tears were forming in Marion's eyes, and she looked shocked.

Brodi gave her a quick hug, and moved to the sink. She looked down into the mess, and nearly gagged. Flies covered unrecognizable food items on a tower of plates, bowls, cups and glasses in the sink that had taken a long time to accumulate. She could tell that sliced tomatoes had been a recent meal; red mushy rounds lying like soft petals on the flower-patterned china plate, but they had been hideously transformed by a black and white mold into a grotesque pile. Two flies didn't even budge from gorging themselves on this delicacy as Brodi loomed over them. She waved her hand and they, with 10 other flies, took flight over the sink area of the kitchen.

"I'm just going to let some fresh air in here," Brodi said, quickly cranking open the bay window Beth had been about to open above the sink. The cool Spring morning air felt so refreshing in this fetid mess. She located yellow dishwashing gloves under the sink, and began to exhume the pile of dishes there, like an archaeologist finding an Egyptian tomb. The noise of the clanking cups and dishes, and now the rushing hot water in the sink pulled Marion back.

"OK, Mom. I know you get confused sometimes. Dad's actually been dead for over 20 years now. Remember? You've been on your own for such a long time." She smiled at her mother and reached out to hold her hands. "And we *have* to do something here, mom. This is really not safe for you anymore."

"I do get confused, Marion, don't be angry with me. I'll get to the cleaning, dear. Brodi, don't bother with those dishes! I don't see what all the fuss is about. Goodness. I just get so tired lately." She looked around and her crown of white hair seemed dull in the morning sun coming through the plate glass doors leading to the porch. Brodi's eyes took all this in, and she realized that Beth's hair was an unwashed mess, that her dressing gown had stains down the front, and that the sliding glass porch door was dirty with a film of dust. A wearable device, such as Brodi was envisioning, could function in many areas to help, but the needs here were so much greater.

CHAPTER 6

Two weeks later, after a thorough cleaning at Beth's, and time at home with Marion evaluating options for where Beth would live, Brodi was once again traveling for work. While Brodi felt the stress of the impending changes in her home life, once en route to her destination she focused laser-like on the job before her. She needed to travel to review the progress on her prototype being developed by the Florida firm, and discuss further refinements to the plans.

Brodi had enjoyed coming down to Florida, for the meteorological break, even though she alternately despised and envied the culture and lifestyle. During her brief stint here, right after her UNC master's program, she had enjoyed the seemingly easy culture. There was something so sweet about never worrying about the weather, or what to wear. Jacksonville enjoyed hot, hot summers, generally in the 90s or 100s with a ton of humidity, but air-conditioning was everywhere. The car, your house, the office, the stores, the restaurants, the gas stations, the bathrooms. Everywhere. So Brodi had adapted. Polo shirts, white or khaki shorts, and sneakers were the order of the day. She had had a wonderful place in Atlantic Beach, a duplex with a lanai from which she could see the ocean through the palm trees, and listen all night to the surf breaking on the sand. After a day of wrestling with the electronics department managers, glitchy computer chips, broken solder joints, misread spec sheets, snarky engineers, fried circuit boards, and senior leadership at her company, she had reveled in getting home, taking off her work clothes, donning shorts and a T shirt, grabbing a soda, and heading out for an evening stroll on the beach.

Brodi smiled at the reverie as she arrived at her destination. RXX Enterprises, Inc. was a leader in portable medical devices worldwide, and proud of their footprint here in Jacksonville. The corporate offices stood amidst a myriad of corporate campuses with ponds and lakes that dotted the Florida landscape. A sense of power and wealth radiated from these buildings. Brodi was pleased that her new company, Medtronol, could design simple electronic devices that became components in the RXX line. Her portrait picture had appeared in the RXX Annual report more than once (*Our Strategic Partners*). Very satisfying.

Her meetings that afternoon started with the usual banter with the

RXX staff, many of whom swiveled in their chairs in their work cubicles to greet her as she walked past them to the conference room. Her warmth and knowledge about the lives and families of the various RXX employees made this kind of time more than a simple ritual; it solidified relationships. Susan's son was now in college at UF (Go Gators!), while Carolyn's boy was making his way in the corporate world of sales. Jeff's father had begun his decline and early sink into Alzheimer's; Brodi and Jeff could commiserate here. Dorothy was not in the office, so Brodi left a quick hello on a Post-It and stuck it to her computer monitor, *Sorry I missed you!*

Brodi headed into a conference room with Ted Miller and Chelsea Dennison, her two main contacts at RXX. After a bit of catching up, Ted came to the point.

"So what's new with Medtronol?"

Brodi took a breath and started in, "Medtronol has finished designing that new product we talked about briefly when I was here last." She pulled out her iPad.

Chelsea interjected. "Let's get this on the widescreen here so we can all see it without straining our eyes." She manipulated a small electronic interface on her tablet to Bluetooth Brodi's device into the widescreen monitor on the wall. It came to life with Brodi's presentation.

"Voila!" Chelsea beamed.

Brodi smiled and nodded her head. "Much better! Let me show you the device and then take you through various specs. I think you'll find it takes computational analytics with blazing speed and exhibits many new capabilities that you haven't seen before in the wearable sphere."

For the next 15 minutes, Brodi expertly moved through a series of screenshots and spec sheets that demonstrated this new device prototype. Ted and Chelsea exchanged a few glances, and then Ted said to Chelsea, "Are you thinking about the Sapphire ADHD manometer? This could move that ahead with the increased capacity and precision that we were hoping for."

"Yep." Chelsea answered. Never one to talk excessively, Chelsea's engineering mind was always focused on the next iteration or new breakthrough. "Should we see if Carl is available?"

Ted, without answering, reached for the phone sitting on the table. He punched the speakerphone button and then the 5-digit extension and waited while the phone rang.

"Carl Mellon's office," Kim was Carl's executive assistant.

"Hi Kim. It's Ted and Chels meeting in room 325 with Brodi Saunders from Medtronol. Is Carl available?"

"Oh, hi y'all! Hi Brodi! No sorry, Carl's in a meeting for most of the afternoon. Can I give him a message?" Kim was helpful, friendly, and fiercely protected her boss's time and privacy. "Do you want his voice mail?"

"Sure. Thanks, Kim."

"Let me put you through."

Ted left a voicemail with enough information to pique Carl's interest.

"Well, Brodi, I'd like you to meet with us and Carl, but it looks like it won't be this afternoon. Are you staying over in Jacksonville tonight?"

"Yes, as a matter of fact I am. I had been planning to play some tennis tomorrow at Ponte Vedra with an old friend of mine, but I could switch that to after work today and fit in a meeting here."

Chelsea chimed in, "Well, if your device offers the capability you say, and it maximizes the electronics capacity for our other new mobile device, I think we can jump ahead fairly quickly. We have needed a device which could measure the capacitance of the heart rate and the alpha signal of the patient and through telemetry signal the physician or psychiatrist when the patient was experiencing an episode of maximum hyperactivity. Then depending on the therapy currently being prescribed, the psychiatrist could signal the patient to initiate a stress reduction sequence through a prescribed wellness program, DBT, or use a designated pharmaceutical if the patient is on drug therapy. It would allow the doctor and the patient to be in real time contact during episodes of highest hyperactivity, and interrupt the cycle of agitation. I think these devices could be interoperable."

Ted asked, "Do you think we could add in a component of interactivity where the doctor could contact the patient directly on their device?

"We actually have been looking at an app that could enhance that capability, and we're investigating some input from dementia experts on how that could work." Brodi was excited by how quickly the engagement was proceeding.

"Well, this is a propitious development for us, wouldn't you say, Chels?" Ted turned to his co-worker with a big grin on his face.

"Yep." Chelsea replied, nodding portentously.

"Well, anything else?" Ted looked at Brodi hopefully.

Brodi returned Ted's smiling gaze. At this moment, possibilities arose in her mind. Revolving around the devices that Medtronol had consistently supplied to RXX over the years, Brodi envisioned building steadily on the products and incrementally changing them. Her mind expanded to the next 5 years, encompassing new products already envisioned. Brodi could position Medtronol in research and develop the analytic devices that RXX wanted. This would be a new step for them in their corporate relationship.

"Well, Ted," Brodi began slowly, pulling on her earlobe nervously as she spoke. "As you know, we have a number of product lines that can be used for metrics and analytics in various devices. I think our cloud-based caches for individual medical data will prove most invaluable for the implantable devices as well. All HIPAA compliant of course. These days, people don't want to be slowed down to take a pulse, take a blood sample, or anything. I want to be careful, but people want to be able to access their cloud-based information, the internet, and their provider in real time. They want control with the minimum of disruption to their lives."

Ted looked at Chelsea, "Yeah, heaven forbid we were inconvenienced by our diabetes," his comment dripping with sarcasm. Chelsea chuckled appreciatively.

"So we translate verbal instructions or comments into a written record that can be added to the patient record. The patient verbalizes a passcode that sends the record and a flag to the provider's office simultaneously. The voice-recognition software can monitor the content as well as the level of agitation or stress in the patient's voice so there can be a flag for informatics as well as agitation level."

"And this capability is currently in development?" Ted sounded cautiously optimistic.

"We're in beta testing on this. We are ready to share the capability with you at any point."

"Holy crap." Ted looked at Chelsea and they both broke out in a grin, looking like happy monkeys.

"Where are you in the patent process?" Ted asked.

"We've applied of course, and we initiated a placeholder process months ago when we began to see potentials here. Shouldn't be a problem."

Chelsea turned to Ted and said, "I just had a thought about a strategic partner we might investigate for this. I was talking with Sangita in Payer Relations and she was mentioning new contracts coming up with Florida Blue. We may be able to leverage this kind of product in their Health Delivery Systems Options market. Sangita said she wished we had a new product offering to entice a more liberal structuring option."

Ted turned back, "Brodi, we're completely jazzed as you can see. Medtronol has always brought us great product and development potential, but this could bust open another channel in the Health Delivery market completely. We are definitely interested."

"I thought you might be. I've got a very rough video describing this, let's show it to Carl when he's ready."

Ted and Chelsea were all smiles as they left the conference room, and headed toward the elevator. Ted's cell phone rang, and he turned his back slightly to them for a shrug of privacy in the hall.

He spoke briefly, then turned quickly and gestured to the others standing by the elevators.

"Carl can see us now," he said with a note of urgency and reverence.

As a Senior Vice President in a large corporation, Carl commanded tremendous respect and deferential treatment. His tall, lean stature carried a somewhat aristocratic bearing, and coupled with the thin mustache he sported, one expected Carl to speak with a British accent. In fact it was pure Southern.

As the three exited the elevators on the 8th Floor, Brodi was again struck with the quiet sense of power that the Executive suite exuded. She could glance out the window and in the distance downtown Jacksonville pierced the plane of distant treetops, and the towers of the Napoleon Bonaparte Broward Bridge, a landmark two-towered steel array, pierced the sky to the northwest. In general Jacksonville was so flat that it did look, from here, like a carpet of tree tops.

Kim ushered them into a conference room with glass walls all around, and a moment later Carl greeted Brodi with his gentlemanly smile and a warm handshake.

"It is good to see you again, Brodi!" He said with sincerity, "So what have y'all got for me today?"

Over the next 45 minutes Brodi showed the brief video and discussed the capabilities of the prototype. Ted and Chelsea were enthusiastic, but mildly restrained as they worked to judge Carl's level of interest. As Brodi, Ted and Chelsea slowly wound through their ideas and enthusiasms, Carl looked pensive.

"So ease of connection is important. Reliability of data transfer. HIPAA compliance. And not wanting to disturb the patient; inconvenience them, as you said. I can see that. What if we offered an implantable monitor device that could broadcast to the mobile device through a safe, ultra-low frequency? Then the mobile device could automatically transmit the health informatics, and message the provider with the relevant data. It would enable the patient's sense of ease through the knowledge that his or her health data were being monitored by the provider, and also we could have passive data collection for research and development purposes."

There was a moment of silence as the others digested the idea and its implications.

"Uh, I think that would definitely require FDA approval..." Ted hazarded.

"It's brilliant, I'll say that much, " Chelsea added.

"I have no idea about implantables at this point, but Medtronol can investigate that, I'm sure." Brodi reasserted.

As Brodi left the RXX campus a short while later, verbal agreements and handshakes around, she was filled with an exuberance of success and some real trepidation around the implantable device Carl had suggested. She marveled how strange and wonderful life was, to provide her with the opportunity for a huge business success in this far flung place, and how this could potentially impact the field of uncertainty surrounding her family life at home. An afternoon smashing tennis balls with the club pro on the warm Florida courts seemed like the perfect end to this day.

CHAPTER 7

Back in Amherst the town looked out at four inches of falling snow. It had begun in the night, and now with the sun illuminating the scene, Ben Miller could see that this late spring snow was going to slow everything down today. The flakes were big and flat, and falling rather rapidly. The white cover was fluffy and thick, and softened all the contours. The branches and crotches of the deciduous trees had a white coating, as did the steadily drooping branches of the pines. It was like a downpour in slow motion. Ben loved the silence and the beauty of snowfall, and only wished that he could stay home and appreciate it from the warmth and comfort of their living room. Or strap on his cross-country skis and head out to appreciate the quiet of his local ski trail with the dogs. Even as he sipped his coffee, and gazed at the bushes and trees, he watched the landscape disappear under the snow. The roads would be treacherous.

It was unusual for the snow to fall so heavily and thickly this time in the early spring. A few pastel crocuses and hyacinths had already opened their blossoms, those hopeful harbingers of happy warm spring days. Spring had been steadily surfacing, and in only a short time the warmer winds and sunny skies would prevail. He and Alice had planned to be out in the garden soon. A group of new pansies in pots and 6 new azaleas now gathered snow, and those fantasies of springtime planting were fading under the reality of the late snow.

Ben fully turned his thoughts to his work, obligations overcoming desires, as he surveyed his email inbox. He would work from home this morning as the snow fell. All his projects were moving so slowly, and it seemed in every domain he was waiting for someone else to complete some task before he could proceed.

An email from Doug Stengel caught his attention, and the subject line made him catch his breath.

TO: Ben Miller
FROM: Doug Stengel
SUBJECT: River Property
Time: 03/24 5:45 A.M.
Ben: I've still been thinking about our walk and conversation on

Saturday. I've heard from the developer with some new information which I didn't know before.

I'll need some additional time to think over what you said and get back to you. Doug

The email had two effects on Ben. First he felt a sinking sense of foreboding that Doug had received some juicy offer from the Rhinestone Redneck that was going to be too sweet to turn down. Second, and perhaps more importantly, Doug *had* sent him the email which was at least courteous on his behalf. Doug could have sown up the deal with the developer and not even bothered to mention it to Ben. All in all, though, the message was cryptic and unnerving.

The fact was that over a number of months of talks, Ben had never felt close to striking a deal with Doug. At times Doug had seemed open to working with the Trust on a straight-out preservation of the farm using the Agricultural Preservation Restriction that Ben had introduced to him. The APR was designed to compensate the farmer for the reduced payment from the Trust, and perhaps support an easement for some recreational use of the land. Doug had initially been mildly supportive of preserving the land outright, or at least so it seemed to Ben. The fact that the Trust would purchase the land, and Doug's family could continue to live there during his lifetime had also seemed of interest.

Now with the arrival of this email, Ben wasn't so sure. He hated to be uncertain in situations like this; he was a man more used to decision and action in his work. His habit had always been to stay on solid footing, and not make any unnecessary moves that would disturb things. His challenge in this situation had been the anxiety he felt with Doug moving between talking with the developer, then talking with Ben and the Valley Conservancy Land Trust. Ben increasingly suspected Doug wasn't trustworthy. Doug had more than once said he was on board with the Land Trust, only to be seen with Wayne Thibodeaux in the fields, or even in the newspapers. Was he playing one side against the other? Was he really just a kind of political animal after all, looking to get the best deal? Doug was hard to read, and harder to fathom. Did he want to preserve the valley he knew and had grown up in, or did he want to provide a nice nest egg for his retirement, and his children? From what Ben could piece together about Doug, the farm was turning into heavy weight for Doug. Ben slammed his fist on the desk as though he could break through these circular thoughts like ice on a puddle. His coffee sloshed over the rim of the cup.

"God damn it!"

He decided to step away from the computer, strap on his cross country skis and take advantage of the quiet early morning and the still falling snow. "Here Rusty! Here Frieda!" He called the dogs and laced his cross-country ski boots. He wrapped gaiters over his ankles, and cinched them to his calf, to keep the snow off his pants and socks, and out of his boots. He left the house by the back door, which headed into the garage. The dogs danced expectantly around him as he fished his skis and poles from the rack along the back wall. Frieda let out a low growl that morphed into a kind of a happy bark. She was always vocalizing something. Ben surveyed the fast falling snow as he strapped the skis on and headed toward the woods across the street. The dogs began their dominance dance, growling and snarling at each other, as though only one could be the leader of the pack. Ben glided down the driveway and glanced up and down the street, but it was too early for traffic. He turned into a meadow that entered the conservation land, now covered in a beautiful blanket of white snow. The dogs plowed a trail and now burst upward and outward with each bounding leap. Ben established a rhythm to his cross-country stride, push-glide, push-glide, push-glide, push-glide. He could feel his thighs and calves tighten as he worked to establish as long a glide as possible. The meadow was flat with a slight downhill grade.

Ben was reminded of a meeting the neighbors had in this very meadow the previous fall, when they tried to understand the grass mowing schedule that the town was following. That summer, the meadow had been mowed in June, and then not again through August. The meadow had become so wild and the grasses so deep that neighbors had begun avoiding it now, whereas for years it had been a gathering place for kids, families, pick-up ball games, frisbee throwing, soccer games, kite flying, picnics, watching the stars, and occasionally a sleep-over for the young kids who want to sleep outdoors but not too far from mom and dad. Previously the Town had mowed the meadow every few weeks, and the grass had been like a ball field. The Assistant Town Manager had offered to meet with the neighbors at the meadow after many of them had tried unsuccessfully to get the Town Department of Public Works to continue to mow the meadow as it had done for 20 years. The meeting devolved into an officious politician trying to placate the locals, while appearing reasonable and slightly avuncular. He explained that the Town had just this year realized that the meadow was not really supposed to be mowed as it had been, since it was technically conservation land, and not a park. The neighbors were adamant about getting the mowing reinstated; the official had been placating but non-committal. Grassroots meets tie and suit. Ben remembered that everyone had felt shined on, but then curiously, the meadow had been mowed regularly through the rest of the fall. It made for easier skiing in the winter for sure. But as he reflected back, Ben realized that situations were often more complex, more nuanced than one-side-versus-the-other portrayed. Maybe that was true in the situation with Doug Stengel as well.

Ben and the dogs headed into the woods along a faintly visible path that started at the far side of the meadow. As usual, Frieda was taking the lead and racing along on her own. She was following some dog sense of adventure, and her leaping over downed logs and branches was so graceful and effortless. Rusty was as exuberant, in his own way, but more plodding and lumbering as he charged through the under-brush. He often chased after Frieda, a happy support to her adventurous-ness. Frieda leading the way and Rusty bounding along behind, with a frequent stop when two heads went down in the same spot, and butts and tails raised in the air, sometimes followed by intensive digging. Some living or dead animal was discovered, and after a brief kerfuffle, one dog and then the other bounded away again. Occasionally Ben had to force-fully call them, especially if it appeared that rolling in the dead thing was about to commence. What was it with dogs and rolling in the dead thing? And then Frieda or Rusty would come happily, joyously, bounding up to him and, like as not, jump up to share the bounty of the scent. Often overpowering and nauseating. The mystery of the animal kingdom. Ah well, Ben loved the dogs for all of it.

Ben admired the snow-covered branches of the deciduous trees, and the weighed-down skirts of the hemlocks and white pines. The pow-dery snow was magical, and all was quiet. His breath came in white puffs of frosty swirls as he worked his arms and legs. Now breathing heavily, he could feel himself starting to sweat inside his parka, and stopped to unzip the gussets under his arms to let cold air into his core. The dogs came back and jumped on him expectantly; he some-times had a hidden treat for them in his pockets. He shooed them off, since the combined weight of the two dogs hitting him simultaneously was enough to knock him off balance. And topple over he did, landing butt first in a mound of snow, laughing, and the dogs now jumping on him and licking his face. He pushed them away, his "Get off me!" too muffled in chuckles to sound authoritative. He struggled back to his feet and dusted snow off himself.

The trail had been traversed before this storm; faint tracks dented beneath the new snowfall. The new snow made the tracks smooth, and evened out the places where dogs and walkers had broken the continuous tracks. Ben could see a way into the distance between the trees, and the dogs now ran perpendicular to the trail as they tracked a rabbit or deer that had passed recently.

His eye was caught by a movement through the trees ahead and to his left. Even though he knew these woods, and knew there were no real dangers out here (black bears were not frequent here and probably still hibernating at this point), he still felt a slight anxiety. What was he seeing? A red checked jacket, gliding through the trees ahead. Ben also saw another dog, and then saw his two turn suddenly and bound toward it. His two were totally friendly and safe, but it would be disconcerting to have two medium-sized dogs running at you in the woods.

"Rusty! Frieda! Come! COME!" his voice rose and strengthened the second command. When his dogs were in their instinctual mode, it was hard to snap them out of it.

His dogs turned almost simultaneously, and began running toward him, their tongues hanging out the sides of their mouths in a happy pantomime. They rushed up and stopped at his feet, panting heavily. Both turned to look over their shoulders at the approaching person and dog.

He didn't recognize the person, nor the dog, which was unusual. At this end of town he knew most people coming through the woods at 8:00 in the morning. He waited for the approach. The woman appeared to be older, moving a bit cautiously on her skis.

"Morning! My dogs are friendly!"

"Hi. So's mine."

"OK dogs, go ahead," He said, and the two dogs turned and ran up to their new best friend. Lots of tail wagging and butt sniffing ensued. The new dog was a mid-sized German Shepherd, bulky but not overweight. By contrast Rusty and Frieda looked small. They began to jump and dance around each other as they got the sense and rhythm of their three dog dance.

"Nice morning!" Ben said by way of starting small talk.

"Yep. It's pretty all right. Couldn't wait to get out into all this white fluffiness!"

"Where did you start?"

"Over by Mt. Pollux. Live up there."

"I just came in from the meadow. Such a perfect morning. How old's your dog?"

"Rex is 3. He's still a puppy at heart, and loves other pups."

"Yea, they are getting along. My two are both about 2. Rusty and Frieda."

"Nice dogs. Real pretty. Are they purebred?"

"Well, Rusty and Frieda are actual brother and sister chocolate lab mixed with something else. How about Rex?"

"Pure German Shepherd."

"Beautiful dog," Ben said.

"Thanks, he's my best buddy."

They stood for a few moments in silence, watching the dogs play. The dogs were now running around, jumping and dancing as though they had known each other forever. Rex chased Rusty, with Frieda in pursuit until she would jump playfully on Rex. Rex would drop, or roll over, playfully growling, and the all three would be tumbling in the freshly fallen snow. There would be moments when all three would pause, like the end of a music passage, before they would begin again. It was choreography.

"It's great to see him play like this. He doesn't get enough time with other dogs." The stranger commented.

"Yes, they love to socialize. Name's Ben, by the way" he said, glancing at the woman.

"Rhonda. Nice to meet you."

"Nice to meet you, too. Now that we're talking, you look familiar, but I can't figure out from where," said Ben.

"Well, it's Amherst. We could have seen each other at the Farmer's Market or Amherst Cinema for all that. Lived here most of my life since I came to UMass as an undergrad in the 1970s. Also, I think people get to look familiar. "

"No, I want to say I've seen you at a party, at someone's house or something. Maybe a meeting at the UU?

"Well, you could have, except I don't go.."

Rhonda looked directly at Ben, with kind and intelligent eyes. Ben felt certain they had met at some point, but let it go.

The dogs continued to romp and play in the snow. Now Rex was leading Frieda and Rusty on a wild chase around the trees, in and out and around at a fast clip. They all suddenly stopped again, tongues rolling out of the sides of their mouths and hard panting.

"I'm not inclined to stop this right now."

"Me neither."

"So what do you do?" Rhonda asked.

"Oh, I'm an attorney, mostly corporate law, and I do some pro-bono work as well. You?"

Rhonda leaned in on her poles. "Well, I am a semi-retired engineer. I started a medical device company and worked there most of my career. Now I go in and bother the employees mostly. Sometimes they ask me to work on something, but I think it's mostly so I can feel helpful. I don't have much to offer in terms of anything new, really. Lots of the more recent discoveries are by the young folks I hired. You know what they say, hire people smarter than you are to really shine. That's been my motto."

"So, is this the place Brodi Saunders works? She's a friend of mine."

"Well, we actually provide some electronics to her firm. We manufacture, then they build the devices. As a matter of fact she's working on something right now."

"Oh, yeah." Ben watched the snow still falling steadily from a slate gray sky. "That's a coincidence that we both know her. Brodi comes and helps me out with some of my pro-bono work sometimes. Now that I think of it, I think she's mentioned your name."

"What's your work involve?"

"As I said, I'm a lawyer. I work for a small firm with an office in Amherst, and I also volunteer with the Valley Conservancy Land Trust."

"Sounds like important work on both accounts."

"Sometimes the day-to-day work is a bit crazy – lots of details and wording on documents that have to be very precise. The VCLT work is always righteous as far as I'm concerned – protecting your valley, as the saying goes. Brodi's going to take a turn on the VCLT Board this coming year."

"Got kids?"

"Me, yes, two. Jeremy is 17 going on 50 – he's a wise old soul in a young man's body, and Sophia, who is 15 and finding her own way in life. How about you?

"Kids are grown and left the area. My son's 30 and is living in New York City, which I don't understand. He's a filmmaker. My daughter's studying marine science at Woods Hole."

"Sounds like they are doing well."

"I'm proud of 'em. You never stop worrying about them though, I'll tell you that."

Ben nodded. "I believe that! Sophia seems like she's headed in the right direction, and she can be prescient beyond her years, but I worry about her nonetheless. She's made some difficult choices."

Rhonda shrugged. "Kids have to make their own choices sometimes, to see what works for them. And I think especially with girls, you want to empower them, and give them the support to trust their own intuition, their own judgment. Nothing is more powerful than knowing your parents have your back, and will be there to support your life choices. You're not always going to be around to help them avoid mistakes."

Ben nodded appreciatively. "True enough. I can see where my wife and I have had to let go of control bit by bit as both kids navigate their engagement with the world." Ben scratched his head through his knit hat.

Rhonda said, "Well, good to talk with you. I'm getting chilly, so I think I'll push on. Maybe we'll run into one another again. Rex!"

Ben replied: "Good to meet you too. Happy Ski!"

The dog came bounding and ran alongside Rhonda.

Ben watched her turn and glide away. He mused on how *small world* this Valley actually was. Of course it was small by population standards, but Ben thought six degrees of separation were actually a few more degrees than you needed around here. People knew people. And if they didn't know someone, they knew someone who knew that person. Or they were going to meet that person skiing in the woods at 8:00 on a snowy morning.

CHAPTER 8

"I always get so nervous before a dinner party," Marion laughed at herself as she bustled about the kitchen. She held an aluminum cookie tray of homemade dinner *chapatis* in her right hand as she bent over the stove, pulling the oven door open to a cloud of steam. A dishrag draped over her shoulder slid onto the open oven door as she began to close it.

"Oh, shit!" she grabbed the dishrag as the oven slammed shut. She laughed again.

Brodi bustled in the adjacent dining room, getting wine and beer glasses out of the glass-fronted cabinet on the built-in shelves. She glanced through the doorway at Marion, hearing the expletive, and smiled gently.

"Not to worry, hon. It's going to be a great evening with friends. Your food will be awesome, as always. Folks will mingle."

"I appreciate your confidence, but people are arriving in 45 minutes! Have you even taken a shower?"

Brodi sensed the stress emanating from the kitchen. Sometimes she would walk into the kitchen and offer to pick up some aspect of the preparations, say, making the salad, and it was a welcome offer of assistance. Marion would look over at her gratefully and she would smile, and the tension would drop like a summer heat wave with a cool front moving in over the Holyoke Mountains. Nice. But other times a gesture of assistance would be met with resistance as though it were a sign Marion couldn't handle things. Brodi took a deep breath and put the last glasses on the sideboard. She tried an easy-going approach: "Anything I can do?"

Marion said, "Honey: would you mind making the salad while I get the casserole finished?"

Brodi moved swiftly, and gratefully, into the kitchen.

Marion turned to the curry casserole, chopped the fresh lemongrass and added coconut milk to the simmering Dutch oven on the stovetop. Bright orange sweet potatoes, maroon kidney beans, yellow onions, garlic, crisp celery, dark green peppers and curry spices simmered in a savory vegetable broth. As she raised the lid to add the coconut milk, the steam drifted over to where Brodi stood washing lettuce at the sink.

"That smells awesome," Brodi offered, glancing over her shoulder at Marion's back, rocking as she stirred the casserole. There was sensuousness in the gentle rhythm. Brodi stole over to the stove, and gently kissed Marion on the top of her head, her hands squeezing her shoulders. Marion hummed softly at the contact. A smile creased her warm cheek. A promise of later fires warmed their thoughts.

As the guests arrived, their focus shifted to the steadily growing group. A dinner party for twenty people was a bit of a stretch for them, as they usually enjoyed having one couple or family over at a time. But as Marion and Brodi had sat together a few weeks earlier, planning out the invitations, the list just seemed to grow organically, and they arrived at 20. What fun!

Brodi noticed how initially it seemed as though the group made a conscious effort to integrate each new person or couple coming into the door, entering the living room, and saying hellos. There was the usual: "Hello, I'm Michelle."

"Hello, I'm George. How do you know Brodi and Marion?"

Then at some point, and a social network researcher might be able to untangle this, the group just could not sustain the expansion, the energy, the personalities, the social anxieties, the confusion, the urge for each person to be able to talk, or need for attention, to contain itself as one group, like an amoeba growing until it split in two, and all at once there were two groups, or three, and a thoughtful host would skillfully observe and navigate the ensuing multiplicities. When the group went to two smaller groups, the conversation would naturally start back up, or continue, with some adjustments owing to the reconfiguration. Brodi was happy to see that as the Garcias entered the room everyone found a group home, as it were. The newcomers, Diego and Marcella Garcia, skillfully moved between the groups introducing themselves around; Brodi was not needed there. She noted that Ben was paired off with a guy, George? Or Geoff?--Brodi didn't know him well–who was a writer that Marion knew. Ben and George/Geoff both stood facing one another, slightly obliquely as men will (and holding their drinks at chest height, like a shield). Brodi noticed the kids moving toward the den, and the widescreen TV, which was fine. Marion was with a clutch of women, Alice, Marcella, Eileen Johnson, and Audrey Hodges. They were animatedly discussing the upcoming town council elections, and the concern over the new school location. People clearly had strong feelings one way or the other. It was Amherst, after all.

Brodi wandered over to Ben and the other guy. Diego followed.

"So what do you write?" Ben asked and sipped his beer.

Brodi stepped right in and hugged Ben. "Hey Friend!" And turning, "Is it Geoff? George?" She offered her hand.

The guy smiled slightly and shook hands, briefly. "It's George. George Leon."

"Sorry, you were just going to say what you are writing, and I recognize your name. I've read some of your work in the *Recorder*. Yes?"

"Oh thanks," George seemed a little embarrassed. "Yeah, I was on staff for a number of years, but now I freelance, and write my own stuff."

Ben seemed impressed. "Yeah, I remember. You wrote a piece on the carving up of the valley farmland a while back. You gave a nice shout out to the Valley Conservancy Land Trust. I'm on their Board."

"Right. I was proud of that piece actually. I found a real pulse beat of people who want to keep this valley pristine, and just like it is. They don't want to see anything change. And I discovered these awesome well-integrated community members who are committed to preservation and are actually working every day to do that. I loved talking with Christine Brown at Valley Conservancy Land Trust. She's a visionary."

"She's awesome. And we've got our eyes on the Stengel parcel in Hadley out by the river. Christine is doing some behind the scenes work on that."

"Yes, I kind of wish I were writing about that. Dan Lewis at the *Recorder* is covering that now, and I think it's kind of a big story." George pursed his lips and shrugged, then took a sip of wine.

Diego chimed in, "Yeah. I mean, what's up with that guy from Georgia anyway? He's got so much money that he thinks he can just muscle his way in anywhere and buy whatever he wants?"

"Completely unacceptable if you ask me. But money talks." Ben replied sardonically.

Brodi weighed in, "Well, I think Doug Stengel wants to make back some of the money his land lost in value as the economy tanked and land prices have plummeted. Also those floods last summer really hurt the valley farmers. You can't fault that really, but," she added quickly, knowing her audience, "still, you wish he could simply appreciate the value the land holds in its present state. My god, it's so beautiful!"

"It's not just aesthetic, Brodi," George enthused, "For instance, the Connecticut River and the flyway are used by migratory birds coming down from Canada in the fall, and heading back up north in the spring. They need the open water and land for stopping and resting along the way. They eat the tender spring greens. There are flocks of Canada geese that have used this migratory corridor forever, and you know, it's believed that they need to return regularly to their same markers to find their way. There is apparently one flock that Fish and Wildlife has banded that comes down actually from Hudson's Bay, and uses the big bend in Hadley and the Ox Bow as their marker for stopping."

Ben said, "Didn't know that! You can't put a price on that, or the larger ecosystem value of having contiguous parcels of open and undisturbed land going down to the river from the hills and the Holyoke Range. You've got black bears, bobcats, deer, and coyotes who use that as forage land. Once that's gone, it's gone for good."

George added, "I wrote a piece about a decade ago about Doug's great grandfather, Martin, who farmed the land in the late 1800's. Interestingly, Martin was a bit of a historian himself, and he wrote tales his parents had told of flocks of thousands of geese that would come through in the spring and fall, and the raucous calls and honking, even at night, that could wake you up from a sound sleep. And during the day the sky could darken as a huge flock swept past overhead. Amazing stories. Martin's grand-dad had a troupe of Native Pocumtuk people still living at the edge of the river in the 1800s."

"I love this valley!" Diego interjected. "Just this morning, I was hiking along Amethyst Brook and saw the first wildflowers along the trail. It's astonishing how many different kinds of plants there are out there, and the different shapes and colors of the flower. The yellows, whites, pinks, blues and reds can all mingle together like they were planted in a garden."

"That's right! You know, VCLT hopes to buy the Stengel property. Being on their Board, I have walked that land,--" Ben gesture to Brodi, "Brodi's come along–and it's beautiful. Right now those green shoots are coming up through last fall's brown stubble, and you can see the geese footprints in the softening earth. There are deer prints in the mud around the various puddles and vernal pools in the woods there. It's very precious. It *has* to stay as farmland, for my money."

The group went silent for a minute, each one taking a sip from their drink, and reflecting on some private thoughts – flowers and deer, geese and trees.

"Do you think he'll go with the land trust?" Diego queried.

"It's really anybody's guess at this point." Ben shook his head.

"There is something to be said for the innate feeling of steward-ship," George gazed slightly up and into the distance as he spoke. "You wonder if some ancestral blood beating in his veins calls to him from his great grandfather, or great-great-grandfather, and reminds him of the re-sponsibility of being the current owner of the land. That mantle has been passed down to him for generations, and with that must come some ex-pectation of maintaining the tradition, the family ways. When I inter-viewed Doug, way back when, he certainly hinted as much, but I have to say that I don't know whether it felt like a burden he wanted to shrug, or a mantle he wanted to assume."

"Are there any kids who might step up?" Diego inquired.

George answered: "As I recall, no! Oldest son killed in Afghani-stan, daughter lives locally but doesn't seem interested. Youngest lives out of state."

Just then Marion clinked a fork on her wine glass. "Dinner is ready! It's buffet style, so grab a plate, the food is here on the sideboard, and find yourself a seat wherever!"

Appreciative murmurs followed, and guests remixed and flowed into the dining room to grab food. George attached himself to Diego and Marcella who stood in the informal line. He noticed an apparently single woman up front with two other women, two men just behind, and vaguely wondered if she, too, was a singleton at the party. Even though Amherst prided itself on being progressive, and modern (while simulta-neously being rooted somehow in this rural New England soil), the fam-ily groupings were still primarily couples with kids. Marion had skill-fully set up a kids table at the side, and 5 or 6 kids were already seated there eating and loudly interacting. Two younger girls, maybe 4 years old, seemed to be enjoying the attention of the others who were older. Two teenage girls whispered conspiratorially together. Two older boys, one African-American, sat opposite one another, making jokes about the things teen-aged boys find funny. As the people moved through the serving line of food, people found their seats around the long dining table or in the living room on the sofa or easy chairs. Compliments erupted throughout the group for the delicious stew, warm, fresh-baked wheat chapatis, salad, the delicious cucumber-mint yogurt raita, and jasmine rice Marion had created. Marion graciously accepted the praise, and smiled, being sure to point out that Brodi had made the delicious maple-mustard dressing for the mango-coleslaw salad. Conversations drifted to a higher energy level for awhile, as the eating infused commonality and cohesion across the crowd. A few mentions of favorite TV shows arose, and some excitement was generated through the discussion of *Ted Lasso*, *Russian Doll*, and other current offerings.

Conversations then fractured into smaller groups clustered around the table or in the living room. Other favorite shows discussed, then more locally focused topics – the Hurricanes chances in the state hockey tournament, the ongoing Amherst problems with the school administration and the town's opposition to building a new elementary school. Chuckles surrounded the discussion of the perpetual library rebuild. Amherst's politics never seemed to get resolved, and the debate of the moment always created two passionate sides.

George found his attention drawn to the same woman, now seated two to his left, and he kept trying to engage her in a conversation across the man sitting in between. It seemed her name was Audrey, and she was a tutor of math. She had her own small business that she ran out of her home, and then she also went into the Middle School to work with the girls there. George's questions to Audrey, over the man in the middle, were like tennis balls lobbed over a net, returned in a desultory fashion by Audrey. Audrey's efforts to directly include the man in between did not dissuade George from continuing.

Audrey asked, "So what do you do?"

Man: "Teacher."

Audrey: "And what do you teach?"

Man: "Different things–math and science."

Audrey: "Oh! I am a math tutor, that's a coincidence. And I teach Zumba."

Man: "What grades do you tutor?"

George jumped in too: "What age kids do you tutor?"

Audrey grinned: Uh, 4-9, and I guess, 9-14!"

The conversation continued as they ate.

* * *

After dinner as folks got up for coffee and dessert, Brodi again scanned the room for isolated guests. Most people had continued to mingle with their tablemates from dinner, although a few close friends had reformed. Brodi caught Marion's eye and smiled and mouthed "I love you" as she watched her from across the living room. She was with her women friends and they seemed deeply engaged in a serious topic, judging from the expressions of intensity and focus, and the overly sincere nodding of heads as they listened to one another. Brodi thought she would ask Marion later about what engaged such conspiratorial intensity.

Brodi strolled over to Audrey, standing somewhat apart from others at the coffee service table.

"Did you enjoy the curry?"

"Oh my gosh, that was so delicious!" She turned to face her and her eyes widened. "And the jasmine rice was so tender and flavorful. Was that cardamom for spice? I loved it."

"Marion is an awesome cook, so she's the one to ask about that," Brodi loved to shed some praise on Marion and her cooking, since Marion herself was so self-effacing in that regard.

"She seems so easy and natural with all this; I'd be a total wreck with this many people," Audrey said, giving a little chuckle. "I can teach a room full of women doing Zumba, but a roomful of conversation is not my thing."

"Marion loves your Zumba class! Now she can't wait for Saturdays to get out there with you!" Brodi responded.

"Zumba is just exhilarating, and fun. It's a dance party. The music really does it all. I don't have to do anything but dance."

George drifted over, joining in the dyad.

"I can't dance, actually." He said as a way of entering.

Brodi and Audrey turned to him with a quizzical look.

"Well, I heard you say you don't have to do anything but dance, and I am totally flat-footed myself. No sense of rhythm." He took a sip of coffee.

Brodi made introductions. "Sorry -- Audrey, this is George. George; Audrey. Well, personally I love the Saturday night contra dancing at the South Common Church. Marion and I get out there every month or so. I love the bluegrass music."

"I've gone to that a few times, too," said Audrey. "I like that the caller tells you what the steps are in advance. Helps you feel more comfortable with the songs. And it's so much fun with a group like that, everyone dancing together. And there is a lot of encouragement to learn the steps."

Ben came over at that point, and joined the enthusiasm about the contra dance. He and Alice had been with Brodi and Marion a few times.

"You and Marion want to go next Saturday, Brodi? It would be fun!"

"Sounds like a plan. You want to come along, Audrey?"

Audrey reddened. "I 'd love to go, but I don't want to be a fifth wheel."

"Nonsense! Marion would love to have you along. And maybe you'll find someone to bring."

"OK, we'll see."

George worked himself gamely back into the conversation. "OK, I have never been to a contra dance myself. Now, I still can't dance, so I would probably stand on the side."

"*You can't dance, so I assume…*" Audrey sang a short line from a song.

"Little Feat!" said George. "I haven't heard that in years. I love that song! "*In a bag you couldn't carry a tune!*"

Audrey chuckled, "It's a great song. I remember hearing that so long ago, and that line has always stuck with me."

"Ah!" George's eyes lit up. "Little Feat" is one of my favorites. I saw Paul Barrere at the Calvin Theater a few years ago with Fred Tackett. So sorry that he passed."

"Me too! " sighed Audrey. "So sorry that Lowell George is gone, too. He was one of a kind."

"I know…" George sank into reverie. Then rebounded.

"Hey, want to get together for coffee sometime?"

Audrey fairly jumped at the topical change, but smiled.

"Uh, sure."

"How about we meet next Saturday at Amherst Coffee at 9:00?"

Audrey's eyes darted from Brodi to Ben, who were both smiling and nodding.

Ben turned to Brodi: "Shall we make our exit?"

"Let's do!" They nodded, turned and walked away.

Ben and Brodi caught up with Elisa pouring herself some coffee.

Brodi said, ""Hi. It's Elisa, isn't it? I know you go to Zumba with Marion and Alice sometimes."

Elise responded with a warm smile. "Yes, and you are Brodi! I've heard so much about you from Marion!"

Brodi smiled. "Nice to have you to our home. This is Ben Miller. Elise is another Zumba aficionado."

"Pleased to meet you!" Elisa smiled.

"Nice to meet you as well. You're my wife, Alice's friend. Architect, right? Where are you an architect?" Ben asked.

"I work with Rodale Associates downtown. Our office is right above Amherst Coffee."

"Oh, yes! My offices are kitty-corner across the street above Antonio's Pizza. What kind of architecture do you work on -- residential or commercial?"

"Well, mostly we work with whatever comes in the door! I often do residential work, since I love the classical styling. Our office is really branching out though, taking on lots of new projects."

"Sounds interesting. Is that good for you?"

"Well, sometimes! The senior partner took on a really big project, which is taking lots of time. Some architects are planning and drawing like mad, so the rest of us just keep going on our projects. I am working on a renovation on a lovely old Victorian here in town myself."

"Wow, I'll bet that's pretty interesting."

"Oh, yes, and Alice is such a good friend! She always listens to my complaints! Between the listening and the dancing I am a new person when I am done. But I tell you," here she leaned closer to Ben, "I think the senior partner is drafting up some plans for that big property along the river everyone is talking about, and I think they are planning to showcase those plans at some Planning Board meeting soon. Because our office is on this night and day." Elisa had clearly had a few drinks, since she was telling this story with some dramatic flair.

Ben tilted his head. "But…that property hasn't even been sold yet. It's not clear who is going to buy it, and what it's going to become. I don't get it." His head started to spin with this tidbit of information.

Elisa turned as though walking away, saying over her shoulder, "I'm just telling you. This is a big project for our office, and there is a tight timeline." She shrugged her shoulders. "Nice to meet you, Ben." She walked toward the front door.

Elisa wasn't alone. Sometimes at dinner parties, when one person or couple starts to take their leave, it is like a cork pulled from a drain, as others went to gather coats and say goodbye, and thank you, and gush about the food, and swirl down the drain out the front door. Within minutes nearly all the guests were saying goodbye.

Marion felt herself relax and take in the compliments. She appreciated that her cooking was good, and these endless and unanimous doorknob compliments made her feel reassured, but also tired. Or maybe it was coming down from the nervousness of prepping and anticipation. As she said her goodbyes, she wrapped Brodi's left arm in her arms, hugging her to herself. Brodi for her part leaned into Marion, and smiled as well. Alice, Ben and Audrey were still talking in the kitchen as Alice rinsed the last coffee cups.

Marion walked back to the kitchen, telling Alice to stop.

"You don't have to do that," Marion scolded. "I can take care of that later."

"It's no bother," Alice replied over her shoulder from the sink. "Besides, you put on that enormous spread and dessert. So yummy!"

"Zumba tomorrow, ladies?" Audrey asked.

"Oh, not for me," Marion said. "I'm exhausted."

"I'll bet you are, " Audrey said. "But if you are interested…"

"I'll be there," Alice said. ""I've got to work off the pounds I put on from this delicious dinner!"

"Well, maybe I'll go, " Marion felt herself wavering. "I know it would be good for me."

"You can shake out those bad vibes from this turmoil we're stewing about," Alice encouraged.

"I know!" Marion exasperated. "I am worried about my mom's advancing dementia, and then I get so riled up about the Stengel land sale. It's so infuriating that one man can have so much influence in this Valley. To think that we could lose another 300 acres of farmland to a developer is unthinkable. It was one of the earliest farms to plant tobacco for God's sake –"

"And used slaves," Alice interjected.

"Well, there is certainly that side of things, too. It is hard to reconcile that horror from the past with our beautiful valley. And his family made good money and survived in farming for generations. You'd think he'd have some loyalty to the earth and the community!"

Audrey broke in, "This is where I head out!" she said brightly. "Hope to see you tomorrow!" She quick-hugged everyone and disappeared.

"She left in a hurry," Ben observed.

"Well, it is weird for her with Doug Stengel being her dad." Alice said. "They aren't close at all, but still, it's awkward for her to get caught in conversations about him."

"Of course it is. I can't imagine what it must be like for her," Marion said."

Brodi said, "I keep forgetting that Doug Stengel is her father; she's just Audrey to me."

Alice said, "It's not like that's really part of her identity. She's her own person now, and everyone knows she teaches and dances. And everyone likes her, unlike her dad. AND," she emphasized, "Life goes on! How about George and Audrey going out for coffee!"

"Well, there's that, " said Ben.

"And, it still must be hard to have your family be a potential topic of conversation even at a dinner party you attend. If you are all in, then you've got to get ready to defend them. But if you have some mixed feelings, then you end up just feeling yucky and wanting to change the subject." Marion understood those complicated dynamics.

Ben was carefully placing dirty glassware into the dishwasher, and added in, "You know, I wish I had remembered Audrey was connected to Doug, somehow. I would have liked to talk with her about him, get her take on her old man. He's a kind of cypher in a way, and it pisses me off! He should just make up his mind and go with one thing or another!"

Brodi looked thoughtful. "You know, Ben, first off, I wouldn't ask Audrey about her dad. Seems like a touchy subject. But for my two cents, it dawns on me that Doug may be either more cagey than you give him credit for, a Wile E. Coyote kind of guy, or he may just not be honestly sure which way he's going to go. He may listen to you, think, that sounds good, then hears from the Rhinestone Redneck and think, the money sounds good. He may actually be of two minds about the whole thing."

Marion poured herself another glass of wine, and sank into one of the breakfast room chairs. "I'm pooped! I've got to sit down for a minute." She took a drink of her wine. "Mmm. Thank you two for staying to help clean up. I think it was a successful party!"

Alice took her wine over to the other side of the table and sat. "Marion, you always create the most delicious meals! It was actually an elegant menu and so good! I loved that curry! and the jasmine rice was perfect. Chapatis! Raita! I don't know how you do it -- making it all look so easy!"

Marion smiled. "30 minutes before the guests were supposed to arrive I was ready to tear my hair out. It seems like nothing is going to be ready on time, and I'm still not put together, and we're running around the place.

"You know, though," she reflected, "My mom was quite an entertainer in her day. I remember her and my dad having dinner parties with tons of people -- all different people -- coming over to the house. My brother and I were expected to help out, too, setting the table or cleaning the living room; we had our chores before guests. I can vividly remember looking at folks in our living room with a glass of wine --" she held up her glass, "And just looking so animated, also so relaxed, and having a good time. I wanted that when I grew up."

Alice raised her glass to toast Marion, "Well, here's to Beth and the influence she's had on her amazing daughter!" They clinked glasses and sipped. "How is Beth, by the way? Have you started talking to her about next steps?"

Marion glanced at Brodi, who made a slight grimace. "Well, I've tried to talk with her, but she's pretty set in her ways up there. It's almost as if she knows when the conversation is going to turn to the subject and she deftly sidesteps into a different topic. It is so hard! I feel like I am being the most disloyal child! And she'll do something that is so full of everything she always was -- witty, insightful, gracious, kind -- and I'll get confused thinking she's really still OK."

Brodi added, "In another vein, I've been working with this group in Florida to develop a kind of smart watch for folks with Alzheimer's, and we're hoping to have a prototype to help Beth. It has reminders, and information, and can help with appointments. I'm hoping to get one for Beth soon. It may help her keep track of things."

"It really will only postpone the inevitable, though, Brodi," Marion interjected.

"True, true," she agreed. "But even a few months of normality in this situation would be so helpful. It would buy us some time to figure out what's right."

Marion sighed. "It's all so sad really. And scary. Not knowing what's coming." Alice got up and crouched down next to her, rubbing her arm gently while looking into her face. Ben walked over and threw his arm around Brodi's shoulders, gently patting his friend's arm. For a few moments, friends with friends, nothing needed to be said. The air was pregnant with all the feelings, sadness and relief, love and uncertainty, possibilities and eventualities.

In the silence of the kitchen, the background music slowly filled the quiet. Gently strains of Chick Corea's *Spain* drifted in from the other room. The melancholy opening music fit the mood of the moment. As the tones of the electronic keyboard moved to a more sprightly and jazzy mood, the four friends smiled, Brodi tapping her feet, eyes closed, and let herself be taken into the music. Sometimes music filled spaces that were already full of feeling, already full of human experience, human suffering and human hope. Each person shares the moment, privately and together, each person hears the music, and somehow gets transported to somewhere, sometime, and someplace. Music is a magic carpet, a healing journey, a dynamic vessel that is almost guaranteed to move you.

As the song wound down at the end, Brodi sighed. "A full day, a full evening, and finishing it off with friends. Always appreciate that."

CHAPTER 9

Audrey Stengel Hodge wasn't sure that she had the details right. She often felt so uncertain, so unsure of herself. Ever since her painful and protracted divorce 8 years ago, she felt like her life had been turned upside down, and she never felt like things were solid, like, *solid*. She was always repeating things to remember them. Sometimes she said them under her breath, over and over, as though the repetition would drill them into her memory bank.

"Milk…milk…milk…milk…"

Then with dismay, she would get home from the grocery store missing the one thing she wanted for her bowl of granola in the morning. Conversely, there were often moments of clarity, and those were pure gold, practically bringing her to tears. By some seeming miracle, at 11:00 PM, she remembered that it was her brother's birthday. Her brother lived in New York, and was usually out on the town late, so she could still call and wish Ryan a happy birthday and not be late. She could crawl back out of the deep pit of uncertainty and panic. This, however, was one of those moments when uncertainty clawed at her belly like a tiger.

She had made a date (was it really a *date*?) to meet George at Amherst Coffee at 9:00, but could it have been 9:30? She suddenly wasn't sure of that. And she worried that it was supposed to be Sunday, not Saturday. She looked at her phone again. 9:02. Maybe it *was* Sunday? Oh God! This was torture. She should never have agreed to meet up with him, especially after just meeting him at the party at Brodi and Marion's house. She was really nervous. She dragged her fingers through her layered sandy blond hair, and checked herself in the window reflection. At 50, she felt she was beginning to look her age, and she hated it. There were the first signs of gray hair coming in. And her face now had furrows running from the corners of her nose down past her mouth. Wrinkles! And she often had circles under her eyes even when she got a good night's sleep. Fortunately, she still had the body and strength of a dancer. This morning, she wore a baggy white cardigan sweater over a loose green tunic, black Capri leggings that were casual, but somehow stylish too. She thought she looked OK, but damn, she just wasn't sure and worried that she was just fooling herself.

She looked past her reflection in the glass and spotted George getting out of his car across the street in front of the Jones Library. OK, good. Right day and time! George looked a bit disheveled, Audrey thought. His hair, now thinning, was obviously not combed or brushed, and his shirt, a blue striped Oxford, was wrinkled; she could tell even from this distance. His khaki pants also were a bit rumpled. Men, she thought. She hadn't needed to worry so much about how she looked; he obviously didn't. Still, when he stood up, Audrey could see that George took care of himself at the gym. Broad shoulders and a firm barrel around the middle, and he moved with the grace of someone comfortable in his body. He reached for his manbag out of the backseat, then apparently thought twice about it, and tossed it back. Audrey smiled; is it a meeting or a date? Slamming the door he turned, looked quickly both ways, and hustled across the street.

As George came through the front door of the coffee shop, his face broadened into a big grin upon seeing her.

"Sorry I'm late. I tried to finalize one more book chapter before I had to head out the door. It's great to see you again!" The words came in a rush of nervousness, and he unconsciously tried to smooth the ruffled hair.

"It's OK. It's only a few minutes, and I was worried I might have the wrong day or time. I had two glasses of wine the night we made the date!" Audrey was smiling, a bit nervous herself, but also amused at how *excited* she was to see George.

"Did you order anything yet?" He ventured.

"No, I was waiting for you," she replied.

"Oh, sorry." George responded quickly.

"No, I didn't mean, like *waiting*. I mean, I wanted to order with you!"

"Oh!" They both laughed.

They got their drinks (black coffee for George and a mint green tea for her) and sat at the cafe-level counter that ran around the wall in front of the window. All around them were folks with their morning caffeine and their laptops. Couples were talking and laughing.

"What a lovely morning," Audrey murmured.

"Gosh, yes. I can't believe how lucky we've been so far this spring. The cool nights and mornings, then the sun slowly warming up the valley through the day. All the daffodils are coming up and the fruit trees are blossoming. It's been heavenly," George enthused. They each

took a sip from their steaming mugs. They engaged in small talk for a
few minutes – weather, Saturdays, springtime, distal subjects.

"So, you are a writer?" Audrey curved the conversation closer to
home. "What you are writing about now? I mean, I don't want to jinx
your mojo by talking about it."

George was looking at her with a cocked head on one side, and a
slight smile on his face. "No I can say," he drawled slowly. "I am working on a slice of the history of this area, going back to the first settlers,
and talking about the families and their connections and struggles. It's a
book length manuscript."

"So, are you focusing on specific families?"

"Well, I am using a few families that have good historical records
as examples of what life was like. I have interviewed some locals about
their fathers and mothers and grandparents. They inherit traits and pro-
pensities and idiosyncrasies."

"So some inner dynamics as well as the economic and community development issues?"

"Well, yes. They inherit land and money and bad debts and family legacies. This place has a colonial history that has shaped what it is
through the families that lived here."

Audrey smiled and shook her head. "Well, that's a pretty interesting point of view. We are all a mixture of the history and culture that
came before us.. Would you be interested to know that my middle name
is Stengel?"

George gave a quick, short jerk in his seat.

"Like, the Stengels from Hadley? Like Doug Stengel?"

"Yep. My dad."

"But I thought you moved here four years ago from Connecticut.
Isn't that what you told me at the dinner party last week?"

"Yes. And that's true. I did move here from Connecticut, but it
was really moving *back* here. I left in 1989 to go to college at Yale, got
my degree and settled into life there, got married, then divorced. And
now I moved back here."

"Oh, OK. So I have actually researched *your* family a bit, and
have been writing about them and their presence in the valley, in Hadley.
I even interviewed your father when I wrote for the *Recorder*. One of our
stalwart, long term pioneer families. Maybe you can read some of the
material and let me know if it's accurate. Or maybe you've got some old

juicy stories…"

"Well, we are landowners and farmers from way back. Tobacco, cattle, then branching out to feed corn, now organic produce. The farmstand on Route 47. And of course, selling off lots of land to keep things afloat. I wasn't interested in all that so I had to escape, and did that through my brains. Worked my ass off to get into a good school. Looking back I am sure it helped getting into Yale that dad was reasonably well-connected. And my grandfather's brother went there. Legacy kids get a big boost in the application process."

George smiled in mild disbelief. "Hey! I'm sure you had plenty of smarts yourself to get into an Ivy. That takes brains and dedication. But wow! I had no idea you were related to Doug, and how curious we're sitting here. Normally I'd be interviewing you for my research!"

"Well, let's leave it at getting to know one another as friends, shall we?" Audrey took another sip of tea.

George looked intently at Audrey closely for a moment. He took a sip of coffee, and glanced out the window. People and traffic were picking up, and a number of folks on the sidewalk were going one direction with empty canvas bags, and coming back in the other with fresh produce, flowers, and bread.

"Looks like the Farmer's Market is getting busy," he commented, changing the subject.

Audrey smiled. "Yeah. I am going to head over there to get my weekly veggies and flowers when we're done."

When Audrey turned her head to the right, looking over her shoulder out the window, she could sense George studying the side of her face. She knew he could see the hint of a scar that ran the length of her jawline, puckering just below her ear.

She turned back, smiling.

George smiled, "And you are a fitness instructor, is that right?"

She laughed. "Sort of! Zumba's my latest passion," she laughed. "I just love learning new choreo and getting moving with a bunch of women!"

"That's so cool! I've done it once or twice at my fitness club, but I feel like a lumbering bear out there. The moves are so quick and complicated."

Audrey chuckled. "You just have to let your body move how it wants to move. I tell my ladies there is no right way, just make it your way! It is such a release and so energizing!"

George smiled and nodded. "And you teach as well? In school?"

Audrey corrected him. "I am also a private math and English tutor."

George arched his back, stretching a bit. "Really? Like with what kinds of kids? Or do you work with adults?"

"Well, I taught junior high school for almost 20 years in Middletown. I loved the kids, they are so inquisitive and full of energy at that age. It was amazing to watch them develop and grow. But then the district switched to a 7-8 middle school format, and they went to a modular schedule. I kind of lost some interest. Then the bureaucracy seemed to grow, and more and more pressure came in to score high on the state assessment test, and it became really unpleasant."

George nodded, "Yeah, older kids, more attitude."

Audrey agreed, "Yes. I lost some motivation, too, after my divorce settled out. It had seemed that my work kept me going when the divorce was most difficult, but then it kind of petered out for me. I think I wanted a change of scenery."

George only nodded. This was a story he knew from experience.

Audrey continued, "I still had some good friends from growing up around here, so it seemed like a good fit all around. Move to a place I love, be near to my roots again, and start over fresh. An old high school friend who now teaches at Amherst took me over to the high school and middle school to get introduced and within short order I had a full load of kids to tutor. "

"You know, it's often the old friends whom we can count on when we need them. They know us and are willing to help us out," George agreed.

Audrey shrugged, "Yes, so then I heard about Zumba, took a class at the North Hadley Community Center and I got hooked on that. I got Certified and now teach a class there every week. I am starting a class at the Amherst Senior Center, too. Life is pretty good again." Audrey stopped. Then snorted and laughed. "Well, now you know my life story!"

George had been unconsciously stroking his chin while he was listening. "Wow. I couldn't tell my story so succinctly, or elegantly. Thank you." He dipped his head in honor. "And, do you have kids?" he asked.

She took a deep breath, sighing. "No. No, Frank and I didn't have kids. At first when we started out we thought we didn't want to have kids. Too much trouble, and what's the payoff? Then I realized a bit too late that I actually did want kids, only to discover Frank had been having an affair with a colleague at work for a year. When I confronted him, he announced that he was leaving. Turns out she was pregnant, so the ass-hole – sorry – wanted kids after all. I was shocked, and then the night-mare of our separation and divorce proceeded from that."

"Ouch. Sorry. Didn't mean to bring up a sad subject."

"Oh, it's alright. You would probably know it anyway at some point. It's in the past and behind me now. But it was hell for a while. What about you? Married? Kids?"

George's eyes flicked away. "No kids. And I'm divorced, too. Another sordid story, I'm afraid to say. I've lived in this valley since I came here to go to UMass. A *long* time ago," he chuckled. "I got my journalism degree, and stayed on as a reporter for the *Recorder*. I met my wife while doing a story on the Fish and Wildlife Service. She was a fish biologist and was working on the salmon repopulation along the Connecticut. It was an inspiring story at the time, with lots of hope for reintroducing species to the big rivers, like the Hudson, and restarting the wild Atlantic salmon. Anyway, Jeannie was so involved in her work she really didn't have time for anything else it turns out. And we just faded away. It was like we ran out of gas." He shrugged his shoulders.

"How could that happen?" Audrey expressed annoyance.

He was surprised, and ran his hand briefly through his thinning salt and pepper hair. For a moment he looked fully his 50 years. "Well, our spark came when I wrote the cover story about the salmon and she was featured. Suddenly she was being interviewed on the radio – WFCR and WRXY. People would recognize her and we got invited to some nice parties. She was being hailed as an environmental hero, and we fell in love over that. When the excitement died down, and she got back into her work, it was really the drudgery of the scientific process, and she just lost herself in that. When the salmon didn't repopulate and the program got into trouble, she withdrew even more. And I couldn't go get her. I guess I pulled back too." George imagined mild disapproval from Audrey, and he struggled not to withdraw, but sit with it.

"Well, that's a sad story, too," She offered.

"Yes, it was. And, like yours, in the past now. It's been 10 years since we've been divorced."

Audrey, threw back the last of her tea.

"Do you want a refill?" George asked. "I'm buying."

Audrey grinned. "Very gallant. I *would* like another cup, but I want to get to the farmer's market."

"Can I get us cups to go, and walk over with you?" George's desire to keep up the conversation and prolong the visit was apparent, and Audrey responded. They had broached a few hard topics already, and he wasn't backing down, or running away.

"Yes, sir! You may buy me another cup of tea. Thank you."

They walked through the small parking lot and down the short alley to Pleasant Street, where the full bustle of the morning was unfolding. Cars filled the street in both directions, and people wound their way past on the sidewalk. Under the budding linden trees, they walked down to the crosswalk, and over to the Farmer's Market, which was really busy. A young man strummed a version of *Gravity* by John Mayer ("*It's working against me...*") on a guitar to add some music and to the single row of stalls set up on the Town Common. Fresh spring produce in shades of lush green lined the alley down the middle – it was a mixture of leaf greens, lettuces, kale, and some early peas and beans; an abundance of produce and riches. Audrey pulled a multi-colored wadded cloth shopping bag from inside her big leather purse, and strolled over to one stand with a happy farmer standing in front.

"Good Morning!" the farmer bellowed, as though speaking to the entire assembled crowd, but he was looking directly at Audrey.

"Good Morning, Sam," Audrey replied, "How's business?"

"Couldn't be better," replied Sam. They hugged briefly. "Already sold out half of the produce and it's not yet 10."

He was the picture of a healthy, robust farmer, -- apple cheeks, a full bushy brown beard, a green canvas apron covering a generous belly– with his dirty, farmer's jeans atop brown, and also dirty, work boots. His burly suntanned arms emerged from T shirt sleeves, even though it was still early spring. The sweat on his brow indicated that, for Sam, it had been a busy morning, and perhaps a late night the night before. But his smile was infectious. He glanced at George trailing slightly behind Audrey.

"Top of the mornin' to ya!" Sam beamed at George and seemed to revel in George's momentary discomfort.

"Hello, hello!" George replied. "How are you doing?" He

sounded casual, but Sam, and Audrey, could tell he was a bit stiff.

Audrey smiled. "This is George. We've just met for coffee and a chat."

Sam glanced once at Audrey, head cocked and one eyebrow raised.

"Lucky guy," Sam nodded knowingly. "Audrey's a great woman. She and my wife have known each other for years. Went to Hopkins Academy together. Worked on their family farms which were down the road from one another. What do you do, George?" Sam engaged George in small talk while Audrey looked over the leafy greens.

"Well, I am a writer. I've been a newspaper reporter, and now free lance."

"Cool! Have I read anything of yours? What's your last name?" Sam sounded like a father interrogating a kid trying to date his daughter.

"Well," George started in for the second time that morning. "My last name's Leon; you may have read some of my columns in the paper a while ago. Now I am writing a historical account of this area, and actually I just discovered that I've got Audrey's family in there."

"Do you now?" Sam pursed his lips, narrowed his eyes and nodded his head knowingly. It was one of his signatures. "My wife Rachel's family too, then maybe. Stokowski. Polish corn and potato farmers that came to Hadley in the mid-1800s."

"And Joseph married Emma Bartlett whose family had emigrated from Ireland escaping the potato famine. 1855. Yes, I have them in there as well. I'd like to meet Rachel."

You can," Sam looked around. "She's right over there at Good Hill Farm. Hey Rachel!" Sam boomed out over the crowd.

A tall woman with long, dark hair pulled back behind a scarf turned in a stall two spaces down. The look on her face was quizzical. When she saw Audrey she smiled. She held up her right hand with two fingers extended. She'd be back in two minutes. She turned back to the woman at that stall, and began to tally up what she'd bought.

"So that's pretty cool that you are excavating some of the old family stories from around here. And I believe I have read one or two of your pieces in the *Recorder*. Like your style," Sam commented. He was still talking to George, but he was also bagging up the green garlic scapes and mixed salad greens a customer had brought to him. "3 bucks," he said to them.

"How about things happening now?" Sam wondered aloud.

"Well, I am not going into current events in my book, " hedged George. "That is still unresolved. Besides, there are plenty of old stories and old tales to go around from 100 years ago."

"Yeah," Sam looked over at a woman feeling early spring snap peas. "They were picked this morning. I grow them in the greenhouse so we can have some early ones. Some are a bit firm, but they'll soften up by dinner. The heirlooms have the best flavor. Want to try a bite?" Sam reached to his left and skillfully brought up a cutting board to trim off the ends. These are Eisenhower purples. Come from New York originally. Try it." He speared one section with a paring knife, and thrust it over to the woman, who daintily plucked it off the blade and popped it into her mouth.

"Mmm. Oh my gosh, that's incredible. What flavor!" She looked as surprised as Sam looked pleased.

"Try it!" Sam turned to George again with the proffered bean pod.

George was a bit more sanguine, snapping the bean in half to inspect the inside before crunching it in his mouth. He gave a kind of groan as he closed his eyes. "Jesus. That's heavenly. So sweet and crispy."

Sam was proud of his produce, and others came closer into his stall, eyeing the proffered beans, and gasping and groaning. It was snap pea orgy, purple bean run amok, spinach decadence, butter lettuce fandango. People were buying things right and left, Sam was bagging beans, making change, and talking to 6 people at once, and George turned to see Audrey and Rachel talking with heads bowed together just outside the stall in the sunshine. Almost at once they both glanced at George, smiling conspiratorially.

He walked over to the two, smiling back at them.

"Hello, you're Rachel. I'm George."

"Nice to meet you," Rachel stuck out her hand, and George felt the strength and firmness of her grip. She was a farmer, no doubt.

George said, "I heard that you and Audrey went to high school together. It's so good to have old friends."

"We like to think of it as long-term," Rachel responded, "But yes, old too, I guess."

"I didn't mean it that way," George quickly interjected, a bit red in the face.

Both women laughed. "I'm just making fun," Rachel replied. "It's another beautiful day for the market. The season is starting out well. It's so great to see so many people here. I think a lot of them are spring break vacationers who have come in to check out the town. I see a lot of new faces."

Audrey looked around, appraisingly. "Yes, lots of new faces, aren't there? And somehow you can pick out the tourists."

George glanced around again. Yes, older men with bright new Tully hats. Women in new shorts and pastel colored T shirts under open coral colored windbreakers. Younger kids looking about with wide eyes, and sullen teenagers with heads bowed, hair dangling in their faces, smart phones at the ready, and airpods poking out of their ears. Somehow these families belied their non-native status. It was a tacit recognition, like a too-bright flower on a daylily that really shouldn't be standing at the side of the country road. All signals saying, *not really from here.*

"How's your mom?" Audrey asked Rachel.

"Oh you know, she's fine. She takes the kids while we're at the market on Saturdays, and they love to work with her in her garden. She misses Dad, you can tell, but she's coping with being on her own. She asks about you, how you are doing."

"I'm fine!" Audrey colored slightly. "You tell her I'm fine. I love teaching Zumba; it's my new thing. I love getting out there and shaking it. You should come to a class sometime. You'd love it."

"Hey, you two want to come over for dinner tonight? Love to catch up." Rachel seemed to perk up at her own invitation.

"Oh we. We 're not. We're not really. Well, you..." Audrey seemed as caught off guard as George felt on the spot. Audrey looked at George. George, raised his eyebrows and his shoulders simultaneously. His ears also rose up, making his glasses do a little hop on his nose.

Audrey was even redder in the face. "Would you want to go to dinner at Rachel and Sam's? I mean, do you have any plans tonight? Any other plans?" She smiled and slowly shook her head, clearly confused herself. This morning she had to steel herself to get out of the house for a coffee date, and now her friend had cornered into a real dinner date with a guy she barely knew. She did *like* George, but getting together in the evening with someone was a big step for her. Since her divorce she was very cautious about any guy.

George's smile was broad, soft, inviting and unequivocal. "I don't have any other plans. I'd like to go out to dinner and get to know Rachel and Sam better. How about you, though? Any *other* plans?"

"Oh, no. No. I don't have other plans. I mean yes. I'd...sure, be happy to go. I'd like to go. If you would. " Audrey stumbled through her responses, clearly nonplussed.

"Great!" Rachel looked back and forth between the two of them, beaming.

Audrey looked down, a bit embarrassed. Her longtime friend had pushed her to conquer a small hurdle that needed breaching. But that was her friend Rachel, whom she had known since junior high, who had known Audrey through losing her brother and her mother, and who helped to guide her through the most terrible and gut-wrenching separation and divorce. Rachel had known that Audrey needed to enter into new territory, open up to new friendships, new potentials, new possibilities. Audrey, who had been so crushed, smiled at Rachel with a squint in her eyes, like seeing the sun again after a long time.

George picked Audrey up around 6 and they drove into the fertile farmlands just west of Amherst. The first corn was rising up, almost a foot now, boosted by the high temperatures of the early spring and the prodigious rains they had been experiencing. As they drove and talked about the spring and the crops, Audrey felt easy with George, and enjoyed the beginning stages of getting to know him.

George asked, "So you've known Rachel since junior high here in Hadley?

"Yep. Hopkins Academy, class of 1987. It was quite a year and we promised each other we'd never part. Other than moving away for over 20 years, it's been pretty true." She laughed out loud. "When you are a kid you think the world's never going to end."

"And you were headed out of town at a dead run, I guess."

Audrey shook her head slowly, "Yes, I was off to an out of state school, and Rachel was staying in town and going to UMass. We were naïve. I was headed to this urban hoity toity school, and she was staying here on the farm."

"Well, you found your way back home."

"Yes, I guess I did."

Rachel and Sam lived on a low hillside just north of the UMass campus, and when they arrived the sun was sinking in the sky, and dusk was falling.

As they went inside, Rachel was just heading upstairs with little Jennifer, who turned to see Audrey coming in the door.

"Audwee!" she screamed with delight. She ran over to Audrey, who scooped her up.

"Hi Jennifer! How's things?"

Rachel came over, shaking George's hand. "Hey! I was hoping to get her into her pajamas before you two arrived, but no luck. Aunty Audrey is here!"

Audrey and Jennifer were indeed having a very intimate moment, turned slightly away from them, and talking animatedly about something. George looked on in amusement. Audrey was a natural with this little girl.

Sam emerged from the kitchen, wiping his hands on a dishtowel. "Hey you two! I see that the likelihood of early bedtime has just disappeared. Oh well!"

George proffered the bottle of wine they brought, and Sam made a great show of inspecting it. He wore an exaggerated frown.

"Lakewood Vineyards Reisling 2019. Hmm. Was that a good year? "

George reddened. "I actually don't know myself. I asked the guy at Amherst Wine Shop and he recommended it. Said 2019 was a nice dry year, lots of heat in the summer with some cool nights just before the harvest, which apparently sets the sugars just right. And it's supposedly very aromatic."

Sam laughed. "Well, to my mind that means we should open it right now! Follow me!" He turned with the bottle and headed back into the kitchen. George dutifully followed, catching Audrey's eye for a moment.

Rachel said, "While they are opening the wine, can you and I work to get this little one into her pjs? It's really her bedtime."

The two women trooped up stairs, Audrey carrying Jennifer in a piggyback.

Back downstairs, Sam popped the cork on the wine, and grabbed four glasses from the glass-fronted cabinet above the granite counter in the kitchen. Something bubbled on the stove and George spotted bread already sliced on a cutting board.

Sam poured all four glasses, and picked up two, handing one to George.

"L'Chiam!"

George nodded as they clinked glasses. "L'Chiam!"

The four sat around the table eating, drinking and laughing. Audrey couldn't remember feeling more relaxed with someone in a long time. George was a good talker and a good listener. He was full of interesting stories, and laughed appreciatively at various anecdotes. She decided before dessert that having him come back to her house after dinner was just the right plan.

CHAPTER 10

Ryan, Audrey's brother, half absorbed the breaking TV news. He had been waiting in a sports bar with a cold Opa Opa India Pale Ale to meet his sister for dinner when the news broke.

"This is WWLP TV 22 news, and we are breaking this story of a plane which has disappeared en route to the Hartford airport tonight. The private Lear jet was due at the Bradley International Airport around 6:00 PM this evening, and has been out of radio contact for over an hour. We will take you live to Amber Gold at the airport…"

Apparently the Federal Aviation Agency couldn't really explain yet what had happened, and the news story broke into all kinds of television, cable, and radio station programming all across the region.

It seemed that three businesspeople, from a land development corporation based in Atlanta, had been en route to western Massachusetts on business when the plane encountered the major early spring storm passing through. There were gale-force winds, thunderstorms and heavy rain in the area. The cold polar vortex at elevation had caused some sleet and hail. So far no crash site had been located.

Ryan tuned into the details being spun out about the plane and passengers. The private jet, a Cessna 1500 twin engine with a sleek golden exterior, wood panels on the inside along with a deep crimson pile carpet, Herman Miller-designed seating and recessed lighting, had been piloted by a young former Air Force pilot who had 3000 hours of recorded flying time behind the stick. The plane had been purchased from Cessna only 5 years before, and the pilot was very familiar with its handling.

All this information was being pumped into the airwaves with pictures of the three business partners and their families, and the pilot with his two dogs. Ryan listened with mild interest to the news cast, and could tell that the station was getting close to returning to its regularly scheduled programming, given that other than the disappearance, which was truly a mystery, there wasn't much to report. Of course, as there was a local connection, the local news anchors were milking what they could from the story.

His IPA was delicious and he was slowly working his way through a small bowl of mildly stale mini-pretzels that had appeared along with his drink. The waiter seemed friendly enough, and if Ryan wasn't meeting his sister he would have tried to figure out a way to engage him in further conversation. Ryan was pretty sure the guy was gay. He was handsome, had a nice biceps and a flat belly, which his tight black T shirt showed nicely, and tight jeans outlined muscled thighs to good advantage. Ryan was gay and single, so, available.

He took another sip of his drink, and glanced casually around the bar. The Smoky Top was somewhat nondescript in a funny way. There were wooden booths with red faux leather seats, small tables with smoothly lacquered wooden tops, and a bar with a nice wooden counter and high stools with the same red leather cushions. Lots of single men populated the bar, and a few couples, but Ryan had the sense that this bar could really be, well, *anywhere*. Come to think of it, maybe most bars could really be anywhere. No, that was not true. He had been in bars in Scotland and Ireland – pubs – that seemed to be steeped in the local flavor of that place. So what was it about The Smoky Top? Maybe it was the clientele? Lots of guys with ball caps either frontwards or backwards, and worn blue jeans, and plaid shirts. The women seemed friendly and known to one another, a nice local vibe. Two or three tables had groups of middle-age men that could be gay or straight or whatever. Ryan thought bemusedly that the folks looked like *folks in a bar*. It seemed obvious, but it was also a type, or the environment. Alcohol loosening insecurities and inducing warmth and friendship. He sipped his drink again, and the waiter ambled over.

"How's everything? Want anything else?" He smiled, and his face momentarily transformed into truly handsome, with smile lines appearing like old friends along his cheeks, and crow's feet deepening along his high cheekbones. His left eyebrow raised slightly with the smile, and Ryan felt his body's response to the innuendo.

"Well, that's a good question." Ryan slowly drawled, nodding slightly while contemplating the question. "I do want another ale, yes, but I don't want to get too much of a buzz going before my sister gets here."

"Oh! You're meeting your sister?"

"Yeah. I'm in from out of town. I grew up here, Hadley. We made a plan to meet here after she gets off work."

"Where you from now?" The waiter seemed inclined to have a little conversation, which was nice. He made a pass over the table top with his dishrag, brushing the pretzel crumbs to the floor.

"Oh, I live down in Jersey now. Across the river from NYC. My family's still into farming here, but I didn't want anything to do with that, so I got the hell out of Dodge when I could."

The waiter looked confused. "Dodge?"

Ryan chuckled. The waiter looked to be in his 20s, so an old TV reference was probably lost on him. "Sorry, that's an old reference from 1950s TV Westerns. You know, John Wayne, *Gunsmoke*. It just means I left my hometown as soon as I could after high school."

"Oh." The waiter seemed slightly put off by the comment. "So what about that beer? Want another now, or wait?"

"Oh heck, I'll take it now, and nurse it slowly until she gets here. It'll seem like I've just had the one anyway. Hey, have you been paying attention to this plane thing?" He nodded toward the TV hanging at an angle from the ceiling.

"Oh yeah! It's so strange! It just disappeared right? And those guys were coming up here, too. I think I may have seen one of them here in the bar at one point – he looks familiar. Totally creepy."

Ryan scrunched up his nose. "They came here? Amherst?"

"Well, yes! They had evidently been looking at turning some local farm into a business and living complex of some sort. Kind of weird. Disappearing like that. I'll get your Opa Opa."

He turned and wove through the warren of tables back to the bar. Just then, Ryan saw Audrey come in through the door, shaking off an umbrella. She scanned the crowd looking for him, and smiled broadly when their eyes met. She gave a happy wave and came over.

He got up from his chair and gave her a hug. "Hey sis! How are you doing?"

"Doing well, Ry. How are you? You look good! Have you been here long? Sorry I'm a little late."

Ryan looked at his sister appraisingly. "You are looking really good, Sis."

"Yeah, well, an hour of Zumba a day keeps your blood moving."

His sister grabbed his arm and they steered back to his table by the window. On the way, they passed one of the TVs and Audrey glanced at the picture, which at that moment showed the faces of the three people who had disappeared. The caption: "Plane disappears in

Connecticut" emblazoned above the faces. "Presumed crashed" also appeared at the bottom of the screen.

"What the -- ?" Audrey stopped in front of the TV. "Oh my God!" Her hands went to her mouth, as if holding back the next words she was going to say. Shock registered on her face.

She looked quickly at Ryan, then back at the TV. Audrey became transfixed by the story unfolding before her, and seemed to have forgotten her brother. Ryan had made it back to his table, and had sat down on his stool, and slowly sipped his resupplied beer while he watched his sister's reaction to the news story.

The local TV station was based in Springfield, 15 miles down the road and the largest city in Western Massachusetts. This was big local news, and the reporters figured they could really ride this story considering its local angle.

Apparently possible crash sites were being speculated, in Western Massachusetts near Mt. Washington, or northern Connecticut in the forest. It was still raining pretty hard in the mountains, but even so the plane would have been pretty far off course to crash out there. If it had crashed.

Ryan signaled the waiter and mouthed, "Reisling," pointing to his sister before the waiter got to the table. The waiter stopped in his tracks, nodded, and headed off, returning shortly with the grapefruit-colored liquid in a wine goblet.

Audrey turned and looked at her brother, a cascade of emotions ran across her face. He sat quietly. Ryan had learned when they were kids that Audrey needed space to allow her feelings to settle before she could speak. The words, when they came, spilled out like water sloshing from a bumped glass.

"Oh my God, I am shocked! This is *so* unbelievable! These were the guys who were trying to buy Dad's farm! Dad is going to be in a tizzy with this. I wonder if he knows? Should I call him? Wayne Thibodeaux was an *asshole*, but this is horrible."

"Wait! These guys wanted to buy *Dad's* farm? That's crazy?"

"Yeah! They have been in the news and the papers since they were coming up from the South, and making big noise about the development they were planning. That guy loved making the news! Some rich old white guy who likes throwing his weight around. Dad felt like he had an ace in the pocket with Wayne, since he might be able to sell the farm to him. Now it looks like that's gone."

Ryan thought for a moment. "So maybe Dad can't sell the farm? What will he do?"

"Oh, I don't know. This is all so sudden."

Ryan took another pull from his IPA. Audrey sipped her wine.

"Wow, I had no idea about this. So, you knew these folks, or what?" Ryan was nonplussed.

"I didn't know them, no. But they were coming *here* to meet with *Dad!* These guys had plans to create a big combination condo and retail center along with a river marina. They were wooing Dad on one side, and then Dad had the Land Trust wanting him to preserve the land for all eternity on the other, but not offering much money. Of course everyone and their mother had an opinion on the matter, and told him so. Dad's been grumpy for months about this."

"Dad's been unhappy his whole life, Audrey. Face it. He's been a sour, unhappy man from the beginning. Whatever this was," he said gesturing with his beer bottle at the TV, "This is just the way grumpiness is playing out right *now."*

"Oh Ryan, Dad's not always unhappy. He sees lots of good things and he enjoys lots of things. He's getting old though."

"Hey, we're all gettin' old, sis. I'm 48. Life's not easy in the big city, either. "

"But it's the life you chose, Ryan. You could have stayed here."

"No fuckin' way."

"I mean lived here in the valley with your family, your friends. Places you know. The Valley is totally inclusive in its outlook. Very progressive. Instead you had to head off to Rhode Island and go to that fancy school, and become an artist, then move to New York and live in some crummy apartment where people in the building sold crack and you nearly got mugged three or four times. One of your so-called friends was *selling* drugs for God's sake. What the hell kind of life is that?""

Ryan glanced away through the window, rain-soaked and liquidly reflecting the neon lights of the beer signs. The rain was falling heavily in the light of the street lamps outside, wide puddles covered the parking lot.

"Look, sis, I came up here to see you and have a nice visit. It's been way too long. I really don't want to fight or rehash old wounds. I feel badly that this thing has happened for Dad, but honestly, I just don't have any juice left to feel sorry for him."

She sighed, put her arm around his shoulders and gave him a squeeze. "Sorry, Ry. It has been so long. I feel like I have to cram everything into a few days – even the arguing – before you'll disappear again."

"I was here on a book tour of little New England bookshops in 2019 when *Green Light* was released. And before that you came to New York in 2015 to check out my bohemian lifestyle."

"Oh goodness, yes. That long? Anyway, New York was scary to me. But how are your books selling?"

"Not too bad. 5,000 copies of *Green Light* and the serialized version online. An indie animation group is making a short film version, and I'm learning CGI graphic design through that. The company's finishing production over the next few weeks, so I have a little break right now. Hence the visit."

Audrey smiled widely. "That is so cool! So you're rich and famous now?"

He chuckled. "Definitely not rich, and famous among a small cadre of 12-24 year old boys who probably still have acne and tend toward the anti-social. But it helps pay the bills, and it's fun, and I still get to create."

Audrey pressed, "You gonna see Dad while you're here?"

"Not if I don't have to."

"It would be good to see him; he'd appreciate it. Especially now."

"*Sis!* Stop being so pushy. I haven't talked to Dad in years, and haven't seen him in over a decade. And that visit is embedded with burn marks in my brain. He doesn't write or call me either."

"Ryan, he's old and proud. He loves you in his own way, and he definitely misses you. Besides, he's softened up. We're all he has left. He asks about you. Wonders if I've heard from you, and how you are doing."

"He could ask me directly, Audrey."

"Ryan Stengel, from whom do you think you got that stubborn streak, anyway?"

"OK, OK, maybe I'll give him a call. I feel sorry for him if this thing," he nodded at the TV screen, "Means his business deal got messed up."

"Thanks, Ry. So, I am famished. Dinner?"

"Su--u--re," Ryan sounded a bit hesitant. "Here?"

"Oh gosh no! Are you kidding? The food here is terrible! They don't call it barfood for nothing (she made it sound like *barf-food*). We're heading into town to one of my favorites, Johnny's Tavern."

Ryan paid the tab, and the waiter gave him a sideways glance of annoyance as they walked out.

Audrey waved him toward her late model black Honda CRV. They climbed in as the rain increased in intensity and they shook the rain off as the car warmed up. Audrey looked at her brother and smiled.

"He was cute...think you'll follow-up? "

"Maybe...probably not." Ryan looked uncomfortable.

They both noticed someone with a jacket slung over his head running toward their car from the bar. He was dodging puddles as he ran, coming up to the passenger's side of the vehicle. Ryan recognized the waiter from their table, and rolled down the window.

The waiter thrust a piece of paper at Ryan. "Hey. I know you're in town just visiting, but if you wanted to get together for a drink or something, here's my number."

Ryan took the paper, and smiled. "Thanks! I'll text you!" The waiter smiled back and then turned to dash back through the rain to the bar.

Audrey smiled, shaking her head. "Well, the first step taken!"

Ryan smiled shyly in return. "You never know..."

"You know I liked that guy you were seeing when I visited you in New York. André? I was hoping you two might make it as a couple. You have your mysterious ways, Ryan, but you are smart, funny, and you are good looking for a middle-aged guy. Apparently..."

"How about you, sis? Dating?" Ryan deflected more discussion on the waiter, or past loves. He loved his sister, but over time she had naturally taken on a kind of mothering role, maybe naturally, after their mother had passed away.

"Well, as a matter of fact I am. Dating. It's early days yet, but he's a nice guy. Name's George and he's a writer. Also divorced, no kids, so we have that in common. We met at a dinner party and then had a nice date."

"That sounds promising. Is he all into Zumba too? Or does he have some other sports thing?"

"He loves to hike and bike and cross country ski. He works out at the gym. He loves to fish. He really likes being outdoors, he says, and we are planning to go for a bike ride this weekend if the weather gets nice. Doesn't look promising right at this moment though." The rain picked up a notch in intensity, drumming on the car roof as the windshield wipers slapped furiously at the water rushing down the glass. Most cars were moving at a crawl through the puddles and rivulets in the road.

"Glad you found someone, Audrey," Ryan nodded.

Ryan looked over at his sister again. She had a vague, wistful air about her. Ryan realized that Audrey had never really seemed happy, at least not as an adult. He didn't actually know her that well, of course, since they lived so far away and his penchant for long periods of silence was not conducive to staying in touch.

They had arrived in town, and Ryan noticed the new buildings that were transforming the small college town. They passed a 5 story brick and glass office and apartment building on the corner of Triangle Street, and another 5 story building along East Pleasant street going up. It totally changed the look of the town, made it feel cramped. Audrey turned left on Kellogg, then right into the parking lot behind the coffee shop.

When they came through the front door of the restaurant they were enveloped by the warm and savory smells from the kitchen. The interior was taverny with wood walls and sconces, and pictures of horses and horse racing on the walls. The hostess knew Audrey and smiled warmly when they entered.

"Hey Audrey! How are you!" She came over and hugged her.

"Hey Barb! So great to see you! This is my brother, Ryan, up from New York."

"Hey Ryan, Nice to meet you! Welcome home!"

Ryan smiled and shook the proffered hand..

"Let me show you a table we have in the back. Just opened up." Beth grabbed two menus from the stand in the front, and moved easily through the crowded restaurant. Audrey and Ryan trailed behind. The customers seemed happy, talking, laughing, and enjoying the food. Ryan glanced at plates as he passed, noting braised seafood, fresh green salads, and French fries elegantly served like a bouquet of flowers sprouting from a deep metal cup.

Audrey and Barb chatted briefly as they settled in. Then Barb bustled off, stopped expertly to clear some plates from a neighboring table, smiling and chatting along the way.

They perused the wonderfully diverse menu, everything from comfort food appetizers, soups and salads to entrées with creative sauces and presentations. The server was friendly and helpful, and knowledgeable about wines to pair with the dinners. Audrey opted for smoked salmon steak on a bed of fresh greens, and Ryan went for a slider and the fries.

Ryan pursed his lips for a minute. Thinking. "OK, so what is going on with the farm? I try not to care, but since this whole thing has come up I am curious."

Audrey smiled. "So you *are* interested in what's going on with Dad and the property? I'm glad. It's a pretty big deal around here, since a big development could reshape the whole economy. Of course whichever way he goes could affect all the local towns. It puts a lot of pressure on Dad, and you can see he feels the stress of making a decision that so many people are going to be affected by. I just wish he'd make up his mind and be done with it."

"Do you care which way he goes?" Ryan asked.

"I'm not sure. I love that farm, and wish it would stay like that forever. Of course if he does sell it to the developer for big money, you and I would probably inherit some good cash. So there's that."

"I don't even want to think about that," Ryan mused. "But, it would be nice…"

The drinks arrived. Nodding silently at the waitress for the service, Ryan held his glass in two hands on the table, almost as though praying.

"OK, Sis, so this is the story. I do care about Dad, but I never felt that Dad ever wanted me involved in the business at any level except as a hired hand. He was happy to have me work on the farm, like as a kid or in high school, but I never got any indication that he actually wanted me to be the one to take over some day. If anything, it seemed like you were the one to get the nod to go to buy new equipment, or when he wanted to assess buying up adjacent properties. He seemed to look to you for advice, or your opinion. He never even asked me what I thought. From my perspective you were the heir apparent. At least after Mike died. And sometimes I felt like Dad resented the fact that I was the son who survived. It was like I was shut out of it..."

"Ryan, you never showed any interest! Dad never saw any glimmer on your part to want to learn about farming! You always ran off to play with your friends or be with your girlfriend as soon as chores were over!"

"He never even asked if I wanted to learn! He was always comparing me to you. "'Your sister could drive that tractor easy.' 'Audrey can plow in a straight line down the rows.' What was I supposed to get from that? I was never going to match up!" Ryan stopped to take a drink as the dinner plates were put before them.

They began to eat in silence, each in their own thoughts and feelings. Their server swept by and asked, "How is everything?"

Audrey managed a wan smile, "Wonderful."

The server appraised them for a moment, then reached for Audrey's wine glass. "Another Riesling?"

"Sure, thanks."

As she moved away, Audrey leaned forward and spoke in a lowered voice.

"Ryan, Dad loves you. He misses you. He's too proud to say anything like he's sorry, but he knows he never knew how to connect with you. He's getting old, Ry, and his health is failing. He's trying to decide what is best for the farm as he faces retiring. He actually needs us both, though he would never say so."

"OK, whatever. He's an asshole, though."

"Ryan, cut the *poor me* crap. Dad did his best, and he lost Mom which was a huge blow to him. He also lost his oldest child, for God's sake! He's been a farmer his whole life, and he's *survived*. He's really not sure which way to turn, and he feels like there's no one he can really trust for advice. He has over 300 acres of land right along the Connecticut that everyone drools over. There are three or four streams that cut through the property as tributaries, and they have fish in them – trout and some small bass."

"You sound like National Geographic or something..."

Audrey grimaced. "He farmed that land his whole life, as did his father, so that's all he ever knew. Our family name is well-respected in town because of him. And, that land is worth millions to a developer. He could literally sell it all and make millions of dollars! Millions! And just walk away from this impossible life. It's hard work, and he's done it for over 70 years. He's done, but can't figure out the best way to close that chapter. I think he would appreciate hearing from you right now, and knowing at least his kids will support him in making the decision."

Ryan made a moue with his mouth as he listened to his sister. Her passion made sense in so many ways, but there was a part of him that had spent too many years in opposition to his father; he wasn't sure he could switch to a different stance. His anger and resentment had simmered for decades, and it didn't move easily.

Ryan was erecting the wall that came as second nature when he felt attacked or criticized. Audrey could sense it, and she admitted to herself it was a great strategy. Most people had no clue that Ryan was gay when they were kids, certainly not their parents, although their mother claimed she had known from an early age. But Audrey had only suspected, since her younger brother never said anything, and he had actually dated girls in high school. She hadn't seen that those relationships had been a cover, so he could keep his true self hidden and safe.

She looked at her brother, slowly eating his burger, and he was staring into middle distance space.

"Ry, look, I'm sorry. I just want you and Dad to at least bury the hatchet. It's painful for me to see the distance between you two, knowing that there could at least be some sense of connection."

Ryan smiled, "You have always been good at softening me up. We'll see."

CHAPTER 11

"So I wonder what this'll mean for the sale of the Stengel property?" Brodi wondered aloud as Ben smoothed down the coat of the coal black horse. The news of the plane disappearance and the missing three business people aboard had been in the news for a few days now.

They were standing next to Ben's daughter's horse, Lightning, in the barn at Muddy Bottom Farms. Muddy Bottom was almost a euphemism at this point; the barn had seen better days and all the equipment was falling into disrepair.

Lightning had a white blaze along his nose that sparkled against his black coat, and Ben actually enjoyed helping Sophia by caretaking the horse on occasion. He massaged her glossy coat with long, gliding strokes of the brush.

"Well, The Trust is speculating whether Red Dirt Associates will continue with the offer for the property now that Wayne Thibodeaux has disappeared," Ben said. "The push for purchase may have been his personally, with others following reluctantly. He was gung-ho and very aggressive, in his easy-going, Southern drawl kind of way. He could talk others into a plan that they didn't really want to follow. When I spoke with Doug briefly he seemed a bit at sea about what all this would mean."

While the certainty of a plane crash remained up in the air, and under investigation by the FAA, there had been hints in the press that some routine maintenance which hadn't been done to the equipment might be revealed. It was known now that the Georgia developer had been en route to Hadley on another junket to woo Stengel for the property. While Doug Stengel was himself a hard-scrabble farmer, with a life coaxing crops from lush loamy soil, he wasn't one to rush into decisions, which at times had driven Ben mad. And he had strung Wayne Thibodeaux along as well.

Ben changed brushes to the grooming comb and continued with his rhythmic stroking. Brodi watched her friend's practiced movements.

"You look pretty natural grooming horses, Ben."

"My mom's cousins had horses, and showed them at meets and events. Sometimes when we'd go out to the country to visit, I'd get to ride with my cousin, Betsy. She was an outstanding rider – won lots of competitions – and we'd just hang out in the barn. Our moms would be in the house talking – and getting smashed as it turns out – and we'd just be in the barn with the horses.

"Uh, sounds like an escape to me," Brodi added.

"It was a great time; I think it was really relaxing for both of us. My cousin always seemed more comfortable around the horses, like she knew how to relate to them, and they were reliable in the way they acted. She showed me how to groom a horse, although I was always an unsteady rider. I rode at summer camps too, but it was a cross between a thrill and terror for me. I once got thrown off a horse because I hadn't cinched the girth strap, which is kind of a basic thing, as it turns out. Got a slight concussion then."

Brodi absorbed this bit of information. "Wow, and you still let Sophia ride even though you were nearly killed riding as a kid?"

"I was actually really glad when Sophia showed so much enthusiasm with horses, since she's such a cautious person. Alice and I let her find her own way with it. I was a bit nervous when she voiced an early desire in owning her own horse, but then – you know Sophia – she is a determined young woman, and has demonstrated responsibility with the horse and with everything else – homework, track and cross country, piano. She does it all on her own, no reminders. Lightning is a kind of reward."

"So, do you ride with Sophia?"

"Well, we've been out a few times, but I still feel awkward and Sophia's a perfectionist when it comes to form and commands and such. I think I embarrass her, so mostly Alice and I watch her ride. Proud parents."

Ben finished grooming and patted Lightning's neck and rubbed the white blaze on her nose. The horse responded with a swish of the tail and a noise of contentment.

"Lemme feed you, beauty," Ben said to the horse.

A silver Toyota Prius swung into the parking lot just at that moment, slowed in the dust and gravel, then came to a stop just outside the open barn doors. A slight young man with silvered sunglasses climbed out of the driver's side door, looking into the barn doors.

"Hey, Sanjay! What are you doing out here?" Ben called through the doors to the young man, who then started toward the barn, removing his sunglasses and squinting into the bright morning sun.

"Hey Mister Miller," said the young man. "I had to drive to come find you out here. I couldn't get hold of you. Left messages. Your wife said you were here when I called your house. She said to come find you." The young man seemed agitated.

"Sanjay, this is Brodi Saunders." "Oh, hello, Ma'am." Sanjay extended his hand to Brodi. His grip was surprisingly soft, and Brodi was worried that she would crush the young man's hand when they shook.

Ben pulled out his phone and swore. "Shit! My battery's dead. So what's up?"

"Well, there have been a few calls to the office today, and also an email that sounded somewhat urgent. Some guy's trying to reach you to talk about the Stengel property. He's from Georgia."

Ben glanced at Brodi with an expression crossing worry and annoyance. "I wonder what the hell that is?"

Sanjay ventured, "His message only said it was urgent he speak with you. He didn't indicate anything else."

Ben seemed momentarily conflicted. He ran his hand over his short-cropped graying hair, then once over his face, clearly not welcoming the news.

"OK. OK. It must have to do with Thibodeaux's disappearance. But why call me? Their conversations with Doug Stengel are their own negotiations." He started pacing around the yard next to the barn in circles, looking intently at the ground. Sanjay stood a few steps away, staying quiet.

Brodi cleared her throat. "Ben, look. I don't think you have enough information here. If your phone's dead, why don't we get in the car, you can drop me off, and then head back to your office with Sanjay. I'm sure you can figure out what to do when you get there. Let's put the horse away; does it need food or anything?"

Ben looked at his friend, small relief creeping across his face. "Right. Thanks, Brodi. Yes, Lightning just goes into his stall on the left. I'll lead him back there, and if you can get some oats from the bin over there and pour them in his trough, that would be great."

Sanjay headed to his car, and spinning the Prius around a bit too fast, gunned his car out of the barnyard. As fast as a Prius could go anyway. After securing the horse, Ben and Brodi followed suit.

* * *

Back in the downtown Amherst office, Ben hurried into his private office and flicked on his computer, then tapped the speakerphone to listen to his messages.

"Hello Mr. Miller, this is John Engle from Red Dirt Associates in Atlanta, Georgia. I wanted to connect with you to discuss the Stengel Property. We are aware that your client, Valley Conservation Land Trust, is interested in buying the property from Mr. Stengel. As you may know, our associate, Wayne Thibodeaux, has apparently disappeared and perhaps perished in an unfortunate plane accident up there, and Wayne was our principal on the negotiations with Mr. Stengel. I would like to urgently discuss our mutual interest in the property at your earliest convenience. Please call me at…"

The tone of John Engle's message indicated urgency, and Ben was wondering what the urgency was. It was Saturday morning, after all, not the business week. The conversations with Doug Stengel had proceeded, if not glacially, then at least slowly and episodically up to this point. In fact, Stengel had not shown any clear indication that he was going to sell to anyone in particular. Doug was a classic older farmer, moving along when it seemed time to do so, but content to let things simmer for days or even weeks at a time. Having worked with many of these local, long-term farmers, Ben had learned to adapt to this pacing, and let the seller define the terms. Valley Conservation Land Trust came in with an offer that was slightly or significantly below the asking price, and even approached farmers or landowners before they themselves were really thinking of selling. The primary bargaining point was preserving the land, perhaps allowing the farmer to continue farming as long as he or she wished. Then another farmer continued to use the land for crops or livestock while preserving the rural character of the valley. When Ben was in conversation with a farmer in general, many were already thinking pretty hard about the APR, and understood it provided compensation only for the agricultural value of the land. It was often the farmer's heart that spoke to them about preserving their farm.

So why would this guy from Georgia want to speak with him? It really didn't make any sense.

Ben glanced at the email that had come in from the same John Engle, and saw that it was essentially the same message. Pushy. And the guy wasn't giving him anything to go on to let him know what was up. Glancing out the window at the Pleasant Street intersection the office overlooked, Ben could see diagonally across the street to Amherst Coffee, where patrons sat outside with their to-go cups at the outdoor tables. He imagined himself sitting out there, too, enjoying a late Saturday morning coffee in the sunshine. No worries, talking about nothing in particular. Heavenly. But he had to call this guy back. He was stalling. He noticed Elisa someone-or-other come out with a coffee, and turn around the corner and head into the architect's office. He recognized her from Brodi and Marion's dinner party, and was remembering her comment about the architect's office being under some pressure apparently about the Stengel property. He wondered what that office was working on, or for. He glanced at the second floor windows and saw a number of folks there in the offices through the windows. Hmmm.

He looked through the interior window in his office wall to see Sanjay sitting at his desk in the main room. He caught Sanjay quickly glancing down at his computer monitor, as the young man had been watching him.

He walked to his office door. "Hey Sanjay, thanks for coming to find me. Sorry my phone was dead. Listen, I am going to call this character back and find out what he wants. What are you doing here in the office on a Saturday, anyway?"

"Oh, sorry Mr. Miller." (Sanjay was always apologizing). "I was just taking care of a few things on the East Pleasant Street sale that I thought would be good to get done over the weekend. When I saw that the message came into the general office account I thought you would want to know. I am sorry I had to bother you on your weekend."

Ben shook his head. "Sanjay, it was TOTALLY the right thing to do, and lucky for me you were here. I don't want you to work here all day, though. It's a beautiful Saturday and you should be out enjoying yourself."

Sanjay just smiled, acknowledging the praise. He turned back to his monitor and began furiously typing.

Ben turned back to his desk, punched up the number into his phone and let it ring. While he waited for the answer he gently tapped a pen on the legal pad he kept at his left hand.

The phone was answered. "John Engle."

"Mr. Engle, this is Ben Miller calling from Amherst, Massachusetts..."

"OK, Miller, thanks for calling back. I wasn't sure your office was operational on a Saturday. I wanted to assure you that Red Dirt Associates was going to be strongly pursuing the purchase of the Stengel Property in Hadley, Massachusetts, despite the untimely plane disappearance of our associate, Wayne Thibodeaux." The energy coming through the phone was unmistakably forceful and aggressive, again, to Ben's ear, strangely countered by the soft, Southern drawl the man had. Ben recognized an asshole when he heard one.

So what was this about? A pissing contest? A chess move? An obfuscation? A stalling maneuver? A scare tactic?

"Look Mr. Engle, I am sorry about the loss of your associate. I can't imagine what your firm is going through with him being missing and possibly dead..."

"That's why I am calling you, Miller. Red Dirt Associates is proceeding full bore on this property, as per Wayne's wishes and instructions. While we grieve the loss of our associate, our business must go on, and we have a team picking up where Wayne left off."

"OK. I think I understand, and of course Levin & Miller Associates are unable to discuss any particulars of client business. So if you can assist me with the reason for your call..."

"Mr. Miller, it's all over the news and you are quoted in your capacity as the attorney for Valley Conservation Land Trust that you are part of the negotiation with Mr. Stengel on their behalf. I wanted to let you know that you might want to re-consider the pursuit of this property, since Red Dirt Associates will be making a significant offer to purchase, and we feel certain that Mr. Stengel will realize the potential for massive financial gains through our offer, not to mention getting to see his property turned into an economically viable income generating establishment."

A-ha. That was it. This guy wanted Valley Conservation Land Trust, through Ben, to back off in pursuing the Stengel estate. Ben smiled to himself. For some reason this property here in little old Happy Valley had gotten under their skin there in Atlanta. How interesting. And this was their opening gambit to be the only buyer in the market.

"Well, look, Mr. Engle, I appreciate how hard it must be to approach a seller of a property so far away from – where did you say, Red Dirt, Georgia? –"

"Atlanta!"

"Oh yes, Atlanta, well, I know Hadley, Massachusetts is a pretty good hike from Atlanta, Georgia, but there are some sensibilities here about our valley, and what it means for us here to preserve our landscape. So there are some factors that you might not be taking into account here."

"Honestly, Miller, you don't frighten me. We've bought property all over the South and the Eastern seaboard, and we know what it takes to turn a commercial property into a viable venture. We're expanding into New England, which we see as a huge potential market. Stengel will see what we have to offer. Valley Conservation Land Trust might as well back off. Lots of other property on the market up there, I'll bet. More in your league."

"John, I 'm not sure you appreciate our little communities up here. Your buddy, Wayne, seemed to respect people's way of life in his travels. He spent time getting to know Doug Stengel as a person, and a farmer, and I know he even got to know some other folks up here. Maybe you want to take a trip up here yourself to see what's going on in our little Happy Valley."

"Don't worry, Miller. We'll be up there soon enough. Goodbye." And Engle hung up.

As Ben hung up the phone, he was sweating. He wasn't used to being spoken to so forcefully right off the bat. He had avoided criminal litigation when he studied law for exactly this reason. He wasn't a great debater, nor was he good at arguing. He was methodical and down to earth. His heart raced, and he felt a little queasy.

Sanjay looked over at him as he got up from his desk. Ben nodded to him, then turned to look out the window and collect his thoughts. He felt attacked, and ambushed. Why in the world had Engle been so antagonistic? It didn't make sense. What was it about this property that made him so aggressive? He looked out his window, over the two story brick building across the street, and he could just see the tops of a few hills in the distance. The sun was illuminating the trees on the slopes there, and he remembered how much he loved this valley. This was the reason he was so keen to help out Valley Conservation Land Trust. Now he was a warrior in this fight.

Ben typed a long email to the Executive Director of VCLT detailing the telephone conversation and his recommendation relative to moving ahead with the purchase of the Stengel property. He had to in-form and advise VCLT on all developments, but this one also put a bad taste in his mouth. He stood up and walked again to the office door.

"Hey Sanjay, it was really good that you fielded this call. This guy is from the Atlanta developer's office; you probably heard of them on the news. They are pretty keen to buy the Stengel property, and it turns out they want to scare VLCT off the purchase. So now I am offi-cially sending you home. Finish up and let's get out of here and enjoy the rest of the day." He smiled, and turned to pack up his things. As he got up he glanced again across the street, and noticed that the lights were still blazing in the architect's office. And he could see there was a group of people there, all hunched around one computer terminal. Busy for a Saturday.

CHAPTER 12

The actual Vernal Equinox falling on a Tuesday, Old Jim held his equinox healing ceremony on the previous Sunday, hoping for a better turnout. The daylight arose on a foggy and chilly day, with rain having fallen at night. The grass was soaking, but Jim held these *earth-based* rituals rain or shine (or snow or shine). The wet weather definitely affected fire ceremonies and using drums. Jim did not like using the drums in the rain, as it could warp the wood frames, and damage the intricate carving and paintings on the sides. Plus the drums sounded dead in the damp.

Jim was one of the many white people who had felt a connection to nature-based spirituality, and spiritual paths. He believed that had been his true calling from the realm of the spirits, and he practiced his own form of cobbled-together rituals and prayers and activities, trying to honor the shaman's path, and following a four-fold way. It had made sense to him from the very first time he had entered a sweat lodge ceremony some 30 years previously in California. Old Jim's spiritual practices were no more easy to trace in origin than a mongrel dog's lineage. It all made sense to him, in some non-linear way, and those looking for a feeling-based spiritual experience were drawn to Jim and his practices. He held minor cult status among a small band of post-hippies and back to the land types. A few young Millenials had also aggregated onto his coterie.

Old Jim had been conducting his solstice and equinox healing ceremonies for years, and it always attracted 15 or 25 people. The ceremonies were held either at sun-up or sundown at the Sunwheel stone circle at the University, which itself had been installed by astronomy professor Judith Young and used to teach astronomy about the rising and setting of the sun relative to the changing of the seasons. Dr. Young, in her lifetime, had a wonderful way of sprinkling some myths and legends about the solstices or equinoxes, along with some hard-core science in her lectures out here. The University didn't seem to mind Jim out here doing his thing.

The stone circle looked like a miniature Stonehenge. A group of large, 8-12 foot high gray Chester granite stones stood in a circle about

60 feet in radius at the cardinal points, with smaller stones sitting at various points along this circumference. If you stood at the center of the circle, on a small hunk of granite set in the ground, you could align these smaller stones with points on the horizon where the sun rose or set on each of the equinoxes and solstices. At Stonehenge, and other Neolithic settings like Carnac in Brittany, the stones apparently served a ritual purpose for the ancient peoples, and Old Jim, like many others around the world, tried to recreate those rituals on those days sacred to the pagans.

As he was unloading his truck, a silver Accord pulled into the parking lot. Jeremy smiled and waved to Jim through the windshield.

"Hey Jeremy!" Jim said as Jeremy exited the car. "Good to see you!" He was putting on a Mexican blanket multi-colored vest, the patterns and colors looking traditionally indigenous.

"Hey Jim! Jeremy replied. "Good to see you, too!" They gave each other a brief hug.

"Hey! How was your winter?"

"Awesome, " the youth replied. "I'm playing guitar, and a few of us formed a band. It's really cool."

"That's wonderful!" Jim enthused. "What kind of music? Have you played any gigs yet?"

"Well, we do some hip hop, blues, and some Latin stuff. I include some of the African spiritual stuff in my lyrics."

"Sounds good! Do you have any songs you'd like to share with us today? I've always got room to add in material from participants in the ceremony."

"Hmm. Well, I am a little nervous about that. The songs are really for the band, and I don't know how they'd do out here. Also I am really a guitar player, and only noodle around on the drums when I'm here."

"Can you sing the song, and we can add rhythm on the drums?"

"I guess so…" Jeremy seemed uncertain, not sure how to back out of this.

"Great!" Jim abruptly turned with his plastic tub of regalia and walked over to the stone circle center, where he put down the tub, took off the top, and began fishing out various ceremonial items.

Jeremy felt a wave of panic come over him. Was he going to sing a song, and perform it in front of the assembled group? This sounded awkward, and potentially embarrassing. Something about Old Jim's natural acceptance and even offhanded way of inviting him into the ceremony was disconcerting. He felt included, but then precipitously thrust into the limelight.

Jeremy often felt off-kilter in social situations. For starters, he was the only person of color in his family, and he knew that most people saw *that* first. He had become aware of it when he was little, and it used to make him mad, and then hurt. Of course, his mom and dad and sister loved him unconditionally, and that was good. But there would be times when they were out as a family, say at a restaurant, and they'd be laughing and enjoying themselves, and suddenly he would feel someone staring at them. It was tiring, really. Somehow, when he was here, Old Jim's demeanor made him feel welcome and accepted for who he is. So that was good. But what would he sing?

Jeremy walked around in the morning mist, making a trail in the dewy grass, and feeling his sneakers getting wet. He felt like he needed to offer the song like a gift to the group, and that would be a way for him to step up and be more comfortable with it himself. He wanted to be his own person, standing on his own feet, and recognized for himself and what he could offer to the world. It was a way of being comfortable in his own skin on his own terms.

Old Jim took a lighter out of his bucket of things, and he laid it beside an abalone shell. He then took a plastic bag of some organic matter out of the bin, and opened it. He reached into the plastic bag and grabbed a handful of some whitish-green leafy material.

"What is that again?" Jeremy asked. He couldn't remember what the herb was called.

"It's *artemisia*, sometimes called mugwort," Jim answered. "A friend brought it to me as a gift from the woodlands in Vermont. It's used to smudge yourself, and some people feel it cleanses you. It's like taking a spiritual bath. I use it at the beginning of the ceremony."

"Oh yeah. That's cool." Jeremy liked the organic elements of Old Jim's ceremonies. He remembered how they had used a rattle and a bell the last time. Jim turned and looked around the 10 or 15 people who were standing or sitting inside the rock circle.

"Everybody: Welcome! Gather round and find a place in the circle." Jim's tone was warm and inviting, and the creases around his wise eyes deepened with the generous smile he bestowed on the gathering.

"Today we celebrate and honor the first day of spring, the Vernal Equinox. This is the day that the number of daylight hours is the same – equal – to the number of night time hours – nox. Equinox. This is a phenomenon of the Earth's revolution around the Sun, and it comes up once a year, and many ancient people have celebrated this day in a ritual way, as the time to celebrate the ending of winter, the coming of the sun and heat, the lengthening days and the planting of crops. Many cultures around the world, including current indigenous cultures, celebrate this day."

"We celebrate that the earth provides us with sun and rain, and the deep brown earth that will accept our seeds, and bring forth our plants and food for this coming year. We celebrate emerging from the long winter sleep, our long time indoors, in the dark, and back into the light. We recognize the magic of this time, and the knowledge that plants and animals respond to this turning of the seasons, to this place, and we honor farmers and planters who are just now creating this year's harvest. It's the beginning.

"Too, we realize that we all can enter this time with hope, and with a renewed commitment to ourselves, our families, and our communities. We can inwardly plant seeds of hope, or determination; we are readying ourselves for some next phase of our lives. Perhaps there is something we are going to grow within ourselves, perhaps there is some new awakening that we feel is growing internally. We celebrate all this today as well. Perhaps you can celebrate some new elements coming into your life that strengthen you and sustain you." Jim gave them all a moment to reflect on that.

"Too, this day also may be a time to let some things go. Perhaps there are some old ways or old patterns that no longer serve us. There may be thinking patterns or behavior patterns that we wish to shed. Let's not put those seeds into the soil again. We are done with those. Let's move into a new time, and a new way of being. Let's agree to let those go. *To everything there is a season, and a time to every purpose under heaven.*" So what is your purpose? What is your intention? Let's support that, and let's validate that today.

"Today is a day to celebrate all of it." Jim turned and picked up the half Abalone shell, now heaped with the silvery green leaves of the mugwort.

"First we light the *artemisia,* and use its smoke. Some people believed that this simple act helped to purify them, body, mind and spirit. It's called smudging, and you take the smoke all around your body in a sacred manner, allowing the smoke to cleanse you." Jim set the lighter to the gray-green leaves, which began to smoke as they caught fire. He let the fire catch, then gently blew out the flame, so that the leaves smoldered in the shell. He set the shell before him, as he sat cross-legged on the blanket he had laid on the ground. He leaned forward, cupping his hands as if to capture the smoke, and drew his hands over his head, as though pouring water cupped from a mountain stream over his head and shoulders. He then repeated the gesture over his chest, arms and legs. Then he passed the shell to Jeremy, who was sitting to his left. "You can say to yourself a prayer, or a blessing, while you wash yourself with the smoke."

Jeremy liked the smell of the smoke. It was sweet, and pungent. He mimicked Jim's gestures as best he could, imagining that the smoke was indeed cleansing him, purifying him. He felt a little changed in this action, somehow; he wasn't sure quite how.

As he passed the shell to his left, he turned to pick up the drum, following Old Jim's nonverbal head nod toward the instrument. He began to beat the drum as the others, one by one, smudged themselves in a quiet manner. Something was shifting here, some odd deepening, or reverence, or silence. Jeremy was aware that he was somehow moving more inside himself, even as he was beating the drum with the beater stick.

As Jeremy beat the drum in a steady beat, over and over, he began to discern slight variations in the sound. It was a rhythmic sound, but the drumstick made a slightly different tone with each beat. Sometimes it sounded deep, and then it would be flat and shallow. Then it would sound like it was resonating in a cave. The beats were about two to a second, and the steady beat was kind of hypnotic. He began to feel a bit lightheaded, or something. He was losing a sense of time passing, and even of the present moment. Old Jim was singing a chant which repetitiously accompanied the steady beating of the drum now. Jeremy started to lose track of time passing as the drumming continued –boom-boom-boom-boom-boom. Jeremy felt that he could almost mimic the low chanting Old Jim was singing, apparently from another culture or language.

Jeremy was rocking gently back and forth as he drummed; aware that his body was moving, but he was not consciously doing so. This seemed cool, but a bit scary, too. He was swaying from his waist up, back and forth as he drummed, forward to two beats, backward to two beats. The feeling of being out of time, being a little high, mildly dizzy, intensified. He closed his eyes to stop that feeling.

As soon as he shut his eyes, Jeremy imagined a scene before him: He was watching an open field, full of the stubble of crops already harvested, and behind this a hedgerow of trees, their leaves showing brilliant fall colors. Jeremy's eyes flew open as he continued to drum. He felt a brief panic, realizing he had gone into some kind of trance, or maybe was falling asleep, and almost dreaming. Old Jim was still chanting, and shaking a kind of rattle to the rhythm of the drum. The others were now also sitting with eyes closed, listening to the drumming and rattling, and also swaying to the beat of the drum.

Jeremy took a deep breath and closed his eyes again, and again, he was transported to some place where the fall colors in the trees surrounded an open field with dried yellow corn stalks. He was in the field himself, and he felt very comfortable in that place. It felt like it was *his*. He felt a moment of confusion, since the only place he felt was his, generally, was his room, or his house in Amherst. But this vibe was that this place was his. Weird. But he let himself go with it, feeling that drumming beat and rhythm. Jeremy was in a dream-like state, he was dreaming but he was awake. He could smell the smoke, hear the drumming, feel the intensity of the people all around him, but when he closed his eyes he was right back there in that field, standing there, looking at the corn stalks in the sunshine, feeling the wind blowing, seeing the reds and golds in the autumn trees.

Jeremy wondered: "Why am I seeing *fall*? Why am I seeing the crops harvested and the colored leaves of autumn?" It felt very strong, and very real, and he was confused. He felt like something was telling him something, but he didn't know what. He felt like he was learning something about himself. It wasn't an unpleasant feeling, but more new, and unfamiliar.

Opening his eyes momentarily, he caught Jim looking at him, and Jim nodded to him and smiled. *What did that mean? Did Jim know what he was experiencing? Did Jim want him to stop drumming? Did he want him to continue?* Then Jim smiled, and closed his eyes, and continued a new chant, again in some language Jeremy didn't know or understand. He decided to keep drumming and keep his eyes closed.

This time when he closed his eyes, Jeremy was again transported to the cornfield, the same cornfield, and he was standing near a barn and looking out from a different perspective. His sister, Sophia, was there, and she had her horse, Lightning, by her side. She was happy, and smiled at Jeremy, and he felt so good, so open and free at that moment. Her presence was comforting and reassuring to him. It was all right. So Jeremy let himself go with it, and in his vision he watched Sophia mount her horse, and she set off across the field along a dirt path, galloping along. Her long brown hair was streaming behind her, and she was smiling, and leaned forward over Lightning's long black neck, and she and the horse seemed as one being, one entity for a moment, as they galloped away. A voice came to Jeremy, *it is a blessing.*

Jeremy opened his eyes again, and caught Jim's eyes, who nodded, and slightly changed his chanting rhythm. Jeremy knew it was coming time to stop the drumming, and Jim slowed to a stop, and so did Jeremy. Jim then shook his rattle quickly for a brief burst. Once. Twice. Three times. Then there was silence for a while.

Jeremy remembered he would be singing a song shortly, and was still wondering what song he would sing. He was struggling with the songs he had written; they didn't really seem to fit here. Most of his songs were ones he'd written, either by himself or with his friends, and they mostly centered around things that mattered to him and his friends – girls, school, being bored and hanging out. There was angst and there was ennui and there was sarcasm, some humor, but it didn't really seem like a good fit for this situation. He was drawing a blank. And feeling mild panic. This was like performance anxiety without his usual props and supports – his bandmates and his guitar and a microphone. Shit.

Old Jim spoke: "We welcome into this sacred space our hopes and dreams, our fears and our failures. Our passions and our secret drive. Feel free to speak into the circle anything you wish to articulate or say. Please know this is a sacred space, and please honor one another's confidence. Remember that sometimes what people say in this space has never been spoken before, and so it may be struggling to be said. We do not share anything said in the circle outside the circle. Does anyone want to share anything?

He waited in silence.

Someone spoke. "I feel very content. I feel held in this space." Jim nodded.

Another: "It feels so good to be with people after the pandemic."

Someone else, "The drumming made me feel comforted, and it was like a warm blanket around me. I didn't even mind the chilly mist."

A third person was silently crying. "I feel so sad. My husband died this winter, and I've felt so alone. We were married for 25 years, and since he died I haven't known what to do. Coming to this circle was the first time that I have been with other people, really." Jim nodded again, looking with kind eyes at this woman.

The woman sitting next to her reached over and took her hand in hers. She then spoke. "I have never come to a ceremony like this before today. I lost my husband 10 years ago, and I still think of him everyday. I miss him. And over time things have shifted, and now I feel like Life is calling me along, inviting me forward. When the drumming was happening, I closed my eyes and I could see a scene in front of me. It was our church, and I saw that the doors were open, and people inside were beckoning to me. I felt like I was being welcomed back into the fold. The flock. It felt so good."

Others also spoke, one by one, and each had something different to say. As Jeremy listened he realized that each person was voicing something deep and meaningful to themselves. It felt important, and it felt, well, sacred was the best word he could come up with. There was silence for a while, and then Jim asked, "Anyone else?"

Jeremy said, "I saw a field of corn in the fall. There were autumn leaves all around; it was gorgeous. My sister was there with her horse, and she was really happy. I don't know what it was all about, but I was peaceful."

Old Jim crinkled his eyes, with a half smile on his lips. He nodded again, seemingly knowingly.

He asked Jeremy: "Do you have a song for us, Jeremy?"

The moment had come. Jeremy took a deep breath, a nervous smile, and it came to him. An old song his Dad really liked. He cleared his throat and began to sing:

"Love is but a song we sing,
Fear's the way we die,
You can make the mountains ring,
Or make the angels sigh,

Though the bird is on the wing, and you might not know why,
Come on, people now, smile on your sister
Everybody get together
Try to love one another right now."

When Jeremy got to the chorus, many others joined in singing, even Old Jim. He had heard that song so many times, from his parents during their old hippy days. The Youngbloods, a group from Northern California in the late '60s, and a kind of anthem of those times. Somehow this gathering had dredged that out of his memory banks. Now that he was singing it he realized it was just right for this crowd. The message of the song was just the kind of uplifting message that was needed here. We are all all right; we can make it together.

Each person was invited to take a handful of blue corn kernels from a woven grass basket that Old Jim passed around the circle at the end. Old Jim prefaced passing the basket by saying, "Take some kernels of local corn, held sacred by the many peoples, and consider what corn you wish to grow in your life as we enter Springtime. What are the places you wish to sow your seeds, what are the elements of your life you wish to nourish, to support? Where do you wish to plant something new, is there something new that is being asked to come forward in your life? Let these seeds be a symbol of that for you. Consider planting these seeds as a visible symbol of what you want to grow."

As Jeremy reached into the woven grass basket, he hesitated taking corn kernels for a moment, barely perceptible to others, while the images he had seen during the drumming played before his mind's eye. The sense of fall, the plowed fields with the refuse of the season's corn stalks seemed still visible in his mind. And here was corn. Weird. The fall leaf colors, and the sense that he knew that place, that it was a specific place for him. He treasured that feeling of being home, right there. What was that?

He took some seeds and held them tightly in his hand, almost saying a prayer that he didn't know how to say, to ask to be in that place, to ask to be part of that place, because of the feeling he felt there.

When the ceremony was over, Jeremy paused near Old Jim, who was packing up his things near his truck.

"Hey Jim, can I ask you something?"

"Sure, Jeremy," He responded. "What's up?"

"Well that was really cool. I liked the drumming and everything. I was just wondering if people have visions or stuff like that in these ceremonies."

Jim paused in his packing and looked fully at Jeremy, appraisingly. "Like how do you mean?"

"Well," Jeremy hesitated, unsure how to proceed. "Like I was, like, dreaming or something. I was totally seeing this place, a corn field that was plowed, and fall leaves changing in the trees, and blue sky. There was a raven flying in the sky, and it really seemed so real. Was that a vision?"

Jim's face fell into an inner reflection. Then he raised his eyes to Jeremy. "Was this a familiar place? Do you know it specifically?"

Jeremy shrugged. "No, it just felt familiar. But it was clearly around here somewhere – the trees, the farm fields. "

"Was there any voice telling you something, or were there words in any way?"

"Oh no! Oh no. Nothing like that. Just what I saw. And felt." Jeremy paused for a second, then,: "Oh, wait! Something like 'It is a blessing.' Yes, there was a voice that said that!"

Old Jim nodded. "We sometimes get confused about what has been known traditionally for indigenous peoples as visions, or signs, or ways that either the spirits or maybe our intuition has guided us. Because we are so disconnected from our spirituality in this modern world those abilities have now been denigrated as crazy. Crazy talk! Hearing voices is now considered a sign of mental illness. In the past, in some indigenous cultures, that might have been known as the spirits talking to you, or even guiding you. If a person had those kinds of visions, or experiences, that might mark them as a visionary, or a healer. A shaman. People in a tribe might come to know that person as having some power, or some connection to something greater than themselves. It would be considered a gift, an ability."

Old Jim paused and looked up. The mist of the morning had cleared, and the gray clouds seemed higher in the sky than earlier. It wasn't quite so chilly and cold as it had been. He lifted the container which was filled with his ritual artifacts and nodded to Jeremy to grab the blanket that had been spread on the ground. Jeremy picked it up, folding it carefully, and carried it to Jim.

"So, Jeremy," Jim continued. "Did you feel like this vision or imagery was something special, or something in particular? Did you have a feeling it was important in some way?"

Jeremy thought for a minute. "Well, maybe. I had a feeling of excitement, kind of. I felt like I was having some experience that was kind of fun, and kind of different. I don't know. There was definitely something else going on. For sure."

"Well, there you go then," Old Jim smiled. "That was a special thing just for you, and it means something to you, for you. You just gotta keep that vision or idea in your heart, and in your mind, and things will slowly gain some perspective about it for you. You may have some way of connecting to that place, or it will come to you in some other way. Stay open, Jeremy. That's what this is all about; stay open."

"Yeah but, how will I know what it means, if it actually means anything?" Was he supposed to do something? Was he supposed to follow-up in some way? He now felt like Old Jim was keeping something from him, and he felt annoyed.

"Can't you just tell me what this is supposed to mean?"

Old Jim put his hand gently on Jeremy's thin shoulder. "Jeremy, I know this seems distressing, but I really can't tell you what this means, or what you are supposed to do. I am not that wise, and I don't see into the future, and am not an interpreter of these kinds of visions. You are really going to have to stay open to what is coming, and what other signs you might get along the way."

"Like what kind of signs? What will they look like?"

"Jeremy, I don't know. I have no idea what is being shown to you, and how important or relevant it is. That is really for you to know, and you may not have an idea about that for a long time. You have to be patient, and you have to trust."

"But trust what? Or who?"

"I think this is one of those times you need to trust yourself, and trust that it will be revealed at the right time."

Old Jim smiled at Jeremy, and his confusion, "So, treasure what you've been given. I'll be interested to hear more about it when I see you again. You'll be fine!"

Jeremy said, "Are you sure?"

Old Jim smiled. "Yes, I'm sure."

And with that, Jim boarded his truck and started it up. "You OK?"

Jeremy shrugged. "I guess so."

"See you soon," Old Jim was waving, then drove out of the parking area.

Jeremy stood there alone. He looked around, at the now empty stone circle, at the trees in the distance, with their new growth on their branches, and then up at the sky. The gray clouds were breaking up, and blue sky could be seen in the background. Jeremy felt an odd sense of calm, and curiosity. He wasn't frightened, which is what he imagined he would have thought if someone had said, *you are going to have a vision.* No, he was definitely kind of calm, and even a little excited. He was cool with not really knowing what it meant, or what he was supposed to do. There was something about not knowing, actually, that made sense to him. How could you know what was in the future, anyway? He didn't really believe you could see the future. Fortune tellers were just trying to make a buck. You had to be patient.

As Jeremy got into his car, he thought to call his sister. She picked up right away.

"Hey" he said.

"Hey, what's up?" Sophia always sounded like you were interrupting her. Terse, quick.

"Nothin' much. What are you doing?"

"I just finished breakfast. Why?"

"I dunno. I was just wondering what you were doing."

"What? Why?"

"Well, I went to this equinox thing, and I sort of had a vision or something. I could imagine being on a farm, and you were on Lightning. It was pretty weird."

"That sounds totally normal. What was weird about it?"

I'm not sure. Maybe nothing. Maybe it was totally random. I don't know. It just seemed like it might be in the future, you know? Like something that is going to happen in the future." Jeremy realized how silly it sounded as he said it.

"So - ?" Sophia wasn't connecting to what he was saying at all.

"OK, well, nevermind. It was just like it seemed like something. I don't know. Like maybe you might think of something."

"Uh, no. I mean, I like riding Lightning, but that's totally normal. Are you OK?" A glimmer of concern in her voice.

"Fine! Fine! Yeah, I am great. No worries. Look, just forget it, and I'll see you later." Jeremy hung up the call. He was unsure of himself, but he couldn't help feeling something special was coming.

CHAPTER 13

The ecstatic dogs raced across the school soccer field in the steady cool drizzle, oblivious to the rain and thrilled to be out of the car. Late March was continuing its one-step-forward-one-step-back dance toward spring, and this cold, soggy afternoon was a step back for sure.

Ben walked slowly along, cutting a diagonal across the field toward a trailhead at the far corner. He had the dog leashes in his rain parka pocket, and felt the raindrops occasionally hitting his face. He could tell his hiking sneakers would be soaked by the time this walk was done, but it didn't really matter. He was preoccupied. The Stengel Farm. Doug Stengel had been as inscrutable as ever when last they talked, at first being gruff and dismissive of Ben and the Land Trust, and argumentative when Ben reiterated all the reasons to protect the land in perpetuity.

"I'm going to be dead and gone, Ben," he'd sniped, "What do I care if the land is open or developed? If I develop it, I end up with a handsome retirement for myself and a wonderful inheritance for my kids!"

Ben couldn't argue the money angle. The Valley Conservation Land Trust was appealing to a greater good. Not to mention there was a ton of paperwork to be done seeking approval for the APR. Ben acknowledged to himself a growing fondness for Doug, despite Doug's gruffness, and a wish that he somehow could produce more cash for the Land Trust offer.

Rusty and Frieda had by now circled the field twice and raced down the neck of the trailhead in front of Ben. Ben witnessed them barreling onto a series of wooden duckboards across the wet muck. The dogs skillfully maneuvered the duckboards and charged ahead again.

Ben slowly navigated the wet and slippery duckboards, and thought back to the discussion he had with Alice this morning after she had returned from Zumba class.

"You know, Ben, I think the dinner party actually made Audrey revisit the whole issue of her dad's selling the family farm. After class today she came over to me and Marion and talked about her dad being a died-in-the-wool land conservationist. Always was. She talked about when she and her brother Ryan were young, their dad used to scold them for racing around on ATVs, making dirt tracks across the fields or in the woods. He'd be furious, and explained how even a dirt road would take years or even decades to grow over in the woods. He'd talk about the loud noises that would scare the nesting birds in the trees and scare the wildlife. Audrey wanted to communicate who her dad was."

Ben knew Audrey only peripherally, mostly through Alice taking Audrey's Zumba class and other friends of friends. He only met her once or twice. And Doug was known publicly as a farmer of a large local farm, and a shrewd businessman. But in this instance Audrey apparently wanted others to know a side of her dad he didn't broadcast much publicly. It was so interesting how people had private and public sides. The side we wanted to have people see, the side of us we wanted people to think of, or remember. The side we were proud of, the side that put us in the best light. The side that let others know we were good, or honest, or thoughtful, or smart, or funny, or respectable, or courageous, or...something. So Doug must somehow have that inner split too. It was...Doug wanted people to think he was a simple farmer, had come from farming stock and his family had worked that land in Hadley for almost 300 years. He wanted people to see his weather-beaten face and his deep blue eyes, and his shock of white hair coming out from under his duck-bill cap, and think, *salt of the earth.* Hunter, farmer, family man. Getting by on his wits and hard-work. But that was the very public side of Doug. Ben also needed to connect with the private side of Doug Stengel, and to be able to speak to that person. And through Alice Audrey had given Ben a nugget of information.

Ben himself was not a crafty person. He was really not devious, or strategic even. He had in fact prided himself (there was that public/private persona again) on being basically straightforward and direct. He was not a strong personality, but he was steady and got through things. But he wondered: would some craftiness be useful in this instance? He began to imagine a conversation with Doug that might navigate toward the deeper waters of Doug's desire to protect his land.

A pronounced yelp, and loud barking brought him back to the present, and Ben realized the dogs were into something up ahead. He called them:

"Rusty! Frieda! Come! Rusty, Frieda! Come!" He called again and finally he heard a few more barks, and then the Rusty, rain-soaked and mud splattered, came barreling back along the duck boards with his tongue hanging out. Frieda came along more slowly, and limping. Ben noticed a red gash on Frieda's side that was oozing blood.

"Come here, girl," he said to her, and she whimpered as he gently touched her near the wound. It was deep, and the blood was coming freely now. She was really injured, and limped awkwardly to accommodate the obvious pain she felt.

"Come on dogs. We are going home."

He turned and walked purposefully back to the car, looking down repeatedly at Frieda, who was walking slower and slower, and whimpering. She kept turning her head to lick the wound. Rusty was obviously distressed as well. He looked from Frieda to Ben, and back again. Ben was going to have to pick Frieda up and carry her; she was slowing down so much and obviously unable to walk. She lay down in the mud, the rain soaking her as she looked plaintively up at Ben. He knelt down, pulled out his phone and speed-dialed Alice. The phone went straight to voicemail.

"Honey, I am heading to the veterinary emergency. Frieda got injured somehow on our hike, and she has a really bad wound on her side that needs attention. I am heading to Valley Vet right now; it's 1:30."

He stuffed the phone back in his pocket, and gingerly went to pick up the dog. She whimpered more loudly as he picked her up. At about 50 pounds, she was heavy. As the rain picked up, the duckboards through the swampy muck were even more slippery than before. He walked carefully, and the dog just slumped against him. Her weight was throwing his center of gravity off just enough to make him unsteady, requiring almost baby steps for Ben. The rain increased in intensity again, and he realized there was a chance he wouldn't make it back to the car. Frieda had now almost drifted into unconsciousness. His phone began to vibrate in his pocket, but he couldn't reach it, and didn't want to stop to put Frieda down to answer it.

He could look ahead through the gray curtain of rain, and saw the end of the duckboards through the murky light. He was close to the edge of the field, which was good. Just then his right foot slipped on the wet board, and planted firmly in the brown muck next to the board, the jerking motion caused him to lose his balance and he went down on his right knee, trying desperately to not to drop the dog. He wrestled his body to stay upright, and then his glasses slipped off his nose and fell in the mud. He couldn't see. He glanced frantically around but his vision was not good, and he couldn't tell in the gathering gloom, rain, and puddles which glistening light might be a reflection off his glasses lens. He couldn't go on without them, so he placed Frieda gently on the boards, and dropped his head closer to the mud, looking and feeling with gentle pats on the surface for the glasses. The water was cold, the mud clammy, and the glasses could be anywhere. Rusty was whining and circling his, and he told him to "Stay away!" with frustration. Then he felt the bows of the glasses with his right hand, and grabbed them from the puddle into which they'd fallen.

He shoved the glasses back on his face, frustration nearly causing him to break them. Impatiently flicking mud and water off the lenses so he could see, he again knelt to pick up Frieda, and carried her the rest of the way back to the car. The rain was pouring down by this time, and Ben was soaked through. Frieda was clearly in distress, as was Rusty, who was whining even more than his sister. Ben got to the car, and gently placed Frieda in the back seat. Rusty had jumped in ahead and sat next to her, whimpering. Ben drove quickly out of the parking lot.

He arrived at the vet and carried Frieda into the clinic. The technician took one look at the gash on Frieda's side and ushered him into a treatment room. She had the receptionist call a vet immediately. Ben had laid the dog on the examining table, and stood speaking soothingly to her, and stroking her head. The gash looked deep and ugly, and he could barely stand to look at it. It was frightening. Frieda laid her head on the table and was panting.

The vet, Dr. Kenwood, came in, and inspected the wound. Ben knew Dr. Kenwood, and knew her kindly, grandmotherly demeanor and slightly rounded look belied an exceptional mind and skilled clinician. She quickly checked the dog's eyes and listened to her heartbeat, then said, "We'll take her in and get this sewn up right away. She's lost a lot of blood already. Do you know how this happened?"

"She was off in the woods where I couldn't see her. I heard her squeal, and she came back like this."

"Looks like it could almost be an animal wound, or perhaps barbed wire." The vet tech brought in a wheeled cart and they gingerly lifted her on, and then wheeled her out of the examining room.

Ben turned back to the waiting room and sat down. He checked his phone and saw a text from Alice. *Be there in 20 minutes.* Sent almost twenty minutes ago. He realized that Rusty was still in the car, and he went back outside and leashed the dog, bringing him into the waiting room. Rusty seemed to know instinctively that this vet visit wasn't for him, and was alert and sniffing around for his pal. They went into the waiting area, and Ben sat down, Rusty 's head appeared in his lap, and he stroked it, talking quietly to Rusty.

"You're worried aren't you, boy? She'll be OK. She'll be OK." He stroked the soft head, and gazed into the deep brown eyes. He saw the pain, the fear that he felt there.

A sudden commotion as the door swung open and Alice and Sophia burst into the waiting room. Both looked apprehensive as they rushed over to him. Rusty's tail began a frantic wagging as he gave a short bark of recognition.

Ben was relieved they were there. "She just went into surgery. Dr. Kenwood didn't say much, but she was obviously concerned."

"What happened Ben?" "What happened Dad?" two questions simultaneously.

"Oh, we were walking into the woods behind the school, and I heard a yelp, and then these two came running back and Frieda had this giant gash on her side. I carried her back to the car, and we drove here. The vet thought it might be an animal, or barbed wire. Oh God, I hope she makes it!" He grabbed Alice and Sophia in both arms and they hugged together there. Rusty stood beside them, expectant, anxious, tail wagging sporadically as he glanced around the waiting room. Then they sat down in a row on the bench seat. Alice and Sophia instinctively sat on either side of Ben, hugging him even though he was still soaking wet. Blank, frightened looks from all three. A quiet desperation filled the room. Rusty lay down at their feet and put his face on his front paws. This waiting, waiting filled with hoping, and praying, praying to God, to some possibility that everything will turn out OK, that a miracle could occur, that the clock could be turned back, anything to avoid a sad and dismal scenario for Frieda.

An hour later Dr. Kenwood emerged through the doors leading into the back of the vet hospital. She spotted them and walked straight over to them.

"It was a very deep and ugly wound. It went through to the rib-cage. I tried to sew her up the best I could. She lost a lot of blood, and

I'm frankly not sure she will last through the trauma her body has sustained. She is still with us, but she's out for now. We did the best we could."

Her words were not hopeful, yet not definitive. The ambiguity was palpable there.

"Is she going to make it?" Ben was beside himself with fear and anguish.

"I can't say. Often those kinds of wounds prove fatal. But she came through the surgery, so that is a good thing. We gave her a blood plasma transfusion to replace some of the blood she lost. Sometimes with dogs they fight through it on their own. She is sleeping right now, and we have her sedated to help her rest. That is probably the best for now."

"Can we see her?"

"I don't think that's wise right now. She'll probably be asleep for a while, so why don't you go home and we'll call you."

Dr. Kenwood looked from one to another of the family with a look of deep kindness, but they read no hope in her expression. They each felt adrift, not hopeful, yet not quite despairing. What was to be done? There was only waiting.

"OK. Thank you, Doctor."

"She has to get better!" Sophia stated.

Ben steered Alice and Sophia to head out the doors, and they walked into the parking lot. Rusty trailed along behind, his head hung low.

"Shall we go home, or just hang out and wait for a call?" Alice was shell-shocked.

"Let's head over to Barnes & Noble and browse, and maybe get a coffee. It's close by and we can get back here quickly if we need to. Let's hop into my car." Ben knew the waiting would be worse at home, especially if they needed to return quickly. Alice had grabbed Ben a towel and dry clothes when she left the house en route to the vet. He gladly made a quick change in the parking lot. Ben also toweled Rusty off and left him with a rawhide bone in the back seat.

Barnes & Noble was a welcome distraction. They each wandered into a different aisle, picking up books at random, then putting them down again. Sophia found herself in the animal section, where she got engrossed in a horse book. Ben and Alice stopped at the New Arrivals, reading the posted reviews and glancing over book covers and jackets.

"I left a message on Jeremy's cell, but he's at band practice, so he hasn't called back."

"He will be so upset. He loves that dog. He loves both dogs."

The conversation lulled again. They each got distracted by a book, and then got a coffee and sat down to read in one of the comfy chairs provided. After a bit the phone rang in Ben's pocket. It was the vet.

"The vet wants you to come back to the hospital," said the technician. "Frieda's awake."

Ben was thrilled to get this news, and they purchased the books they had started reading and headed back to the car. They arrived shortly at the vet hospital, and left the windows cracked for Rusty in the back seat. Rushing through the doors into the vet, they saw the technician.

"Come on back," she said. They followed her through the swinging doors into the back surgery, and to the kennel, where they came up to Frieda's cage. She lay on her healthy side, and her head was up and she wagged her tail weakly when she saw them.

"Oh, girl!" "Hi Frieda!" They all smiled with relief seeing that she was back with them. Alice cried with relief, tears streaming down her face. The technician opened the door to the cage, and warned them to be gentle. They each stuck a hand through the door and gently petted Frieda on her muzzle, head and neck. Touch was the bond of reassurance they all needed.

"Can I bring Rusty in to see her?" Ben asked, realizing that the dog was as much a part of the family as the rest of them. "He's in the car."

The vet tech looked puzzled, and said, "Let's talk to the vet about that."

Dr. Kenwood showed up just then, with a slight smile on her face.

"Look like she'll pull through. She's a tough girl. That was one nasty wound, and I think it was probably an animal, so I've started her on a rabies regimen. It will take a good long time for that wound to heal, but I would say she is going to make it."

"Oh, god! I am so relieved," said Alice. "I was fearing for the worst."

"Can I bring Rusty in to see her?" Sophia asked the vet.

She looked at her appraisingly. "Well, I think that's a fine idea. He can't get her riled up though. She needs to rest."

"Oh I won't let him." Sophia fairly ran out before turning around to her father.

"Keys?" He fished them out of his pocket and threw them to her.

A few minutes later Sophia came in, pulled by Rusty at the end of his leash.

Rusty pushed his way to the cage and stuck his nose in at Frieda. Both their tails were wagging furiously as they licked each other. The family laughed with joy at such a sight.

"That's enough, boy," said Sophia, pulling him back. Rusty was having none of it. He forged himself back to the cage, and practically jumped up into the cage with Frieda.

"No, no!" They all went to hold him back.

Dr. Kenwood said, "It's too much. She really needs to be resting now. Let's leave her alone and then you can check in tomorrow. She needs to rest under observation here tonight."

Pulling Rusty by the leash, they exited the recovery room and went into the waiting room. Dr. Kenwood came out.

"I am glad she is so alert, and so responsive. It's obvious that she is as relieved as you all that she's awake. I want to remind you that Frieda's so alert partly due to the medications that are masking the pain. Once she is quiet again, I think the trauma and pain will pull her back into sleep, which is what she needs. I suggest that you all go home to try to relax yourselves, and we can call you with an update, or you can call us to check in."

Looks of uncertainty were exchanged all around.

"Well, OK, we can go, I guess," said Ben, not sounding as sure as he hoped. "It's 7:00 PM now, how late can we call?"

Dr. Kenwood looked at her watch. "The answering service kicks in at 10 PM. Why don't you call just before then?"

"Will do. Thanks, again, Doc."

Dr. Kenwood turned to go, and the family turned as a group to the exit. Once in the parking lot, Alice's phone rang. It was Jeremy.

"Hi Jeremy. Where have you been?"

"I was at band practice. What's going on with Frieda?"

"She's OK now. She had an accident while Dad was hiking with her. She got a big gash on her side that required surgery to repair. She's resting at the vet." Alice was always succinct and excellent with the details.

"Are you still at the vet?"

"Yes, but we were thinking of heading out for dinner. We're all wiped out here. Do you want to meet us at Gonzales's restaurant for dinner, honey?"

"Yeah. I'm starved."

"OK honey, we'll head out now and see you in 20 minutes." Alice clicked off.

She laughed. "Food is always a good motivator for family contact!"

Then more soberly, "I'm hungry too, now that I think of it. This has been a real rollercoaster. Sophia, do you want to ride with Dad or me?"

Sophia was thoughtful, "I'll ride with Dad, I guess."

As they drove to the restaurant, Sophia seemed very quiet and thoughtful.

"Worried about Frieda?" asked Ben, looking over at his daughter. "She'll be OK, I feel sure of it."

"Yea, it's scary. But I also had a really nasty conversation today at Robin's. Dad, is it true that if the Stengels don't sell their property to that guy, or whatever, that our whole area will just die economically?"

"Absolutely not. But what do you mean? "

"Well, Robin's dad is a real estate agent, and he said to her that you were trying to block a big development out there because you just wanted us to stay in the olden days, and only have farmers out here. She said you were against this area growing. I told her to shut-up and then Mom called and came to get me, so that's how we left it."

Ben was silent for a few moments.

"Sorry that happened, Sophia. Your friend shouldn't have gotten mad at you and blamed you for what I am doing…And I had forgotten that her dad worked for Happy Valley Realty."

Sophia sighed. "It's so complicated sometimes. "

"Well, I am sorry you are stuck in the middle," Ben replied, trying to stay even-keeled. "But I guess she caught you off guard. And it sounds like she's taking her dad's point of view on this. He's a realtor, of course, so making money through real estate sales is his way of think-ing about this."

"Yeah. Robin's always talking about how great her dad is, and how much money he makes. She's always saying, 'Oh he sold this house for $500,000' like we're supposed to be impressed. Most of the kids just try to ignore her."

"Money's a powerful motivator, there's no doubt. But money is not the only reason to do something. I think of this property, which is so big and it's never been developed, and think, if this gets sold and turned into houses and buildings and condos, that's it. It's gone. It will never go back to farmland again, or woods. Or, it could be left to evolve on its own, and not cultivated for farmland, and eventually we'd have another 300 acres of woodland right along the river. How awesome would that be?"

Sophia seemed still unconvinced. Ben looked over at her, and saw she was staring out the window at the darkened streets. As they approached the town center more streetlights and buildings lit up the night. More people were walking along the sidewalks and entering bookstores, restaurants, coffee shops, and the movie theater. Many peo-ple were animatedly talking, or smiling, and there seemed to be a good vibe all around. Sophia's eyes studied and cataloged the happy group-ings, feeling even more morose and saddened in comparison.

Ben remained quiet for a bit, letting the conversation drift away and die. He knew his daughter needed space to process the day.

As they parked the car, Jeremy and Alice stood mutely, the lights of the restaurant reflected in the remaining puddles around them. Ben and Sophia exited the vehicle and joined them, the family clutched in a group hug for a minute in the gathering gloom.

"Let's go get something to eat," Alice finally said, and they turned as one with that suggestion.

CHAPTER 14

As they followed the hostess to their table, Ben spied Brodi and Marion in a booth across the room. Glancing up at that moment, they made eye contact. Without skipping a beat Brodi's hand went up and she motioned Ben and family over. Ben steered the weary group over to say hello.

"Hey Ben, Alice, kids. How are you doing?"

"We're exhausted. We just have Frieda at the vet emergency, for a horrible accident…"

"Oh my lord. You poor people!" said Marion. She stood up and hugged Alice, then Sophia. "Here, sit down here and we'll have the waitress set up this table here."

The hostess helped to settle them by sliding the second table against the end of the booth. Marion readjusted and they sat down. Brodi made sure everyone put in a drink order and then they turned their attention to their friends.

"What happened? Will she be OK?" Marion was hovering next to Sophia and gave her a quick squeeze across the shoulders.

Ben looked very pale, but then he briefly recounted what had happened.

"Anyway, Kenwood did quick surgery and sewed her up. She's recuperating now. We just came from there, and will know more in a few hours. Problem is, she lost so much blood. It was just oozing out."

Marion again. "Oh my! That is so scary. You must all be in shock." One look at their friends' faces told them so.

"Let's get some food into you," Marion took charge, flagging the waitress over. "We want two orders of nachos, please. And the hot artichoke dip. After you put the appetizer order in, we'll order the rest of the meal when you come back."

"How are you holding up?" she asked Sophia and Jeremy. "You look like you could use a hug."

Marion leaned over and hugged first Jeremy, tightly and closely, and then Sophia again. A proper hug. The physical contact seemed to bring the kids back into focus. The terrified look in both their eyes lessened.

"I hope she's OK. I was scared." Sophia acknowledged.

"I didn't even get to see her! It's so weird," added Jeremy.

"And no wonder! She's your sweet girl!"

Alice perked up somewhat with the attention and the solicitous behavior.

"It was awful for Ben; lucky he responded quickly. It may have saved her life."

Brodi laid a firm hand on Ben's forearm, lying on the table. "You have always been good in a crisis," she said. "Quick to respond and level headed. I remember when Jeremy fell out of that tree and broke his arm. You knew exactly what to do."

Ben gave a half smile. "It's pure instinct."

It was quiet for a while as the drinks and appetizers arrived. Warm nachos with plenty of cheese, and hot artichoke dip with warm pita chips soothed the traumatized family.

As a nurse, Marion could identify the initial shock starting to wear off. Color began to return to wan cheeks and the kids started eyeing the other tables, looking to see if any friends were in the crowd.

Ben ran a hand through his short graying hair. He seemed older and wicked tired.

"That was the most scary thing I've seen in awhile. Having Frieda show up with that gash on her side! And it was pouring rain, there was dirt and water everywhere. It didn't help that I was so damn distracted about the whole Stengel property thing. It's constantly on my mind these days."

"Ben, you're freaked out. That's natural, but let's stay focused." said Brodi.

"And having something tragic happen heightens your feelings about everything," added Marion. "We observe that in the hospital all the time. Even insignificant things can assume larger than life importance."

Ben rubbed his head again, in nervousness. "With everything happening with the Stengel property, I just can't handle the additional stress of the dog. I'm just so wrapped up."

Marion intervened again. "Ben, I think you should come over to our place tomorrow morning and you and Brodi can talk through a strategy for that. It seems like maybe time is of the essence, and you don't think things are moving along the way you'd like them to. I could make you breakfast and you two could spread out your battle plans on the dining table."

Brodi picked up the cue. "Best idea I've heard yet. I'll have the coffee ready by 8:30."

Ben glanced from his one friend to the other, then caught the looks among his own family members. His shoulders sagged a bit, and he rubbed his eyes. "Sounds like a plan."

After a few clicks, Marion shifted the conversation topic.

"So, Jeremy, how's the band coming along?" Marion addressed the young man directly, with open inquiring eyes.

"Pretty good. We had practice today…it seemed like things are coming together pretty good."

"*Well,*" corrected Ben.

Jeremy rolled his eyes. "Well. I mean, we are adding a guy who can play bongos and congas, so it seems like a more island vibe just seems natural. We played around with some reggae stuff, even tried out *reggaeton.* It's got a very hip vibe. The band seems ready to try some new stuff, so it's cool."

"Not too crowded with two drummers?" Brodi asked.

"Nah. We have a more traditional drum kit, so Bennie's congas and bongos are a completely different thing." He gave a sly smile. "More of a Natti Natasha kind of vibe. Anyway, he may only play on a few songs anyway. Until we figure out how to add some more songs he can jam on. I can switch back and forth from drums to guitar, too."

"Antoine thought his sound was cool," Sophia added casually.

"When'd you talk to him?"

"He texted me last night!" Sophia casually replied.

"He was texting you while we were playing?" Jeremy asked.

"Yeah. So?" Sophia's response was a challenge.

Alice cut in. "Last I heard you thought he was a *tool.*" The adults chuckled at the term.

"Mom! I didn't say that." Sophia reddened. Her head dropped between her hunched shoulders. "I didn't even know him before. He's actually OK."

Jeremy gave a non-committal moue. "He said he knows about recording, and has some equipment. I don't know about recording just yet; I think we're still a bit rough."

Sophia jumped in, "No way! Last weekend when I heard you

guys, you were awesome! Oh my god!"

"See," said Alice, "Even your sister approves!"

Jeremy shook his head. "You guys don't understand. We can't just play good – *well (to his dad)* – we have to practice 'til it's perfect!"

Brodi smiled. "If anyone's got the ear for it, it's you, Jer. You have a pitch perfect sense for what sounds right."

Jeremy's head bobbed up and down not in an actual nod of acknowledgement, but in a secret pride in his father's friend's support.

"I actually think that music is always going to be a side gig," he ventured. Heads turned to him.

"Like what do you mean?" His mother asked.

"Well, like, I love music, you know, and it's cool to be able to jam with other kids and get some songs written. And it's great to have this to fall back on. But like," and here he paused, "It doesn't feel like my whole life, you know. Like for our drummer, it's really his whole life. He wants to be with the band, and he wants to get the band going and into a recording studio. He's like, pushing the band."

Alice said, "And you don't want to push the band?"

"Well, it's not like that exactly, but kind of. I mean, I love making music, but I just feel like it's not all of who I am. Music doesn't define me as a person. I have more complexity than that. I have more dimensionality. Like take the planet. The planet's really in a scary place right now. There's so much bad that's happening – all the plastic in the oceans, all the species going extinct, global warming, climate change, pollution – it just goes on and on. It's really sick! Like tragic. And I feel like I want to do something about that before it's too late."

Ben made a quick surprised expression, but recovered quickly. Only his friend Brodi caught it.

He carefully checked in. "That sounds pretty good. I think doing positive things for the planet is always going to be the right action. Look at Greta Thunberg; she's a firebrand, and very focused on the environment."

Jeremy scratched his head. "Yeah, I just don't know what to do! There is so much! It's kind of overwhelming actually. Greta Thunberg is actually doing something. Like she sailed to New York to meet with the United Nations! I wish I could just drop out of school and travel around telling folks about the trouble we're in."

Marion smiled at Jeremy. She reached out to squeeze Jeremy's forearm. "I love hearing your passion around this. I hadn't heard this before. And you are absolutely right – it is overwhelming! I feel like taking out the recycling is so small when our environment is tanking."

Sophia turned to her brother, "You do get pretty pissed off about the way things are going. Especially over the past three years."

"Yeah, it's true." Jeremy agreed with the assessment. "I've been kind of quiet about this, but it really bothers me. I guess I think if I am not doing something about it, I should just shut up."

Alice's eyes widened. "Here comes the food!"

The waitress brought over a full tray of plates, along with another waiter who held two plates in his hands. The steaming food was distributed around the table and there was the prelude to eating that always preceded a meal in a restaurant. Napkins into the lap, silverware distributed beside the plate, glasses shifted to make room for plates, hot sauce shaken onto enchiladas, warm tortillas slathered in butter. It was almost like an orchestra tuning up before a performance.

Classically, the waitress said, "Can I get you anything else right now?"

Heads shaking, "No thank you!"

Everyone dug into their food. Appreciative murmurs of satisfaction. The food was providing a distraction, as well as nurturance. Comfort food.

Marion was the first to surface from the eating.

"So, Jeremy, I am thinking that you could do something locally that would feel like you were doing something for the planet. You know, start a campaign about plastic straws, or using reusable food oil to power cars or lawnmowers or something."

"Mmm. Yeah, maybe." He picked up his soft drink, and fingered the straw. "Like this straw here. It's plastic. And that's no good. This stuff is floating all over the planet in the oceans. It doesn't go away. I could work to get restaurants to begin using paper straws."

Alice nodded, "You could do that for your environmental science class project."

"Yeah, I guess so." Jeremy's lack of enthusiasm in that idea was apparent. Ben could tell the young man desperately wanted to be engaged in something, but it just wasn't clear to him what that was.

"You'll figure something out," Ben smiled encouragingly. "Maybe there will be classes in Environmental Studies at Oberlin you could take."

Marion turned to Sophia and the conversation as well. "So, will you come to Zumba with your mom Saturday? I love having you along, and Audrey put out on Facebook that she's choreographed some new songs. I think Pit Bull."

Ben looked quizzical. "Pit Bull? Like, *Fireball*?"

Sophia smiled. "Well, yes, dad. But probably from this decade."

Ben seemed nonplussed. "Oh, I had no idea. Brodi, were you aware that Pit Bull has continued to make music?" Looking for allies.

Brodi made a sideways face. "Well, in fact, I have danced a few times to *Fireball*. And I do know he's continued to make hits. He's very catchy. And I think my wife thinks he's quite a hunk. Right, Marion?"

Marion smiled. "That would be correct. Yes." She smiled at Sophia and Alice. They both nodded.

Marion continued. "Audrey has caught a little fire herself it seems. I've noticed that she is introducing new songs – one or two – at every class now. She is dating that new guy, George, so I conclude we are the beneficiaries of that new mojo."

Alice chimed in. "I know! Last week Audrey had that new outfit – all pink and yellow and green. And the sparkly eyeshadow! She looked dazzling. I was so excited that she had gotten a new vibe going on. Of course, she's always so upbeat and personable. But clearly she's got something new happening in her life. It is infectious."

The rest of the meal moved along with more mundane topics. The tension from when they sat down had dissipated slightly, and the families could enjoy one another's company as they might on any other night.

The waitress came by the table and smiled at each in turn. "Did anyone save any room for dessert? We have our signature Molten Chocolate Cake, or Hot Apple Pie? We also have three flavors of sherbet: Mango, Watermelon, and Sassafras."

Brodi turned to the table. "Dessert anyone?" While the adults initially demurred, the two kids enthusiastically went one each for the first two. Then Ben and Brodi both emerged with seemingly reluctant orders. Only Alice and Marion remained steadfast.

After dessert, they all got up to go. Putting on coats and walking out to the front, Brodi turned to Ben.

"See you around 8:30 tomorrow? Coffee will be ready."

"Sounds good. I may have to deal with the vet, of course, but assuming there's nothing to be done for Frieda I'll be there."

CHAPTER 15

Ben and Brodi had talked about various developments following the plane's disappearance. The whole incident had slowed the movement on the Stengel property sale as attention was focused on the possible location of the plane and its occupants. And then there were Wayne Thibodeaux's associates who had already started their assault.

It had been a few weeks since the plane went missing. Initially, with the terrible weather, there was a huge search initiated in the area surrounding Hartford, and especially to the west, although the area was fairly populated and the crash would presumably have been noticed. The plane could have gone down somewhere remote, like the large swath of forest just to the west. It seemed so odd that in this modern day there would be no trace of the aircraft over the continental US. The weather had come in late, and hard, with 70-80 mile per hour wind gusts. Microbursts had been identified. The plane was a small, twin engine Bombardier LearJet Challenger 350, with a cabin capacity for 10-12 people, so it would have been able to navigate through weather.

The experienced pilot had been working with a consortium of developers and the Rhinestone Redneck had been one of the regular passengers. Wayne was the CEO of the high-profile Red Dirt Associates, so he was expected to travel fancy and showy. The company was known for its regular cross-country ventures to accumulate more real estate and develop cheap, affordable properties filled quickly with businesses and merchants that began producing rental or leasing income to the building owners. Fast real estate acquisition and development was their standard. Depending on the outcome of this particular situation, the jet-hopping practices might get somewhat curtailed.

The problem in terms of locating the plane, which was assumed to have crashed at this point, was that the airline company was also somewhat well known for not re-checking in with air traffic controllers or altering their flight plans at the last minute. This apparently threw off any competitor developers who might be tracking the company and the potential deals it was negotiating, but it was a bit paranoid, however much a part of the company culture it remained.

When the news originally broke about the missing plane, it was assumed that the pilot had diverted the plane from its intended flight path and landed at some remote airport with little or no long distance communications. The storm came in fiercely; a Nor'easter with slashing winds and torrential downpours, so most people had hunkered down, and planned to ride out the storm in the comfort of their own home. As the hours turned into a day, then a few days, concern rose quickly that Wayne Thibodeaux and his associates were in fact dead. He had been such a larger-than-life figure that many people assumed this might be part of a larger stunt to gain publicity for his organization, and that he would re-appear at some point. Alternatively speculation arose from Red Dirt Associates that some competitor had sabotaged the plane to land a blow to the impending real estate deal.

The television reports had started out with minute-by-minute updates on the incoming knowledge about what had happened. Then that coverage began to trickle down. The 24-hour news cycle was only so focused and intensive, then it needed to get on with another story that was going to grab the short attention span of the public. *How about those Red Sox?*

It had been speculated that the plane might have gone down in a body of water, given the total lack of any crash site or debris reported. Since the plane had gone down in a blinding rain and windstorm, it could have been blown off course and gone down in the forests. Speculation turned to any forests, or local bodies of water, and came to rest on a large reservoir to the west of the airport, about 20 miles away. It appeared that a number of trees on the eastern shore of the reservoir had been shorn off toward the top, some almost halfway down, which could be due to microburst action but also intimated that a plane coming through at a low angle could have been the cause.

The Barkhamsted Reservoir had been created in the 1930's when Hartford, Connecticut was expanding their access to water. The population was growing steadily and water resources for the city were becoming a concern. Buying up land all around the reservoir had proven easy at the time. With the Great Depression going on, many people had been selling, getting rid of timber and housing that they could no longer afford. The city quietly and steadily bought land, and in consideration of the upcoming flooding that would occur with the damming of the river they began selling off the logging rights to local firms who stripped the hillsides of the large trees that had been there.

The Town of Barkhamsted considered itself a little "place out of time" and "quaint" so they were not ready for the media frenzy that descended on the town when it was decided that that plane had probably come down in their reservoir. News trucks and reporters were seen now standing on street corners, interviewing residents (no one had seen or heard anything), various views across the reservoir, and later of boats criss-crossing the waters with dredging equipment. The town opinion became split fairly evenly, on the one hand some loved the attention, the diversion from the mundanities of regular life, and thrilled with every nuance of the search. Then there were others who wished this had never happened to their perfect little town, and who were annoyed and disgusted with all the media frenzy. These folks were rarely the ones being interviewed on television, of course, since their attitude and demeanor on camera were not pleasant, and they often were monosyllabic when asked questions. They felt the town was being ruined and they weren't afraid to say so. They blamed just about everyone for the unending sifting through the meager details of the disappearance. A Mr. John Hay called a reporter a "f* * *cking moron who should just leave us the f* * *ck alone" during a live interview (edited for viewing). This pretty much summed up that point of view.

As with any situation where a vacuum of information existed, the background noise of idle speculation started to become more pronounced. Sometimes on the news there would be the occasional interviewee who would raise the specter that somehow the plane had been involved in illegal activities, perhaps running drugs, or laundering money, and so what was likely to be uncovered was in fact an act of sabotage to bring the plane down intentionally. The logic thread ran something like: kill Wayne, as he was the kingpin of a vast fortune that had been made from illegal activities such as this. Weren't these guys well known for their flying here and there across the country? Wasn't it well known that the company flew all over, sometimes to Mexico? They were probably smuggling drugs or perhaps illegal aliens across the border, then distributing them via their fleet of LearJets to other parts of the country.

The fact that this kind of wild speculation could even get any traction was largely due to the real lack of data on this particular flight, and the odd bits of information on previous Red Dirt Associates flights

– unfiled flight plans, uncharted flights, a strange malfunction on a previous flight. It made for a good late-night story, but it really didn't hang together well over all. Even the news reporters were getting tired of chasing the tail of this story, since it kept going around in circles like a dog. Try as one might, one couldn't quite catch the end of the darn thing.

The Department of Conservation for the State of Connecticut was naturally ready for emergencies on their various properties. They were ready for weather events, lost hikers, drowning boaters, fires, car crashes, and folks having heart attacks; what have you. They comprised first responders, fire fighters, park rangers, forest wardens, as well as concessionaires, maintenance crew, janitorial staff, and lifeguards. So in some respects the elevated activity that now ensued with the search of a potentially lost airplane was something they could activate around. And this also provided good footage for the camera crews and newscasters. The issue was two-fold. One, they weren't completely sure the plane had gone down in the 8 mile long reservoir, nor where in that sinuous length it might be. And then the reservoir was actually well over 100 feet deep in its greatest depth, so the remains of the plane could be really, really down there.

In order to fill in the whole story, reporters also descended onto Hadley and the surrounding area, and tried to work in the story of Doug Stengel's property, and his desire to sell his land, and the "impending sale" of the acreage to Red Dirt Associates. There were reporters trying to interview Doug, who remained intransigent in his unwillingness to talk. Lots of footage of Doug running a tractor, or sowing crops, or baling hay, all from a respectful (and legal) distance. Then they spilled out into the surrounding area to talk to people there, which produced the same bifurcated response you saw down south in Barkhamsted. Some people were thrilled with the idea that there would be additional money generated through the sale of the property, and others bemoaned the loss of the rural character of the valley should the sale go to Red Dirt Associates. No one knew Wayne Thibodeaux, but many folks had seen him or heard of him. A reporter ferreted out the lead that there was some contest to the whole sale, with Doug considering also a sale to Valley Conservation Land Trust. This led to interviewing the Executive Director of Valley Conservation Land Trust, and her beautifully articulating the vision

of a preserved farming community that was transitioning away from traditionally viable crops, like tobacco, or corn, to a growing diversity that
helped to feed the local communities, rather than being cash crops that
left the local community. While this vision was well integrated, it served
to highlight the seeming nefarious intention of Wayne Thibodeaux.

Townspeople from small communities have a unique ability to
join together to protect what they have, and who they are. Even as ill-
defined as values and common interests might be, it was fascinating to
see the towns each slowly coalesce around their shared understanding of
who they are, and what they stood for. Barkhamsted, Connecticut and
Hadley, Massachusetts slowly evolved their story about this tragedy and
mystery to come to a common stance: This was an unwelcome intrusion
into the life of their community, and they would tolerate it for now, but
they would not allow it to continue for long. A bit of New England sen-
sibility and down-to-earth practicality emerged.

What also connected the two towns now was the shadow of the
apparently recently departed Wayne Thibodeaux. Wayne became a
larger-than-life figure in the eyes of the newspeople, and his life and
times were writ large across the evening news and daily social media. He was "missing and presumed dead," for accuracy's sake.

Perhaps the most intriguing element of the unearthing of the most
trivial details about Wayne was not so much his penchant for Skol chew-
ing tobacco, and the disgusting habit of carrying around a cup into which
to expectorate the foul brown liquid, not to mention leaving said cups
around when he was done with them, nor was it his eye for turning a
property into a goldmine of income when it had been developed. That
talent was well-known in southeast real estate circles. The Rhinestone
Redneck sobriquet was both acknowledgement of his incredible wealth,
symbolized by a large diamond earring stud worn in his left ear and the
diamond encrusted Rolex watch he wore to great effect on his left wrist,
as well as his protracted Southern drawl, which he would enunciate and
extrapolate when it suited him. And the plethora of large sparkling
stones his wife sported.

Ben and Brodi both listened to one of the local NEPM reporters
who had touched on a little-known side of Wayne, a deeper and perhaps
more elusive quality he rarely shared. Wayne Thibodeaux had grown up
on the outskirts of Atlanta, Georgia, in the little town of Newnan, about
40 miles southwest of the city. It had been a typical small Georgia town

back in the day, although now completely changed demographically as Atlanta had sprawled outward, the suburbs growing like an expanding fungus in all directions. Back then, Wayne had grown up on a farm; his father was a farmer of cattle and crops. Wayne always said he learned the value of land from growing up on a working farm, but it was also apparent that he had grown some spiritual roots into that red Georgia dirt. His connection to that farm, that land, had in fact given him an appreciation of land that went far beyond any monetary value. In addition to monetary value, he could appreciate less tangible dimensions like aesthetics, the beauty of a good summer rain falling on rich soil. In quieter moments, and to only a few close friends, Wayne had waxed almost poetically about the cycle of life that included a human life, but one that was connected to place, to stories, to trees and animals, both wild and tame.

Ben listened intently as the reporter had asked Doug Stengel in a quiet moment about his impression of Wayne Thibodeaux. She had stopped in at the farm on a whim, and perhaps it was her silver 2006 Nissan Altima with the dent in the front fender that had relaxed Doug enough to get him to talk about the man from Georgia, and his impressions of him. In fact, Doug had described one summer meeting with Wayne, when Wayne had arrived at the farm, unannounced, and asked if they could walk the land together. Doug had paused when describing the meeting to the reporter, and had himself turned to face across the fields, and took a deep breath. He spoke somewhat quietly, and, the reporter thought, respectfully, about Wayne's connection to the farm, and the land itself. Doug mentioned that he could sense a deeper pull on Wayne, something he himself had felt, but it did seem strange since Wayne had only visited the farm a handful of times. Doug described the walk in the fields that day, and how Wayne had merely turned up his collar as the mottled gray August sky had loosened its grip on the moisture that now began steadily to fall, darkening the rich loamy soil. Wayne had this day come more dressed for a farm walk, with waterproof half boots from L.L. Bean, blue jeans, and a North Face rain shell. Doug described a man comfortable with weather, with getting wet, with talking with a farmer about his land, his crops, his vision for this season and the next. Wayne himself transformed before Doug's eyes that afternoon. He had become a fully-fleshed out person in those moments. Doug had seen a man who really listened to the land, and heard what it had to say. It was as if the falling rain had not only wetted the rich soil, but moistened the inner memories of the man himself.

Of course, that bit played well on NEPM during the *Morning Edition*. Light smooth music played as the segment aired and the reporter led into her description of her conversation with Doug Stengel. It added some flavor and color to the overall story of Wayne's disappearance, and a new twist since most of the media portrayed Wayne as an incredibly successful developer who was known for high-rise development, multi-use residential and office complexes. He was that, but the reporter had added this new dimension. Of course, that kind of personal interest story was only of interest to a certain few folks who could relate to a sense of place, who could imagine themselves as a young person with a particular, indescribable sense of *who they are* and *where they are* as interlinked identities. There were some people who just naturally fit into a land-scape, or a place, and inhabited it with a surety and sense of belong-ing. Who looked out their window at a scene, perhaps with a vista of a distant mountain, or body of water, perhaps a closer view of a yard, or some trees, a garden, and knew this was where they belonged. These folks could hear about Wayne's sense of longing and passion for a place to be and they understood. These were the folks who had their driveway moment listening to Morning Edition and having a renewed appreciation for where they lived, and the trees and soil and rocks they knew. On the broadcast Doug relayed that time with Wayne, and his own feelings, so intimately that when Ben talked to Brodi about it later, he, too, was touched by his own often unspoken feelings about land connection.

It seemed that perhaps Wayne was indeed searching to reconnect with that sense of home or place or whatever it was that he had lost or buried deep inside himself. It certainly seemed that he thought he had found, in Doug Stengel, a kind of kindred spirit, or a mentor who had found that sense of connection to a place. Ben reflected that perhaps this had been someone who was on the cusp of finding that in his life. Un-fortunately for Wayne, that quest was cut short. And his story would end up like so many others, whose deepest dreams and inner holding of mem-ories and passions would quietly fade away along with the person them-selves.

Meanwhile, about a month after the plane went down, a young Barkhamsted girl, Mary McLeod, whose parents were quietly resigned to the fact that their 13 year old daughter would often cross the street and head into the woods of the reservoir with the family dog, Ralston, came across a bright red PFD caught in the branches of a tree limb that had half fallen into the reservoir. Mary was intrigued by just about every-thing, so she definitely noticed the life vest, and was curious how it got there. She noted that it was fairly new, although clearly water-logged. After looking it over for a bit, she did not remove it from its ensnared predicament in the tree branches, but mentioned it to her mom and dad upon returning home later that morning. Mom and Dad thought to call the local police to report the sighting. The police came and asked Mary (and her Mom) to take them down to the edge of the reservoir to see for themselves. Of course, the route that Mary had taken that morn-ing, and the route she led the four Barkhamsted constables, with the po-lice dog and Ralston, around noon that day, wound through some bram-bles and thickets of prickers, not to mention patches of poison ivy. When the police spotted the red life vest they nodded knowingly, for they did have relevant information that convinced them that this PFD had come from the missing plane.

Another round of searches began in earnest in the reservoir now. There was another smattering of small lake craft, there was sonar, and divers, and the hullabaloo of a circus. Not dissimilar to what had occurred three weeks previously, but there seemed to be an increase in intensity, perhaps driven by the understanding that the previous search had, in fact, failed. The life vest indicated that the plane was likely some-where in this reservoir.

Another onslaught of news reporters. Another round of inter-views of Barkhamsted locals and officials. Another rehash of Wayne, his dealings, his company. *Deja vu* all over again as someone com-mented.

And then there it was. Apparently overlooked earlier, well, ob-viously overlooked earlier, the plane was found at perhaps the deepest point in the reservoir, near what once had been Barkhamsted Hollow, founded in the 1700s. Due to the steep sandstone cliffs that had been just upstream from the Hollow, where the plane had come to rest, it was easy to understand that sonar and divers had just missed the wreckage in their earlier search. That plus it being over 100 feet down. While there were some who groused about "how could they have missed it before?" most were willing to acknowledge that a sleepy little town had never before had to deal with this kind of search and rescue operation before.

Captain Nick of the Newtown Underwater Search and Rescue actually found the plane on his dive into the narrow defile. He had a long history of dives, mostly in the Long Island Sound and elsewhere in the open ocean, and located the wreck on his second attempt. Nick wondered why he hadn't been on the original search crew three weeks ago, but really, at least it was found. He had a few turns on the nightly news describing finding the wreck, and determining that the bodies were still in the fuselage of the downed plane. No survivors. The plane was raised from the reservoir by a large cantilever arm from a helicopter, the video showing on the late night news was of a big crumpled hulk coming up from the surface of the lake, water pouring off of it as it was slowly flown to an awaiting flatbed trailer in a nearly parking area. The ambulances with the bodies had long since left the scene.

Wayne Thibodeaux's wife and kids were interviewed about their reactions to finding the wreck and the confirmation of Wayne's death. They were all in shock. There were the surviving partners in his firm, and people would note the apparent lack of grief they demonstrated in their interviews with the local news outlets. The tragic crash of a private plane killing all aboard had taken to its watery grave the answers to questions, such as why had Wayne had been so enamored with that farm in Hadley, Massachusetts? And what spark had been kindled as he had walked those dirt tracks on Stengel's Farm with Doug Stengel, such that his farming roots had tingled with faint memories? And what reticence to buy the farm and convert it to another commercial development had prompted Wayne's snail-like pace to make a clear offer to Doug for the farm? Whatever the answers to those questions, things were about to change.

CHAPTER 16

The Lear jet landed at Bradley airport, outside of Hartford, Connecticut, around 11:00 AM, and the three businessmen exited the plane and walked briskly across the tarmac, entering a black Chevrolet SUV awaiting them. They all wore long black rain coats against the weather, over finely-tailored black 2 piece suits and power-projecting red ties. Each wore sunglasses against the bright spring day. Arranging an SUV with black-tinted windows to meet them on the airstrip was orchestrated to impart power, money, and prestige. The only problem, from John Engle's viewpoint, was that no one was paying attention. This was Hartford, Connecticut, not New York City, or Washington DC, or even Atlanta from which they had originated.

The SUV rolled smoothly up I-91 toward Massachusetts, and the three executives were each on their cell phones to their respective clients and assistants, conducting rapid-fire business and legal deals. In the greater scheme of things for their firm, this particular deal was small peanuts, but they recognized that in New England, one's reputation could rise or fall on the success of one deal. And this was their first foray into the region.

John Engle was the current COO of the firm, spearheading the deal that Wayne Thibodeaux had shepherded essentially on his own. John was in his mid-fifties, and his short cropped gray hair and chiseled jaw communicated an almost predatory air. He chewed gum rapidly, his jaw muscles clenching ferociously. He spoke in short staccato bursts, and communicated intensity to everyone around him.

John was orchestrating this meeting with Doug Stengel at the property. He had strong-armed many clients to sign a deal that was in the firm's favor with veiled threats and intimidation. This was the tactic he was planning for today, and assumed they would be back on the plane about 4:00 heading back to Atlanta. He planned to be home with his wife and kids by 8:00 PM, in time to tuck the kids into bed, and have late night sex with his wife. A satisfying end to a satisfying day.

Mick Peters was the corporate lawyer in charge of contracts. Mick was in his late 30s, and was paunchy and soft in shape where John was tight and angular. Mick's expensive suit was a bit more disheveled on him, but he used his slightly less focused style to put his clients at ease. And off-guard. They didn't recognize the sharp, decisive mind behind his easy smile. In his briefcase were the documents Doug would need to sign. In fact, there were multiple copies with different scenarios based upon price negotiated, payment schedules, and other contingencies. Mick was good at speaking to clients with a style of kind engagement so that they felt there was no way he could be doing anything untoward. Which was his strategy. If they signed a contract with Mick, likely they might be paying a premium for something he had glided over in his presentation.

The last member of the trio, Bruce Schwartz, was the contractor and design person for the firm. His title was Chief of Strategy, but he covered a vast waterfront of responsibilities long before a shovel entered the earth on a project. He had a keen eye for surveying a job site, envisioning the placement of buildings, landscape, and even the amount of work and effort that would be required to get the project to completion. While John and Mick worked to get this seller to sign his name on the contract, Bruce would be eyeing the property to set the stage for the first assault. They could have equipment and workers on the ground within days or weeks of the contract being signed and finalized, and Bruce was an expert at making this happen.

As the large car roared up the interstate, John phoned Doug Stengel once again to let him know they were en route. They had made a hasty plan to come up here to Massachusetts to re-engage Doug on the sale of the property to their company, Red Dirt Associates, and to affiliate themselves to Doug. They knew that Doug had a connection to Wayne, but they weren't sure what the relationship entailed at this point. Wayne had been a very intuitive businessman, and operated primarily from gut feelings, John knew. Wyne had been charismatic, and people usually were enamored with him when they first were getting to know him. He put people at ease, and often made promises that he could not later fulfill, but as the face of Red Dirt, his broad, smiling countenance was exactly what most prospective clients wanted to see. They had used his face in advertising, and his quotations could be seen on billboards and in magazine ads. No one had heard of John, Mick and Bruce, and the three of them were actually OK with that. This situation was unusual for them since Wayne was out of the picture, but in the interest of time they felt it was necessary to get on a plane to move things forward.

The car turned off the highway, and headed east. They noticed the enterprises along Highway 9 – gas stations, small restaurants, small businesses, strip malls, what looked like mom and pop stores. It was small town USA, but this clearly wasn't the quaint side of town, if there was one. This was the commercial corridor, where sales tax dollars were likely a welcome relief to a town budget. All three men were aware they carried with them the potential to increase the Hadley town coffers substantially if this deal went through. John grinned thinking this deal would be like a Taylor Swift concert coming to town. A huge cash drop, minus the support for the local food bank. And the music. And Taylor Swift.

John turned to the others, "Do we know if Wayne had any contacts with the local town officials – anyone elected, building department, zoning commission? This looks like the kind of hick town where some small-time bureaucrat could easily derail this project."

Bruce replied, "Wayne didn't keep good notes from what I could see. We have a folder on the shared drive with some basic outline of the results of his conversations with Stengel. The notes seem to indicate there was some movement toward a sale, but there are various questions about siting, and scale. Wayne seemed to envision a pretty large project, maybe 24-36 months from groundbreaking to grand opening of the hotel. Anyway, he had even engaged a local firm to begin drawing up the plans on the QT. They are –" he consulted his tablet – "based in Amherst. Next town over."

John cut him off, "Yeah, I'm thinking about any town approvals, that sort of thing."

Bruce shrugged. "Nothing along that score. But you never know who Wayne was schmoozing with, coming up here."

The car turned off the main road and headed north onto a quaint side street that edged the town green. In fact, two parallel streets ran along either side of a green space about 50 yards wide. Stately older Colonial homes, an old brick library and school building faced inward along the outside of this, framing the scene and one could imagine the town meeting space here–fairs, markets, parades. About a quarter mile up, the two roads converged and zigzagged. The road now ran alongside the river levee, rising 20 feet to their left. Shortly they were into farmland. The road wound its way north past farms and farm houses for a few miles until the car slowed and then turned into a dirt farm yard, clouds of dust rising as they slowed to a stop between the farmhouse and barn.

A tall, slightly stooped, white-haired man in a denim shirt and denim jeans was just driving a tractor into the yard from the adjacent field. Doug Stengel was a big man, large-boned as they say, and his weather-beaten face showed years of sitting on that tractor, facing the sun and the elements, and keeping his own counsel. He looked appraisingly down from the perch at them, a slight frown on his face, and then descended the steps to ground level.

John exited the car first and strode over to him. "Mr. Stengel? John Engle, COO of Red Dirt Associates. It's a pleasure to meet you in person. These are my associates, Bruce Schwartz and Mick Peters." Hand shaking and pleasantries were exchanged.

John pushed them forward. "Can we see the property?"

Doug shrugged. "Sure, I'll walk you around a bit, then you can wander on your own if you like. Got 300 acres that runs along the road here – Route 47 – and down all the way to the river. Prime farmland – best in the valley really. But you boys aren't interested in that. You are thinking about commercial real estate. You want to look in the barn?"

"Yes, please," Bruce said. "Early 20th century New England post and beam, isn't it? When was it built?"

"Well, my grandfather built this himself around 1905. It sits where the previous barn stood until it burned down. That barn was built by his grandfather around 1855. "

Entering the barn, they could see the beautiful wooden beams and rafters and the care that had been taken to keep the barn in good working order. The doors on sliding tracks were new and the metal shined. The floor of the barn was dirt, but hard packed and reasonably clean, as though swept. Stretching toward the back, along an aisle, were 6 stalls for animals.

"You have horses?" Mitch asked.

"Well, we board horses for others. Right now there is one. Belongs to a young lady across town. I could take others, but I don't advertise at all."

Bruce turned to his companions. "This barn could be a feature in some way – preserving the rural character, and a kind of outbuilding. Maybe shops or offices."

John turned to Doug. "Did you and Wayne discuss any of his

plans? Did he want to preserve this barn, do you know?"

Doug smiled slightly and cocked his head. "Well, he didn't tell me much of what he had in mind. I would have thought he would have told you; you being partners and all."

He continued. "Wayne did seem particularly keen about the barn. He would always come in here when he stopped by. The way he looked around the rafters, and the way he ran his hands over the posts told me he admired it."

They walked out the back of the barn and gazed into a field with young green corn stalks just reaching calf height.

"This field's 40 acres, stretching over to that windrow of maples over there. Just beyond that's the river field, running down to the edge of the Connecticut. We've got that planted in wheat, oats and barley. This track will get you over there. Want to take a look?"

"That would be great, Doug," Mitch said agreeably.

As they walked John matched Doug's pace. "So, Doug, I don't know if you and Wayne ever got to the place of talking numbers?"

Doug gave a slight moue with his mouth. "Well, son, we talked about that here and there. "

"The property's beautiful, anyone can see that. It's the location--so far from anything–that's a bit tricky. Hadley's a sleepy little town with not much going on. I understand the University of Massachusetts is nearby?"

"Yep. We get the Ag people here usually once or twice a year to look over what we're doing. They do seem interested in the land, and how we've been farming for something over 200 years."

"Have they expressed interest in purchasing?" John's voice conveyed some concern in the matter. Doug could hear it.

"You and Wayne really didn't talk much, did you? Well, the Chancellor and a few of his folks came by at one point, looking over the property, speculating how it might be used. The Ag school people were the ones who thought it'd be perfect for some kind of field station. That was a little while ago, and I haven't heard from them lately. So it may be just a bit too far from the University to be of much help."

"How soon are you interested in selling?" John persisted.

Doug resented the directness of the question, feeling it a bit unseemly, but John seemed determined to press forward.

He nodded his head thoughtfully. "Well, that's a hard question. You see, son, the thought of selling this land has a lot tied up into it. When I *do* sell, that's it. I'm done with it, and with farming, and then my family's done. It's a big decision and it'll be a big moment. It weighs on me." He stopped walking and looked directly at John.

"Whatever I decide, it would have to be worth it."

All three of the others stopped walking too. Something had just shifted, like a faint breeze that wasn't there a minute before. A little chilly breeze.

John cocked his head and looked at Doug dubiously. "Like a certain dollar figure would make it worthwhile?"

Doug said. "Maybe. Sure. That. And then other things as well."

John pressed. "Like what other things?"

Mitch stepped in at that point. "Mr. Stengel, I'm guessing the money is just a part of this sale for you. Maybe you are thinking about your legacy? Your memory here in this valley?

Doug half-turned to him. "That's some of it, yes. And wondering about the land itself. What does it want?"

It was an odd turn of phrase. None of the three from Georgia had ever heard it, and they weren't quite sure how to respond. For Doug, who had lived on this land his whole life, who had gone out every morning with the sun coming up in the east, over the maples and oaks across the road, slowly illuminating – revealing – his fields and pastures as the light came up – he had come to know that this land had something within it. There was some awareness, some consciousness, some intention that he felt rise up to him at certain moments. It spoke to him in the soughing of the wind in the trees or corn sheaves, or his cows lowing in the pasture, something that was always striving to talk to him. Connect with him. He remembered one morning when a red fox, trotting through the stubble of harvested corn, stopped to turn and look right at him. *That fox* had something to say. So he realized as he stood here, ready to say goodbye to this land, that he needed something more than money; that money in itself wouldn't satisfy him as he turned to the last years of his life. What was it? He wasn't entirely sure himself.

Doug glanced at his three visitors, at the dark business suits, and the red ties, and the sunglasses reflecting everything with crisp mirroring lenses, and he knew they wouldn't be able to answer these questions.

He pivoted. "Well, don't listen to me. I'm an old farmer who's probably spent too much time out here in the sun. I just know that this land is valuable, and when I do sell it, it will have to be the right sale for the right price."

He turned and continued walking along the dirt path through the field.

Quick glances among the other three, and they fell into the pace. Now Mitch took place alongside Doug.

"This is quite a property here, Doug. I can see how you have nurtured a working farm for a long time. We would try to preserve the beauty of this place as much as possible should we be lucky enough to purchase it. I am not sure if Wayne mentioned that he had contacted an architectural firm here in Amherst to create a vision of what we have in mind here. It would be an extensive development, but one which showed off the beauty of this property to its best advantage, while enhancing its utility for recreational as well as commercial use. There would be -- residential availability -- on a large-scale which could be incorporated as well."

Mitch was sweating with the exertion of the walk, and the last sentences were starting to come more haltingly as he struggled for breath.

By now they were passing through a strip of trees and brush, where the dirt trail dipped down and crossed a very small trickle of water. The men in suits had to make a small leap across the wet earth to attempt to avoid muddying their expensive Italian shoes. Mitch was somewhat less successful in this. The splattered mud hit his trouser legs mid-calf. The light brown spots didn't look so good on his shiny black trousers. Then he slipped on some slick mud and his shoe went into a deeper patch. Now the light brown mud was slicked across his fancy black shoe.

Doug continued to walk at a brisk pace, seemingly unaware of the stress this was creating for his fellow travelers. He came upon the berm above the Connecticut River, the surface of which was 30 feet down. The green waters swirled lazily past right to left, a constantly changing pattern of swirls and eddies. The three Georgia men all felt a strange disquietude being alongside this river. The intimacy made them nervous.

"There she is, gentlemen, the Connecticut River. She's the longest river in New England, over 400 miles from the Canadian border to

Long Island Sound. You learn to respect a river of this size. The locals have worked to contain her, so the flooding isn't a danger, and yet you can feel her power and unpredictability. It's hard to know what is more amazing, that this river cut this huge swath of a valley over thousands of years, or that there are a dozen dams along its full length that help to provide electric power to millions of people."

There was a palpable sense of energy. Doug felt it deeply and insistently in his blood. He could practically feel the rumble of the waters flowing past the bank here, in his feet, and he knew that this river would be, should be, flowing past this spot for many generations to come. He could practically see into the past here, when his father, grandfather, and grandfathers going back in time, stood at this spot and knew this river had been there through all that. He glanced at his companions. Two of them had turned their attention in this moment to their smartphones, one tapping with thumbs , and another scrolling through his emails. Only Mitch seemed to be still looking out across the river, at the mountains in the distance. He turned at that moment and caught Doug's eye.

"Wow, it's really pretty. You can't see any buildings from here."

"Nope. This is a pretty wild stretch of riverbank right here. Jim Diskowsky's across the river in Hatfield there. He's still primarily in tobacco, and he's got a long field stretching over to the Main Road, which is out of sight. "

"You know him?" Mitch seemed surprised.

Doug nodded. "Known him all my life. He and I rigged up a rowboat we'd take back and forth across the river when we were kids. Had a landing on either side. Sometimes we'd meet up and go fishing, find a way to anchor near the bank and find trout. We learned how to work the current, and stayed off the river after a storm. Anyway, Jim's kids are taking over his spread. They're talking about marijuana growing, since that's the up and coming crop. Lots of cash there, apparently."

Mitch nodded. "Well, what about your kids, Doug? Do you have kids? Aren't they interested in farming?"

Doug half-turned to Mitch, again with the tilted look of not being sure where to begin. How much to say.

"Well, my kids are kind of lukewarm about the farm. They both are grown and have other lives. They'd stand to inherit the proceeds if I sell."

He turned and started to walk back along the track they had come down. The sun came across the field from their left, and they could feel the warmth coming up in the day. Doug walked more slowly now, surveying the land to the right and left.

John broke the silence. "So, we are looking at a fairly rapid turnaround in our work on the property. Assuming we can come to terms here, we would figure out what kinds of approvals we would need from the town to start construction. Assume there would be some environmental reports and approvals we'd need. What are you thinking, Doug?"

"Well, you all seem pretty keen on this property, but as we discussed, and as I mentioned repeatedly to Wayne, we have perhaps a ways to go here. I like the idea of the money, but I also have some feelings about the way the land will look once I'm gone, and what you are proposing. I've heard a lot of talk, but haven't seen a plan, or a map. No drawings or sketches. It's all a bit jumbled in my mind, to be honest."

John chuckled. "Well, to be honest, Doug, we are offering you a substantial chunk of money in order to buy the property, and once you have decided to sell it, then it will be out of your hair. We will be making the changes and improvements to the property to make it commercially viable. You just aren't going to be involved with any of that."

Doug stopped and looked at John. "Commercially viable? What's that mean exactly?"

"Well, we will have to run the numbers on the commercial building – hotel, office space leases, marina, restaurant income. That sort of thing. We usually build out for a leasehold management company. We'd sell to them or offer things over in stages after we build. What do you think, Bruce?"

Bruce thought for a minute. "The property's ideal for development. The naturally flat fields make great building sites, and there are many sightlines of views up to the hills that we could advantage. I see the construction staging area near the river for the hotel and marina. We'd need a big drive to get larger equipment here, but it's very accessible. I want to find out about the plans that have been drawn up. I guess you haven't seen those Doug?"

Doug shook his head. "Wayne had a group out here once or twice, but I never really met 'em. Seems like they would have had to take some survey measurements. This land hasn't had a survey for decades."

They had walked back most of the way to the barn by now, and John continued his press. "So, Doug, we are going to find those plans in town, and I can bring them by if you like. I have to say that we are ready to go, though. Plans can change, or be changed, and I think we'd like to know we have some tentative agreement."

Doug slowly shook his head. "Well, like I said, I'd like to see some of your big plans here. And I don't know what you've got cooked up so I can envision what this place might look like after I've gone. I would like to see that."

"But assuming you like what you see, you think we can come to an agreement?"

"Well, I'd like to see plans first."

"Of course, of course! But then we can start talking numbers and timelines."

Doug was momentarily distracted by a small silver car turning into the drive just then. He looked over his shoulder at John. "I'd like to see the plans first," then, "Now I wonder who this could be."

* * *

As the small troop of men in suits made their way back to their SUV, someone got out of the silver car, and stood looking at them. He looked briefly at the large black Suburban, and then turned to face in their direction. He raised a hand to block the glancing sunshine, and in that gesture Doug knew who it was.

They approached him, and Doug kept his surprise to himself.

"Ryan," he said. "Didn't expect to see you here."

"Hi Dad. I was in town and thought I'd come out to see you." Ryan glanced from one of the strangers to another.

"These gentlemen were just leaving," Doug said. And to them, "Been a pleasure, gentlemen."

As they climbed into their car, Doug faced them, as though figuratively escorting them off the property. The car started up and they headed out the drive and down Route 47.

Doug turned and looked at Ryan. His gaze was appraising, his face impassive.

"So what brings you here, son?"

Ryan looked down, away from his father's gaze.

"Well, Dad, I thought I would come out and see you. It's been a really long time."

"Yep. You took off and didn't look back. That weighed heavily on your Mother. And me." Doug's gaze was sizzling with anger.

"And that's the story you are telling yourself?" Ryan stood up straighter, trying to level the gaze his father brought from his height. "You are going to make this about me leaving?"

The argument flared up like a brushfire, heat rising and crackling.

"You took off. You left your mother in tears. You came back for her funeral, then left immediately. We didn't speak."

"And if I had said something to you then, I probably would have regretted it. That was time to say goodbye to Mom. It wasn't to make nice with you!"

Doug turned and pointed a long finger at his son. "Don't you take that tone with me about your mother. She was a good woman, who loved you despite how you treated her. Disappearing for months and years. She loved you and was so proud of you. And you couldn't give her the time of day."

"And what about you, Dad? You weren't so excited to have a little gay son, I'll bet. You couldn't wait to see me disappear! I was like a curse on the family. I wasn't Mike! I wasn't going to be that macho son who was going to grow up to be a farmer like you, and so you didn't want to have anything to do with me!" He spun around, and started walking away.

Stopping about 10 paces away, Ryan turned back around.

"You gave up on me when I was 12. You could tell I wasn't going to be a farmer like you, and you figured I was lost. You barely gave me the time of day after that." He walked slowly back toward his father. "I don't even know why I came out here today. I guess I thought we might somehow start over."

Doug had reddened, and he opened and closed his mouth.

"You don't have any idea how I felt or what I think. You were always so wrapped up in your own little world, you never had the time for anyone else. When you left I figured it was for the best. Maybe you would be comfortable with the man you were becoming. I guess not, hearing you now."

Doug turned and started walking toward the barn. Ryan stood for a minute, weighing his options. He could follow his father, chasing the retreating back, or he could leave. Leaving seemed like the wisest option. He turned slowly back to the car, climbed in, and drove quickly away.

CHAPTER 17

Ryan took a deep breath and opened the door to The Black Sheep deli a few days later, en route to a meal with his sister. An Amherst icon, The Black Sheep had been around for decades, since they were both in high school, and it hadn't changed much. Now there was a place for outdoor seating along the sidewalk on Main Street, a nod to the need for socially-distanced dining the pandemic had necessitated. Facing the door was the counter where you ordered your food–baked goods, sandwiches, and salads. Refrigerated cases held drinks and prepared foods for take out. Ryan spotted Audrey sitting down at a table in the window, and pointed to the counter mouthing "I'm ordering food."

Audrey stood up and gave Ryan a hug when he got to the table, smiling at her little brother, though he was 6 inches taller than she was now.

"How ya doin'?" She asked him, searching his face for a sign as to his emotional state.

"Good. Good. You?" As he shrugged off his denim coat he glanced around instinctively, then realized it was unlikely he still knew anyone here in Amherst. He had his coffee and waited for his order to be called at the pick-up counter.

"I haven't been in this place for ages!"

Audrey smiled. "Yeah, our own local deli! I figured "The Black Sheep" would be a fitting place for us to meet! She smiled at him with eyebrows raised. He feigned annoyance. "Remember coming here with Dad and Mom for Mother's Day?"

"Oh yeah. Dad was always so proud to be taking Mom and us out for brunch. Fried pickles! I had to order some of those with my sandwich."

Their food orders were called up and Ryan got up to fetch them. Coming back he slid into the seat.

He asked, "So, am I going to meet the new guy?"

Audrey gave a short snort. "I don't know, maybe. We are still in the early stages of whatever it is. I like him, and he clearly likes me. We've only been out a few times, but it does feel like we might have something…"

"You gotta start somewhere," Ryan added.

"You know, when I first met him I didn't think he was that hand-some, and he's a bit disheveled, so on the surface he doesn't make a good impression. You really have to get to know him, and he is very intense. I liked the fact that he is so smart, and he actually reads people really well. He seemed to understand me right off, somehow. Rachel and Sam immediately liked him, and I trust their judgment."

"He's from around here?" Ryan was looking at his sister over the rim of his coffee cup, and seeing her almost for the first time. He saw how open and honest his sister's face was, and he saw the lines around her mouth and eyes.

"No, he moved here for college and then stayed. So, well, I guess you could say he's from around here – been in the valley for 25 years. He knows a ton about the place, since he's a writer."

"Your first real relationship since you moved back, right?" Ryan asked, as he stared out the window..

Audrey chuckled again. "Uh, no. I tried a few others. All dis-asters. It seems that after my marriage to John, I lost the hang of being in a relationship. I'd be distant, or I'd be too clingy. I'd talk too much, or wouldn't talk enough. Guys would like my independence, and then they wanted me to just be paying attention to them. I could never get it right!"

They were interrupted at that minute by a mother and daughter, the girl about 8, who were walking by their table.

"Hey! Hi Audrey!" said the mom.

"Hi Missus Hodge" said the girl, smiling widely. Her bright white smile, minus a missing front tooth, contrasted with her beautiful ebony skin.

"Oh, Hi Amanda! Hi Cheryl! How are you both?"

The mom smiled. "Amanda completed a full page of fractions all by herself this morning, so I am treating her to lunch out."

Audrey's eyes went wide, and she gave a big smile. "Amanda! You did that whole page?" Amanda nodded emphatically, but kept her gaze at the floor, suddenly shy.

"All by yourself?" Amanda nodded again, and then giggled.

"I even figured out that five sixths plus three fourths is nineteen twelfths!" She said proudly. "That's more than 1!"

Audrey clapped her hands. "That's amazing! Good for you!"

The mother, Cheryl, beamed down at her daughter with her hand resting gently on her head. She looked at Audrey.

"I cannot thank you enough for everything you've done for her. The fractions are only a small part of how she's grown."

"I love working with Amanda." She turned and looked directly at Amanda. "You are a very wise young woman." Amanda beamed again.

"This is my brother, Ryan. He's visiting from out of town. This is Cheryl and Amanda."

"Pleased to meet you. Your sister is a true gift to the children in our community. She is an amazing tutor – it's like she turns a light on inside them."

"She is definitely special! And nice to meet you too," Ryan said, shaking hands and standing up in the slightly crowded space.

"Where are you from?" Cheryl asked politely.

"I'm from New York."

"Oh, that's the big city! Amanda: Ryan is here all the way from New York!" Cheryl worked her daughter in the conversation.

"I've been to New York! Empire State Building!" Amanda smiled again.

"That's right," Ryan said. "I live right near there."

"Well, we won't interrupt your lunch any longer. We just wanted to say hello, and thank you again."

"I will see you Thursday," Audrey said to Amanda.

"Bye, Missus Hodge!" Amanda said as her mother led her away by the hand.

They watched them, mother and daughter, weave past tables to the door.

"She is so smart," Audrey said. "I can see that brain churning whenever we work together."

"You obviously care for her, too," Ryan reflected.

"Well, that family has not had it easy here. As you may recall, there are not a lot of black families here in the Valley, and while people are friendly, racism comes in subtle ways. I sometimes wonder if Amanda hasn't gotten all the attention she deserves," she sighed. "But that's a strong mom, right there, and she is going after what her daughter needs."

"Cool. And they really look up to you. Amanda was all smiles when she was talking to you."

"Yeah, well, I like to tutor."

"And teach Zumba."

"And that. Zumba is just so much fun! I get to host a dance party, and pick all the songs and choreography. It's a riot!"

"Maybe I'll stick around for a few days and come to a class?"

"I would LOVE for you to come to Zumba! The ladies would be thrilled to meet my little brother and have you in the class. Oh, please come!"

"OK We'll see. Does Mr. Writer attend?"

"George?" Audrey smiled. "Uh, no. I actually haven't talked him into coming to a class. I think it's so far out from what he knows, or does…Don't get me wrong. He definitely works out at the gym, but I'd say he's more the pump-iron type of guy. He likes to stay in shape."

"OK. I actually do want to meet him."

"Maybe that'll happen. So how is it being back home?"

"It's weird. Everything is the same, only different. Or maybe I am different. I don't know. " He rubbed his hand across his short blond scalp "I tried to look a few people up, but the ones who stayed seem like just older versions of themselves, not that interesting. Others have left and not come back. I drove by Johnny Marinski's old place. His folks said he'd moved to Boston, and gave me his number and email. They didn't seem too happy to see me. And their back field is a solar panel array now. It's huge – it must be two acres."

"Yeah, a bunch of others have gone that way, too. It's some quick money when they sell the land to the solar developer. The solar farms don't look too bad when you are driving by on 116 or whatever. So, are you going to stop by and see Dad?"

Ryan's eyes widened and glanced sideways. He seemed immediately wary.

He cleared his throat. "Well, I actually did stop by to see Dad a few days ago. Thought maybe we could try again. But that asshole is still pissed at me. Like I left on my own, instead of him kicking me out."

Audrey's voice raised an octave. "You went to see Dad? Just out of the blue? Why did you ever think that would be a good idea?"

Ryan recoiled. "Do we really need to talk about this now?"

"Well, when else are we going to talk about it? I have no idea if you are staying in town for a while, or suddenly taking off again. I wonder, will you tell me that you are going, or will you just suddenly leave? The last time you left you didn't tell me, or Dad, and it took almost a year for you to resurface. You had a whole new life in New York City. You had a cool job. You might even have a 'new friend' in your life. And then you acted like it was no big deal, and like we were always just as close as ever. And Dad was devastated. You disappeared right after Mom died, then you resurface and disappear again…You're unpredictable, and unreliable."

Ryan was silent in the onslaught, feeling the pulsing rage that simmered just beneath the surface for his sister. The quick eruption of feeling had caught him off guard, as it always did with her. His anger flared.

"Who cares what I do? You were always there for mom and dad. You were always the good girl, you always did the right thing. You never disappointed them. You stood by Dad when Mom died. Christ! How could I live up to that?"

Audrey now hissed, trying to keep the volume down in the restaurant. "Don't you take that 'Poor me' tone with me, buster. I did stick around, yes. I knew you were too self-involved to be much help to the family, or me. I knew you were dealing with your *sexual identity*. Did you think we didn't know you were gay? We just wanted you to acknowledge it and get a life! No one expected that it would mean you would make a new life and cut us out of it!"

Ryan couldn't believe what had happened in the course of a few moments. He stared at his sister, feeling attacked and humiliated. It felt like his conversation with his father two days ago. This was how it always was, his identity was under attack, and his past behaviors were being held up to him as his faults. This was why he had to go away to create a sane life for himself. She could not understand how being gay affected his being in the world.

He carefully took his napkin off his lap and placed it on his half-eaten salad. "Well, I guess it was a bad idea to come back after all." He stood up and yanked his coat off the back of his chair and left the restaurant.

Audrey was shocked. People around them noticed and recoiled from the intensity of the exchange. Some of them pretended not to notice, and tried to give them some privacy in this very public place. Audrey grabbed her purse, yanked it open and grabbed a twenty out of the wallet and dropped it on the table. Pulling on her coat, she said, "I'm sorry" to the bewildered waitress, and ran out the door after her brother.

Ryan was walking slowly down the sidewalk as she trotted to catch up. She could see he was crying, but silently. Audrey made a calculated move and threw her arms around her brother from behind. She was surprised to find that she was crying too.

"Oh, Ry! I am *so* sorry. I love you so much and just can't stand that we have drifted apart. I hate it that you live so far away, and you keep your life so private. I wanted us to grow up and be brother and sister together, close. What happened?"

Ryan held her arms that encircled him from behind. He stroked them up and down the forearm, and slowly calmed himself, and her. He turned around and held her and they just stood there for a while.

After a few moments they moved apart, and looked at each other, in the eyes, with tears still sparkling in the midday sun. The each sniffed, and Audrey got tissue out of her purse and blew her nose, while Ryan dragged his sleeve across his eyes.

"Wow. I didn't expect that. I love you, too, Sis. I do love you too. I knew coming back here would bring up some feelings, but I didn't know they'd come blasting out like that."

Audrey grabbed his arm and began walking him down the sidewalk. The warm sun dappled the sidewalk under the big maples along the edge. Audrey leaned her head into her brother's shoulder. They walked a short way in silence.

"Ryan, I guess when I heard you were coming home I figured you were going to bring back some good feelings, some hope and some grace. We need some healing in the family, and I can see that was too much to put on you. You have your own path to walk."

Ryan put his arm around his sister's waist as they walked. "Well, I guess I sort of hoped for a miracle too. I sort of imagined that something magical would happen, and now that I'm here, over the past week, I can see that things are pretty much the same. It's all the same. Same old small town, same old college town snooti-ness. I guess I figured I'd see you and we'd connect..." he drifted off into his own internal reverie.

"And Dad?" Audrey asked.

Ryan slowly blew out a long breath. "Yeah, Dad. I don't really know what I thought about him. About what I'd do with him. What I would say to him. What he might say to me. It was totally impulsive to go out there, and then when we were together…It's so complicated."

"What's complicated?"

"Well, we never really talked about…anything. So, when I got there it blew up pretty quickly. How do you start a conversation that has so much baggage in it?"

"You could start with, "Hi Dad? How are you doing?" You know, at the beginning."

"Yeah, OK. But at some point you have to acknowledge the crap that's just right there. You have to deal with it. What was I supposed to do?"

"I don't know! You were always the one with the fancy words and writing. You can figure it out!"

Audrey pulled them up short. They had walked up the street and around the corner onto Pleasant Street.

"Look, Ryan. Here is my car. I say we get in, and drive over to Dad's. I can call him to let him know we're coming. I know Dad actually loves you; he's just hurt. He doesn't really have anyone else. You could try apologizing. "

Ryan had stiffened with her first words. "I don't know if that's such a good idea…besides, why should I apologize? He was the one who shut me out. He should apologize."

"That may be, but that is not going to happen right away. Come on Ryan. No time like the present."

Ryan looked around. The Amherst Town Hall was across a small parking lot. The elegant brick building oversaw the Town Common, the spire on the corner uplifting the entire scene. Three beautiful wooden planters with Callery Pear Trees stood along the street on one side, giving a green dimensionality to the area. Ryan studied the scene for a few minutes, then turned to his sister.

"OK, I'll go. But I am driving my car. I want to be able to have a quick getaway if I need it."

"Absolutely." Audrey conceded. She was appraising her brother, gray hair at the temples now, and thinning in the back. Gray flecked his beard, too, which he kept fashionably short in the perpetual three-day length men fashioned. Audrey saw the care and worry that had lined his face.

"Tell you what. Lemme go out and give Dad a heads up you are coming. He and I aren't close, but we do see each other occasionally, and he'll at least not be completely surprised when you show up. Give me an hour."

Ryan looked at his sister, recognizing the love that gave context to that statement. She did love him, and she wanted him to feel supported in this first foray back home.

"That sounds like a plan. Thanks. I'll see you out there in an hour." They hugged, and Audrey went around to the driver's side of the car, and opened the door.

"I'll text you the coast is clear." She smiled at him as she climbed into the car.

* * *

As Audrey arrived at the farm, her father exited the barn. He wiped his hands on an old rag that he stuffed into his back pocket.

"Hey, girl. How you doing?" Doug came over and hugged her. "What brings you out this way?"

"Hi Dad! I thought I would stop by and see how you were doing. Spend a little time if you've got it."

"Sure, sure! Gotta work a bit while we chat. You can lend a hand, too, if you don't mind a little grease and dirt. I'm in the barn." He turned and walked slowly back.

"I'm working on this combine harvester. Something's gummed up the knife cutter bar here, and I had to take it apart." Various parts were strewn across the floor, and it was clear that Doug was in the midst of it.

Audrey had seen her dad in this situation a thousand times. He was a great mechanic, not to mention a do-it-yourselfer.

Audrey tilted her head to one side, studying what her father was working on. "What's up with the revolving reel? You've got it detached."

"Oh, shit. I don't even know about that yet. I'm still fussing with this thing." Doug was hunched over the knife cutter bar, using a wrench to wrestle a nut off its bolt. When it slipped he cursed again.

"Son of a bitch! This thing is welded shut!" He grunted again as he applied himself to the nut. It finally gave way. He twisted the nut off turn by turn. After he removed the nut he hit the bar with the wrench and then it came off with a squeaky grind.

"Dad," Audrey began. She too was eying the revolving reel, and seeing that it would have to come apart and get cleaned. She found a monkey wrench and began to loosen a metal nut. She tried to sound casual. "Ryan's back in town. I've seen him."

Her dad flicked his eyes in her direction. "Yep. I heard that from the Masons. Seems you were over at the Smoky Top the other night having a drink."

"We did, yeah. He's doing pretty well in New York. He's got work he likes."

Her father grunted. "Well, he did actually come out here. No idea what the hell for. Trying to blame me for being a shitty dad, I guess. Left in a huff."

"He came back to see us both. He wants to reconnect. And yeah, he told me he came out to see you."

"Why'd he come now?"

"Well, I guess he finally feels like it's time."

"Time for what? He took off out of here like his pants were on fire. Come to think of it, maybe they were." Doug chuckled at his own joke.

"Dad, not fair. Coming out here took a lot of guts, and he said you weren't too receptive."

"Yeah? Well, he wasn't too calm. I could tell he was already agitated when I saw him from 100 feet away. Plus he came out when those guys were here. That was strange in and of itself."

Audrey rolled her eyes. "Those guys? From Georgia? The ones with the guy who died? They still interested in buying the place?" Her interest in the selling of the family home distracted her from her stated goal of getting her brother and father back on good footing.

Doug gave a dismissive wave of his hand. "They are a bunch of sharks looking for a quick kill. Money is burning a hole in their pockets and they need something to do, I guess. And," here he nodded with a pensive look, "It is damn good money for me. Us."

Audrey rubbed her forehead and left a grease smear from the tractor she was leaning against. She was quiet for a minute, thinking about her father trying to sell this land, where he had grown up, where he had raised his children, where he had buried his wife, and now was quite likely going to sell.

"Dad, I know you'll figure out the right thing to do. Look, from my point of view I don't care what you do with the farm, just make your-self happy. We'll figure out the rest later." She sighed and looked around the barn. "And you know Ryan. He is who he is, and you know he's stubborn. He never felt like he fit in around here. He's gay, for Christ's sake. That's not an easy life."

"He could have chosen differently, if he'd wanted. He just wanted to be that way."

"That is not true and you know it! No gay person chooses to be gay. It's the way they are! They have to learn how to accept it, and then find the people who will accept them. Ryan felt tortured his whole life here. Those Hadley farm boys all made fun of him, heck, he got beat up a few times. He was afraid to tell you; didn't know how you'd react."

"How I'd react? He should have just come out and said some-thing."

"That's not Ryan, Dad, and you know it. He was always quiet and to himself."

"Well, he can come out here again, but he's got to lose some of that attitude. Heck, when he came out here the other day, he was looking for a fight. "

Doug took the knife cutter bar and blew it clean with an air hose. He sprayed some oil over the surface and took the rag out of his back pocket and smoothed it clean. He inspected it closely, then wiped the other parts clean as well. He deftly reassembled the pieces in a matter of minutes.

Audrey watched him momentarily, then took out her phone to text her brother: "All clear."

* * *

Fifteen minutes later Ryan's Toyota Corolla turned slowly into the driveway, almost as if it were someone lost looking just to turn around. Doug looked up briefly, then looked down again, recognizing the car. He braced himself for another tumult.

When the car stopped and the engine was turned off, Doug looked up again. His eyes flicked again to Audrey, and he shook his head when he saw Ryan climbing from the car. He stood up, and wiped his hands again, slowly, as he watched Ryan stand in the sunshine look-ing around.

Audrey called out, "We're in here!" Ryan peered toward the darkened doorway in the barn, and began to walk over. His halting steps telegraphing his mounting dread and discomfort.

Father and son approached each other from a long way away. In Audrey's eyes, the coming together took eons, light years, movement as slow as honey dripping off a spoon. It took an eternity for them to cross the space between them, and then they paused. Uncertainty crackled in the air. Tension encircled this pas de deux. What was the next step?

Doug looked Ryan up and down, then said, simply, "Ryan."

"Dad."

"You came back. I didn't think I'd see you again anytime soon."

Ryan said, "Dad, look. I'm sorry about the other day. I came back to see you. And Audrey. And I mucked it up."

"Why come back at all, though?" Doug's inquiry wasn't as harsh as it could have been, but it challenged nonetheless. This wasn't a welcoming engagement, but neither was it open warfare. A skirmish perhaps.

Ryan glanced at Audrey, "Well, I guess it's been a long time, and--"

"It was a long time 15 years ago."

""Yes, and maybe this was a mistake." Ryan turned as if to head back to his car.

"Ryan! Dad! --" Audrey was on her feet, hands on her hips. "Slow down you two! You haven't communicated in over a decade, then you immediately have an argument as soon as you see each other."

She started in again, "Geez, Dad: Ryan is your only living son, you'd think you'd act like you are happy to see him. Ryan: Give Dad a break! You never even told him you were gay, he's had to piece that together from what everyone else told him. Take a chill pill you two!"

Audrey walked over and pulled two old caneback chairs from the side of the barn.

"You two siddown and act civilly." Both men did as they were told, and sat facing askance at one another.

Ryan said. "Well, OK, I left because it seemed you never approved of me and who I was. I've made a good life for myself with friends and good work in the city. I came back here to try and patch things up. I hoped you'd be proud of the life I've made for myself. But I can see you never approved of me anyway."

Doug harrumphed. "You were always too sensitive. Little things would set you off and you'd cry. Cry! Like that's ever going to settle anything. You were never tough when you needed to be. Always complaining and feeling put out about this or that. Hell, your older brother went off to fight in the First Gulf War, and never came back! He didn't complain, he did what was right!"

Audrey jumped in, a natural family therapist. "Dad, it's not fair bringing St. Michael into the conversation. We all miss him, we're all sad, but that was a long time ago. It's not fair comparing. Mike's gone, and Ryan's here."

"The great St. Michael went off to slay the dragons and died trying," Ryan chimed in. "May his memory live on forever, and ever. Amen!" The last dripped with a sarcasm that came from a long time ago.

"I'll ask you not to speak ill of the dead," Doug said. "Your brother did what was honorable, and he felt it was his duty to serve. I have great respect for a serviceman, or woman," he added. "You couldn't serve your country, for whatever reason. But your brother gave the ultimate sacrifice."

Audrey interjected again, "OK, can we please leave Mike out of this? Dad: Ryan traveled all the way up here to see us both. We can at least make an effort." She paused.

"And Ryan, can you please at least acknowledge that this is a little weird, you coming all this way. Why now? For what?" She looked at her brother, head tilted, eyes wide, raising her eyebrows and willing him to say something conciliatory.

"Probably wants to make sure he gets his portion of the farm, is what," said Doug.

Ryan shook his head, "That's not even close! Geez, Dad, look I'm gay, OK? I have known this since I was like 10 or 9. I knew I wasn't into girls, but it was just too crazy. I didn't even know what that meant. Like I was a freak. I couldn't talk to you and Mom, even though I think Mom knew –"

"Oh, don't worry! WE BOTH knew! You were her little sensitive boy! '*Go easy on him, Doug!*' She was always protecting you…"

Audrey again stepping in. "OK, wow! So you knew Ryan was gay. When did you know that?"

"Ever since he was caught trying on your mother's dresses in her closet…"

Ryan winced at this.

Doug kept steaming ahead. "…He tried out her make-up one

time--your mom caught him with red lipstick still on his mouth. He was enthralled with those fashion magazines. I kept hoping he'd grow out of it."

"Dad! For Christ's sake! You don't grow out of it! It is who you are! Ryan's always been quiet and sensitive, so what? And he is finally talking to you as himself. His full self! Why is it so hard for you to just accept him?"

Doug opened his mouth, then closed it again. He pursed his lips, looked away. Tears came to his eyes, and he lowered his head. It was quiet for a few moments.

When Doug looked up they could both see Doug's cheeks were wet. As if on cue a wedge of Canada Geese flew honking across the sky, heading north.

He took a deep breath. "I am sorry, Ryan. I am so sorry. It feels like my whole life has been crumbling around me, drifting away. First your brother is gone, then my wife, then you leave. Now I am looking at selling this farm. Selling the farm! This land was my dad's and his dad's and his dad's, and it came to me and now I can't seem to hold onto it. You kids, *my kids*, don't want it, and so what is the next step? I sell it *for money*?"

The fullness of this moment reverberated among the three of them. Audrey went over and squatted next to her dad, putting her hand on his forearm.

Doug took another deep breath and exhaled, "Ryan, I am sorry for the way I treated you, and sorry for what you have had to go through. I can't imagine how hard life has been for you. But damn, son. Your timing here is shitty."

Audrey had never seen her dad be this emotional, this vulnerable. She hugged him. And he hugged her back. They stayed that way for a long time.

When they slowly released each other Audrey went over to her brother, and hugged him too. Ryan was crying, silently, and Audrey joined him in that. Doug took a handkerchief out of his back pocket and wiped his eyes and blew his nose.

"What the hell's wrong with us?" Doug said, his grimace turning to a chuckle.

CHAPTER 18

Bright sunshine flooded the parking lot of The Woodland Dell as Brodi swung the car into a space towards the front. As she and Marion got out of the car, a warm Spring breeze lifted her hair, and she noticed various groups of people in the grassy areas, elderly folks, some in wheelchairs, moving slowly and carefully around the asphalt paths and perched on the beautifully carved wooden benches.

They walked up the front entrance with the wide automatic doors which parted with a near-silent *swoosh* as they approached, such that they didn't even break their stride. Across the small lobby was a reception desk, the older woman behind the desk smiled warmly at them, her bright blue eyes warm over the half-moon glasses.

"Good Morning! How can I help you?" Her hands were clasped gently over an open book before her as she leaned forward slightly.

Marion jumped in. "Good Morning. We're here for a meeting with Marge Pierson. She is expecting us."

"Oh yes, of course. Let me just ring her. Please have a seat." The kindly woman reached for the phone on her desk and pressed one of the many buttons there. After a slight moment she said something *sotto voce* and replaced the handset.

"Marge will be with you shortly," She said with a smile, then she returned to her book.

The whole vibe was one of peacefulness, calm and reassurance, quiet efficiency and control. Not in a bad way. Marion perched like a cat on the edge of a chair while Brodi wandered between the big picture windows looking out across the lawn, and then over to the bookcase filled with old copies of the Reader's Digest books, recent modern bestsellers, and a few odd travel books. An elderly man sat in one corner of the lobby reading the newspaper, contentedly sipping a steaming cup of coffee. The gentleman was the picture of contentment, for whom time was no longer a concern because he had so much of it now.

Marge Pierson approached them down a corridor, a woman of substantial yet elegant presentation. Her outfit was a beautiful, burgundy red silk blouse accessorized with a string of pearls at the neck over a dark green and burgundy paisley skirt. The large-framed glasses gave her a slightly surprised look. Her tight gray curls framed her cafe-au-lait-colored face and warm smile.

"Good Morning! Are you Marion?" she walked over to her hand outstretched. "Marge Pierson, Director of Sales and Marketing."

"Good Morning Marge, and this is my wife, Brodi," she smiled.

"Good Morning, Brodi! I am so pleased to meet you both," Marge smiled even more broadly looking from one to the other.

Looking directly into Brodi's eyes with a slight smile, she clasped her hand in both of her own hands. Then Marge held open her arms as if to scoop them both up. "This way, please!" And ushered them down the hall as though corralling loose hens.

Brodi had been somewhat upbeat all morning, especially considering that finding someplace for Beth seemed like the most important step they could be taking now. She anticipated the relief they would feel knowing that Beth would be cared for and attended on a regular basis in a facility. She didn't say this to Marion, but felt that Marion couldn't help but agree. Still, she could tell that for Marion there were other considerations – worry about the facility itself, staffing and safety, worry about what her mother would think and how she would react. It was a huge step. Brodi knew that Marion would bring Beth into their home if that seemed like the best option.

And, Brodi hoped that Marge Pierson had faced this same dynamic a thousand times with families who were approaching this facility for the care of their loved one.

"Shall we walk around the grounds before sitting?" Marge said. "It will help us get a feel for the place."

As they walked, Marge was more talkative at times, and at other times let Brodi and Marion take things in at their own pace. Marion's face did not betray any feelings, but her stiff body language told Brodi that she wasn't really receptive. Marge used her regular sales pitch as a way to reassure Marion of the high quality of care that The Woodland Dell provided. She rolled off statistics about size of the campus, numbers of residents, average ages, mix of men and women, number of staff, average daily ratio of staff to residents, meals served, number of activities offered each day, field trips, facilities, etc. When they stopped to review a particular meeting room or activity room, or study a view across the campus, Marge would stop her running commentary and allow Marion and Brodi to absorb what they were seeing. She had a practiced eye for noticing when the guests, as she referred to them, were coming to a point of overwhelm.

"How is this seeming so far?" Marge turned to them, her gray curls tilted to one side. "I know it's a lot to take in all at once."

Brodi responded, perhaps a bit too quickly. "It seems fantastic to me. I can definitely see Beth thriving in a place like this."

Marion remained quiet, and Brodi charged ahead, "I love the recreation room, and the fitness facility. Beth loves swimming, so the pool would be a highlight. I could see her getting interested in the plays, too. I remember her telling me once about the high school musical she acted in, and how fondly she remembered that time. I think she was one of the leads, in fact."

Marion seemed vaguely distracted. "Yes, Mrs. Alonzo Smith in "Meet Me in St. Louis." I remember her talking about that when we were young." She seemed to come back for a minute then, "Brodi, she has never shown an interest in the theater other than reminiscing about that play."

She turned to Marge. "You know, I just don't know. I can't see Mother here. It's all so nice, clean and sparkly, and the furnishings are so new. Mother would feel like a fish out of water here. She's so used to her old-style Cape with the wrap-around porch and everything a bit threadbare. Comfortable. And she's not really that social. Mother's quiet, and a kind of bookworm. I'm not sure that this would be the right place."

Marge looked at Marion appraisingly. She pursed her lips, ready to speak, but paused.

"Marion," she started gently, "You mentioned on the phone that your mother was beginning to show signs of Alzheimer's. Would you like to visit the West Building and see our Alzheimer's facility? That might help you to see the kind of care we can provide. Until she is no longer able to care for herself or might pose a threat to her safety, she could live on our Main Campus here. Then we can offer the best Alzheimer's unit in Western Massachusetts right here."

Marge led them across a walkway that arched over the rise in a hill. A large flat roofed one story building came into view, surrounded by a tall wooden fence with a phalanx of arborvitae trees growing up inside it. Marge paused briefly to discreetly swipe her ID badge at a keypad by the gate, and a short buzz sounded. She pulled the gate open.

A wide yard surrounded the building, with asphalt paths around planting areas, and more carved wooden benches along the paths. The trees, seen from inside the fence, gave a feeling of containment and privacy to this area.

Marge continued her spiel, communicating caring and authority.

"We currently have 20 guests in the West Building, both men and women at various stages of progression of the disease. A full time staff of ten professionals care for the guests on a daily basis, with up to 15 during the work week. Daily activities include story hour, singing group, exercise classes, and art. Three meals are provided in the dining room on a regular basis, and we can accommodate a variety of special diets, including low salt, gluten-free, vegetarian, vegan, and other diets. There is a visiting schedule that also permits families to take their family member on outings with them. The entire daily agenda is designed to stimulate the resident and keep them active to the extent they are able."

Another near-silent sliding door permitted entrance into the building. The residents were already engaged in a variety of activities, although many seemed to be staring out the window or at nothing in particular. To give credit, the staff were in the mix, and one staff had a group of four sitting around a table making some kind of collage with cut out pictures from magazines. One elderly man became agitated with the staff member who was trying to get him to do something, and as his voice raised, another, slightly burlier staff member walked over to assist. It was clear they had used these same tactics in the past – it was well-rehearsed. In fact, as the agitated man got louder and more vocal, the two staff members gently and firmly led him through a discreet side door, where his volume quickly subsided as the door swung shut.

Marge turned to them. "Obviously some of our guests become agitated and disoriented. It's natural in Alzheimer's patients who have progressed to a certain degree. They become unable to maintain their contact with present reality, and it can be distressing. Poor dears. We work to minimize the disruption on the floor, as you can see. Poor Marvin does have those episodes with some regularity, and so we have a standard protocol to get him to a location so he can feel more secure and in control. He will calm down within the next 5-10 minutes, I assure you."

The episode left Brodi feeling a bit uncertain, and she glanced at

Marion and saw similar feelings moving across her face. She felt com-
pelled to speak up.

"OK, I guess it's good to be aware of what may be in store for
Beth. She is not there yet, I can tell you, but we have had one time when
she clearly didn't know who we were and what was going on. It was
scary and very disturbing. In fact, it's what brought us here to The
Woodland Glen." She smoothed her hair absently and looked
around. Now that Marvin had been escorted out, the whole scene had
returned to a state of calm and quiet purpose. In fact, the scene with
Marvin didn't even apparently register for those who were still in the
large activity room.

Brodi found herself looking out across the serene lawn to the arborvitae trees some 50 yards away. A few tall maple trees dotted the
perfect lawn, well-landscaped, with a few beds of shrubs dotted here and
there. The soft brown dirt mounds were beginning to show green shoots
of some bulbs poking through the deep brown mulch. Brodi felt that the
regular plantings and landscaping was intended to produce a sense of
calm, order and serenity.

"Marion, how are you doing? How is this feeling for you?" she
gently inquired.

"That episode was disturbing. It was like a psych ward, where
the patient is being sent off to get a shot of Thorazine or something. Like
the whole idea is to contain the outburst. What is therapeutic about sep-
arating him like that?" Marion turned to Marge with a mixture of fear
and accusation.

Marge responded, "I know that seeing that kind of outburst and
the response can seem frightening, and it doesn't sound like you have
seen that kind of behavior from your mother yet, but please understand
me when I say we know how this disease progresses, and that kind of
behavior is likely coming for your mother. Maybe not right away, but at
some point she will probably have a complete memory lapse which
brings confusion, terror, and often real anger at not knowing what is happening. I believe at that time you will want your mother in a facility that
knows how to handle the situation, and keep her safe. Remember, if your
mother loses her ability to know what is real, here and now, she can become disoriented to the point that she could become confused, and hurt
herself or someone else."

"My mother would never hurt anyone," Marion's voice rose perceptibly, "You don't know Mom, she is a lovely and caring soul."

Brodi intervened at this point. "Marion, dear, we're talking about the disease which is claiming more and more of the mother you know and love every day. Remember the microwave incident? Remember the time she didn't know who we were when we got to the house? We can see that this is coming at some point. "

She thought for a moment. "Can we take a short break and walk outdoors for a bit? Maybe back on the main grounds?"

Marge was quick to agree. "Of course you can. Let's head out here and go through that gate over there. You can have a nice private walk back over to the main building."

Once outside the gate, Marge bid them a short goodbye, and said she would be back in her office when they were ready.

As she walked away, Brodi gently put her arm around Marion, and could feel her sag into her. She was crying silently to herself, and Brodi could feel her shoulders shaking with the sobbing.

"This is so hard. I don't know what to do, and Mom is so fragile and scared right now. I feel so guilty putting her into a facility. This is not the right place for Mom. Maybe we should just try to take care of her at home, like we planned? " The words tumbled out in a jumble.

Brodi sighed, "We can give it a try, Marion. But look at how quickly your Mom has declined over the past few months. She left the pot on the stove that boiled dry and nearly started a fire. The toast she left in the toaster oven that *did* catch fire. She wandered out the door and down the street saying she was walking home to Dalton, which is 35 miles away. Honey, I am afraid of the strain it's already putting on us. It's really too much." Brodi tried to be sensitive, and reasonable. She knew this was a key moment in their decision-making around this issue.

"She's not your mother, Brodi, You don't understand. She stood by me and the family for years, especially when Dad was going through all his shit, and now I'm just going to abandon her to some strangers? I can't do this now."

They had slowly strolled over another rise in the path, and there at the edge of the woods Brodi saw a doe grazing peacefully on the green grass shoots. She lifted her head at their voices, but seemed undisturbed. As she glanced over her shoulder, Brodi saw that it was a small family group. Two white-spotted fawns were also grazing a short distance into the woods from the first. Brodi took in the scene, and then she smiled.

She remembered a time, it seemed so long ago now, when she had been interested in the tales and myths of the Indigenous peoples in the world. She had been drawn to the simplicity of their world view, and the very concrete elements of their spirituality. It wasn't simplistic, but more so natural, and in a way so obvious. Spirit for many native Indigenous tribes was the earth on which we lived. It was the trees, and the sun, and the blue sky, and the deer at the edge of the forest. This was spirit, here and now. There wasn't something somewhere else, a someone or some place where spirit inhabited and you had to do something in this world to get to that world. Spirit was here at this moment. And with these deer so close, so perfect, and just *being*, Brodi was reminded of spirit and its presence. And somehow this calmed her. She trusted that whatever was supposed to be, would be. She really wasn't in charge, and she couldn't control things.

She turned to Marion, "Marion," she said, looking deeply into her beautiful gray eyes, still spilling tears down her cheeks. "I love you. And I love Beth too. We will make this all work out. We will. Let's keep Beth in our home as long as we can."

Marion reached out and grabbed Brodi's arms, burying her face into her chest. She sobbed, relieved.

They walked in silence to the main building, where Marge was waiting for them. When they explained what they were going to attempt to do, Marge nodded in understanding.

" I fully support your efforts to care for your mother on your own. It is not going to be an easy road, so if you do change your mind, please be sure to give me a call. This is a progressive disease, so it will get harder for you and Beth. Of course, we may or may not have an opening at this time, but we can cross that bridge when we get there." She handed them her business card, and walked to the main door with them.

"Best of luck to you both, and to Beth." She shook their hands and then turned as they walked away.

As soon as they got into the car, Marion began to have second thoughts. She was worried that they had made a rash decision. She began a rapid fire series of questions to Brodi.

"I hope we made the right decision. Do you think we can do it? Can we really take care of Mom? We may have to get someone to come in to care for her during the day, don't you think? When we're working?

Brodi nodded, "Sure, we can get some kind of in-home care person when we're at work. We will figure it out."

Marion was still looking at every angle, "What alterations in the house will we have to make? How can we convert the downstairs guest room into a room for mom? She'll need her own private bathroom too. Can you call the contractor to have him come over to discuss that? I wonder how Mom will take it? You don't think she can keep her car and driver's license do you?" The enormity of the tasks before them rolled out in rapid-fire succession.

Brodi smiled. "I can call Valley Home Improvement and have Steve look things over."

Marion was super-organized and efficient at her work in the hospital -- she had to be. The enormity of the responsibilities of the nursing staff fell on her shoulders. She had an insightful mind, and a deep compassion for the people with whom she worked. She was well-respected and loved by all her colleagues. And in this private moment, she allowed all the anxieties and worries about her mother to overtake her. Of course Brodi recognized this, and knew the need we all have to have some place to open up the fears and anxieties and just let them flow. She knew Marion well enough to know that this cascade of worries would eventually subside, and that the amazingly competent Marion would emerge to take charge of the next step.

Marion fell silent, and looked out the window of the car, and wiped the tears from her cheeks.

"Holy shit." She turned to Brodi. "Are we really going to do this? I know it is the right thing to do, and mom will be so much safer and more comfortable in our home, but *Jesus*!" She shook her head in disbelief. Raised her eyebrows up and down.

Brodi took a deep breath as well. "I am in 100%. I know Beth will be more comfortable at our house, for sure. I think it is going to be a wild ride to get us ready to have her living in our home. There is a ton to manage just to get the place ready, and then to get her down here, and then to get her place ready to sell, and then sell it. But we will do it." She reached out her hand and held Marion's hand, squeezing it gently.

CHAPTER 19

The following day the women gathered at the back of the gym after Zumba class. Marion, who only came to Zumba occasionally, was out of breath, her cheeks were flushed a deep pink, and sweat stained her sports bra top. Her skin glistened under the bright light of the gym. Alice and Sophia were gathering their sweatshirts and towels, and laughing about something together; Marion noted the strong mother-daughter resemblance in that moment. They both had their hair drawn back in matching ponytails, Alice's with streaks of gray, and one could see how Sophia's young woman' freckles might recede with time, and how the crow's feet wrinkles might mirror her mother's at some point.

Audrey was drinking deeply from a water bottle as she walked over. She said things to various groups of women as she walked, laughing and occasionally hugging this one or that one. Zumba was a women's gathering and the connection they all felt was palpable.

"That was awesome!" Sophia enthused as she wiped the sweat from her face for perhaps the third time.

"I am so glad you liked it!" Audrey replied genuinely.

"And it's so much fun!" Alice chimed in. "You really keep us moving!"

She was winded, and she was also beaming as they all were. "I love that cumbia song – what is it called?" She mimed a few of the moves with arms raised and twining and untwining as she danced a circle.

"Oh that's *La Zenaida*," Audrey said, "by Armando Hernandez. The first time I heard it, I knew I had to choreograph it. Isn't it sexy?" She danced the steps with her hips swinging in a sensuous arc around a circle.

"Sexy on you, yes," Marion laughed. "I just feel big and bulky doing it, but it's fun."

"Fun is what it is all about," said Audrey. "You've got to move what you've got, and it's sexy every way!" They all laughed appreciatively. Truthfully they all felt a little sexy after the class, feeling the energies moving through them.

"Anyone interested in tea or coffee?" Alice asked. "Quick trip over to Share coffee shop?"

"Sure!" Audrey said.

"I'm in," Sophia brightly. "But, Mom, you will have to pay since I don't have a wallet."

"When do I *ever* not pay?" Alice asked with a touch of irony.

They gathered their belongings, and Audrey led them out into the late morning sun.

"What a glorious day!" exclaimed Alice. She turned her face up to the sun, eyes closed, in a private moment. It would be a lovely spring day, sunny and warm. As they walked, Alice turned to Marion. "Hey, you went to The Woodland Glen yesterday. How was it?"

"Well, it's a lovely campus. And they show it off to its best advantage on the tour," Marion said. "The staff seem OK, and the rooms seem perfectly adequate."

Alice, still sweating, wiped the back of her neck. "Not a ringing endorsement…"

Marion sighed. "It's just so hard to think of Mom living there. It's just so institutional. Brodi and I had first planned to have her live with us, but I know how fast Alzheimer's can progress and how unpredictable someone with the disease can become. Mom can seem completely normal and present and then she can be gone in an instant. She can get very upset and she doesn't handle change that well."

The women entered the coffee shop, and ordered their drinks. They came back outside to a wooden deck with four tables, all with brightly colored sun umbrellas. The four women sat around one table which looked out over the street, where cars were navigating the morning traffic.

"Did someone say something that makes you hesitant about having Beth go there?" Alice asked Marion when they were settled.

"Oh no, oh no," Marion replied. "They said all the right things, and were very reassuring. No, there was one thing, minor really, that has me worried."

"What was that?" Audrey asked. She had grabbed a bottled juice drink from the cooler, and was already almost finished with it. Marion sipped her coffee, and looked away, staring off into the distance.

"Well, one of the patients – residents – guests – whatever they call the people who live there – started getting agitated about something, and he started talking loudly, and seemed to be getting pretty upset. He was yelling. And then two staff members came along and shuttled him through a side door, and he was gone. Just like that. And everyone else acted like nothing had happened. They all just went about their business. It made me feel a little spooky."

"Did they have to forcibly remove him? Did they hurt the man?" Audrey seemed concerned at this.

"Well they seemed to be encouraging him to go with them. They were talking in low tones, and they seemed to be guiding the man, not actually forcing him to go. I don't know, I am struggling with imagining that with Mom. Would they treat her that way?"

"Did the man seem dangerous at all?" Audrey asked her.

"Well, no, but he was escalating, and could have been yelling and maybe even throwing things pretty soon. I guess it was for his own good, and for everyone else's safety."

They sat in silence for a minute, absorbing this.

Audrey spoke. "That sounds very upsetting. I don't know what I would do in that situation. I would be worried too."

"Was your mom with you?" Alice asked.

"Oh no!" Marion replied. She dabbed at her face with her towel. "It was just Brodi and me."

Sophia then spoke up. "Does your mom want to live there? In a place like that?"

"Well, we have tried to talk with her about what she needs and what we need, what we see as the issues of her living arrangements. That is an excellent question, though."

"Well, I was imagining what her life has been like, or what it maybe seems like her life is. She's lived alone for so long, right? And the next thing is that she's coming down to live with you and Brodi. But then she's going -- maybe going -- to live in this retirement place. Maybe she's not ready for that."

"Yes, Sophia, that's true enough," Marion replied, impressed with the young woman's insight. "We still need to talk with mom about it."

Alice looked at her daughter with an appraising gaze. "Of course you are right, Sophia. Beth will need some time to get used to the idea."

Sophia had a big coffee drink in a large plastic cup with ice, and a huge mound of whipped cream on top. She grabbed the straw coming out of the top in her mouth, and gave a deep pull. Then she took the straw in her fingers and played around with it, stirring the drink and mixing the whipped cream into the coffee, lost in thought.

"I think Beth will be uncertain at first, but she will really grow to love it as she becomes comfortable being there." Alice asserted, wanting to be supportive of her friend.

"It's just such a big change, " Marion wondered. "Mom's always been pretty independent, Sophia's right, and I want to make everything perfect for her down here."

" I think you should let her be as free as she can for as long as possible. I think getting locked up sounds horrible." Sophia blurted out.

"She's not getting locked up, Sophia," Alice cautioned. "You make it sound like Marion and Brodi are abandoning her. The plan is for Beth to live at Marion and Brodi's at first. But Beth may reach a stage where she needs real 24 hour care. That's more than anyone can manage without professional help. The Woodland Dell is down the road, really, and they can visit her every day if they want to."

"But suppose Beth was there. Could she go out on her own?" Sophia asked.

Marion hung her head now, defeated. "I just don't know what else to do. I am afraid that Mom could really hurt herself. We were all ready for her to live with us. We have a guest room on the first floor, too, where she stays when she comes down now. We thought we'd turn that into a room just for her. But lately every time we've been to see her, she's more forgetful, more unhinged from reality. She nearly burned her house down for gosh sakes – she put a bowl in the microwave with a metal spoon in it. Luckily it blew a fuse, and then killed the microwave. There were these burn marks all over and the plate shattered inside there. She had no idea what she had done. To be honest, I'm terrified of her living with us and endangering us."

"And I'd worry about Edna, too," Sophia added. "She might be in danger. Dogs can't fend for themselves."

Alice rubbed her friend's back to calm her down. Clearly this was upsetting to Marion even to think about this, and the incident yesterday was still fresh in her mind.

A car pulled into the parking space along the street just in front of them. The loud hip-hop music blaring from the car speakers suddenly cut out when the car was turned off. Two college age women climbed out of the car, both looking fit and healthy in their stretch pants, athletic shoes, and fitted tops. Their animated conversation faded as they entered the shop for coffee.

The punctuation of sound had broken the intensity of the moment.

"It's all really hard," Sophia said, with a note of dejection in her voice.

"That is correct, Sweetheart, " Alice replied. "Getting old is really hard. You just don't know what is going to happen. And sometimes it's left to others to make decisions for you when you can't make them for yourself."

"But how do you know she doesn't know what's going on?" Sophia persisted. "Maybe she does know what's going on, but she just doesn't say. Maybe she feels bad too, knowing that she's putting you in this position to have to choose for her."

Marion looked at Sophia with her head cocked on one side. She furrowed her brow. "You know what? I think you could be right. I am not giving my mom credit enough for the smart woman she has always been. So, just to be clear, Brodi and I are now planning to have her live with us -- *at first* -- and may then need to have to move her somewhere more institutional if she becomes more combative or oppositional and less in touch with reality. But for right now she is coming to live with us, and I am going to explain that to her directly. Thank you, Sophia!"

Marion gave Sophia a big hug then. Sophia looked momentarily perplexed, but then responded to the show of affection in kind.

Audrey raised her coffee drink in the air in a kind of toast. "Here's to strong women who look out for and support each other!" Everyone laughed and smiled, and they touched their to-go cups in a mock toast.

Audrey continued, "I mean really! We have to stand together as women in things both big and small. There are so many times that decisions are made *about us* that can really affect us, without our being involved. When we find ourselves alone, we need to band together to be in solidarity with each other."

"Hear! Hear!" A voice from behind them made them turn around. They all looked at George, standing there with his man bag slung over his shoulder, frumpy unironed shirt and baggy corduroy pants, a half-grin on his face.

"Hey!" Audrey was the first to respond. "Didn't expect to see you here." She leaned in for a brief, perhaps awkward hug, and a kiss on the cheek.

"Hi everybody!" George smiled. "I don't want to crash your party but I was just walking up the street and saw you all here. I'll just grab my coffee and sit in the corner. I just came in to work for a bit."

"Hi George!" "Hi George!" Hi!" all three women responded. Friendly.

Audrey turned back to the group. "You OK if I head over to chat with George?"

"No problem!" "You go girl!" A few knowing smiles and raised eyebrows showed the conspiratorial nature of this ascension. Everyone loves a new love.

Audrey then turned and headed over to where George was setting up shop.

He had his coffee on the table and was taking some notebooks and his laptop out of his bag. Writers everywhere were eyeing an opportunity to sit and work at their craft. George seemed genuinely happy to see Audrey and hang with her, too. Which was another element of the writer's craft. Legitimate distractions from settling down to do the work.

"Hey!" George smiled broadly.

"Hey, yourself," Audrey leaned in to kiss him on the cheek, then slid into the seat next to George.

"How ya doing?" George asked. "How was Zumba?"

"Great!"

George was tickled that his new friend was a Zumba instructor. He had never known a Zumba instructor before, or any fitness instructor really, but he loved Audrey's energy and her enthusiasm. She just seemed so real, and so present.

"I wasn't expecting to see you here. I thought I was coming down for some focused writing time at the temple of caffeinated thinking."

"Well, don't let me bother you. I just thought I'd say hi," Audrey started to gather her things from the table.

"Oh, no! NO!" George reached out to hold her forearm. "I just meant I wasn't expecting to see you here. I am GLAD to see you here."

Audrey gave a quizzical, but momentarily mollified, smile. She took a sip of her drink, and looked around. Her gal friends were pretending not to observe her and George.

Audrey turned back. "So, what were you planning to write about today? The Great American Novel? Some expose about the inequities inherent in our racist, misogynistic political system?" She gave a sweet smile to George to let him know she wasn't making fun, but actually asking.

He laughed. "Nothing so grand in either dimension. Something more local in fact. Kind of more on the local angle of our local disappearing farmland. I heard that another two large fields along 116 are being converted to solar arrays. I'm investigating what they had been used for, and trying to find out the cost benefit. When it comes to solar array fields, federal support for infrastructure installation and deferred taxes, they are looking more and more viable. But it just continues to point to the demise of the family farm around here."

"So if this is a common story, what else are you going to add to it?

"I'm looking at the local angle. Talk about the families directly involved. Personalize it for our friends and neighbors and communities."

Audrey looked at him with her head cocked to one side. Quizzical. "You know, you could almost add in a piece about my family. Have you thought of that?"

George took a sip of coffee. "Well, I have thought of that, of course. The various conversation you and I have had -- "

"The many, many conversations--" Audrey said, teasing him.

"OK, you and I have talked about this a few times, and you have alluded to your dad's situation, AND, I didn't want to pounce on his story like some vulture. I am sensitive enough to pick up the nuances of feeling between you and your brother and your dad. Being close to a story sometimes makes it more challenging to tell the story. It's your story, and it's theirs. You are my -- friend? paramour? -- and I respect you for confiding in me as your friend, not as a reporter or writer. "

Audrey was quiet for a moment. "OK, fair. Thanks. I actually do appreciate that. Maybe I got carried away when I realized my life was running in a parallel stream to your story. "

George nodded, "Yeah, it's a little weird -- your family and my professional writing. If it's any consolation I have been working and writing about these issues for quite some time, and I believe that many locals who are interested in this issue, and who have followed it in any way, would know my name as being associated with it."

Audrey appreciating how he had considered the situation, and knew this was a fairly tight person, for all his unkempt and shluppy appearance. He had rules and boundaries, which in his professional life were very appropriate, but Audrey made a mental note that the apparent rule-bound approach when applied to a personal relationship might cause some friction down the road. Audrey herself was a bit of a rule-breaker, especially when she was younger, and that side of her was always there, walking the line somewhere.

Audrey was Doug Stengel's kid, so she got some respect and was given some lee-way because of that (like the time she was caught smoking cigarettes behind the tool shed at the Hadley Elementary School when she was 10, and saying she was *just experimenting*). She learned that a quick smile combined with her brown freckles and auburn ponytail would get her a pass in many situations. How often had she gotten to school late, skipped classes, missed a homework assignment, or some other infraction, only to have the teacher or administrator say, "Audrey, let's not do that again." Pushing the limit became a regular part of who she was.

"So, anyway," Audrey said after a moment's thought, "Are you going to add in anything about my family?"

George looked at her, brow furrowed. "Look, I can't say I am not tempted with the possibility of finding out more interesting and juicy details about your family and how they -- you -- got to the point of probably selling the family farm. Your family has been here in this valley for generations. Generations! That's amazing in and of itself. Heck, Stengel Road in Hadley is named after your great-great-whatever-granddad, right? I'd love to do that story."

"So?--"

George chuckled. "For starters, I am much more interested in, shall we say, getting to know you more intimately, than I am in adding your family's story into my article and having that feather in my cap."

"Notch on the barrel instead of a feather in your cap?" Audrey laughed.

"Ouch. Not at all. Nothing like that. More like who is this intriguing person? I want to get to know her better."

Audrey leaned back and stretched her arms over her head. She crossed her arms in front and leaned forward on the table. Smiling.

"Fair. So what's your plan?"

"I don't have a plan. I am glad to have the opportunity to make a plan. I hadn't thought that far ahead."

Audrey glanced over at her friends, watching surreptitiously from their table across the room. She smiled at them. They smiled back. Alice gave her questioning look, with her hands raised. Audrey gave an I-don't-know shoulder shrug.

George said, "What are you doing tomorrow morning? It's Sunday. Church?"

Audrey swiveled her head around to him. Shook her head no. Looked up to check her memory, as if checking a wall calendar. "I think I am planting my garden since it's supposed to be nice."

George responded, "Then I am bringing my gardening gloves and old clothes, sun hat, and will assist."

CHAPTER 20

Brodi glanced out the plane window at the glistening blue-green water of the Atlantic. Wetlands and swamps flashed by as the aircraft slowly descended to ground.

When the plane touched down, smoothly and easily onto the tarmac at the Jacksonville Airport, Brodi felt the welcome relief of a safe flight completed. She turned on her phone, seeing a text from Ted saying he would be waiting outside baggage claim. Deplaning, Brodi glanced up at the giant stained glass window portraying a torso with a suitcase at the end of the concourse, a wry comment on all the travelers in the airport.

Seeing Ted standing next to his car, she waved and walked over, appreciating the blast of hot air that greeted her as she exited the air-conditioned terminal.

"Hey Brodi! Good flight?" Ted asked as he opened the trunk of the car.

Brodi hoisted her roller bag. "Perfect. No problems. I worked on some specs for the prototype on the way down. Ready for our meeting."

Ted slammed the trunk and walked back over to the driver's side of the car. "Great! Shall we do some strategizing over lunch, or do you want to drop your bag at the hotel?"

"What time is the meeting? I don't want to cram in too much before then." Brodi replied, buckling into the passenger's seat, and fishing her sunglasses out of her jacket pocket.

"We're meeting with the team at 2:00 PM." Ted looked at his dashboard clock. "2 hours, give or take."

"Let's grab lunch and head over. "

"Sounds like a plan. How's Marion?"

"Well, Marion's doing O.K. She is working to get on top of this transition for her mom, as you can imagine. It seems like Beth goes in and out, some days better than others, and it can really throw Marion for a loop when Beth's having a hard day – emotional, or even belligerent. And her memory's definitely getting worse."

"Sorry to hear that, Brodi. Are you still planning to have her move in with you two?"

"Well, we're working on that, but to be honest, we are also weighing moving her into assisted living sooner."

Ted was sympathetic. "That may prove best. We had to do that with my mom as her memory faded. And hey! All the more reason to get this device going. We have a very rough model to show you today, by the way. I can only imagine how helpful and reassuring this will be for you and Marion if we can get it going soon."

* * *

After lunch they drove onto the campus of the corporate offices, complete with a guard gate along the drive. Ted used his swipe badge to raise the gate, waving at the guardhouse. It was coming up on 2 when they rode the elevator up to the 8th floor, and exited to a conference room.

Carl and Chelsea were in the room already and Carl got to the point. "Brodi, I was sorry not to really focus with you on your last trip; you know the pressure of too many things to do. But I think you will be suitably impressed with what the engineers have been able to come up with in just a few weeks. Chelsea, walk Brodi through what you've got."

Chelsea flipped open a laptop, hit two buttons, and the screen at the end of the room illuminated, revealing a powerpoint, with the RXX logo prominent on the title slide.

Chelsea detailed the specifications of the wearable device they had developed that was almost fully functional as a monitor for various health-related measures. It appeared to be a watch, fairly unremarkable. "This is the GPS tracking component, and this is a voice box recorder that can record a message for the user. This prompt allows the user's name and address to be input as a baseline, so that the person can be located in the event of a wandering episode."

Brodi opened her computer to the calculations she had been working on the plane.

"This is amazing, and you folks have taken this along further than I imagined in a very short period of time. I have been thinking of some capabilities that would enhance the effectiveness. For instance, how about an alarm that signals when it's time for medications, and shows a picture of the medications to be taken at that time? It also prompts the user to input when each pill has been taken, and so records the dosage and time. This adds to the capability we discussed earlier of directly sending the information to the cloud so it could be downloaded at the doctor's office."

Carl cut in. "Brodi, let's look at the prototype we have developed. We can then see about integrating the added capabilities you have outlined." He turned and opened a smooth black box that had been sitting conspicuously on the table. Inside, mounted on a slightly raised cushion, was a sleek banded watch. Carl slid the box across the table to Brodi, who gently removed the device, and slid it onto her wrist. It felt lightweight, and easy to wear. When she tapped the face, it lit up with the red RXX logo as it warmed up. Then a light blue screen appeared briefly with Brodi's company logo – Medtronol – before going to a screen with four small icons displayed.

"Very cool," she murmured.

"Take it for a spin," Carl encouraged. ""We loaded it with a template as though it already belonged to someone."

Brodi tapped the upper right icon on the screen. The device spoke.

"Good afternoon Brodi. It is 2:20 PM on Monday, June 16, 2022. You have no appointments today, but it is time to take your afternoon medications. Touch the pill button to see what you are taking at this time." The voice was a pleasant male voice, simply modulated.

Brodi touched the pill icon at the upper left corner. The voice came back.

"You have three pills to take today at 2:00 PM, so this is a good time to take them – one is a round green pill." The voice paused as an image of the pill floated on the screen. "Find that pill and take it with water please."

Brodi tried to imagine Beth's reaction to this, and suspected at first she'd be uncomfortable. "This is pretty amazing," she said aloud. "I like that it shows a picture of the pill so you can match it."

"RXX wants to be first to market with this, Brodi" Carl responded. "With the Fit Bit, Apple Watch, and other devices, we know that we can't be the only ones looking to enter this space with activity trackers. To be honest, we want you to take this back and we're hoping that Beth might be willing to give it a try. We have five other prototypes for you to take to encourage others to get involved. And of course," he continued, "Tomorrow we want to look at other capabilities you have identified to get Chelsea working on the next iteration. We believe that we can get 10,000 units into the market in 6 months, and we could signal to go on production now if we're ready. And Brodi, we've had a discussion about this. We feel this has excellent market potential. We are willing to underwrite the first 50,000 units until we see how it registers with the market. Then we can discuss the next level of production."

The next day Brodi found herself winging home in the midafternoon, with a new "RememberWatch" in her suitcase, and 5 more being shipped to her offices in Northampton. Brodi had gotten Beth's information including her medication schedule loaded into the model she had in the briefcase for Beth. It could be a game-changer.

She knew that Marion would feel a sense of relief knowing there was one more "pair of eyes" on Beth as she moved about. The GPS tracking ability would be very reassuring.

* * *

Jeremy walked over toward Old Jim sitting amidst the standing stones. It was June 21, the Summer Solstice, and the sun was tipping toward the horizon, although it was still a full hour before sunset.

"Jeremy," Old Jim said. "You are ready to learn the Dance of the Animals today. Summer Solstice, and this Dance, are so important for the deep connection to nature and the land. We are lucky to have a medicine woman here with us today to lead us through the dance itself, just at sunset."

Jeremy's stomach lurched. "I hope I'm ready! I worked on the steps you showed me last time, so I know the beginning of the dance at least."

"Good, good." Old Jim opened a pouch and pulled out a smudge stick of dried mugwort.

He turned to Jeremy. "First, we smudge."

Old Jim stood up, and his long gray hair fell midway down his back as he turned to face Jeremy. He lit the end of the smudge stick, and it briefly flared into flame. After a moment Old Jim gently blew out the fire, and the bright ember amidst the mugwort leaves emitted a pungent smoke, not unpleasant, and somehow it didn't sting the eye. Old Jim cupped the smoke in his hand, and bathed himself in the smoke like pouring water. He started at his head, and worked his way down his own body, then turned to Jeremy. Old Jim waved the smoldering plant wand in a circular manner in front of Jeremy's face, then around his head, then around his body.

"This smudge prepares you for the ceremony," Old Jim explained. "The earth-based worshippers believe that our negative thoughts and feelings could be released through smudging, and this allows us to be ready and receptive to the energies in the ceremony. You can also say prayers for the success of the ceremony, or your hoped-for outcome of the ceremony as well."

As they finished this simple act, a group of 4 people walked toward where they were standing. One was a short, dark-skinned woman, long dark hair flowing down her back, with very wrinkled skin and piercing brown eyes. She glanced briefly at Jeremy, nodded, then looked down again as she walked. The other three people walked a step or two behind her. All were dressed in colorful peasant-style clothing, with designs and images from the natural world woven into the fabric.

Old Jim bowed slightly to the old woman, and said, "Doña Martina, this is young Jeremy, of whom I have spoken."

Jeremy looked quickly at Old Jim, slightly confused, then also bowed his head briefly. "I am honored to meet you."

Doña Martina glanced briefly into Jeremy's eyes, and he felt as though she could see through him.

The three people behind Doña Martina all carried various satchels and bags, and seemed to be helpers to this woman.

They turned and looked at the sun, then found their way to the center of the circle of stones. There a blanket was opened and thrown over the flat stone lying in the center, and various other implements were brought out of bags and cases. Some were instruments -- gourds and rattles, and a beautiful wooden flute.

Doña Martina sat cross-legged on the blanket, and pulled some items from her bag -- a bowl, and some herbs that looked similar to the smudge that Old Jim and Jeremy had used a few moments before.

As people began to gather, they formed a circle around Doña Martina in the center, and sat down cross-legged on the grass. One of Doña Martina's assistants filled a large abalone shell with green leaves, which she lit, creating a thick dark smoke. She walked the circle allowing everyone to smudge, and even this simple practice seemed to calm everyone down, get them into a different mindset. Jeremy wondered if the smell transported him, or was it something else?

Doña Martina brought out a short drum, carved from a single section of wood, and she put water on the leather drum head. She began to beat rhythmically on the drum head, and water jumped up from the surface in beads of water, spraying her. She closed her eyes and chanted in another language. It was guttural, and melodic, and unlike anything Jeremy had ever heard before. Her voice rose and fell in a kind of sing-song back and forth. Her upper body swayed back and forth in time with the chant, and her voice and the drumbeat combined to create a special feeling. They all began to gently sway in time with the drumbeat.

For Jeremy, it reminded him of the equinox ceremony he had attended in the spring. The images had stayed with him the whole time. Something really special transpired that day, although he couldn't articulate what it was. As a musician, he naturally gravitated to music, and rhythm and a beat. Today he also could feel a slight inner shift; a little like being high on weed. The sun just kissed the horizon in the west at that moment. It felt like they were about to descend into some new time, some new place.

Drumming and chanting, rising and falling, the sounds carried everyone forward, upward, into a new place internally and collectively. As Jeremy mimicked the chanting he heard -- he actually didn't know the language -- he could feel the earth beneath his bottom. He was aware of sitting on the ground, but he had a strange sensation of merging, or melting into the ground beneath him. It wasn't unpleasant, but he was aware of slowly becoming more connected to the earth, as though he *was* the earth. As he faced across the circle, beyond the medicine woman, he was aware of a deer standing just outside the circle. Maybe not an actual deer, more a hint, or a suggestion. It had a headful of antlers. It was majestic, but also insubstantial. Jeremy glanced at it, then his eyes traveled to those others around the circle, also sitting, swaying to the rhythm of the drum. He felt a bit dizzy, but somehow the sense of being rooted in place was keeping him present. The mysterious deer looked straight at him back across the circle. Jeremy could tell that others could not see the deer, it was a ghost, or a spirit, or a vision or something. It seemed so -- ephemeral -- was the word that came to him at that moment. Ephemeral. Yes. And yet he felt some power, or some source of strength there. He glanced over at the Doña Martina, and she was looking directly back at him. She knew, and somehow she was participating. He then felt, or saw, this ghost animal come across the circle toward him, walking slowly and purposefully. The animal was walking to the rhythm of the drumbeats, slowly and methodically, like a dance or a march until it was right before him.

Was he just imagining it? This giant stag was now right before him, and looking down at him. He felt himself lifted up, although he was still seated on the ground, but his being was lifted up. He began to move inside the deer, and in a sudden moment, he was inside of the deer. He felt like he was the deer, but he could see his body sitting there on the ground. He was looking down at his body. As the deer he could move his body, and perceive through the deer's eyes. He was both the deer and he *was* himself. He didn't have to do anything consciously, but the deer was moving slowly around in the circle, moving at the rhythm of the drumbeats, as though dancing to the rhythm. The drumbeats were all around, permeating him and everything around him. Jeremy had enough presence to know this was really crazy, wondering if he was imagining this, or dreaming, or making it up. His whole being screamed that this should be terrifying, yet he did not feel afraid.

Jeremy felt moved to stand up, which he did slowly, and he began to tap his feet in rhythm to the drumming. He danced the steps Jim had taught him before, the ones he had practiced. He could sense the deer moving its hooves along with him, and as he swayed his torso, he felt the deer move its torso too. There was a swaying, sinuous movement that seemed to overtake him/them; he wasn't really sure if he was moving this energy himself, or if it was moving him. Even with his eyes closed he could see the deer, or feel it within him and around him. He could see and hear through the deer's eyes and ears, and these impressions were both very exaggerated and also somewhat muted. There was a moment where Jeremy felt like he was going to faint, or throw-up. He felt immediately disoriented, and a little unstable. Now through the deer's eyes he could also see other ghostly animals around the circle. Owl, bear, eagle, weasel, raccoon, all gathered here in this circle. He felt a deep feeling of connection to these other animals, and to the people with whom they were connected.

Then, all at once, he leaped forward, using his powerful back legs to propel him through the air and he landed 4 or 5 yards from where he had been standing just a moment before. Jeremy had no sense of how he had accomplished this feat. That one movement had broken some kind of trance he was in. And with that movement he was moving again, leaping forward in great bounds, and feeling both the strength of this body, and these four legs that moved him forward.

The drumbeats stopped for a moment, then there were a series of four bursts quickly rat-tat-tat-tat, rat-tat-tat-tat, rat-tat-tat-tat, rat-tat-tat-tat, rat-tat-tat-tat. Then the steady drumbeat resumed, but this time it was quicker, more insistent. Jeremy, as the deer, turned back to where Jeremy's body stood, still swaying; he was meant to go back.

The deer spirit body moved to where Jeremy stood, and Jeremy felt the deer un-merge with his body, and then he was standing back in his own body. He felt a little unsteady, and sat down hard. He slowly opened his eyes as others around the circle were doing. It seemed like they were all waking up.

Doña Marina and her assistants said a few words in another language, lit some mugwort bundles and waved them up and down, calling a final blessing to the work.

Old Jim came over to where Jeremy was sitting, resting a hand gently on his shoulder.

"How you doing, Jeremy? Just take a minute to relax."

"Wow, I dunno. It's hard to speak. I was a deer, or something. I was a deer and moving like a deer, and I was leaping around. What was that?" Jeremy's eyes were bright, and he was perspiring.

Doña Martina came over and squatted next to Jeremy. She was smiling broadly. "This boy, he has the visions. He can *see,* and he can *become.* The deer has chosen you, it is your animal. It can bring you power and wisdom. This is a great gift for you, but also for all. The animal is your *familiar.* You can learn its ways, and you can learn its wisdom. It will be like coming home. This is your spiritual home."

She turned to Old Jim. "This boy needs guidance, and support. He will learn more ways with your help, and with the help of others. Have him contact us, and we can help to guide him. If he wishes this."

With that, Doña Martina patted Jeremy on the shoulder, then rubbed it firmly with her old gnarled hand. Jeremy felt energy traveling into his shoulder, and felt a deep calm come over him. He had never felt like that. She moved off and checked in with others there.

Old Jim stayed next to Jeremy, and said softly, "Take some time to integrate this."

Old Jim helped Jeremy to stand up. Jeremy brushed off the seat of his jeans with his hands, and stretched cat-like toward the sky. He glanced around, seeing that others were glancing at him, and also they were all smiling and looking around.

Jeremy started wandering slowly amidst the stones and looking at the trees. The trees felt very solid right now, and that felt good to him. Jeremy felt different inside, but more himself really. Something had shifted, loosened. Jeremy thought that this encounter with the deer spirit -- that was how he thought of it -- was something like the patronus he read about in Harry Potter, but he wasn't a sorcerer. That was fiction made up in a book. This was something else. He had felt it, and he had experienced it. It was, well, it was like a dream. When he closed his eyes he could feel the deer still nearby. Somehow. He was a little scared; he was a little intrigued.

Jeremy wandered over to Doña Martina. "Was that real? Or was I just in a trance?"

She smiled at him. "Very real. That was a gift to you. Keep it in your heart, and we will talk again."

As Jeremy drove off home, he wasn't sure what the right next step was. Maybe there was something that was coming along, something he didn't even know about now. He smiled ruefully to himself. He hadn't known what coming to these gatherings might do, but it wasn't this.

CHAPTER 21

The warm morning sunshine stirred a slight breeze rustling the young pale green leaves in the maples and oaks. The sun was dappled in the garden at this early hour, and George put on his leather work gloves, as Audrey appeared around the corner of the shed with a wheelbarrow filled with long-handled garden tools. The spring plants were beginning to take hold in the rich brown earth, and Audrey anticipated a ton of weeding that needed to be done today. This was fine with her; spending the day in the garden was something she loved, and doing so with George made it more enjoyable.

"Ready to do some work?" Audrey asked, smiling in the sunshine.

"Absolutely," George said. "Show me what needs doing, and I can jump in."

Audrey indicated to George a 16 foot by 20 foot long plot in a raised bed.

"Got to be weeded," Audrey said. "try not to pull out any of the starter plants themselves."

George gave her a rueful smile. "I am not a complete novice at gardening; I just haven't done it much lately. I can see these plants are all about the same height and they are in a pretty straight row, so they look like they are supposed to be there."

"Yep. Basil in that row, spinach in the next."

The sun slowly cleared the treetops as they worked. George dug with a trowel, carefully excavating the smaller weeds that had sprung up among the plants. He had become so completely reliant on the Brookfield Farm share over the last two decades that he didn't really get involved in any gardening to speak of. He puttered around his own yard, but he relished the wild look he had cultivated, and really only mowed his lawn every few weeks. The herbaceous border around his lawn was essentially wild, and not cultivated toward any particular end.

Audrey was digging with a spade in the next bed, really going in deep. George noted the energetic way she was shoving the blade into the dirt, then heaving the dirt up and turning it over. Obviously everything in that bed was going under the soil. Weeds disappeared into the dark brown soil, turned under. Every once in a while a worm would be turned up too, and Audrey turned the worm into the soil right along with the weeds.

George turned his attention back to the raised bed in which he was standing. The earth was slightly moist, and the weeds were coming up pretty vibrantly in the bed. He was building a pile of pulled weeds on the side of the bed when Audrey started talking to him.

"It has been so weird having my brother back here these past couple of weeks. When he left I figured I might not ever see him again, and that has almost been true."

"Yeah, I was surprised when you told me he was back in town. Seemed sudden," George nodded.

"When he left originally my dad was so angry and hurt he could only say 'good riddance,' but I was just watching the last remnant of our family disappear. I ended up blaming Dad, but Ryan didn't want to have anything to do with me, either, so I lost him too."

George grunted his understanding.

"Looking back to high school, Dad was probably just so overcome with grief, and maybe some guilt or shame for what happened to Ryan, and then he was also angry because Ryan ended up acting like such a shit. Ryan would mouth off at Dad, and really was just doing whatever he wanted, there at the end. Dad couldn't control him, and I think he was also scared of Ryan. He didn't know what gay meant. And in the midst of all that Mom is sick with cancer, Dad's trying to cope with caretaking her, then as she slipped away, we're all plunged into grief. And it's all this pain jumbled together," Audrey's feelings and process came tumbling out as she jabbed the spade into the dirt, turning it over like she was unearthing these memories.

George stopped and turned to watch Audrey as the words poured out.

"Now that Ryan is back it's like we are supposed to be happy and receptive, but I still feel ambivalent. I wish he had given us more notice that he was coming back, or engaged a bit with Dad and I about who he is and what he has been doing. I love him, of course, he is my brother, but I feel so conflicted to see him now.'"

As she talked she pitched the clods over and over so that the dirt became more crumbled and more uniform. Audrey's movements were smooth and rhythmic, practiced.

"You know, Audrey," George responded, "I don't know what to

say about Ryan exactly, but I think it is not uncommon for someone to return home after being away -- you know, the Prodigal Son -- and hope that things will have gotten better simply because time has elapsed."

Audrey turned, suddenly furious. "Let me tell you something! He waltzed out of here and left me holding the bag with Mom and Dad. Dad of course acted like he was all fine with Ryan going, meanwhile he became an absolutely grotesque caricature of someone who was totally fine with it. Ryan completely disappeared. I mean, disappeared! I didn't know where he had gone, if he was still alive. He was obviously reacting to all the shit that had gone on between him and Dad, but then he just left. He obviously had been planning his escape for a long time -- probably months -- but he never let on a word. You can't imagine how that felt! I felt so -- lost! I felt ashamed! Like it was something I had done that he wouldn't even say goodbye! That he wouldn't let me know what he was planning, or thinking! I thought we had been so close, and then -- boom! He's gone. And now he just shows up!"

Audrey threw the shovel she was holding down -- luckily away from them both -- and strode away. George raised his eyebrows at the outburst, but kept quiet. He turned back to the weeding, slow and methodical.

When Audrey returned she had calmed down, her eyes glistening and red-rimmed. As George put down his trowel, and got up, she walked over and let him gently gather her into his arms. She allowed herself to be engulfed. She put her arms around George, at first tentative, but then more firmly, then fiercely. It felt so good to hold onto something solid, something real. She appreciated his presence, and his seeming acceptance of whatever she was going through.

Slowly they separated, and George lowered his arms to his side. He was aware of the preciousness of this moment, when silence, punctuated by a few bird songs in the trees, and a wafting breeze ruffling Audrey's hair was a natural punctuation to the poignancy of the present.

Audrey drew a big sigh. "I feel so overwhelmed with everything. Ryan's return brings up all the feelings that I had when he left, and a part of me is frozen in that moment. Part of me stayed in that moment because -- I didn't know! I didn't understand! I was left with Dad, and I didn't even really love him at that point. I was so angry with him for the way he had treated Ryan, but then Ryan fled. Mom was sick and then she died, what the fuck! Now all that's resurfaced, like something you lost in the fall that got buried in the snow over the winter, and it resurfaces in the spring when the melt comes. And all those feelings smell about the same as whatever got buried under the snow and thawed out in the spring.

"Anyway, I am all stirred up now. I need to reconnect with Dad, and find out where he is mentally. I have to overcome my reluctance to interact with him -- he's always so negative. And now that Ryan's here...It's so all jumbled up!"

George said quietly, "Seems like you feel like there is a lot you have to do just because Ryan has showed up. "

Audrey looked momentarily confused. "I guess you are right. I have always been the fixer, the one who gets everything right or who makes everything right. That's been my role and my stance for so long, I guess I just assume that's what needs to be done. Fix it. And Ryan's always been my little brother, always needing help or to have me step in. I guess that's why I feel like I failed somehow when he finally took off. Like it was because I didn't make it right with my dad, somehow, that if only I could have smoothed everything over, they could have gotten along..." She kind of slumped into the soil of the raised bed, looked out across the yard, watching the trees gently sway in the breeze.

"You know us farmers really like to play it close to the vest, not let anything personal out. But here we are, digging in the dirt, and I am like a crazed rabbit. We had a lovely moment the other day when I was with Ryan and Dad at the farm, but inside I just can't trust that it is real. That it will last."

George smiled slightly but kept his own opinion to himself. He took a few strokes of his beard, and nodded.

"I don't think anyone would blame you certainly. From what I can see, Ryan left you in the lurch with your dad. They were about to kill each other, and then Ryan just up and skedaddled. Your dad had all his feelings and nowhere to put them. That required you to manage the aftermath, like you said. And the *rapprochement* seemed sudden, from what you said."

Audrey got up and dusted off her jeans with her hands. She turned resolutely to the wheelbarrow, and walked to where a phalanx of small plants in pots stood in two rows over by the shed. She easily bent and lifted them two by two into the wheelbarrow, and then wheeled them back over to the plot she was working. George returned to his weeding, letting the conversation drift away.

Audrey knew that the truth was that this story had played out a million times for a million families across rural USA. This was their own particular example of it, and it *was* their story. This was a family born from a long tradition of farming and working the land, of being a part of the community of farmers and families that worked the land, that struggled each and every season, and year, to make the most of the land, and the crops, and to work with the weather and elements that they were given. This was a community blessed with beautiful soil that supported a bountiful harvest every year for generations. It looked like the prosperity, or at least the sustainability of this farmland, was guaranteed into the future, as far as the horizon.

And Audrey knew the possibility that there was something more, or maybe even something better, had become that siren's song for Ryan Stengel. Mom had tried to protect him, had allowed him special favors -- watching Disney Princess movies over and over, having tea parties with Audrey and other little girls -- and maybe wondered if he would someday grow out of it. Ryan's way in the world coincided with the eruption of gay liberation movements for those 2 or 3 decades older than he was, and thus the political and the personal collided in the Stengel household. The tensions of how his family first tried to shape and contain him, then just live with him, had built their own brand of pressure-cooker such that Ryan had to blow out, exploding just like the pea soup had exploded literally out of the 1950-era pressure cooker on Doug's mom's stove, when she had forgotten to turn down the gas under the pot as she momentarily left the kitchen. That boiling, drab green slime had covered the walls of the kitchen with a boom! Ryan had practically stormed out of that same kitchen 3 decades later. His time had come and he was not going to be held back, held down, held under anymore. The problem was that it was really Audrey that took the brunt of it.

And now here she was some decades after *that,* still picking up some of the fallout in terms of emotions that could boil over from seemingly out of nowhere.

She shook the reverie from her head. "I picked up these flats of squash and some peppers that I want to get into the ground today. I was thinking of putting in a few rows here, and seeing what would come up. I love zucchini, and with some tomatoes and sweet red peppers they make a mean pasta sauce come late August." She maneuvered the wheelbarrow into place, and she wiped her leather work gloves together, knocking some of the dirt off, surveying the planting spot.

"Do you want to help me get these into the soil?" She asked.

"You bet," George replied. He glanced quickly up at her face, but Audrey was looking studiously into the dirt.

"Let's first get a bit more manure into that soil there," Audrey moved to a pile of bags of steer manure and grabbed one. She swung it around like one might a little child holding their hands in the air.

George asked, "Can I help with that?"

"No, I've got it. You can grab that rake and begin to rake it in, though." She reached around to her back pocket and pulled out a utility knife and sliced the bag open deftly. George watched with appreciation for her economy of motion. Audrey had done this before, many times.

"You know," George said nonchalantly, "When I was doing my research about the area, I learned that your family followed the trajectory of many of the farming families in this area. Started out in the early Plantation Period with corn, then switched over to tobacco and onions when those crops really took off. These sandy alluvial deposits were perfect for those crops, and the proximity to the Connecticut River meant getting the crops out of here, first south via the Connecticut River, and then later via the railroad. The history of farming here is stupendous, and maybe the weight of that is hard for your dad."

George assiduously raked the manure into the soil as he said this, purposefully avoiding looking at Audrey. He knew this was tender territory.

Audrey pursed her lips in thought. "You know," she started, "It's really, really weird that you know so much about my family. And that the knowledge you have comes out in these dribs and drabs as we spend more time together. Like it's actually creepy. I feel like you know things you shouldn't, or something. Like I should get to reveal myself to you slowly over time, and you get to know my story from my perspective. It's so–so–discomforting–to know you know some things from my dad that I might not even know. Like he might have told you things that he never told me."

George wiped sweat from his brow, took a sip of water. "Yeah, I totally get that. Lots of people think that folks just open up and spill the beans to reporters. That somehow we are able to learn the real truth about things. And sometimes that happens. But more often folks are thinking about telling us a story that frames them in a good light. People want to see themselves that way; it's only natural."

"So did my dad open up to you with family stories?" Audrey's question shot out.

George stopped raking and looked over to her. "I don't think anything was too private. Like I said, people know what they say could end up published. So when they talk to a reporter, they will situate their story in a particular orientation to show themselves well. A story in the paper can seem like a real scoop, but that means that the person was ready to tell the whole truth, and the reporter looks good and like they really dug for the story."

George smiled at Audrey, and shrugged his shoulders. He looked actually a bit sheepish in that moment, letting her in on a secret that newspaper reporters knew, but the rest of the populace might not.

Audrey smiled back. "Thanks for saying that. I guess since we've been getting together I have always wondered if there was something about my family -- me -- you knew but weren't saying."

"Nope. For better or worse your dad never mentioned you kids. And really, Audrey, to be honest, your family's emotional story is secondary, to me, of the loss of another farm. Your family is one family, but the real story is what is happening to family farms all across America. The family farm is going down for so many reasons -- economics, aging farming populations, how hard the work is, few rewards, the unraveling of the traditional farming communities, the ascent of factory farming and the industrialization of agriculture. I mean I am sorry about your family and what you are going through, but if you step back it's happening all across this valley, and the next valley over, and the next state over, et cetera. It's real and it's scary, and it's very sad."

"Yea, I guess I can see that."

"Now your family also has the thread of the tale that includes the younger generation just not being interested in the family farm. You and your brother have just found new paths for yourselves, and have had an awakening supported by the changing culture that allows for you to make a move away from your dad's farm. That move began in the 60's and 70's and has escalated. There are tons of retiring farmers getting to the end of their working careers and looking around at no one wanting to take over their farm. What are they going to do?"

"I only know what my dad is struggling with, George. It's personal for us. You're the man with the bigger answers," Audrey started unpacking the starter plants to get them into the soil.

"To be honest, I think the Woofer model is likely the way to go here. I think that finding a young person with the passion or the vision of owning their own farm, and somehow getting them connected to a farmer who wants to pass along what he -- or she -- knows is a great match. It's going to save a lot of farms. There are a good number of young people who realize the value of farming, and who see the beauty of working the land and producing food, but they themselves aren't connected to a farm. Give them an apprenticeship on a farm. Give them room and board, and teach them how to be farmers. They will love it, and they will themselves become farmers that have come to feel that connection to land, to crops, to the cycles of the seasons, and the satisfaction of providing food for others."

George and Audrey smiled at each other, looking down on the four new rows of little starter plants they had put in the ground while they were talking. It was a small accomplishment, but they both knew it would mean something for those plants. For them.

CHAPTER 22

Strategizing enveloped the three Georgians. Since Wayne's disappearance and death, they could tell, during phone conversations, that Doug Stengel's interest in them and their offer was waning. They discussed how to get the interest back, how to seal the deal, maybe even on this trip. The firm had a long history of devouring real estate, and even bamboozling farmers or farmers' cooperatives. They needed to stick the landing with Doug, and for that they wanted some cash in their back-pockets to sweeten the deal. Investors were needed.

They decided en route to another meeting with Doug that they would offer even more money for the property.

"I think we try $5 million," John Engle mused aloud.

"That is certainly more than any land conservancy could hope to raise, and the prospect of all that money would capture anyone's attention," Bruce added.

"You know, we could stretch the truth a bit, and say that we *already had* investors to support that offer, unnamed foreign investors that were interested in this type of mixed-use commercial and residential space..." John let the rest of the thought drift off.

The large chunky car pulled into the dirt driveway leading into the farmyard. A brown hound came slowly out from the open red barn door, stretching into a perfect Downward-facing dog, before yawning and sauntering over to the car, tail wagging.

As they climbed from the car the dog went from one to the next, sticking its nose into each crotch. One by one the men pushed the dog's nose away, looking annoyed and embarrassed.

Doug Stengel sauntered out of the barn, his head cocked to one side, holding a piece of greasy machinery. Seeing them he put it down and started wiping his hands on an old dirty rag. Grease stains covered his jeans and old flannel shirt, and his three day old beard, gray and white, looked pretty natural on his weathered face.

"Howdy," he said.

One of the suits came forward hand outstretched, "Mr. Stengel, good to see you again -- John Engle, from Red Dirt Associates. How ya' doing?"

"Ayuh. Nice to see you," Doug said, at first looking at the proffered hand, at his own oil stained one, and then shook it.

"You remember Mitch Peters and Bruce Schwartz."

"Ayuh," Doug shook each hand in turn.

"Sir, we'd like to sit down and go over our proposal to you to purchase the farm. It's been awhile since our last visit, and we didn't talk about firm numbers at the time. We've put together an offer and have our architectural drawings I think you'll appreciate..."

Doug looked down at his boots, then raised his head, looking at the sky. "You know," he began, "I liked Wayne. He had his big ways, his big talk, but we spent time together. We grew to know and understand one another. When we talked, it felt personal. Like Wayne and Doug just talking about farming. I realized that I kind of missed that in your last visit."

John quickly backpedaled. "You are right. Wayne's death is a huge loss for us, both personally and professionally. Wayne was an amazing person, so full of life, and such a force of nature. We all miss him," he turned to glance at his colleagues, who nodded in agreement.

"Yeah, I knew he was a man who was used to getting his way," Doug added ambiguously. He wiped the back of his neck with the greasy cloth. "Whenever we talked I could feel the intensity of him focusing on me. That's a powerful thing."

Doug turned and started walking along the dirt farm road, the dog at his heels, and said over his shoulder, "C'mon walk with me here. I need to stretch my legs anyway."

The men glanced at one another, then walked quickly to catch up with Doug, who was walking along at a reasonable pace, but due to his height and long stride was already a good way ahead.

The tallest of the group, John, was the first to catch up to Doug.

"Doug, the property is fantastic. We saw this before. We love the prospect from the road, and the broad sweep of the mountains in the background. It's picturesque. We like the wide spread and riverfront for a marina and café. It's a once in a lifetime development in this area for us, and we think, for the region as well."

"Well, John, we'll walk down there and take a look," Doug replied. "It's a big property, and we only saw a bit of it last time. There are quite a few surprises you may not know about. Your buddy, Wayne, was just beginning to appreciate the nuances of the land and the variety of geographical elements. Now you take that open meadow over there," he said, gesturing to his right. "Just behind that hedgerow of trees, that's a wetland area. Actually let's head over there."

They took a spur track along the edge of a field of potato plants, a different direction than what they had walked previously. The dog happily ran in and out of the tall grasses at the edge of the road, sometimes pouncing on small critters scurrying deep in the grass.

Mitch and Bruce held back a few steps from Doug and John as they walked. The road breached the trees and they came into a wide and open meadow. Blackbirds swarmed back and forth across the tall wild grasses, speckled alders, cattails, and milkweed, and water could be seen standing all across the open marshy land. A few dead snags also towered above. The beautiful bird songs added to the sense of tranquility.

"So, this is a designated wetland area." Doug pointed across to a far row of trees. "Over there is the bank of the river, but from here to there it's all wetland. Can't build on it, according to wetlands protection laws. You know about wetlands protection? The good news for me is, I don't have to worry about it. Got plenty of acreage to plant. Of course, mice and voles and woodchucks, maybe beaver and foxes, and I don't know what else all live in there. But then again, I don't have to manage it. Or worry about the soil getting depleted, or anything. It's just there."

Bruce, the Chief of Strategy, piped up, "It's right in the middle of the property, which is too bad. It's a prime site for the residential tower we were planning. "

Then Mitch, "Who actually knows this wetland is here, anyway?"

Doug shrugged his shoulders. "I dun'no. Fish and Wildlife maybe. Department of Conservation and Recreation. The UMass Ag people I mentioned probably also know about it."

Mitch wondered *sotto voce* to Bruce, "We could probably just start working around it, like have a construction road around the edge. Put enough dump trucks of soil back here and it would slowly fill in…"

Bruce quietly chuckled.

Doug went on, "Well, it is likely that with a property this size changing hands, the sale would draw the attention of the regulators. They built a Lowe's in town a few years back that made the mistake of encroaching on the wetlands there. Got fined pretty heavy and had to do reparations. Seemed like a problem for them."

He flicked a glance to Mitch, turned and started walking again toward the water. John Engle caught the eyes of the others and sharply shook his head, brows knitted. He turned and walked to catch Doug.

"In any event this property is wonderful, and we love its rural feel. We do want to retain the features as best we can. Of course, we have big plans for the property, I think Wayne spelled that out to you. We will work around the wetland issue, get Fish and Game in here to tell us what's what. Maybe we make it like a small park area in the center, like where folks can get out for a walk in nature for a minute. We can place a trail around it, maybe one of those raised walkways, and benches for folks to sit on and watch the birds. The birds are nice."

Mitch rolled his eyes for Bruce's benefit.

Bruce picked up the thread, "We are thinking a nice curved drive through the property will go around stands of trees we'll leave for atmosphere and site accuracy. Other than the residential tower you really won't see much from the road anyway. Hints of things through the trees. The signage on Route 47 will be discreet – we are thinking of a rough stone and wooden sign with gold lettering, not too big. It will look nice."

They cut through another stand of trees and stood high above the Connecticut. John waited for the others to catch up. Then he started in again.

"Doug, I am sure you can't imagine the scope of this project we are proposing here. It's going to transform this property but also the area surrounding here. Here, Bruce, let's pull out the architectural drawings for a minute."

Bruce had been carrying the drawings in a metal tube, and gently shook them free. He and Mitch opened them out and held them like a treasure map.

Doug noted the Rodale Architects logo along the bottom edge and an architect's name that looked vaguely familiar – he tried to pull it up but couldn't quite place it – and then he looked at the sweep of the vision. There was a street level view of a shopping mall, a boutique hotel, and a residential tower. The Tower was only 10 stories, but in this landscape it looks huge. Nothing like it for miles around. There was a marina with boats along the riverbank, and a café.

"There will be dozens of construction jobs created with this development. In the shops, hotel, café and marina you'll also see over a hundred permanent jobs. This residential tower will provide 50 units of condominium housing which will induce other businesses to open in this area. The Hadley Mall area will see a resurgence of storefront operations, spurred by this development. If we build it, they will come!" John's eyes were alight with the possibilities of what they were proposing.

Doug squinted, partly from the sunshine, and took in his surroundings. His farm, his family's farm. He had stood on this spot innumerable times, and gazed out across this stretch of the Connecticut River often. He loved turning upstream and seeing the big waters sweeping around the bend, and he could imagine the force of that mass of water slowly carving out the outer bank of the river. Slowly, steadily, over time, carving and carving out the dirt, sand, rocks and making a wide sweeping curve. In his lifetime Doug had witnessed the slow erosion of that bank, and he had seen whole trees succumb to the encroaching river. The strains of *Old Man River* came into his head, and he began to hum the song. Kern and Hammerstein had penned the song almost 100 years ago, and it still resonated with Doug. There was something about the flow of the river, and how it seemed eternal. Doug was wise enough to know the original song had to do with how slaves in the South were forced into labor and cruelly abused to be made to work for slave masters. Doug knew his own family, way back when, had probably had slaves to help run the farm, or at best very poorly compensated workers, perhaps African-American, but that was a long time ago. He just knew his decision had to also honor that legacy.

Doug bent over and picked up a clod of dark sienna earth. "What do you think of this?" He asked his companions.

John chuckled. "Doug, you are the farmer here. To us, as developers, we see potential, and we know that whatever the dirt, whatever the composition, we can build on it, and make a good-looking property. It is in our wheelhouse to turn this land into a profitable business, and we have investors" -- here he made a quick eye contact with his colleagues --"Who are ready right now to put up the cash to back this development. It's going to be a winner in so many ways. Don't be surprised if the Hadley Chamber of Commerce itself comes to realize how vital this development will be for the town, heck, for the region. The combination of leisure, housing, mercantile, and offices will be a beacon for this area in terms of commerce and income."

Mitch took his cue from John. "Doug, as the onsite Project Manager, I can assure you that all considerations will be taken to ensure that proper environmental codes are complied with, and all local construction laws are followed. Our firm has a long history of working in close cooperation with our local constituents on the siting and building of our projects. We deliver on time and on budget, so there should be no adverse reflection on you as the seller in terms of the quality of the project. Of course, we will go before the local planning council or board to make sure we comply with any recommendation they make, but this is a process we have undertaken in literally dozens of projects all up and down the Eastern Seaboard. We've worked in seven different states, and dozens of municipalities."

Bruce again, gesturing at the plans, "See, Doug, here is the marina, and there will be docks and a harbor master's office here," he signalled to the left. "Two docks for boats and other watercraft will project into the river, although we might need to put in some retaining wall to minimize the drag from the river flow right to left here. The actual marina building will have a small cafe/restaurant, which will of course be open to the public as well as marina members. There will be locker rooms on the lower level as well. It will give a sense that boaters from here can really engage in their recreation, and if there is weather, or folks are wet from swimming, tubing, water skiing, whatever, they have a place to shower and get into dry clothes. We've tried to think of everything."

Doug studied the drawing, glancing at the men as they spoke, then looked out. All he could see along the River were the tall maples and oaks and a few weeping willows that stretched out from the bank. He saw two squirrels chasing each other up and down the trunk of an old oak. Somehow that little adagio made more sense to him at this moment than a marina with two docks filled with boats and other watercraft.

"So you fellas have thought this all through, have you?"

John cleared his throat. "Well, we haven't arrived at a final figure, we still have some calculations to do. For instance, we didn't really count on that wetland you pointed out. But I would say that $4.5 to 5 million would be a good figure to start with."

Doug's eyebrows raised and lowered, as if they had just gone over a speedbump at 30 miles per hour. "That's a lot of money."

"Doug, we feel it's fair, given what this property is worth. Of course, as I said, we have to do some additional calculations, but we'd be in that ballpark." John realized his first foray into some negotiations set up the seller to think of an actual figure. It could also soften the seller up to be more amenable to a different figure later. If it turned out the later figure was more, they'd be more likely to accept. If it was less, then there was some explanation necessary. And John knew that Doug Stengel had never considered such a high figure for his land, especially since the land had never been for sale, and there was nothing comparable within 40 miles.

John pressed on. "You know, Doug, the world is shrinking; there is no question about that. What seemed like insurmountable distances are now just minor trips. Think of flying places, and how accessible even remote places can be. Heck, we don't think twice about hopping on a plane and flying up here now to see you. It's, what?" He looked at his colleagues with his shoulder up and his hands out to his side—"an hour and a half? Two hours? Nothing! This complex will be big city, but we will preserve enough open space for it to feel country. The drive into the complex will be through big trees along a winding drive. People will have to take it slow, so they will feel slowed down. So folks from anywhere can come up here for a getaway."

Bruce chimed in. "Yes, and it will be—what?" Again looking at his colleagues—"30 minutes to that new MGM casino in Springfield? People will come for a weekend here thinking they are in this lovely country retreat, but an easy shot down the interstate to a night at the casino! The best of both worlds!" He smiled in a self-satisfied kind of way, nodding at his two colleagues.

Doug smiled a thin-lipped smile and nodded. Careful observation of human behavior would identify a response to this putative argument that was not entirely welcome. In fact, mention of the city of Springfield, along with the fairly recently added casino, had struck a sour note for Doug. Now his mind filled with imagery of stretch limousines turning down a well-lit macadam drive through a grove of probably newly-planted trees to a glass-and-chrome ten story tower right where his current crop of tobacco and corn was coming up sometime in the next few weeks. Not copacetic.

Doug stopped walking and then turned to look back across the field from where they had walked. He instinctively knew that he might need to irrigate at some point. He could feel it; a tacit knowledge grown from decades on this land. He felt a slight shiver and shrugged his shoulders involuntarily. He knew himself well enough not to dismiss an intuition out of hand. Something wasn't quite right here. But did it actually matter?

John was studying Doug's reaction discreetly from the side. He was aware that Doug's silence was probably not an encouraging response. Somewhere along the way they had lost or were losing him. John regrouped.

"Anyway, Doug, what is most important is that you feel good about the sale, and we think $4.5 million would be a reasonable price to pay for this land that you have farmed your whole life." John's tone itself was reasonable. The way he spoke now made it seem like it was the most rational thing to do -- sell your house and land for a large settlement. The way of the world was certainly money -- hard cash. Get as much as you can, as fast as you can. It was prestige, it was power, it was privilege. Empires built, fortunes made. What could be more logical?

Doug pursed his lips, turning back toward the house and barn. "You gentlemen make a persuasive argument, no question. And that fancy architectural drawing does bring the project into clarity. Something is tickling the back of my mind; not quite sure what it is. Let me think on it, and we can talk again. Thanks for stopping by. I'll walk you back to your car."

Doug turned back along the farm road. The three from Georgia turned as a group to walk back to their car. None of them felt entirely certain they knew what had just happened.

CHAPTER 23

Doug climbed out of his powder blue 1966 Chevy K20 pickup, slammed the driver's door, and carried the flyer over to the bulletin board outside the entrance to Atkin's Market. A slew of older and more tattered flyers were posted there – puppies for sale, babysitting, tag sales, guitar lessons, the local playschool, a bluegrass band playing at a local bar, early intervention services, hauling and dumping, all sorts of things to have, do or buy. Studying the layout, Doug found a space that looked big enough for his flyer and he shoved a push pin into each corner to post it. Doug was a simple man in some respects, but he took some pride in having created the flyer using his MacBook Pro, on a Word document, sizing the different fonts to capture attention.

His sign featured Garamond typeface which he had always admired:

Farmhand Wanted
Basic farm duties include:
Haying, planting, mowing, fencing, plowing, minor mechanics
(can be taught), drive tractor and combine
$21 per hour
Looking for 20 hours per week
Contact Doug
413-413-4131

With a slight nod of approval, and glancing around to see if anyone was watching, Doug wandered back to his truck and climbed in. When he started his truck, it roared to life, turning a few heads in the parking lot. He headed out for Maple Farms Foods, which also had a bulletin board for community events.

Now, Doug was not just an old codger farmer from rural Massachusetts. He did live enough in the modern world to know he also had to post a notice on Craig's List and the Hadley Facebook page. He knew that he was more likely to find a farmhand through those social media sites, yet he was also not one to ignore the nearly impossible serendipity of someone looking at a poster on a bulletin board at the local stores. So here he was with a stack of printed flyers on his passenger seat.

Doug needed extra help on the farm just to keep up. Even the two local fellows he had weren't really enough. He had had farmhands over the years, some of whom were full time hands, and for a while in the 1990s and early 2000s he had WWOOFERS (Worldwide Opportunities on Organic Farms), which had proven very fruitful for haying and also grazing. The young people who generally came into town to work for the season were interesting and invested in learning how to farm so they could head out to start their own farm. They rarely stayed more than a season, maybe two.

He needed someone to do more of the heavy lifting and intensive labor, and he imagined a young person, maybe a high schooler, who had that high energy of the young with a willingness to work hard in exchange for a good wage. Of course it would be a cash arrangement, so the kid could pay his own taxes, or not, but there wouldn't be any paperwork. It was an arrangement that included a handshake and an understanding about when they'd show up, how long they'd work, and when they could go home. On Saturday or Sunday he'd feed them lunch, which was a nice extra benefit of the job. Having been a farmer his whole life, working hard manual labor, Doug was known for his two sandwich lunches, starting with good thick fresh farm bread, stacked with ham and cheese, slathered with mayonnaise and stone ground mustard, lots of tomatoes and lettuce. You didn't leave the table hungry. Doug also liked a good cole slaw, made with farm cabbage and carrots, sometimes with raisins, but always lots of vinegar. During the months when the tomatoes were in, Doug had a bowl of bright red tomatoes on the table to eat like fruit. It was a good life, working on Doug's farm.

As he drove along the country road past wide fields of crops, and the occasional solar panel array, he again mulled over his farm options. He knew tons of farmers that had sold, and moved on. He chuckled in disbelief that he could walk away with $4.5 million! Then again, he was resentful that his children had no interest in farming, but he knew it was hard, hard work, and the monetary rewards just weren't there anymore. It used to be that farms supplied the locals with food or feed or animals, and you could make a decent living if you worked hard, and stayed focused on your farm, but now that wasn't necessarily the case. Most of the bigger farms around here had been divided up, slowly or quickly, to try to make the cash you needed just to get by. Here he was, over 80, and he was still working from sunup to sundown nearly every day, and he wasn't rich. Hell, he couldn't think of retiring and just living out his days here. He felt a flash of anger that time and life had brought him to this point, without Fran to soothe him.

He was going to sell the place, one way or the other, and take what he earned and live somewhere else. *Somewhere else*, that rankled him, and scared him. Where was somewhere else? Would he retire to Florida, like other folks he knew? The lure of sun and warmth year-round, fishing and beaches were definitely a draw. His old bones were getting mighty tired of these Massachusetts winters. But he really didn't know anyone down there; his people were all here. So he imagined he would find a small house with a small yard that he could manage, or get someone to manage for him. It was still a ways off – a few years – but he could see that time coming.

* * *

Jeremy drove the car to Atkins Market for his mother. She needed a few things – bread, eggs, a nice Provolone cheese to make sand-wiches with the Black Forest ham she had purchased the day before, and tomatoes. She had mentioned a good black rye bread that Atkins some-times had fresh at the bakery. Since there were a few other items she also made a short list for him. Jeremy didn't mind going to the store, in fact he enjoyed getting out of the house and being able to drive his mom's car – a 2014 black Honda CRV. It had plenty of get up and go, and he could play his music as loud as he liked. Once, before he could drive, he had reached from the passenger seat to spin the volume up high when one of his favorite songs came on the radio. He had blown out the right front speaker in the process, learning that while he liked his music loud, there was a limit. He slowly raised the volume on the ska music he had on now, letting the music fill the car until it was bumping. Desmond Dekker playing *Israelites*.

It was three miles down Bay Road to Atkins Market, just long enough for one song. He waited in the car in the parking lot for the song to finish before he turned the motor off and climbed out. His mom had given him two twenties; he might have a little extra for something for himself. He looked over the extensive candy counter which was conven-iently right next to the entrance doors, and spotted some dark chocolate sea salt caramels. He asked for about four dollars' worth, which seemed like a good amount. Just as he turned away, he thought again and asked for a similar amount of milk chocolate sea salt caramels, which he would give to Sophia.

He fetched the items on the list, getting a half pound of the Provolone cheese, which seemed really expensive. The ham was sliced. He made small talk with the friendly cashier, a girl at his school. He hoisted his grocery bag, and was walking out when something caused him to pause and look at the board of notices. He wondered if there might be a job posted there – something he could do during the summer. He needed extra cash.

He detested the idea of working at Mickey D's, or Dunkin', or any other strip mall chain store. Too sanitized. Maybe something would turn up here. He scanned all the ads – colorful, funny, asking, offering, demanding, cajoling, regaling, describing, until his eyes came to rest on one that just seemed straight up. Farmhand. He thought for a minute. He could do that. It looked like manual labor, which he was down with, and he liked $21 per hour. He could definitely see doing that. He pulled his phone out of his back pocket, took a picture, then typed in the number, double checked it, and then dialed as he walked out to the car. The phone rang a few times, then went to voicemail.

"Uh, Hi, Doug, this is Jeremy. I saw your sign looking for a farm hand and I am interested." He gave his number and hung up. He thought it was a good sign that the sign had been put up today – there was a discreet 6/25 at the bottom of the flyer.

When Jeremy was back home he was making a sandwich with his mom when his phone rang. It was Doug.

"Hi Jeremy. This is Doug Stengel at the farm. Got your message."

"Oh hi, Mr. Stengel. Yeah, I saw your sign looking for a farm hand and I'm interested. I live in Amherst."

"OK. Do you have any farmwork experience?"

"No, no I don't," he added quickly, "But I've had other jobs and I'm a hard worker," glancing up at his mother who was looking pointedly at him. "And I can give you references."

"This is hard, physical work, Jeremy. Are you up for that?"

"Oh yeah! I help my dad around the yard all the time."

Then Doug invited him out to his farm in Hadley, near the river. Jeremy knew the stretch of Route 47 pretty well. He asked his mom to borrow the car in order to drive over there.

When he arrived at the farm, Jeremy climbed out into the bright sunshine, and squinted until he found his aviator sunglasses. Putting them on he gazed across the broad meadows and farm buildings. He had driven past this farm many times, of course, but he had never known who owned it. He saw the Stengel's Farm sign perched on a post in the yard, looking a little weather worn. He walked indirectly to the house glancing around corners and into the gloom of the open barn doors. The contrast of the bright sun outside and the relative shadow in the barn made it hard to see in there. He could make out some farm machinery and bales of hay stacked almost to the ceiling, and a thin cloud of dust danced in a light shaft created where two boards didn't quite come together somewhere on the siding. The barn looked old, like the rest of the farm buildings.

He heard the screen door bang, and turned to see an old man, tall and broad, but bent slightly at the waist coming toward him.

"Hi, I'm Jeremy," he said and smiled. He set himself to get a once-over by this old guy, knowing that he was likely to be scrutinized.

The man seemed easy enough. He proffered his hand and looked Jeremy straight in the eye. "Nice to meet you, Jeremy."

"Good to meet you too, Sir. Nice place you got here."

"Thank you. If you mean big and sprawling and needing attention you'd be more correct. So, you haven't done farm work before?"

"No, Sir. I have helped my dad in our yard a lot. I saw your sign and thought it would be a good job, though, working on a farm, outside. I've always wanted to learn about farming."

"Well, you would learn that here."

"I live in South Amherst, so I was just down the road at Atkins Market when I saw your sign looking for help."

"That's pretty good – I only put it up about an hour before you saw it. So, do you have any experience driving a tractor or any other rig?"

"I have my license, so I drive a car, and I mow our lawn with a ride around mower."

"That so? How big's your yard?"

"About an acre I guess. Usually takes me about an hour or so."

"Well, I got 300 acres here, young man. Guess you're glad you wouldn't be mowing that."

"Yes, Sir!" Jeremy smiled at that. "What do you farm here – crops, animals?"

"Mostly crops at this point. Mostly corn, soybeans, butternut squash. I still have a good section of tobacco. I keep cows to milk and also for the beef, so there's grazing you see over there. Also there's hayfields. So there's cutting and baling the hay in the early summer and fall."

"Wow, that's a bunch of different crops!" Jeremy said.

"Yep. I do have two regular hands – Jake and Matt – they are full time and know what's what, but we still need more help, which is why I'm talking to you. They've been with me for about 5 years, and they are both local Hadley boys. Right now they are out in the back field near the river, getting the second planting done."

Jeremy looked out past the red barn, and across the wide swath of early corn to a windrow of trees. He could just make out a break in the trees, and he imagined the river field beyond that, out of sight. Jeremy could visualize himself sitting on a tractor, and driving slowly across these fields, dragging a haying machine, or something that would stir up the soil in the spring and late fall. He didn't know the name of the machine, but he could certainly envision it, and he could even hear the sound it made as it moved slowly across the landscape. He turned to Doug, who was watching him.

"I like the feel of the place, sir," he blurted out. "I mean, it's really cool."

Doug was silent and too, looked out at the horizon. He was a thoughtful person, and also had honed his sense of people over years and years of being quiet, and just noticing. He felt that he was a good judge of a person, not as in, you're guilty or you're innocent, but more as one who could deeply feel a person, and know intuitively if this was a good person, or someone who might lie to you, or try to get something out of you. For instance, those fellows from Georgia set his teeth on edge, even when they were speaking in sincere tones. But Jeremy seemed like a good young man, still forming who he was, but ready to work hard and learn the farm trade.

"OK, son, I think this could work out. Let's give it a try and see how it goes. This is a cash deal; I'll pay you for the hours you work the week you work 'em. We can go up to 20 hours in a week. You want to start now?

Jeremy grinned – this was easier than he imagined! "Yes sir!"

They shook hands, and Doug asked him to follow him into the barn.

A tractor was sitting off to one side of the barn, and Doug climbed up into the seat. He talked through the steps of starting the engine, handed Jeremy a set of headphones, then started it up himself. As the machine roared to life, he raised his voice, giving Jeremy directions on what to do to get things going.

"Climb up here and stand behind me," Doug yelled.

Jeremy gingerly climbed over the mechanical structure and stood athwart two iron beams holding up the haying rigging in the back.

"Ease your throttle up, like that, and then disengage the clutch with this lever," Doug moved it easily into gear and the tractor came to life.

Doug swung it in a wide arc and drove out into the sunshine. He drove a bit across the open dirt drive and came to the edge of a field of pale green grass about 3 feet high. The tops were tipped with seed pods waving in the breeze. He braked, and disengaged the clutch and the tractor came to a stop, idling.

"OK, your turn." Doug swung down and Jeremy climbed over the seat and sat down. He looked carefully at the various knobs, levers and gauges.

"You're gonna hay a line along the edge of this rye field. *Secale cereale*. It's winter rye and good for grain. First you drop the cutting edge -- like this -- and start it– there–and then drive. Not too fast, not too slow. Stop when you get to the edge near that creek there."

Doug watched as Jeremy moved through the steps and then, with a slight lurch, he was off. Jeremy drove a bit slowly at first, but then seemed to realize he could go faster and sped up. He looked around instinctively at the place he had cut to see the pale gray-green grasses lying like fallen soldiers in the field. His hands were strong, so he could manage to keep the machine tracing a straight line along the edge of the field. At the end, he slowed down and stopped as instructed.

He turned around to look at Doug, who was now 100 yards away. Doug motioned for him to turn around and come back, so Jeremy carefully re-engaged the tractor, swung around in a u-turn, and began cutting the next row. Even with a tight turn, as tight as he could hold the wheel, he could only come about one cut's worth away from the previous line. He decided to just run a straight parallel line where he was. When he got back to where Doug was standing, he stopped, and then turned the tractor off. Doug was nodding his head in approval.

"Very nicely done, young man. You're a quick learner and careful. You figgered out how to cut alternate rows. I like that. Now next time when you come to the end, you can slow down, and just swing the u-turn without stopping. When the field's done one pass, you'll have cut/uncut/cut/uncut all the way across, like stripes. Then you turn and do the uncut ones.

"How much time have you got today?" he asked Jeremy.

Jeremy pulled his phone out of his pocket, and glanced. "It's 2:00. I can stay 'til about 5:00, I guess. I can come again tomorrow."

"Three hours will get you about half way today. If you want, you can continue like you have, and then finish with the tractor in the barn."

Jeremy nodded, inwardly very happy. He put the headphones on, cranked up the tractor, and swinging a tight turn, started on his third row.

Jeremy connected his music to the headset via Bluetooth, and listened to one of his favorite bands, Mogwai, which he loved. The strong guitar with bass over heavy drums fit the kind of sound he was looking for with his band. With the music cranked up, *Ceiling Granny* really grooved with the noise of the tractor under his seat. He noticed how the rhythm of the tractor's engine and the gears allowed him to bounce to the music too. Mogwai had been around awhile, but somehow that indie sound, hard rock alternating with some real romantic ballad type songs really fit for him. It was similar to his sister's favorite band, Coldplay, so they had some overlap in what they might listen to. With his headset on, he really couldn't hear the tractor of course, it was more like he could feel the tractor. Feel the vibration through his body. He turned around to look at the row of fallen grasses behind him. It was really so mesmerizing to watch the steady falling of the tall grasses. The sheaves fell in a steady line and a regular pattern. Jeremy thought, *this is real, this is the earth. This is the bounty of the earth.* And he had a sense of connection to it.

As he reached the end of the row, Jeremy moved to turn the tractor in a tight circle, and he anticipated the strength he would need to turn this machine around. He gripped the steering wheel and swung it, and, no, it wasn't like a car, turning easily. He felt the weight of the machine as it turned and the mower turned and it required maneuvering to get it around. Somehow his first two turns hadn't felt this challenging, and then he stalled the thing. It stopped with a clunk, and the suddenness of the stop nearly threw him off the seat.

Doug was watching from a ways away, and started walking slowly over to him. Jeremy saw that he didn't seem mad or anything.

Doug said, "Son, here's the first lesson, and it's good to get it out of the way. You can't whip this thing around like your Honda CRV there. You have to respect that you are moving a whole system here, and it's all connected. The way it turns is more like a battleship than a car. You have to respect it. You slowed way down on that first pass, which is really what you have to do. Here, let's raise the mower, and then restart the tractor and turn it around. Doug deftly raised the mechanism, and then restarted the tractor, which roared back to life. He slowly turned the tractor around. He dropped the harrow, and then vaulted off the tractor one-handed.

"You keep going." Advice for a tractor; advice for life.

* * *

Audrey and George were traveling along Rocky Hill Road from Amherst into Hadley, Audrey driving her white Nissan Rogue along one-handed. She preferred having the windows open if it was warm enough; the early summer breeze was just warm enough for that today, and it allowed her to turn up the volume of the radio so she could hear over the noise of the car and the wind whistling past. She was singing along to Taylor Swift, one of the new ones. Audrey appreciated that George had been familiar with Taylor and her music, and since hanging out with Audrey he was apparently finding some of the songs were growing on him. He seemed to especially like, *You Need to Calm Down*, from a few years ago. The political rhetoric had been especially loud back then, and given that the president at the time was especially vituperative against anyone who showed any difference; George had really resonated with the lines,

"And control your urges to scream about all the people you hate/' Cause shade never made anybody less gay." George would sing along with that one in the car.

Audrey had called her dad and left a message on the voicemail to say she was stopping by. It was pretty unusual for Audrey to just go over, and taking George with her felt like some kind of step. Audrey and George weren't sure exactly what kind of step. They were clearly dating, and seeing each other regularly, and having sex on a regular basis (which seemed to suit both of them very much). So, introducing your boyfriend to your dad felt safe, right? Appropriate? Normal? Something. Audrey knew George's anxiety was likely heightened since he had met Doug a few years back when he was writing that piece for the *Recorder*. George had interviewed Doug and quoted him in George's article, along with a flattering picture of Doug standing out in his field amidst the then knee-high rows of corn. Anyway, *this* would definitely be awkward.

Rounding the corner and heading north on Route 47, Audrey decided to switch songs and go for something else; a little harder. George was ready; Audrey would switch music abruptly in the midst of a song. He hated that, but he realized it was her way of staying with her mood. *Maldida Boda* came on; one of her Zumba songs. It was like Latin rap music, and the beat moved Audrey to dance back and forth in her seat as they buzzed up the road. Not George's cup of tea, but he also knew what the music meant to Audrey; it was a lifeblood for her, taking her to the place where her endorphins really kicked into gear. The rhythm, the beat, her smile said it all.

They arrived at the farmhouse, and Audrey parked, and was out of the car in one fell swoop. George was struggling to get his seat belt off when her car door slammed shut. Off she strode to the house. He could hear her yelling, "Dad? You outside?"

Doug was walking back from the fields off to the right, purposefully with his head up, but his expression was inscrutable.

"Hi Dad!" Audrey went over and gave her father a quick hug. "How're you doing?"

"Audrey," Doug responded. "Wasn't expecting you today. What brings you out here?"

"Oh I called to let you know I was coming," she quickly replied. "Guess you didn't hear my message."

"Guess not," Doug agreed. Then he caught sight of George. "You're that fella from the newspaper. What brings you here?"

"Hi Mr. Stengel, er, Doug," George fumbled out. "I'm with Audrey."

Doug looked quizzical. "Like how do you mean, with Audrey?"

"Dad, we're seeing each other. Like dating."

"Oh. That so?" Doug seemed nonplussed. To George, "Can't get enough of my family, eh?"

"Actually, Dad," Audrey interjected, "George had no idea who I was when we met. It only came out later. Anyway, I wanted to have you meet him with me."

Doug nodded, lips pursed. "OK. So now we've met again. That's it?"

Audrey sighed. "No Dad. I also wanted to come out here and see how you are doing. How things are going here on the farm, and hear about your plans."

Doug pulled a red bandana rag from his back pocket, and wiped his brow. "Well, we're in the middle of the season right about now, so we're looking at the first harvest of rye and the hay. I have some row crops coming in and the second planting of beans coming along."

The tractor came into view across the field and they could hear the low drone of the engine.

"Who's that?" Audrey asked as she squinted into the afternoon sun, shading her eyes with her hand.

"Oh, that's Jeremy. Amherst kid I just hired. C'mon, I'll introduce you to him, and we can see how he's doing." He started walking away along the farm road; Audrey and George followed.

George took a few quick steps to catch up to Doug.

"Doug, I think that article got some good publicity for farming when it came out. I hope you liked it."

Doug half turned to George. "That was a while back, but yes. I think you got your point across. I am certainly aware of the challenges I am facing. Your story was about farming all across the valley here. You were trying to talk about farming in general. Good to get that information out there."

"Of course." George had to take a quick two-step to again walk next to Doug, whose long stride was outpacing him. Audrey was by now a few steps back, but she seemed happy to let them walk together.

"If you don't mind my asking, and not professionally, what are you thinking about this place now?"

Doug glanced over at George again, "Well, to be honest, I am weighing my options."

Audrey jogged a few steps to catch up.

"Dad, we haven't had a lot of conversations about this. But it's still in the papers. Farming's not my thing, as you know, even though I respect how you and mom worked so hard for this farm. And you stuck with it even after mom died. Looking out across these fields makes me so proud of you for your sticking with a really hard way of life for your whole life. And it was just not for me."

"Damn it, Audrey, I know that! I am realistic enough to have seen you and Ryan turning away from this life even when you were kids. You tried to be helpful to me and your Mom, but it just wasn't in your blood somehow. I get that!" Doug seemed annoyed.

"But, Dad, I still love YOU!" Audrey grabbed her father's arm. He was forced to stop, and turn to her. His face was flushed, and he pressed his lips together. Doug looked down for a moment, shoulders sagging.

He sighed. "Yes, Audrey. I love you, too." She threw her arms around her father in a tight embrace. He tentatively, then more genuinely hugged her back. They stayed like this for a moment.

"Dad, you've got to do what you have to do. Whatever you want to do, it's OK!"

Now Doug wiped his eyes with the red bandana. He blew his nose. "Let's not have this in your next article, George!"

George smiled. "Doug, I have feelings for Audrey, that's why I am here. I care about her, and by extension, her family."

"Hrumph," replied Doug.

They had come up to the tractor, and Jeremy had stopped the engine and was sitting there.

"Hey Jeremy, it's looking good! This here is my daughter, Audrey, and her friend, George. Sorry, son, what's your last name?"

"Hey," Jeremy said to the two new people. "It's Jeremy Miller. Nice to meet you."

"Audrey Stengel Hodge," Audrey said. "Hey, you're Alice's son! Sophia's brother? They come to my Zumba class!"

Jeremy smiled and nodded. "Yeah, that's my Mom. And sister! So you're the Zumba teacher? They really dig your class!"

"Small world, I guess," Doug smiled.

"Small Valley," George retorted. "Every time you turn around you run into someone who knows someone you know. It can get claustrophobic." He raised an eyebrow.

"Wait," Doug looked at Jeremy. "Is your dad Ben Miller? With the Valley Land Trust?

"Yep," Jeremy now looked mildly distressed.

"Shit! Did you know that I am the guy your dad is trying to get to sell this farm to the Trust?" Doug stood almost staggering. "What the hell!"

Jeremy now looked very uncomfortable. "I didn't know! I have heard my dad mention 'Doug' someone, but I really didn't pay much attention. And I never figured you were the guy."

"Well, I *am* the guy." Doug shook his head bewildered. "So what are you thinking now? Are you hoping to make this an easier sell to your dad?"

"No," Jeremy mumbled. "I just wanted a job for the summer."

Doug stood shaking his head. "Well, this is a fine thing. I guess you can have your job, but I wish somehow I knew who you were already."

Audrey smiled and looked over at Jeremy. "Don't worry. Your dad is a good guy, and my dad is a good guy. They will figure out what they are going to do, and it doesn't really have anything to do with you."

She turned to her father. "Dad, you aren't planning to sell the farm this season anyway, are you?"

"Well, you never know. Those Georgia cats came sneaking around here earlier. They are offering a pile of cash for this place. Very tempting, I must admit. Then I meet this young man and he's ready for farming, with his back-to-the-land vibe. I don't know. And him being Ben's son, well, that's a kicker."

"Holy shit!" George scratched his head. "I need a.program to keep track of this!"

CHAPTER 24

A few days later, Jeremy met up with Matt and Jake in the barn, and all together they took the two tractors out to the river fields. They had developed a comfortable way of working together, despite a slightly rocky beginning. There hadn't been any overt racial tension, perhaps surprising given that Matt and Jake were white Hadley farmboys and Jeremy was a young black man from Amherst. Glances, and chuckles between the Hadley boys did not go unnoticed. Jeremy had felt these kinds of snubs from other white kids over the years. After a few weeks, along with Doug's adult presence, Matt and Jake had become consistently impressed with Jeremy's work ethic and his quiet focus on what needed to be done. While the two of them tended to joke around a bit when they were on their own, when they all worked together it was a different story. Jeremy was engrossed with the work, and the other two young men faded into the background for him. They in turn focused more on the work as well.

This day they plowed under weeds and tangles in the second field in preparation of another crop – this time fava beans, which could grow with relative ease and rapidity in the summer heat. They all knew that Doug was very serious about rotating his crops so as not to deplete the soil. Two rotations in a growing season was about what could be handled, and the fava beans would lock a good amount of nitrogen into the soil for next year. The three boys agreed that fava beans were yucky, but hey, they didn't have to eat them; they just had to plant them and help them grow.

Jeremy was on the first tractor, moving slowly up the rows of weeds covering dry and clumpy soil he plowed under the rich dark loam. Jeremy had learned that not every farming community had this kind of rich soil base upon which to grow. He had heard his father talk about soils for a long time, extolling the virtues of this ancient floodplain. He glanced down and smiled; his skin was the same rich dark color as that newly turned soil! Odd coincidence: Humus/human.

Close to lunchtime the boys all felt hungry, but they took a break only when Doug told them to do so. Usually Doug was pretty reliable when it came to lunch – 11:30 – but on a few occasions he hadn't showed up until noon. One time Matt and Jake had stopped working at 11:40, and rested in the shade until Doug showed up, not happy. That was the last time that had happened.

Just at 11:30 Doug appeared through the hedgerow heading back to the house, and he was walking with someone – a girl. Both Matt and Jake perked up a bit, but Jeremy was taking a long drink of cold water and wiping his brow. He recognized Sophia even from that distance.

"Wonder who that is with Doug?" Matt voiced aloud. "Looks pretty."

"Maybe she's family," Jake added.

"That's my sister, Sophia." Jeremy said, and gave the two other guys the opportunity to look at Sophia, turn to look at him, look quizzical, and then say simultaneously, "What?"

"I'm adopted, OK?" Jeremy was slightly defiant in answering, and the other two picked up the tone in his voice.

"That's cool, that's cool," Matt responded. "No offense. I was just confused for a minute."

"Your sister in high school?" Jake asked nonchalantly. Jeremy had seen enough guys' responses to his sister to know: 1) guys noticed how pretty she was; and 2) there was always a roundabout way to get information from him about her. He was a means to an end.

"Yes, she's in 10th grade at Amherst High, and she has a boyfriend," Jeremy added this last bit of information for effect.

"Oh," the only response.

As Doug and Sophia walked up the boys turned off the tractors. Doug looked across the field nodding slightly.

"Matt and Jake: This is Sophia, Jeremy's sister. Sophia: Matt and Jake."

"Hey!" the boys said.

"Hey," Sophia flicked a glance at Matt, eyes lingered a bit longer with Jake, who returned the gaze.

Doug continued, "Very good work this morning, by the way. You earned your lunch." He made a face as he looked at his watch. "Guess you can knock off 'til 12:45."

All three farmhands thanked him, and Matt and Jake took off jogging to the farmhouse, Jake taking another look over his shoulder at Sophia.

"I walked your sister over here so she could see what you're up to." To Sophia he said, "Your brother's a hard worker. This land always seems to be fighting you, so I appreciate a guy who can fight back."

Jeremy smiled at the compliment.

"I'll let you two walk back to catch up, and then you can join us for lunch, Sophia."

"Thanks, Mr. Stengel."

"Thanks, Doug."

Doug climbed aboard one the tractors after unhitching the furrowing machine, fired it up and drove quickly back toward the house.

Sophia and Jeremy turned and walked back.

"I wanted to see what this new job is all about for you! You've been kind of secretive about it."

"What, now you're checking up on me?" Jeremy's annoyance bubbled.

"No! I was just driving past, and realized this was the farm you were working on."

"Whatever!"

"So, you like this? It seems like hard work and being out in the sun all day must be hot."

"Nah, it's OK, I guess. It doesn't take a lot of brain power, and I can feel myself getting stronger. Even driving the tractor takes some strength to hold it steady and nurse it through the hard clods. When we're bailing or shoveling the grain, and moving the big bins of corn, that's really hard work."

"Wow. Didn't know you actually liked hard work," Sophia smiled. "And how about these guys?"

"Doug's pretty cool, and I actually don't mind the other two, Jake and Matt. They graduated from Hopkins Academy a few years ago. They are simple guys, and *working to live* is their motto. They aren't stressing about college, or careers. We just focus on the work. It's real different from Amherst High kids."

"Well, Mom and Dad have always said follow your passions, and let that guide what you do. We've been lucky that way, I guess." Sophia fell silent as they walked.

Jeremy said: "Hey! This is the farm Dad's been trying to buy for the Land Conservancy!"

Sophia started: "What! That is so random!"

"Oh my God! A few days ago that Zumba lady came out here, and turns out she's Doug's daughter! She knows Mom -- and you! For a minute I thought Doug was going to be angry with me that I didn't say who Dad was, but I didn't know it was a thing!

Sophia wrinkled her nose. "Audrey was here? She's Mr. Stengel's daughter? Mind blown!" She made the brain explosion gesture with two hands.

When they got back to the farmhouse, Doug had some sandwiches and a pitcher of iced tea on the picnic table, along with some potato chips and apples.

He smiled. "Let's sit and have lunch." Matt and Jake were already eating at the table.

Between bites, Jake said, "Sorry we didn't wait. Starving."

"Yeah, no worries."

"I'll bet you get hungry working out there all day!" Sophia was looking at Jake. He glanced back at her again.

Doug spoke up, "You boys are doing a great job on that field out there. Of course, it's easier since we got that good rain the day before yesterday. Soil's softer and easier to break up."

Sophia looked up. "I guess you know all about that kind of thing."

Jeremy piped up: "Doug's told me about this! This soil's been like this forever, right?"

Doug smiled. "Pretty much."

Jeremy smiled. "That's cool. I guess it's always going to be good for planting then."

"Well," Doug scratched his head under his cap, "That's an interesting point. Soil can get depleted. That's why you have to spread manure, or rotate the crops through. "

Jeremy thought for a minute, then asked, "So do you use cow manure or horse manure?"

Doug snorted. "Good question! You can use either. You definitely want to use cow manure if it's fresh. Fresh horse manure would burn the heck out of those crops and roots if it's not composted. Too much ammonia. We do use our horse manure since we compost it for a bit out back."

"And do you use the manure you get from your cows in the field down the road here?"

"Yep. All those Bessies produce a ton of manure!" Doug nodded. "We are also experimenting with an anaerobic digester that essentially decarbonizes the manure so it doesn't contribute to global warming. That's the digester over there ," he pointed to a low building away from the barn.

Matt and Jake looked at each other. "That's the funkiest work -- spreading the manure. It stinks so bad!" Jake made a face as he spoke. They both laughed. "We'll let Jeremy do that job when it's time!"

Sophia spoke up: "Speaking of horses, you have a couple of horses here. Are they yours?" She spoke to Doug.

"Nope. I board 'em. Sally Roche down the road in town boards one here; the other ones with a UMass graduate student. I like having horses around; used to ride them some myself. Love the feel of that powerful animal under me, especially when they get galloping through the woods. And they're beautiful to watch."

"Would you consider boarding any more?"

"Have you got a horse? Sure! We have the stalls. Have Jeremy show you around the horse barn there. From my viewpoint, it's not too much trouble, really, and it helps with the income. I just buy the hay and expect folks to keep their own stalls clean. They pile the muck into the digester as well. Some we let compost a bit before spreading it. What is your horse called?" Doug looked at Sophia.

"His name's Lightning. He's been my horse for about 5 years, and I board him close to my house in Amherst. I love riding him."

"So why board him here? We're farther away, I expect." Doug seemed unconvinced.

"Well, Jeremy's coming here almost every day now. School's out and I was thinking I could tag along some days and be here with Lightning. Besides, it would be so cool to ride along the riverbank."

Jeremy chimed in. "Or I could look after him on days you didn't come out. Maybe even ride him sometimes."

Sophia smirked. "You'd have to learn how to saddle him up."

Doug laughed. "I got thrown once when I was a kid, totally my fault. My cousin and I had snuck out one Christmas Day when we got bored with the family chit chat. Thought we were being sneaky. Took out two horses, and I forgot to check the girth strap and got on the horse when the girth was loose. Once that horse got going, he realized I wasn't secured and he shifted quick one way and then another and off I went. Got a concussion. Went to the emergency room on the sly. My cousin and I had to fake it when we got back home like nothing was wrong. Anywho, you want to learn how to properly saddle a horse before you get on for a ride."

Jeremy smiled ruefully. "Well, OK. I did ride a few times at camp when I was younger, but I probably need to be reminded about some things."

Sophia smiled. "Probably I can remind you about some things…" They both laughed.

Jake piped up, "I ride some. Had my own horse when I was younger."

Sophia nodded. "That's cool. What kind of horse?"

Jake shrugged. "Some Appaloosa that my dad had and he let me ride."

Sophia nodded, then to Jeremy, "So, what do you think Mom and Dad will say if I ask them to board Lightning out here?"

Jeremy stared into the middle distance. "I dunno. I guess they might think it's weird that this is Doug's farm and Dad's the one who is trying to get him to sell it. And it's a lot farther from our house. But you're driving now, so that shouldn't be an issue so much. Of course you'd need a car." Jeremy had just enumerated all the reasons that their parents would likely be opposed to Sophia's boarding the horse.

He continued. "But, here's the thing. I am already coming out here every day to work, so we could ride out here together. And maybe you could do some of the work for the other horses that are boarded here. You might actually get paid for that, too. So there's lots of reasons to bring Lightning over here. I think you just talk to Mom and Dad kind of easy. You know, like it's no problem. Casual."

Sophia nodded. "I can see that. It would be very cool to be coming out here to ride, and like you said you would be here too. I think it could work."

One last appraising glance toward Jake.

CHAPTER 25

Looking back, Ben realized he should have had some warning that he was about to get sandbagged when both Sophia and Jeremy appeared in the kitchen simultaneously Saturday morning. Not only were they not yawning, but looking pretty perky and smiling. Most days they were generally on completely different morning schedules, like ships passing.

"Good Morning, Dad!" Sophia came over and gave him a hug. Jeremy followed suit, and gave his father a hug as well.

Ben exchanged a glance and a raised eyebrow with Alice.

"You two are up early for a Saturday," Ben commented, cocking his head to the side with an unexpressed question.

"Yeah, well, I am heading into the farm to work this morning," Jeremy said. "Doug wants me for a full day today."

Alice chimed in. "That's wonderful, Jer. So this seems like it's working out for you!"

Jeremy nodded while pouring himself a cup of coffee. "It's awesome. I love being outdoors all day. I love working hard and watching stuff happen."

"That's so cool!" Alice seemed pleased that this work had touched her son. "What's special about it?"

"I love riding the tractor in the fields. I like feeling the earth getting worked with the equipment. And, yeah, so Doug's got a horse barn, and I have gotten to help out with the two horses he has there. I have mucked out stalls, and even taken them out to brush and curry them," Jeremy added. "It's been pretty cool, and he even has a few empty stalls that he is thinking of boarding out as well."

Sophia seemed to perk up. "Maybe I could board Lightning there! Then when I went riding, I could visit you too. It would be so great!"

"Oh, yeah, we could even drive over together in the mornings, and you could ride before the day gets too hot," Jeremy said.

Sophia quickly jumped back in, "Oh, right! And the fields and trails go down to the river. It would be so awesome to ride by the river there, and since you're working there, it would be easy."

As Ben was washing his breakfast dishes in the sink, he was listening to this half-distractedly.

He added, "Well, we have paid to board at Muddy Bottom through the end of the year. That's a chunk of money. And I've never heard you say anything about anything being wrong there."

Alice asked, "Is something wrong with Muddy Bottom Stables?"

"Well, a lot of times I go there to ride and no one else is around. And it's kind of a dump. It's creepy."

"You never said anything!" Alice voiced alarm.

"I didn't want to worry you and Dad."

"Honey, you should have said something! Now I am worried!"

"Mom, it's really no big deal. I can take care of myself. But now that Jeremy's somewhere where I could be, too, it would be so great," Sophia went over and placed her arm around her brother's shoulder.

Alice's eyes watered and her face reddened slightly. Heartstrings.

Ben continued with the checklist on why-this-won't-work in his mind. "It's pretty far away. Muddy Bottom is 10 minutes away, and it's 25 minutes to Doug's."

"But Jeremy is going there almost everyday anyway. I can ride with him," Sophia said.

"You do know that I am strongly lobbying Doug to sell his place to the Trust. It feels funny to suddenly have us boarding a horse there," Ben rubbed his forehead.

"Oh, Doug's cool with it. I sort of asked him about this yesterday," Jeremy offered.

"What? You've talked to Doug about this?" Ben's voice rose perceptibly as he turned from the sink.

"Hello! Can I come in?" Marion poked her head around the back door as she helped herself into the kitchen. "Thought I'd just stop in and say hello!"

Marion and Alice were often over at each other's house, sometimes knocking but often not when they went over. Best friends.

"Hi Marion!" Alice said. "Your timing is perfect! You can referee."

Marion brushed back her grey curls and pulled herself erect. "I thought I heard raised voices. Where is my coffee?"

Ben turned and pulled a cup from the cupboard. "Let me pour

you one." He poured the cup and got the half-and-half from the fridge.

Sophia jumped right in. "Marion, I want to board Lightning over at the Stengel property where Jeremy is working."

Marion sipped her coffee, and looked at Ben. "I thought the Trust was angling to buy that property. What happened to that?"

"We still are! This is a whole new thing that just came up before you walked in."

Marion turned to Sophia. "What brought this on?"

"Oh, Jeremy started working at the Stengel Farm recently and he's there almost every day, so it seemed like a no-brainer to board Lightning there too."

Marion's eyes narrowed. "There is something else...I can feel it."

Sophia looked away for a split second. "Well, Lightning is now all alone at Muddy Bottom Farms, and he needs some companionship. Mr. Stengel has two other horses in his stalls."

"And you would go out on the days your brother is out there working?"

"Yep! I could ride and groom while Jeremy works!"

Marion turned to Jeremy. "And what's in this for you, young man?" Marion loved these kids, and had known them all their lives. As she looked at Jeremy, she saw the tall, athletic, handsome young man he was becoming. She even noticed some biceps growing under his T shirt from his work on the farm.

"I thought it would be a good fit for Sophia's horse. I could even look in on it on the days she wasn't out there, maybe even ride Lightning myself."

Marion sipped again. "Mmm, hm. Yeah, well, it sounds like a good idea – family bonding and all." She turned to Ben and Alice. "What's the downside?"

Ben quickly said, "First we've heard of it. We've got a $4,000 boarding cost we've already committed to Muddy Bottom for the year."

"And you've paid for the whole thing?"

Ben demurred. "Well, no, we pay installments. But we have an agreement. Plus we've had Lightning there for years. It would feel strange to yank him out of there now. I'd have to explain to Larry, and he's not someone you want to get on their bad side."

Marion nodded. "True enough, everyone knows that. But everyone knows Larry is not going to suddenly be hard up for cash if you don't board Lightning there. He owns half the town. What do you think, Alice?"

"I love the idea of the kids being together more," she smiled at her children. "They would be looking out for each other. Spending time together. And the horse might get more attention."

Marion nodded. "What about the distance? The Stengel property is out in Hadley, and that's, what, 25 minutes? Seems far away."

Sophia said, "Yeah, but, I'd actually go out more often since Jeremy's out there almost every day."

Ben rubbed his salt-and-pepper hair. "This all seems so sudden. Out of nowhere. I keep feeling like there's something else in there, too…"

Marion's eyes got wide for a moment, then narrowed.

"Jeremy! Are you working with any OTHER farm hands? Any other young guys?"

Sophia reddened. Jeremy glanced at her, then away in the distance.

"Well, yeah. There are two guys from Hadley who work there…no big deal. They're nice guys. Cool." He shrugged noncommittally.

Marion turned to Sophia. "Young lady, look at me. Is this the reason you suddenly want to change your horse to board out there?"

Sophia turned an even deeper shade of red, if that was possible. She looked down, then her eyes shifted away, then she looked at Marion. "Not really," she said in a very small and somewhat unconvincing voice.

Marion nodded her head. Her intuition was very strong, and in cases like this it was always right on.

"That's a big commitment for a cute little farm boy," she said, half mocking.

Marion turned to Alice, who had been quiet through this exchange. Marion also knew that Alice, who was an excellent mother, was a few steps behind where her daughter was in the love and relationship world. Marion had certainly noticed what a gorgeous young woman Sophia was becoming, with her long wavy dark hair and her beautiful chocolate brown eyes, and her figure was developing very shapely. Marion was sure that Sophia was capturing the attention of most if not all the boys, and the ones who really knew her, and knew how whip smart she was, would fall head over heels for Sophia in a heartbeat.

Marion arched her eyebrows. "Well, Alice. Time for some motherly advice, or at least a comment."

Just at that moment Brodi knocked at the back door and poked her head in.

"Hey folks! Any coffee left for me?" She wandered in too, just as Marion had. Looking around the room, she sensed the drama of the moment.

"Did I," she cleared his throat, "Come in at a bad moment?"

She absorbed the tableau of characters around the kitchen and breakfast counter. There was tension, and something else. She crossed to the coffee pot, and reached for a mug from the shelf.

"Well, Brodi," Ben started, "It seems that some cute farm boy has convinced my daughter to move her horse over to Stengel's stable."

"Dad! No one told me to move my horse. You guys have this all wrong!"

Sophia was almost in tears at this point. Marion moved to her side and put her arm around her, protectively.

"That was poorly worded, Ben. " Ben shut his mouth and looked contrite.

Marion turned to her wife. "Sophia and Jeremy had a brainstorm to move Lightning to board over at the Stengel property where Jeremy is now working. There are many good reasons to do so, including the kids being together more, since Sophia could ride while Jeremy is out there working. It also appears," here she cleared her throat, "*Just* by chance, that there is an attractive young farm hand there who may have caught Sophia's eye. No biggie."

She turned again to Alice. "Well, mother?"

Alice smiled. "I think it's an excellent idea."

Sophia's eyes widened, then began spilling over with tears. "Oh Mom, do you?"

She went over to her mother. They hugged each other.

Brodi sipped her coffee, then turned to Ben. "I take it you're the one with reservations, councilor. What's your supporting argument?"

Ben wiped his face with his hand, shaking his head slowly from side to side.

"I don't know where to start. Feel like I've said it all already. You don't make a decision like this based on a passing infatuation. But honestly, I just think it will look strange to have my daughter suddenly board her horse at the property we are trying to secure for the Trust. The optics just look wrong."

There was silence. Everyone took a moment to sip coffee. Sophia sniffed, still hugging her mother. Jeremy walked with his cup over to the kitchen window and looked out at the back yard. Frieda and Rusty were dodging back and forth out there, probably on the scent trail of a squirrel or rabbit, Frieda still hobbled slightly from her accident. Jeremy spoke to the group.

"Listen, this was all my idea. I didn't think about the Trust working to buy the land, Dad. Honestly that has not even been in my mind at all. I go out there almost every day now, and I really love it. I like working, I like being outdoors, I don't even mind it when it's rainy, because we always have things to do. It's cool being around the horses and the other animals as well. I like working with the guys, and Doug is just such a character, he is fun to be around, even when he's all gruff and angry."

Ben tilted his head. "And -- ?"

Jeremy scratched his head. "Maybe I won't work on a farm forever, but this has really been a great thing for me. I have a purpose, and I know what I am supposed to be doing. It feels good. And I thought that Sophia would appreciate having Lightning out there as well."

Ben asked, "And the other guy?"

Jeremy glanced away momentarily, "Well, yeah. Jake graduated from Hopkins Academy, and he works there full time. He's really nice, and he's actually smart. He played baseball at Hopkins, and he wants to go to college maybe next year. He and Sophia met one time when she stopped by."

Ben said, "Which was yesterday? So you're playing Cupid?"

"DAD!" Sophia screeched. "Stop it! You're being mean! Jeremy's just being helpful!"

Ben backed off. "Sorry. Sorry. I'm just still taken aback about all this. It's really sudden and out of the blue."

Brodi stepped in. "Hey, Ben, let's you and I step outside and confer for a minute. I've got an idea. Grab your coffee." She guided Ben out to the back yard, and the dogs came over with tails wagging and

Rusty barked a few times for good measure. Ben absently grabbed the tennis ball the dog had in his mouth, and threw it across the yard. Rusty took off after it, while Frieda wagged her tail furiously.

Brodi came right to the point. "Ben, you're all wound up about the Stengel property, with good reason. You've put months into this gentle selling job with Doug, and keeping the rest of the Trust board with their eyes on the project. It would be a massive coup to get that property listed with the Trust, and to preserve that kind of farmland along the Connecticut. It's to your credit that that transaction is still on the table."

Ben looked at her, head cocked.

Brodi went on. "I just think you're projecting your anxiety about that onto this new development with the horse." Looking directly at Ben, she lowered her cupped hand and Rusty neatly dropped the ball into it, and backed up, tail wagging. Brodi tossed the ball again across the yard.

"You're right. You're right. You know me well, Brodi," replied Ben. His mouth was set in a firm line. "And it's feeling like the sale is so tenuous right now. Doug has been pretty stand-offish lately, and he says he doesn't appreciate being pushed or forced into a decision. We haven't really talked since Jeremy started working out there, and I've wondered if that has shifted his thinking. We'll have to talk if Sophia's horse is going out there – heck, I'll be paying his boarding fees. How is that supposed to look? And what if he sells to the Georgia guys -- Sophia just has to move her horse again. It's all twisted up together.'"

This time Rusty brought the ball to Ben, and dropped it at his feet. He looked up at his owner expectantly, tail slowly wagging, head cocked to the side. Ben leaned over to pick up the by-now slobbery ball gingerly by his thumb and forefinger, and gave it a toss.

"The signals are all crossed in terms of what we are trying to do or say. What I'm trying to do or say. Am I wanting a place for my kid to have a job, or do I want to get this property preserved as farm-land?" And now, do I want my daughter to have a boyfriend, and board her horse out there, or do I want the sale? The other Board members were already a bit confused when they heard Jeremy was working out there. It seems almost unethical."

Brodi listened. "Yeah, I can see that. It puts you in a difficult position." He nodded his head and looked pensive. The dog continued to run and fetch the ball as it was tossed. The summer heat slowly climbed as the sun rose in the eastern sky. The friends were still standing in shadows, but the bright sunlit patches shone golden.

"Listen, Ben. This whole effort to get this property for the Trust has taken over your life this past year. It's been endless. Can you step back for a minute and think about this from Sophia's point of view? What's best for her? She seemed pretty relieved when Alice said she thought it was OK."

Ben was hesitant. "Well, it's all so sudden for Sophia too, and she's usually pretty level headed."

Brodi saw an advantage and pressed it, "Try to think about it if it weren't at Doug's barn. Would that make a difference in this?"

Ben's face tightened, and reddened. Brodi could see her friend struggling with some emotion, almost a physical struggle to contain it. His eyes darted back and forth for a moment. Then he took a deep breath, and visibly relaxed.

"OK. Maybe you're right. What IS best for Sophia? Maybe a change of venue for Lightning would be a good thing for the horse, the kids...But dammit, the fact that it's Doug's barn is a factor. We're not talking about some random farm somewhere. It's like the kids are ganging up on me!"

Just then Alice and Marion came out into the sunshine from the house. Marion had her arm around Alice's waist and they were laughing.

Marion looked up. "You two come to any conclusions? We had a brilliant idea. We are going to drive out to the barn and have a look for ourselves."

Alice chuckled. "Into the belly of the beast." She smiled warmly at her husband, then her smile faded as she saw his haggard face.

"How're you doing, honey?" She inquired of her husband, and let Marion's arm slip away as she approached Ben, and rubbed his arm affectionately.

"I'm not sure," Ben admitted honestly. "This whole thing's caught me off guard."

"Of course it has," Alice leaned in and kissed his cheek. "We're all still processing. That's why Marion's idea seemed so logical. Let's go see the place first. We can drive Jeremy over for work and take a look around."

Ben leaned into Alice, encircling her shoulders with his left arm and bringing her to him. He kissed her fiercely on the top of her head. "That sounds like a good idea. I have seen the barn, of course, and I KNOW it's in excellent shape." He gave a short laugh. "Heck, I'd even buy it."

Everyone laughed, tension dissolving.

"So the scouting party will head out, and report back," Marion said.

They all turned to head back inside.

* * *

Sophia had called to let Doug know she was coming out with her mom to look over the barn, and Doug seemed fine with that. Marion, Alice and Sophia all exited the car simultaneously. The morning sun was warming the recently turned earth. All three women lifted their noses into the air, as the smell of brown earth rose.

"God, that's a great smell," Marion said. "I remember that smell from when I was a girl."

Another vehicle was in the driveway, one of those huge black Suburban SUVs. A man stood by the driver's door, taking off his sunglasses.

"Hello!" Alice said amiably. "Is Doug around?"

The man grimaced. "He's around the back of the barn."

The three women exchanged glances and walked over to the barn door, glancing inside. Sophia decided to walk in, almost as though her horse were already here. "See, it's nice!" Heading in one direction the women could see an aisle with a row of three stalls on either side. Next to the door were racks for horse saddles. Two saddles rested on two of the racks, and six others were empty.

"See, he already boards two horses now, so Lightning would have company," Sophia wandered over to the two occupied stalls. Two beautiful horses were in those stalls, one named, "Mindy" and one named, "Painter." The horses extended their heads over the half doors, and Sophia scratched their noses respectively.

A summer rain had started up outside, and at the far end of the barn three men came in. Each was a bit wet, though two of the men seemed less excited about the rain. The other, Doug, shook off his cap.

Doug spotted the three women, and walked over toward them.

"Hey, Sophia," He looked at Marion and Alice. "You must be Sophia's mom," extending his hand to Alice, "And I don't think we've met -- Doug Stengel," he offered a hand to Marion.

Marion smiled at the big man. A warm and friendly face. ""I'm

Marion Saunders, Sophia and Alice's friend."

Doug shook her hand, and then turned to Alice. "Guess I've met the whole family now!"

He looked over his shoulder. The men in suits stood at the far end of the barn, silhouetted by the wan light from outside.

"We're here scoping out the barn that Sophia hopes to bring her horse to," Alice replied. "We wanted some independent confirmation that all was well. This is a nice-looking stable."

Doug nodded appreciatively. "Got two others who board their horses here. It's not a major element of our work here at the farm. Really we provide the space and some mucking out, but mostly folks take care of their own horses."

"Is there water in the barn?" Alice tried to think of what sort of facility was needed for horses.

"Yep. And there are heaters we can use in the barn when it's cold if necessary. So, Sophia, you obviously talked with your mom and your friend about boarding the horse here. What's your thinking about that?"

Sophia perked up. "I'd really like to! It's pretty cool here, and it would be awesome to come out here with Jeremy when he's working."

Doug nodded. "Yep! And I wouldn't mind the additional boarding fees, I won't lie. Got two other boys working here, as you know, so there are eyes and ears on the animals."

Sophia reddened. "Uh, oh yeah..."

Alice and Marion smiled at one another. Marion turned to Doug. "So who are these other farm boys?"

Doug laughed and raised his ballcap to scratch his head. "Those two! Matt and Jake have been helping on this farm for years, off and on. It's hard farm labor, but they know it, and it suits them. Neither one's a farmer at heart though. Now," here he spoke directly to Alice. "Your son, he's got the dirt under his nails for sure. He pays attention, he's thoughtful, and he's got an appreciation for what it takes to do farming right and it doesn't scare him."

The men in suits walked over to where they were standing.

"Hello!" Both men smiled. "John," "Mitch" they both smiled and nodded their heads.

"Hello," the women said collectively.

Doug interjected, "These folks are here all the way from Atlanta, Georgia, and they are hoping I sell this farm to them!"

The two men smiled, and nodded. "Doug has been very generous with his time and his consideration of our offer. We're hoping he's ready to agree to a very healthy sale!" The soft southern accents were very pleasant to listen to, even if it made the men sound slightly slow mentally.

Another quick glance from Alice to Marion, who countered, "Word has gotten around about your interest in the Stengel Farm. Even predating your involvement."

The men's raised eyebrows and sidelong glance at one another belied their own anxiousness.

Well," John chuckled humorlessly, "Our former colleague, Wayne, was the lead in negotiating with Doug, here, but we've been involved behind the scenes for many months."

Marion continued. "Yes, we're sorry for the loss of your partner. That was such a shock! You must be devastated."

"Well, it was devastating originally, of course," the second, Mitch, agreed, "But we knew we had to stay in touch with Doug to continue our discussions."

John turned to Doug. "Doug, we do have to be on our way soon, but we're wondering where you might be in terms of our offer?"

Doug glanced down at that moment. "Well, John, I am very flattered with the offer, of course, and that you have come all this way to discuss it. I don't know quite what to say right now."

"But you are strongly considering this? I mean, this kind of offer won't stay on the table for too long," John gave a shrug of his shoulders, meant to convey his inability to change this fact.

Doug looked down, and scuffed his boot in the dirt on the floor of the barn.

Doug responded. "Oh, yeah. I will be thinking about it and talking with you boys at some point in the not too distant future!"

The two men looked at one another, then turned to Doug. "Well," John said, "Again, Doug, we are very interested in getting started on our exciting development. We hope to hear from you very soon." They each reached out to shake Doug's hand.

The two men turned to the women, "Ladies, pleasure meeting you," and left.

Doug gave a sigh. "Those two are quite a pair! Lots of money they're offering though. Lots of money."

"Money talks, as they say," Marion surmised. "Hard not to listen."

"Well, let's just say that it's tempting, but it's not everything," Doug replied. "There is history. Like roots in the earth. Money can sound good, real good, but I want to be sure I'm making the right decision. Not easy."

Sophia asked, "Should we wait on bringing the horse out here? Maybe it's not the right time?"

Doug shook his head. "Nope. If you want to bring him here, you do it. I am not selling this place right away in any event. Likely not 'til the end of next season at the earliest."

Sophia smiled. "Mom, Marion, what do you think?"

Alice was reflective. "I don't know. Lightning has been at the other barn for years now. It's be a big change for him."

"It will be great for him," Marion chimed in. "I've got a good feeling about this. Besides, it's good to make a decision and go with it. Don't dilly-dally around."

CHAPTER 26

Brodi took coffees for herself and Ben outside Amherst Coffee and set them on a table on the Amity Street sidewalk. Ben had Frieda and Rusty on a leash, tied to the seatback. Both dogs took in the scene. Chill. It was early Saturday morning, and the friends often went downtown to grab coffee while Marion and Alice went to Zumba class. Marion always invited Brodi to go along for some exercise, and she always declined. Zumba just wasn't her jam. Today she and Ben were going for coffee, and then taking the dogs on a hike, so exercise was going to happen.

She looked around the street as the Saturday morning crowd picked up. The early morning Farmer's Market crowd was moving through with their cloth shopping bags slung over their shoulders, eagerly anticipating the prospect of lettuce, zucchini, onions and kale. A few early morning bicyclists also flew past, in colorful bike outfits.

Ben sipped, and then commented, "That was some situation last week at Stengel's Farm, eh? I couldn't believe those developers just brazenly trying to muscle into that property. I don't think they really understand the psychology of working with a guy who's owned the farm his whole life. Doug's a tough old guy, but I think inside he's got a tender heart. Not to mention he is very savvy. That's what I am angling for, anyway."

Brodi replied, "Um-hum." She glanced into the distance, not really taking in the street scene in front of her, and not really fully listening to Ben. Ben looked over, and realized that this whole situation with the property had completely dominated their conversations for months now.

"Hey, Brodi," he pivoted, "How are things with Beth? Still planning to have her move down here?"

Brodi flicked a glance to Ben, and then took a sip of coffee. She deeply sighed.

"It's worrisome, Ben," she started in, "Beth is clearly going downhill, and we have to bring her down here soon. Her Alzheimer's is progressing, and at this point there is no guarantee what she knows, what she remembers, or if she is safe. She still has long periods of lucidity and clarity. Then she'll slide into forgetfulness and torch something in the microwave, putting it on 10 minutes when she meant a minute. It's kind of unnerving, really. Two weeks ago we went up there and discovered the milk jug in the cupboard for the glasses.

"Oh geez, I didn't realize. I'm sorry," Ben commiserated. "It must be hell for Marion."

"Yeah, she's taking it pretty hard. She is like a rock most of the time, and geared up to deal with everything, but then she'll just crumble. It is so hard for her to have her mother there one minute, and then have her gone. Scary really."

Ben said, "I am so sorry to hear that. And you?"

Brodi shrugged. "It worries me, for sure, but you know it's really different. You remember my Mom died just after we were in college. I loved her but she never fully embraced my being gay. When she died of cancer, we made some peace but we weren't close."

"Yeah, that was hard for you, I remember. Your mom couldn't even come to graduation."

"Don't remind me. And Beth is not my mother. I have some emotional distance since this isn't the woman who raised me. I love Beth, and she is very dear, but I have perspective. I realize that getting old is fraught with challenges in any case. Beth has some quirks that actually are annoying, and with Alzheimer's progressing, she can be a pain sometimes. We are also looking into placing her in a facility. That'll bring other issues, like cost. Again, I can handle that kind of thing, but it's got more complexity for Marion. Sometimes there is guilt, then resentment. It puts a strain on us."

A man coming down the sidewalk had two golden retrievers on leashes, who passed by, the four dog noses and wagging tails creating a brief flurry of activity. The owner gave a brief jerk on the leash to pull the dogs back. "Sorry!"

"No worries," Ben responded, "Everybody seems friendly. Tails are wagging."

"Maybe sometimes too friendly," the man called over his shoulder as they bundled away.

Ben turned back to Brodi. "Sorry to hear all that. Weren't you working on some wearable device to help her out?"

"Oh yeah," Brodi perked up. "That's coming along. I have a Beta-tested prototype which I'm hoping will really help Beth. She's going downhill quicker than it may be ready, but it could definitely serve others. I've been working with this team down in Jacksonville that are ace manufacturers."

Ben asked, "So, what is it exactly?"

Brodi laughed, and explained the device. "I am tickled that it's coming along so well."

"Wow!" Ben was impressed. "Sounds revolutionary for an Alzheimer's patient!"

"The engineering was really interesting. These devices can be programmable at a very discrete level. Another fun part of this has been that I haven't had to do much with this except guide a group of UMass Engineering School grads who are supervised by my friend, Rhonda. It's kind of fun to hang around these smart young people here, then coordinate with the manufacturer in Florida. "

"That is so cool! Oh, yeah! I met Rhonda out cross-country skiing one day at the end of winter. She was out with her dog, and she complimented your leadership on the project," Ben added.

Brodi smiled broadly at this recognition. There were moments when timing seemed everything, and in this case, the poignancy of working to get this all to come together was like a symphony, with all the different parts of the orchestra moving toward the finale. Chords interweaving, notes counterposing, harmonies expanding, dominant, tonic, syncopated. And in this symphony with all the parts coming together, they might be missing something key since they were still in development – and they needed to get it right.

She continued, "We have the prototype here and Beth is wearing it, so that's a start. The technology is a bit too much for her so far, and she forgets to wear it sometimes. We'll see."

Brodi sipped the last of her coffee with that sobering thought, and rose to go. "Shall we?"

"Let's take my car," said Ben. "C'mon dogs!"

They walked back to Ben's car, and the dogs leaped expectantly as soon as he opened the door to the back seat. They muscled one another and there was a slight growl of warning as they established their own territory in that confined space.

Brodi was still reflecting on the re-awakened thoughts about this new device, now coming closer to being ready for the market. She was excited that this could help Beth, but also she thought of all the other Alzheimer's patients, families and providers that could benefit in the future. A feeling of pride arose in her chest. After all, it was her model and idea; she was the one overseeing developing it, so why shouldn't she feel some sense of ownership?

Part of the next steps was to bring the first group of devices out to be used at the Amherst Senior Center, which had expressed interest in seeing how the devices would be accepted and used by the members there. Of course, many of those folks did not have Alzheimer's, but using the devices for tracking whereabouts, medication management, and simple safety was very appealing to the Amherst Senior Center staff. It was unfortunately true that in this day and age, so many of their clients were on their own in town, or did not see their children and grandchildren with enough regularity to have the family know some of the intricacies of their daily schedule.

Brodi suggested they swing by her house to pick up their dog, Edna, to come along for a hike. Enda was a puppy, so would need to be leashed to do some hiking. As they drove to Brodi's house, gray clouds began amassing and the sky turned darker. A steady rain was falling as they pulled into Brodi's driveway. Brodi went into the house and escorted Edna into the back seat with Ben's two dogs. The dogs all knew each other, so there was minimal growling and only minor shifting around as the first two dogs accommodated the third animal into the enclosed space. Edna was the smallest of the three dogs, so she maneuvered between the other two and found a spot along the closer window to sit. Brodi climbed back into the front seat.

"Looks like it's going to rain pretty steadily."

"Yes, well, we've got hiking boots and raincoats, right? *There is no bad weather, only bad clothes.*"

"Yep. And the dogs don't care."

Recently Ben's favorite trail had become the Sweet Alice Trail, which snaked up the Holyoke Range hillsides to the Notch Visitors Center. It was a steady uphill without too much elevation gain. Mostly in the woods, it was not as soggy as if it had been in the direct weather that morning. Frieda was still a bit tender after her surgery, but she bravely trotted along near Ben and Brodi. Rusty took the lead, with Edna straining at her leash just behind.

After entering the forest, they forded a stream on a simple footbridge. The dogs splashed through the creek, emerging damp and happy. They chased one another up the far hillside. The rain provided a steady hissing noise as it dropped through the forest canopy and sifted its way to the forest floor. Brodi let her imagination be taken by the rain, falling here in the forest and also into the far land one town over, where they had been just the other day. The late spring and early summer had been particularly rainy. Climate change was upon them; every day you could read more stories about how the weather and the earth were reacting to the steady erosion of the protective field that the earth had for billions of years.   It was both mind-boggling and frightening that the rate of earth changes progressed more rapidly. The year past had seen another record of droughts and wildfires in the western United States, while in other parts of the world, torrential downpour of rain produced record-level flooding (the irony was so apparent), life threatening heat waves nearly everywhere. Brodi's appreciation of the falling light drizzle increased as these other disasters and weather challenges literally rained down in other areas of the country and the world. Humans seemed incapable of holding the thought that we (humans) were responsible for this global disaster, and therefore responsible to change the direction that humans were moving as a species, thereby increasing the likelihood that this disaster would be increasing, expanding, and going who knows where.

Ben's comments intruded on these thoughts, and belied his own obsession. "I wish I could divine what would influence Doug to work with VCLT. This little corner of the world could do our part for climate change, and preserving land, especially forest and farmland, is the way here. You look at Hadley along Route 9 and you see what a mess it can become, grabbing up the available land and converting it into vast swaths of asphalt parking lots and box stores. It is soulless, really. I know that being able to add Doug Stengel to our list of farmers who have converted to preserved land will be key. He is well-respected among other farmers. It is no surprise that an increasing number of long-term, multigenerational farming families are watching their off-spring turn away from farming. It is hard work, long hours, and to a great extent unforgiving in that one successful season, or even one successful crop does not guarantee ongoing success. This year could be the perfect mix of water and sun, and next year it's a total bust. Climate change is throwing more chaos into that mix as well. In my darker moments I wonder why anyone would want to become a farmer in these precarious times."

Ben trailed off as the rain increased in tempo and intensity. Now it was actually raining, and they both zipped up their jackets, and pulled their rain hoods over their hats.

"Wow, Ben," Brodi interjected. "You make it sound like we're standing on the precipice of global climate catastrophe and the sale of this one farm could spell doom or repentance for us all!"

"Brodi, it's this easy. If Doug Stengel sells his farm to those developers, that land is going away. Probably forever. There is no going back. You put in an asphalt road, all that macadam for parking lots, you tear up the ground for water and electricity and cable and sewer, et cetera. You pump millions into development. No way that's going back to cows and corn. All the local wildlife living among those trees -- deer, raccoons, possums, owls, hawks -- are all displaced. That's why this is so critical! This is the fulcrum point for this property, and it's the fulcrum for dozens of other properties in this area. If Doug sells to the developers, everyone else is going to feel like he or she can do that too. And slowly the landscape changes, slowly its buildings and malls and commerce. Jobs go there, money goes there. It's insidious really. "

Just at this moment the dogs came bounding back from some adventure in the woods. Brodi had let Edna off the leash and she was out with the other dogs now. All were moving quickly, including Frieda, and Ben noted the dog's ability to keep up with the other two. He was relieved to see her prior injury seemed to be fading into the past. Long pink tongues hanging down from open mouths signaled a successful investigation of a mouse hole or a chipmunk tree, or perhaps even a deer run. The trees and bushes surrounding the trail were glistening from the falling rain, which lent a shimmer and sparkle to the variety of greens throughout the dense undergrowth. Brodi and Ben savored the sound of the rain on the leaves, and the softness of the light filtering through the foliage. Both appreciated the benefit of the tall trees and dense bushes to help them hold the thoughts and feelings that came with reflecting on their lives. What a privilege to be able to get out into the woods! What a gift that tall trees and running brooks can offer!

Ben's mind drifted to the steady uplift he felt in walking through the trees -- troubles melting away, perspective changing. It was a kind of magic, really, when the simple act of lacing up sturdy footwear and setting one foot in front of the other could provide the respite from difficult times, troubled relationships, turgid dilemmas, tragic losses, humiliating defeats. Equally he had felt the beauty of a sudden victory, a hard won battle, an impending merger, a graceful turning, a welcomed relief, a bright opening, quiet celebrations of big and small moments in life.

The steady rain contributed to this sense of weighing time and options. A moment was approaching from which there was no turning back. For herself, unknown to Ben, Brodi wondered if the sense of impending importance was being triggered by two cups of espresso coffee or if being out here with Ben enhanced the sense of foreboding she felt. Ben did have a habit of catastrophizing situations, and making their meaning ever more portentous than they actually were. He had a flair for the dramatic, this was certain, and so Brodi's natural tendency for calm, rational progress was highlighted in relief.

Brodi nodded, somewhat to herself. "Ben! Tell Stengel he can easily get enough for a comfortable retirement, and he can feel secure that his farm is going to remain as farmland in perpetuity. This will be his legacy, and a gift to this community long after he has gone. Heck, the publicity that could be generated from the sale of his farm to VCLT might be enough to attract the attention of other investors for the Trust. That is four or five strong arguments in your favor. Does VCLT have a set selling price they are considering?

Ben was caught off guard with Brodi's sudden insistence. His foot slid on the muddy path and he went down on his butt in the mud. "Ooff! Ow!"

"Are you OK?"

Ben got back up. "Yea. Just having a moment, I guess." He wiped off his pants. "So! VCLT works to adequately compensate the landowner at a rate about 50-60% of the going market rate, along with the Agricultural Preservation Restriction from the States of Massachusetts. The rate varies because the landowner can claim a tax credit of the difference in selling price as a donation to VCLT. This can be key for the sale. The enhancement factors you mention allow the landowners to experience multiple benefits while enhancing the altruistic nature of preserving the land in perpetuity. The hook is hopefully more emotional than practical in the sense of what they could get from selling it outright to a land developer, such as the situation that is presenting itself here."

Brodi nodded. "Bingo! You have to press that point!"

Ben paused and stretched his back. "But really, the bottom line is the landowner has to see some value in land preservation. Of course, there are various options -- keeping the land in their name until they die, retaining the land title. They can offer land easements for the use of the land while they retain title, so that farming or hiking or other public uses can continue. Lots of options there. But ultimately the land is going into the land trust domain.

"Now, Doug's property has the beautiful feature of the riverfront shoreline. We have been so excited to possibly preserve that element since we first talked with Doug.   Let's face it, protecting the river shoreline is one of our top priorities at VCLT, and we want to make sure that we can value this property in that light."

Ben turned to Brodi. "This has really helped me clarify how critical getting this property is. I've been going nose to grindstone these past months, trying to work my regular job and my volunteer work with VCLT.   It's been driving me crazy in a way. So stressful, and yet nothing has been fitting into place on any side, so I've been really agitated and grumpy. Now I can see it's because of how important this whole thing is for me. I am completely invested in making this purchase materialize. Maybe overinvolved. I have to stay focused, but I also have to get some perspective on all this. I've been feeling like it's life or death."

Brodi   looked   pensive   too.   "Maybe   in   a   way,   it   is."

CHAPTER 27

As Ryan pulled into the driveway of the farm, Doug appeared at the door of the farmhouse, pushing open the screen and letting it bang shut behind him. He walked slowly and purposefully down to the car as Ryan got out. There was an awkward moment – hug or handshake? – that evolved into a strange handshake – one armed hug – pat on the back.

"Hi-uh," Doug said. "Didn't expect you back so quick. You doin' OK?"

"Yeah, Dad," Ryan answered. "You?"

"Oh fine. Fine," Doug responded, turning to the farm. "Well, she's still here." He surveyed the fields and far trees. "Every day something new."

Doug peeled back his baseball cap, scratched his head, and replaced the cap, a practiced movement. "I was just greasing the hayer since that yonder field needs to be mowed. We'll bale that and sell it. The boys are working the lower field by the river to get the corn in, and the other field with the butternut squashes. Matt's leaving at the end of the summer; he's decided to go back and try community college again and get his degree, so I"ll be down another farmhand. That Jeremy is a good worker, serious and dedicated, but he's still learning the trade. He can follow directions, though."

"Hey Dad," Ryan chimed in, "Actually that was why I came out here again. I had a thought. I think I am going to be around for a while, don't know how long, and maybe I could chip in a little. You know, do a few things here and there for you."

Doug looked at him strangely. "You mean like farm work? You haven't done any farm work for 20 years. You're too soft."

Ryan cocked his head, and made a face. "Like how do you mean? Like I haven't worked for the past 20 years? Or I'm gay and that means I can't do physical work? What are you saying, Dad?" His defensiveness was right on the surface.

"Whoa, slow down now," Doug held up a hand. "I just mean you ain't been here doing any kind of work on this farm. And, I don't think you've been doing anything requiring hard, physical labor since you've been off in the big city. I could be wrong." Doug studies his son, now a man in his own right, with crow's feet around the corners of his eyes, and a bit of gray hair at the temples. Not a kid anymore.

Softening up a bit, he says, "You know, I really don't understand what you have been doing or what you have been up to, for a long time. All this time has gone by and suddenly here you are. And who *are* you, now? Before you left, I knew you were "different," but we never talked about it. I think your mother probably knew what -- who -- you were, but she was careful. She always said you were sensitive, you were more thoughtful, you were more creative, all that. Like you were so delicate we had to be careful not to break you.

"Ryan, I am getting too old to be farting around not saying what's what. If you're homosexual so be it. That's who you are. It's not for me to judge. But why now?"

"Dad," Ryan sputtered. "Look, I had to get the hell out because I couldn't be myself here. I was going to disappoint you and mom since I wasn't going to be a farmer, and wasn't a strong and virile man. I was just me, and I knew if I didn't get out I was going to scream, or do some damage I was going to regret. You never understood me!"

"Well, shit!" His father turned about and walked a few paces away. "You never even tried anything I had to offer. You always seemed so damn scared, and so damn sure you couldn't do anything. You've got to try! You try it, and you try it again. You try, and you fail, and you try again. That's just the way it is. No one does it perfect the first time."

Doug looked away toward the fields. He wanted to shake his son. Get him to understand. He never knew how to talk with him, how to connect. Back in the day Ryan had been a quiet boy, and he'd been hard to reach because he was always into his own little world.

"I never knew you because you never talked to me! I'd ask how you were, or what was going on, and you would turn away from me, walk away. I had no idea how to reach you! I left it to your mom to be the one to reach out to you, and then she was gone," Doug turned around in a circle as the words tumbled from his mouth, looking down at the dirt the whole time.

Ryan crouched down and picked up a small rock in the driveway. Turning quickly, he hurled it into the field as far as he could. It sailed among the corn and dropped from sight. "Shit!"

The two men looked at each other, glaring, wary. Doug looked away toward where the rock had disappeared.

Nodding his head, he glanced back at Ryan. "With a throw like that you could have played outfield for the Golden Hawks."

Ryan huffed a deep breath. "I hated baseball. I only played in middle school because I thought you and Mom wanted me too. I couldn't wait to quit."

"It broke your mom's heart in a way. Not your fault," Doug added quickly, hands up in surrender. "But she thought it was a way for you to be with a good group of guys and make some friends."

"You were *always* pushing me like that. I was never comfortable playing sports and being so *visible*. I felt like I was always going to make a mistake. Even when I did something OK, I knew I 'd mess up the next time. And then you and Mom would be down on me for that."

"You know," Doug interjected, tilting his head down and raising a pointed finger toward Ryan, "We NEVER came down on you if you were trying. If you were giving it a good shot, we let you be. If you weren't trying, well, that was a different story. Stengels always give it their best shot."

"Yeah, right. More like, *as long as you can do it perfectly*. I was never going to measure up in your mind. There was always something a bit wrong, something not quite right, not quite up to snuff. Face it, Dad, I was never going to be good enough in your eyes. For sure never going to measure up to St. Michael. That's why I left. Get the hell out of here and find myself someplace where I could be me." Ryan's face was blotchy and his neck was red. He was breathing hard.

Doug was still looking away, but he turned back around and took Ryan in. "OK. OK. Maybe I was too hard on you. I was trying to give you the direction I thought you needed. You took off for a reason, your own reason, whether it made any sense to me or your mom. I won't apologize for how I was as a father except to say I only wanted the best for you."

Both men were quiet for a while then. Doug wandered over to a tractor pulled to the side of the drive. He unsheathed the oil dipstick. He yanked the rag from his back pocket and tested the oil level. Appearing satisfied, he slipped the dipstick back into the metal sleeve.

"Come over here and let me show you how this thing works," Doug said over his shoulder.

For the next two hours, Doug showed Ryan how to start the trac- tor, how to get it running smoothly, how to attach the haymaker, then how to engage the gears and drive it into the field. They drove to the far north field and proceeded to mow down the timothy grass. Doug had Ryan stand behind him on the rig, and shouted his commands over his shoulder as he deftly worked the tractor's forward motion and the hayer's rhythmic churning. After two rows in the back, Doug had Ryan settle into the driver's seat, and stood in back as Ryan engaged the gear and set the haying blade. Doug noted Ryan's concentration, how intense! Doug could sense the tension in Ryan's shoulders slowly relax as each passing row was completed. "You got it," He shouted over the mechanical noise.

The two men together attended to the task at hand, and through that some understanding flowed from one to the next, and back again. It was as if each were slowly letting go of their end of a tug-of-war, and the rope slipped to the ground, nearly forgotten. Doug became lost in the rhythm of haying a field which was in his bones, almost from the time he was born. He knew each step in this ballet of moving across a field of grain. He saw that Ryan was allowing himself to be the novice, tasked with learning this skill that he had resisted so completely when he was young. Ryan mentioned that he knew nothing about machines, or equipment. For his part, Doug shared the wisdom of experience; encouraging Ryan at each moment. He saw Ryan rise to this challenge, to meet this task as the honest work it was. Somewhere deep in his DNA, Ryan had a farmer awakening. Not that he was born to this work, although in fact he had been, but more that when he relaxed and allowed himself to be guided, an inner part of himself could awaken to join the process at hand. It wasn't easy, but it felt facilitated by something which was beyond words, beyond a simple description.

When the field was mowed, Ryan stopped the tractor, and turned off the key. The noise immediately quieted down and the engine chugged to a stop. Ryan wiped his brow with the shirt on his forearm. Sweat glistened on his brow. Doug took the same cloth from his back pocket, doffed his cap and wiped his brow.

"That's good work right there. I didn't think I'd get to that today," Doug demurred. "Here's water." He reached into the console under the seat and found two plastic water bottles there.

They both drank deeply.

"You did a good job. Are you up for some baling now, too? We can go get that baling machine."

"I can give it a try. That wasn't too hard, really. You just concentrate." Ryan's shirt was also sweaty from the heat and exertion. He lifted the front of his shirt and wiped his face. Doug noticed firm stomach muscles under the shirt.

"You got yourself six pack abs! Quite an accomplishment for a middle-aged city boy!"

Ryan had to grin. "I am not all soft and pushy. I get to the gym down the street four or five days a week." He paused, then added, "After I left college I got a job working in a runaway shelter for teenagers in the city. I was helping kids who were like me, lost and needing a place to live while they figured out their lives. Unlike me, I learned that most of them had been abused in their homes: physical, emotional, and sexual. So they were victims. Lots of them were gay, or lesbian, or questioning their sexuality or sexual identity. For many of them that's what was underlying the conflicts they had at home. I could relate to that. Also, sometimes there was violence in the shelter, and I figured I needed to be strong just in case some of that was either directed at me, or I might have to intervene. I started going to the gym to bulk up. I've kept up the practice."

"Sounds like tough work. Didn't know you did that." Doug pursed his lips. "How long did you keep it up?"

Ryan sighed, stretched his back and unkinked his neck. Riding a tractor for 2 hours was not easy work. "For a few years. Just working with those kids dealing with the traumas they experienced was draining. I was able to shift a bit when the whole urban gardening movement started up. I was able to help connect the kids to an urban farm a buddy of mine started in an old abandoned lot down the street. Believe it or not, growing up on our farm gave me some head start on how to think about gardening, so I could help out planting and help the kids get involved in gardening, see where their food came from. That kept me going for awhile."

Doug pressed his lips together for a moment, "I never knew any of this! You had a whole life there…"

Ryan nodded. "Yea, while I was doing that work, I started writing on the side. It was a long process, and I always felt that my writing wasn't getting the attention it deserved. I'd come home tired, or discouraged, or just burnt out from dealing with the kids all day. I would want a break, and wasn't in the mood to write. I added in drawing, since it seemed easier somehow. I realized I had my priorities off. I needed to reduce my workload so I could devote more time to writing and drawing."

"And now you've got, what, 4 books?"

Ryan looked at his dad sideways. He wasn't aware that his dad even knew he was a writer, much less a published author. "Yes, that's right. And a fifth is coming out next year."

"Mighty impressive. When you were a kid I had no idea you had that much to say. You were mighty quiet. I couldn't get a word out of you." Doug didn't seem to be sarcastic, more matter of fact.

Ryan smiled. "Well, maybe I bottled it all up and it's coming out now."

"Maybe so. What are your books about?"

Just then Doug's phone buzzed in his pocket. "Woop! Hold on there, let me see who this is."

He fished a pair of reading glasses from his breast pocket with one hand while he fished the phone from the opposite hip pocket. Ryan noted it was a flip phone, which didn't surprise him. Doug peered with a facial sneer at the small screen on the phone.

"Looks like Georgia. Better take it." Opening the phone he said, "Hello. Doug Stengel."

From the conversation Ryan could tell that the Georgia developers were putting a pretty hard sell on his Dad.

"Yes, yes, I know you boys are eager to move ahead...No I don't really have a timeline for making a decision to sell...yes, you did mention a dollar figure for your offer..." Here Doug's eyebrows rose as one: "Yes! Five million dollars even is a lot of money, yes it is...I appreciate the additional...And no I never thought it would be anywhere near that much...Of course I think that's a generous offer, but let me say, you boys are in line to make a sweet profit with that fancy development, and I know someone there has run the numbers to say it's worth it...No I am not ready to tell you it's a go right now...And I don't know when exactly...That's fine. You can call me on Friday to see where I am at. Goodbye."

Doug flipped the phone closed and put it back in his pocket.

"Really, Dad? Five million for the farm? What is that all about?"

Doug rubbed his chin with his fingers. "Well, if you'd been

around you'd know this whole story. Bottom line is that these jokers from Georgia -- just thought that up -- Jokers from Georgia, have big plans for a development right here along the Connecticut. Marina, club, tower with apartments overlooking the river, shopping and restaurants. That whole shebang. It would topple Hadley right over I think. But it's a vision I can tell you. And I can't even wrap my head around $5 million. No siree."

"You gonna sell it to them?" Ryan was curious, but felt detached, like this was happening to someone not related to him. Like it wasn't even real. Who would be willing to pay $5 million for this farm? "I can't believe they are offering that much!"

"Me neither, me neither," Doug agreed. "That amount of money is just unbelievable. It never crossed my mind that we could be looking at a sum like that. I could retire and go anywhere, do anything. And that would leave a huge inheritance to you and your sister. We'd all be easy."

Ryan looked guilty. "Dad, I could never accept that money from you. It wouldn't be right after I took off."

Doug gave a frown. "That's nonsense. Just 'cause you did what you had to do doesn't mean you aren't still family. Heck, if I died and left you this farm as it is, then you wouldn't be so happy. This place is a wreck, truth be told. Like a lot of farms, just going on a wing and a prayer."

Ryan sighed. "This place is special, Dad. It's got your years and your family -- our family -- in the soil. Heck, you buried Mom out there in that little cemetery plot. Just because I don't want to farm it doesn't mean it doesn't have real value as a farm. It's just not for me."

Doug looked away across the newly mown field. "There's this other group that is interested in the farm, too. The Valley Conservation Land Trust. They buy up farms and promise to keep them preserved as farmland. Of course, what they offer is dust in the wind to the hurricane the Jokers from Georgia are offering."

"But the land stays a farm?"

"Yep, the land stays a farm. Like it's always been, like it should be."

"So --?"

"So, $5 million dollars is so--! Hard to walk away from that."

* * *

Unbeknownst to Doug, when he hung up the phone, John Engle

was only a few miles away in the hallway of the Hadley Town Offices. He was preparing to head into a meeting with the Hadley Planning Board to begin lobbying to have zoning bylaws changed from Agricultural to Limited Business for the farm. John was just hoping to be able to report to the Planning Commission that a sale of the property was imminent, or under contract. The Red Dirt Associates swept into the special meeting they had arranged with the Clerk and the Commission. Bruce Schwartz presented their architectural plans and the new 3-D model of the build-out. The team was very smooth in their presentation, including an architect from the Amherst firm who had drawn the maps and constructed the 3-D model. Mick Peters made sure to mention the $5 million offer for the property, and the estimated construction costs of $50 million, as well as the estimated annual tax revenue of $10 million for the Town, including: sales tax from the retail, marina, and restaurants; property taxes from the commercial properties; and assorted licenses and fees.

While some of the Planning Board were mildly impressed with the presentation and especially the life-like, 3-D rendering of the 10 story tower looming above the retail spaces alongside the river marina, questions remained. Eyebrows were raised at the potential of $10 million in local taxes generated. One could imagine spending those. But changing the zoning seemed like a major shift in town planning policy. The whole swath of the riverside along the Connecticut River from the South Hadley town line north to Sunderland town line had basically been agricultural land since forever. If they granted an exception to the zoning for this, what would come next? Board Member Tim Murphy scratched his beard and wondered about wetlands protections - the land was pretty damp along the river there and the Town did not want to get on the bad side of the State of Massachusetts Wetlands Protection Act. Somebody would need to look into that along with the architectural plans. Tim also raised, may it please the Board, a possible need to confer with the Town Agricultural Committee, which after all, was charged with promoting the valuable and storied agricultural history within the town and highlighting the current agricultural businesses that are within the town. This kind of huge change of land which had been dedicated to farming should get some kind of approval or waiver or whatever it was. All agreed on this, and referred the Red Dirt Associates to the Agricultural Commission, the Zoning Board of Appeals, and the Conservation Commission

for review.   They noted the unusual nature of these reviews being con-
ducted prior to the sale of the property being finalized.

Back in the hallway at the conclusion of the meeting the Red Dirt
Associates congratulated themselves on taking this first step in the approval process for the construction.   They felt they had smoothed the
way for quick approvals once Doug Stengel agreed to the sale. Meanwhile Tim Murphy wondered with a few colleagues what Doug Stengel
thought of all this, since it was still Doug's property. Doug was known
to be a careful thinker, and often a voice of reason when it came to new
ideas, or potential changes in the town. Seemed as though the cart may
be in front of the horse, and Tim thought he would stop by Doug's on
the way home to check.

CHAPTER 28

Marion was driving fast up Route 9. Faster than she should be, really. When Beth had phoned her, ostensibly to check in about plans for Sunday dinner, Marion had alarm bells ringing in her head from the moment she had answered the phone. Beth had sounded cheery, and had gone on about how wonderful it was that the lilacs were opening up all around the yard in the still cool morning sunshine. But when Marion had asked Beth how she was feeling, Beth had faltered a moment before she had launched in, and then had called her Jess. That had sent Marion into a mental tailspin, and she had interrupted:

"Mom!. It's Marion! Your *daughter,* Marion!"

"Oh sorry, Dear? Yes, of course. How silly of me!" And she had giggled and continued right along. But Marion was not fooled. Her mother had completely forgotten whom she had called, and to whom she was talking. She butted in again,

"Mom, I'm coming right up there. I'll be there in an hour. Don't go anywhere!"

And so, after texting Brodi to let her know, she found herself driving like a bat out of hell, willing the car to go faster and the slower drivers in front of her to get off the road. As she blew through Williamsburg past the cute country general store, she thought for a half second that she should be on the lookout for the sheriff deputies who liked to wait semi-hidden off the main road to catch out-of-towners just like her speeding through their sleepy little country town.

But Marion was terrified about what she might find at Beth's. After the last visit up there with Brodi, she knew anything was possible. Those early signs of decline -- unclean dishes, overflowing trash, stacks of unopened mail -- were all there. But then, instead of getting a cleaner or in-home help, they had hemmed and hawed together about where Beth would live in their home, and what accommodations they would need to address to make Beth a little apartment in their home for her. Their home was plenty big enough, and they'd fix up the little bathroom on the first floor next to the guest bedroom, and move all their stuff out of the large walk-in closet there in order for Beth to move in her things. They had spent a few weekends slowly sorting through many years' accumulation of stuff, but they had gotten bogged down with what to save, what to toss, and what to take to the Goodwill. It was a monstrous chore, and it had sapped their energy. For Brodi, Marion knew, there was the dread that came with realizing that Beth *was* moving in with them, it was inevitable, and Brodi had acknowledged being inwardly terrified of the responsibility. For Marion there was the deep sadness she felt knowing that she was losing her mother so quickly.

As Beth entered Columbia, she took the turn onto Main Street perhaps a bit too fast and right in front of an oncoming car. She heard the screech of brakes and the blast of the driver's horn as she rounded the corner. A quick glance over her left shoulder caught sight of how close she had come to an accident.

She pulled up in front of Beth's home, and her mother was there at the front door.

"Marion! Whatever is the big rush! You must have been speeding to get up here so quickly! Dear me, it's not like the house is on fire." She held open the screen door for Marion as Marion practically jogged up the front flagstone walk.

Marion kissed her mother on the cheek, and held her tightly. She pulled back and looked her mother deeply in the eyes.

"Mom, how are you? Are you OK? I am so worried about you. You called me Jessica on the phone!" Marion surveyed her mother's house and had a strange feeling of vertigo, as though she was about to pass out. As she looked around the home she saw that it was neat and orderly. Things were put away, books were on the built-in bookcases alongside the fire hearth in the living room, and the old faded Persian carpet looked recently vacuumed.

"Mom, it's... all cleaned up in here." She remarked.

"Why, yes, Dear. I actually just did the carpet before you arrived, but it's been picked up."

Marion thought back to their last visit, when the kitchen had been a disaster, the sink full of unwashed dishes, and the dining table had an accumulation of days worth of unread *Berkshire Records*. She glanced around the corner into the kitchen to see that only a teacup and saucer rested on the counter next to the sink. Plates, cups and bowls were nestled comfortably in the dish drainer on the other side. Marion gave a sigh.

"Mom, what's going on? You called me Jessica. You are for-

getting things right and left. Brodi and I are fixing up a room and bathroom for you in our house..." her voice trailed off as she tried to justify
the images in her head with what her eyes were seeing now.

Beth was nonplussed.

"Marion, I *am* getting old. I am forgetful sometimes, and yes, I
may have temporarily gotten confused on the phone, but I am basically
OK. You and Brodi are jumping the gun, and it's very upsetting for me. I
am just trying to live my life in a good and peaceful way, and you are
pushing me to move in with you two. I am just fine, as you can
see. Now, let's sit down and have a cup of tea and talk sensibly." Beth
moved into her sunlit kitchen and hefted the teapot on the stove. She
turned on the burner under the teapot and opened the cupboard above to
find the tea.

"Earl Gray for you?"

"Yes, Mom, that would be great." Marion sounded defeated in
her response. Just then her cell phone rang in her purse. She pulled it
out and glanced.

"It's Brodi. She's calling me back. I should take this." Marion
swiped her finger across the phone's screen and answered.

"Hi honey...I am up at Mom's. .. Everything's fine, I
guess....No, she's fine too...Yes, I am just as confused...She called me
Jessica! That was very troubling...Brodi! ...Look everything's fine right
now. No, you don't need to come up here. I'll call you on the way
back...Bye honey."

Marion clicked off her phone and placed it back in her hand-
bag. Beth was bringing two teacups over on a small round silver tray,
with a sugar bowl and small pitcher of milk.

"So, you told her I was going off the deep end, and now you are
a little embarrassed. You should be." Beth chided Marion as she placed
the tray on the dining table.

They sat around the corner at the table; Marion could glance out
the French doors into the sunlit back yard. The sun on the yellow day
lilies was beautiful, and Beth and Marion sat and enjoyed their tea as
they chatted as they had for years. Marion marveled at her mother's enthusiasm and vitality then, and wondered how long it would last. She
wished for it to last forever, to be like a dream come true. Looking at
Beth, her long gray hair pulled back in a simple bun, and her faced carved
with the story of her life, Marion felt a deep love and appreciation for

her mother spill over her. She wondered what to do to help her mother's current state of mind.

It came to Marion in that sunlit conversation that despite the apparent oasis of lucidity she was experiencing with her mother in that moment, perhaps even because of it, the fact remained that Beth needed to move down to Amherst soon. Marion's mind sometimes circled around a decision, like a predator circling its prey, but once the point of attack was identified, the sudden movement was swift and sure.

"Mom," she reached out to cradle Beth's free hand in hers, "It's time for you to move to Amherst."

Beth seemed taken aback. "But I'm fine, dear! Everything's wonderful. And you know I love the summertime blossoms and warmth in the yard here. It's fine."

"Oh, mom," Marion sighed. "It's not really fine. I know it seems fine at the moment, but it's not fine. You can't be in denial about this, and neither can I. I realize now that I've been on a roller coaster with you these past couple of years, and what keeps me going is the hope, the hope, that you are not falling into permanent la-la land, And hope is not a strategy! Hope is what keeps us frozen into inaction. The beauty of this moment, the love I am feeling for you now, gives me the strength and the clarity to know that this is what we HAVE to do. Who knows when the next outer-space conversation is going to occur with a person I don't know inhabiting the beautiful body of my mother? It sends me into a tailspin. I react like a bomb has gone off, like it's world war three and I'm a nurse in the ER dealing with the incoming wounded and maimed. Mom, I know HOW to respond in those crisis times, I did it for years working as an ER trauma-care nurse, but I don't want to be that way with you. "

Beth withdrew her hand from Marion's grasp and folded both her hands in her lap. A tear slipped from her right eye and traveled down her cheek. She began to silently cry, her shoulders heaving, and she looked down at her hands. "I'm so afraid, Marion," she whispered.

Beth grabbed a napkin and cried into it, tears of fear and sadness wracking her body. Marion stood and went over to her mother, wrapping her arms around the tiny woman's frame and holding her. "I love you, mom," she said into the softness of her mother's hair, and she gently stroked her mother's back.

They remained like this for a few moments. Slowly Marion

straightened up, wiping her own tears away. She continued to rub her mother's back in circles, and looked down at her mom. Beth, too, wiped her tears and looked out across the yard, flowers in the sunlight, wind gently swaying the willow in the back, newly formed leaves a gentle green in the sun. The lilac bushes around the edge of the grass were showing their pastel colors -- pink, lavender, red. Beth had looked at this same view now for decades.

She sighed, "This may be my last summer up here…"

Marion absorbed the view into the back yard. She too, had loved this little view into nature for many years. As now the unfolding seasons began turning to color and light, so too the burgeoning green of summer was the promise to come. The willow would be flush with dark green leaves waving in the hot summer sun, and the roses and lilies would add their hues to the palette of colors. In her mind's eye Marion could see the yellow leaves falling in the cooling breezes of autumn into the deadened stalks of the dying plants, and then the snow falling gently and creating a magical blanket of white across the yard in winter, gray squirrels making tracks in the snow as they scurry about in their wintertime survival strategies. This view, ever changing yet comfortingly the same, would be hers and her mother's no longer. She sighed deeply.

"I love this view, Mom," she said wistfully. "I'll be sad not to look out over the yard."

Marion realized a new chapter coming in her life, a change from the stability of her marriage with Brodi and their two-career lifestyle. She would now welcome her mother into that life. Beth stood and gently wrapped her arms around her daughter's waist, and leaned into her.

Marion sighed again. "Oh Mom, we are going to make this work, you'll see."

She squeezed her mother, and then gently moved away. "If we are sure about this, we should think about what needs to get done." She immediately went to her mother's desk and took a pad of paper and a pen back over to the breakfast table.

As Marion began making her list of things to do, Beth moved the tea cups and saucers back to the sink, and washed up. What Marion couldn't know was what preoccupied Beth next.

Beth then looked into the living room, and into the den, and had a momentary overwhelm with the scope of the tasks before them. It had been decades in this house. Her life with her husband, the raising of the kids, the years of entertaining, and just plain living were swirling around her. She experienced an odd sense of disorientation come over her. She turned to look at Marion, and suddenly she was in another space. Beth knew she and Marion had just had a big conversation, but she suddenly couldn't remember what they had talked about. She felt a mild panic, knowing they had discussed something important, something perhaps life-changing, but she just could not remember what it was. She looked around the room again, looking even for clues, but all she saw was her daughter writing something intently on a pad of paper. She looked out into the yard at the sun falling on the bright flowers, but that gave her no clue. She panicked again for a minute, but thought she should sit down and perhaps something would return to her memory. As soon as she sat down, perching on the edge of a chair like a bird, the feeling of panic deepened. She thought perhaps she might have written something down, somewhere, to help herself remember, and then she thought of her little book, her little red-covered writing book. She went to her desk and found it lying there. She opened the cover.

On the first page were these words:

YOU ARE BETH >>>>

YOU LIVE AT 55 COLUMBIA STREET, COLUMBIA, MASSACHUSETTS.

YOUR TELEPHONE NUMBER IS 413 – 555-2222

YOU ARE 85 YEARS OLD (IN 2021). YOUR BIRTHDAY IS JULY 17, 1936.

YOUR DAUGHTER IS MARION. HER WIFE IS BRODI.

YOUR SON IS DANNY. HIS WIFE IS JESSICA.

Beth looked at the writing and recognized it as her own. The letters were block capital letters, which was not her usual way of writing. She wondered why she had written this in this way. She turned the page.

YOU HAVE THE BEGINNING STAGES OF ALZHEIMER'S DISEASE. THIS MEANS YOU FORGET THINGS AND PEOPLE. SOMETIMES YOU FORGET WHAT YOU ARE DOING OR WHERE YOU ARE GOING OR WHY. IF YOU ARE IN YOUR FORGETFUL PLACE, IT IS BEST TO SIT DOWN AND REST UNTIL YOUR MEMORY RETURNS.

Beth looked at this with only a mild recognition. She didn't remember even writing this, and it felt like an odd betrayal. How could she have written all this and not remember? Was someone playing a trick on her? Would Marion do that? Marion was really caught up in her own thing at the moment and didn't even notice that Beth had gone into the den. Beth wondered if Marion even knew what Beth was thinking, if she knew that Beth was having a moment of panic and insecurity.

Marion looked up from her writing, turning her head to the side and studied what she had put down. She looked up and saw Beth at her desk in the den.

"Mom, OK I started a list?" she began. "We could even begin on this now if you want. Really there is no reason to put things off."

Beth looked at her daughter. "What? I was just going to work in the yard today, and trim back the dead material and do some mulching."

Marion looked startled, "What are you talking about, Mom? We are going to get going on the move! That's what we were just talking about!" She gave a gesture of frustration, and a moue of aggravation.

Beth twisted her hands together in her lap. She didn't know how to respond, and was afraid of her daughter's obvious displeasure. When Marion had her mind set on something, she was intransigent, and her mother had known this since Marion was a little girl. She gave a high-pitched giggle, which Marion knew meant that she felt nervous.

"Oh, Mom, you don't remember what we were just talking about, do you?"

"Yes, of course I do, dear! I was just remembering something…" her voice tailed off.

"Mom?"

"Well, it was just such a nice day. I thought a bit of yard work would be good for me. Get outside in the sun. Vitamin D and all that." Beth smiled broadly, giggled, hoped her sunny disposition would get Marion off her back.

"Mom! We were just talking about getting you moved *out* of here! Packing, sorting, throwing things out! Giving to Goodwill! Not pruning the damn roses!"

"It's too early to prune the roses, dear. The soil's not warmed up enough for the roots yet. I was thinking of some mulching and the fruit trees."

Marion's head dropped onto her chest. A sign of resignation. She had seen this a thousand times with her patients suffering from early onset dementia in the hospital. Still, it was heartbreaking here. She picked up her phone.

"I have to call Brodi," she said with resignation as her mother smiled.

Speed-dialing her wife, Marion felt her lower lip and chin quiver, feeling the tears of frustration and grief overcoming her.

Beth, for her part, smiled and headed out the back door, apparently to work in the yard.

Brodi picked up, "Marion?"

"Hi honey! Listen, after we talked mom went off the deep end again. She walked away for a minute and now she can't remember what we were talking about a minute before. She just went out to work in the garden like she's going to just go on living here forever. It's scary. I started writing a list of things we would need to do to get her moved and she's acting like that is as far away as the moon. I just don't know where to start or where to begin with her!" Marion could hear the panic rising in her voice, and she knew she was on the edge of a breakdown herself.

Brodi was cautious and reassuring. "Marion, it's going to be OK. Let's just slow down and think this through…"

"Brodi! You're not up here seeing this! She's flipping back and forth, in and out and she could injure herself, or worse! She's not safe anymore up here by herself!"

"OK, OK. I hear you. But we're not moving her down here today, and you said earlier the place looked immaculate, like it used to look after your dad died."

"Well, yes, but just now she totally flipped into this Twilight Zone. I don't know who she was! She needs to get moved down to our place right away."

Brodi heard the urgency, and the increasing panic in Marion's voice.

"OK, so we need to start this process now. I get that. And it will still take a few weeks to get this all in order, and planned out. Do you want me to come up?"

Marion felt defeated. "No. Let me sort this out and I'll call you back. Bye." She hung up the phone. Took a deep breath. Thought.

Resolved. Marion pressed the Siri key on her phone. "Siri, call Alice."

The phone suddenly spoke back.

"OK. Calling Alice. Which number, home or mobile?"

"Mobile"

"OK, calling Alice…mobile"

There was silence for a moment, then Marion spoke.

"Hi Alice….yes, I'm fine, well not fine exactly…well, its mom. She has been having a harder and harder time, you know, we've talked about this….I'm here with her now…anyway I think it's time. I was hoping that you and Ben could help Brodi and I do this…move." This last said in a very low voice, watching Beth the whole time.

"I'm not sure – maybe even later this week or next weekend?….Oh my god, thank you. OK I'll call you later. Bye."

She took another deep breath, and called Danny. Left a crisp message about the imminent move. Setting a plan into motion.

Marion ran her hand through her graying hair. She deeply sighed. "OK, Mom, what is next?" It was rhetorical, of course. Marion's brain was racing with tasks to be done. "OK, we need some care coming in for the next – let's say two weeks."

Marion again asked her phone for "in home care Western Mass" and heard back "OK, this is what I've found about that." She studied a list, scrolling through, frowning and then dialed.

"Hello, this is Marion Saunders, I am a nurse, and my mother, Beth, lives in Columbia. She is going to need daily care starting right away for the next few weeks."

"Beth, uh, Elizabeth Mae Carlton…85…July 17, 1936…55 Columbia Street…Columbia…01343…Medicare…" Marion was responding to question after question. She was completely tuned into the nuances of this type of exchange. This was repeated daily in doctor's offices, social service organizations, government health care exchanges, hospitals, dentists…you name it. The endless capturing and storing of mundane details. One had to report the same information to every medical or social service office encountered. Important for the wheels of bureaucracy to turn, yet so trivial in comparison to the depth of this issue.

"OK…When can…tomorrow? What time? Yes, I can be here….Thank you! Thank you so much! Goodbye."

Now Marion truly sighed, a full bodied, things-are-getting-handled sigh. She began to feel her feet again, a small indication of the relief she was feeling in this moment. She called her work to say she had an emergency and would be out for the next few days.

Her mother came over to comfort her, and rubbed her back as

Marion sat in the chair.

"It'll be alright dear." Marion was conscious of the irony of the situation. Here was her mother comforting her, as her own life was slowly falling apart.

The moments of a change in a life, the times when a life trajectory turned slowly, or quickly, was often one of poignancy, and also absurdity. The turning of time, and relationship, and future scripting could appear so different at different moments. And it could change, and one's idea about it could change, and one's feelings about it could flip back and forth so rapidly. Perhaps absurdity was always underlying everything. Perhaps there was an underlying humorist in every situation lying in wait to burst forth, or just poke its little head up, and create an apron of levity to any situation.

Marion was suddenly reminded of Brodi's grandmother's funeral service. It was arranged by her estranged son, Brodi's dad, who was so socially inept and distant from everyone. There they were in the funeral home, mourning the death of a wonderful and loving woman, listening to some minister whom no one knew (selected by Brodi's father) talk endlessly about "our dear Mary." Mary was this and Mary was that. Spoken in measured and reverent tones. Only, no one knew Mary Elizabeth as Mary; she had been known her whole life as Polly. And so this moment of memorializing became one of suppressed giggling, every time the minister mentioned, "our dear Mary."

With that fleeting memory, and the smile it brought to Marion's face, she wiped away a tear, and turned back to her mother.

"OK, Ma! What's up next? Should we begin to pack up?"

CHAPTER 29

As Audrey arrived at the gym on Saturday morning, the sun was glistening through a myriad raindrops dangling off the branches of the trees around the parking lot. Thousands of rainbows and shimmering colors everywhere she looked. Magical, she thought. The intimation of potential illumination.

As she set up for her class in the large gym, she turned on the music to set up the vibe she wanted. Upbeat, happy, energetic. Responding, she nodded her head to the beat as she unfurled her hot pink ZUMBA banner, and mounted it high on the wall with the help of a short stepladder. She loved the round Zumba logo, a stylized woman with elbows jabbing and knees lifted in movement, surrounded within a circle. Everything about ZUMBA was captured there.

Her women (she often did think of them as "her women" – not possessively, but more like a tribe) had gotten closer together and more connected as time had gone on. Many women came faithfully every week to her classes. Shouts of "Hey woman!" echoed above the music, and high fives and hugs were shared around the room. Alice and Sophia came in together, along with Marion, and like the others they couldn't help but smile when they entered the gym. Audrey gave a happy wave to them as they dropped their sweatshirts, towels and water bottles in a small pile around the perimeter.

Audrey started them off with Stevie Wonder's *Boogie on Reggae Woman*, as a kind of warm-up, an old familiar song to many of the women that would naturally get them grooving to the beat. A new cut, *Shake Your Boom Boom!* was very upbeat and by the time they had danced and shouted their way through that one everyone was smiling and sweating. Audrey knew these women loved to dance, and especially in this time of cultural upheaval and environmental uncertainty, when every day women, and black people, and poor people, and immigrants, and children were under intense assault on their rights and their bodily autonomy, this was the church of Zumba, this was a spiritual awakening and communion. This was release! So they prayed to *Baille*, they used their bodies to harmonize with the universe, they aligned their energies with a Divine Feminine, and created a neural network of intention and understanding. The dance was a trance that carried them into the depths of their soul and allowed them to tap into the universal truth that in there was survival, and resurrection. Truly empowered women.

An hour of moving, dancing, shaking, and shouting left them all sweating and exhausted, and exhilarated. More high fives and hugs, bright pink faces and wide grins. Many of the women came over to Audrey to hug her and tell her how amazing she was, how inspirational, and she reflected that praise right back to them. Each woman left feeling the glow of recognition and camaraderie. "I see you!" was the benediction as they walked out the door. Audrey wandered over to where Marion, Alice and Sophia were picking up their sweatshirts and toweling off. She gave each of them a hug and exchanged excited praises for the workout.

"It's going to church and praying with our bodies!" said Alice.

Audrey nodded. "I have said that myself."

She looked at Sophia, "Good to see you Sophia! I love it when you come and shake it up with us!"

Sophia grinned and wiped back a sweaty strand of brown hair from her brow. "I love it! I feel so good after Zumba!"

Marion took a long pull from her water bottle. Wiping her face she said. "I *really* needed that. What a great reset."

Audrey tilted her head. "How are you, Marion? It is so great to see you here!"

Marion smiled, "Well, at this moment I am great! I feel energized and more relaxed than I have felt in weeks, to be honest. I am facing the prospect, a bit daunting, of moving my mother down here from the Berkshires. She's 85, and this will be her first move out of our family home!"

Audrey looked concerned, and sympathetic. "That is a huge decision."

Marion nodded, "Yes, and it has to be done. Really there is no time to lose at this point." She wiped her brow with a towel, and then swiped around her neck. "Last weekend I was up there after she had a kind of episode. She totally forgot who I was, and right before my eyes she kind of flipped into one of her fugue states. Didn't know why I was there or what we had been talking about a minute before. It was scary. I immediately called home health to have a day worker come in on a regular basis."

Audrey pursed her lips as she nodded. "This is the sad fate of so many older women in our culture. It's like they get untethered from reality, and they slip away from us. That happened to my aunt before she died. I hate to say it but men can be totally useless in these situations. My uncle had no idea what to do -- he was in denial that Aunt Betty was getting so bad. Anyway, it was so sad to see, and you feel so helpless! You just want to connect them back to their lives!"

Alice stroked Marion's back in sympathy. "We will help in any way we can, Marion. You are not alone in this."

Sophia piped in, "I'll help you get your mom down here. What can I do to help?" The three women looked at her.

"That is a wonderful offer, Sophia," Marion responded, looking the young woman directly in the eyes with tears glistening in her own. "Really kind. I – I am not sure what you can do right off the bat. "

Alice witnessed Sophia's compassionate nature stepping into the forefront. It was Sophia moving into her own relationship with Marion, and Audrey, too. Claiming her space in the circle of women. And the beauty of Marion's response – recognition, acknowledgement, affirmation.

Audrey also touched Sophia's shoulder. "That's a great offer Sophia." Turning to Marion, "Lots of help offered here. We can make this work, you just let us know."

Marion looked relieved. "Well, I have been talking to the folks at the hospital. They do have a dementia unit where I can take Mom for some testing, maybe a day program. Once she's down here we can do that.

Marion continued: "We've made the decision that we are moving Mom next weekend. Are you all available on Saturday? We can cavalcade up there and get this process moving."

Sophia seemed a moment concerned. "I was planning to exercise my horse Saturday. Maybe I can change that to earlier or later..."

Marion said, "We're heading up there at 9:00 AM. Can you work around that?"

Audrey said, "I'm coming up, too. I think an extra set of hands will help."

Heads nodded. Brief eye contact around the circle. The plan was made.

* * *

Brodi was back in Jacksonville on a hot, muggy Florida late summer day along with Rhonda. The sun blistered as they drove to the RXX offices on the south side.

Rhonda's UMass team had implemented some design improvements suggested by Brodi, which had been communicated to RXX, from the preliminary results on the pilot testing of the device for the Alzheimer's patients, and it was ready for the next stage of production.

At RXX, after quick re-introductions with Rhonda, Brodi started in: "Is Carl joining us?"

Ted looked slightly embarrassed, "He's tied up, but he told us to go ahead."

Rhonda said, "I'd like to hear about the electronic specifications my team messaged down to you last week. We configured those modifications you discussed the last time Brodi was down here. Are there any issues there?"

Chelsea shook her head, "None whatsoever. Your team has been thorough, meticulous, and rigorous in terms of the research and design. We have already forwarded your specs to our design-build department and you will be joining them after our meeting here. I'll walk you over."

Brodi leaned in, "OK good. So back to you, Ted. Production?"

Ted nodded, considering. "O.K. I'll just jump in. We are really excited that the testing on the prototype has proven highly successful. My team is pleased to see this product taking shape, and now to have data is fantastic. We are ready to move into production at any point."

Chelsea added, "We had 10 volunteers use the device. Brodi, appreciate you trying some things out with your mother-in-law on this, too. The raw data we have collected was forwarded to our medical team. We used HIPAA complaint transmission channels to ensure privacy, and to test that capability. The IT folks couldn't detect any slips in terms of privacy protocols, and the fact that we are using the cloud for storage means it is practically seamless."

Brodi added. "I like the simplicity of the design, and how easy it is to use. The listening interface will allow the watch to potentially scan for any information related to timeframes, medications, or other biometric data that could be troublesome. It can then query the user about reminders, or even to contact providers if need be. That feature would need to get programmed, of course, in order to preserve privacy. By the way, the brief setback relative to my mother-in-law's testing it out resulted from a medical event."

Ted responded, "I'm sorry to hear that."

Brodi responded, "Thanks! It's been tough but we're hopeful things will improve there. This device may ease some of the burden for Beth, but it will definitely help others down the line."

Ted nodded, "One thing we need to finalize is the cost of the computer chips. Availability has become an issue with restrictions on rare earth metals now. The Chinese are putting on export restrictions and the pipeline is closing there for chip production. Import tariffs are going to play a factor too. We have all heard about supply line disruptions during the pandemic, so we're trying to move quickly on this. Carl was worried about timeframes."

Rhonda looked puzzled. "Don't you have everything you need? I thought we were merely checking the biometrics to make sure we had the kinks worked out and then you were ready to go into full production."

Ted replied, "Our development team also just wants to make sure we have a ready market to begin distribution. They are coordinating with the market analysis team to see what our potential competitors might be up to. The initial costs of development are pretty steep, so we want to make sure we can cover those elements quickly with early sales. We can't be vulnerable with the development of a device that is this expensive."

Brodi seemed pensive. "Ted, I basically assumed that our meeting today was for handshakes and the directive to roll initial production. What are we missing?"

Ted seemed to wince fleetingly, then said, "Well, Carl wants to be sure this is the right thing, and we are walking a thin line with this being a medical device, which might categorize it such that the FDA needs to be involved. We are looking at a possible way of marketing this as Fitness or Lifestyle, which makes it look like other devices which are currently on the market. Basically available for anyone."

"Uh, OK. Was there a reason you just thought of this?" Brodi seemed nonplussed.

"Well, usually medical electronics are not of concern to the FDA. In this case, there will be protected medical information being transmitted, which makes it a bit more sensitive. The fact that they are transmitted directly to a physician's office could be challenging. We have to be ironclad with HIPAA regs, as we've discussed, and our lawyer thought we might think of a new strategy around marketing that would steer clear of any potential FDA or CMS involvement." Ted spoke with his hands spread wide, a look of submission.

Brodi shook her head. "So you wouldn't be marketing it to physicians who work with the elderly, or AARP, or anyone like that?"

"We haven't honestly thought through that whole piece right now. But potentially, yes."

Brodi and Rhonda looked at each other, then Brodi got up from the table and walked to the window. She gazed out across the treetops, seeing the towers of downtown in the distance. Making up her mind, she turned.

"OK, so what actually changes in putting this thing together and getting production going?'

Chelsea replied. "Nothing essentially changes, except that we probably lose some time in recouping costs of development and production. Getting a device like this to market is expensive, and we were hoping for some rapid uptake by physicians for the elderly and Home Health Care providers, CMS, Medicare. Now we take a more roundabout approach through the wellness channels, which is admittedly softer."

Ted spoke up: "We can probably hit 1000 units within two-three months, three or four at the most. 10,000 by the beginning of next year. We do have a line on wafer production out of Wuhan, if that stays open. Somehow being a smaller producer gets us in faster than say, GM or Ford. They are also scrambling for chips from the Chinese."

Brodi felt deflated. What had seemed so close in terms of production now seemed very far away. She turned to the group. "I have to say that this is discouraging news. I know we have to recoup and keep going, but it flags the momentum."

Ted pursed his lips and tilted his head to the side. "What we know is that this device, when it is fully operational, is a game changer in terms of ADL for people coping with Alzheimer's. This setback related to the chip manufacturing pipeline and concerns about marketing and distribution is temporary, and can be addressed. We hope it is weeks, at most a few months."

He paused and then said, "Let's be clear, Brodi. RXX is ready to sign a contract for production with Medtronol for $100,000 in cash for the development and stake in 5% profits on sales now. If all the hurdles we've discussed today are cleared soon, then the stake goes up to $1,500,000. I'd understand if you'd be reluctant to take it, but it's the offer we can make now despite what the silicon chip market is doing."

Brodi gave a start. "Did I hear you right? $1,500,000 in cash and 5% of profits?"

Rhonda said, "Well I can tell you our share would be very welcome at the lab at this point."

Ted slid a folder across the table to them. "Here's the contract. You can take it with you and discuss it together, and we can talk about it in the morning if you like. If you are ready to sign, we are ready to move ahead."

Brodi and Rhonda looked at one another. "We will look it over tonight and get back to you."

* * *

As they drove away from RXX, Brodi was still stunned with the roller coaster from discouragement to hopeful, and the dollar figure presented to them. They were tickled to think of royalties that could continue to accrue as the device was marketed and sold.

Rhonda was looking at the passing scene out the window, "This contract will infuse our lab with R&D money. Big time."

CHAPTER 30

In the predawn darkness Old Jim shrugged into his Carhartt canvas coat, slipped a headlamp band around his head, flicking on the light, and climbed out of his pick-up parked in the dirt lot alongside the stone circle. Even here at the Autumnal Equinox, the morning was cool, but not unpleasantly so. The ground fog was damp and magnified the cold. Jim freed his scraggly long gray ponytail from under his jacket and dropped it on his back. His gold-rimmed glasses twinkled with the street lights that surrounded the parking area as he climbed from his truck.

Jim turned to the open truck bed and slid a large, dark blue Tupperware container up to the tailgate, then with a heavy grunt manhandled it over to the center stone in the circle. He pried off the lid of the container, and the bright bluish light from his headlamp revealed layers of neatly-folded, brightly colored cloth. Especially for the Autumnal Equinox ritual he loved to create a beautiful altar in the center of the circle. The topmost cloth was from Africa, with a jeweled sunburst batik pattern in the center of a cream colored background. This he unfolded and laid carefully to the east of the granite stone. Next came a deep blue cotton with darker blue shapes like fish swimming amidst swirls of purple and green. This Polynesian cloth he laid to the south. Next an Indian bright orange and flaming red cloth with fiery pulses of gold and yellow, was laid carefully to the west, and finally a woolen Navajo blanket with cranberry red and brown stripes against white was lain to the north.

Jim liked the symmetry of the arrangement, and the way the various fabrics symbolized the ancestors coming from various continents. From the bottom of the container he unwrapped a heavy cast iron bowl, blackened and rusty, with strange geometric shapes cut out from the upper sides, giving the vibe of being ancient and mystical. Jim had uncovered it in a roadside pawn shop along the highway near Santa Fe. He placed this on the standing stone itself, in the center. He placed 4 candles around the iron bowl, in the four cardinal directions. This was the moment that his theatrical eye came into play. He composed the scene carefully, to enhance the feeling that people sought; that they were somehow connected to an ancient ritual despite the fact that Jim was this old, gay, white guy. As he surveyed his makeshift altar, a sedan drove slowly along Campus Drive and then turned into the parking area next to the Sunwheel. *And so it begins*, Jim thought to himself.

The late model Honda drifted slowly to a stop, the car shut off, and the two front doors opened simultaneously. In the growing gray light Jim could make out two folks with dark hoodies pulled up against the early morning cool. They looked young from a distance, and as they walked slowly across the dewy grass, Jim recognized Jeremy..

"Hey, JeremyI How ya doin?" Jim asked. "Welcome!"

"Hi Jim!" Jeremy said, enthusiastically. "This is Sophia, my sister."

"Hi Sophia," Jim said. "Welcome."

"Hi." Sophia shot him a quick glance from under her maroon hoodie, which had "Amherst" stenciled in a curve across the chest.

"Can I help you with anything?" Jeremy offered.

"Sure. Can you grab one or two of the drums?"

"Yeah!" Jeremy followed Jim back to the truck, while Sophia trailed somewhat behind.

Jim smiled, and placed an avuncular hand on Jeremy's shoulder. "That was quite an experience you had last time."

"Yeah, well, something about this really connects for me." Jeremy responded. "I've been checking out some African stuff, listening to African music and reading some things about African spirituality. I like it, especially the part where you connect to the earth and the land as a goddess. Yoruba, and stuff like that." Jeremy let the words tumble out. He reached over the side of the truck and grabbed two cloth-covered Gembe drums by the handles sewn into the cover. He swung them easily over the side of the truck. Jim also grabbed two drums and lifted them.

Sophia hung back, listening to her brother. She had had a sense of something back at the house last night, when Jeremy seemed a bit agitated in the evening. He was obviously excited about something, and so when she asked, "What's going on with you? You're all hyper!" he had immediately stilled himself, but said he was excited about the ritual this morning. He mentioned that he was going out before dawn, and on a hunch, Sophia asked if she could come along. Surprisingly, Jeremy agreed almost immediately.

Jeremy's animation had only increased since they left the house. Fortunately mom and dad were happy they were heading out on this adventure, and had wished them well. Mom had left two packets of Starbucks Via instant coffee on the counter by the stove, next to two aluminum travel mugs. Both Sophia and Jeremy had been psyched to see that, and they happily drank the steaming coffee as they drove to the Sunwheel.

More people arrived, often in groups of twos and threes, and Sophia grinned and shook her head silently as she perused the usual Amherst suspects that would turn up at an event like this. Most people were old, in their 50s, or 60s, with another cadre of 20 year olds. The former were aging hippies; men with long silver hair in ponytails like Old Jim, and the women with either long silver braids, or kinky long hair that sprang like old car seat springs from under straw hats or floating freely about lined faces. Of the younger set, Sophia pegged a few of them for Hampshire College students, long hair and generally scraggly beards on the boys, and long loose hair for the women. A number of them climbed from their cars barefoot, defying the 50 degree weather. Sophia caught a whiff of marijuana smoke as a group walked past. She thought, "Really! Before dawn?"

One young woman was talking to another woman, "The sun's rising in Virgo this morning. Really auspicious. This month will be filled with sexual energy and tension. I could already sense my kundalini rising even before I got out of bed this morning, and my aura was tingling with fiery red energy. "

Sophia had no idea what the woman meant. She was pretty sure the woman was mixing astrology and eastern mysticism, basically nonsense. But, whatever.

Old Jim had walked back to the center stone in the circle, and held an abalone shell which he filled with some green leaves. (*More pot?* Thought Sophia). She wandered over to her brother, who had seated himself on a gray, mossy rock, a beautifully carved wooden drum nestled between his knees. A few other drums had been picked up by others, and people began, as if on cue, to circle up around Jim, close to the outer circle of stones. Jim gave a slight nod, and smiled to the group, turning slowly clockwise. He made eye contact with each person in the group in turn, smiling and nodding. He mirrored the faces of a few people who did not smile back, acknowledging their gravity. He pulled a lighter from his pocket, setting the green leaves alight in the shell. A pungent odor quickly filled the air, and Jeremy leaned over to Sophia and whispered, "Mugwort." Sophia had no idea what he was saying. Jim blew gently on the flames and then they went out, but the pile of leaves in the shell continued to smolder and smell.

Jim held a long black feather in his left hand, and the smoking shell in his right, and using a gentle flapping motion with the feather, he brushed smoke over his head, his shoulders, and down his body, as though bathing. His lips moved silently as he did so.

"First let us recognize that this is unceded land that belongs to the Nonotuck native tribes, the Nipmuk and Pocumtuk. We thank them for stewarding this land. I also thank the many Native and non-Native teachers who have taught me. I welcome you all to the Autumn Equinox. Thank you for joining me at this sacred time, when the earth turns through the season, and we turn with her. We honor the sacredness of life, and the sacredness of the circle and cycles of life. On this day we celebrate the end of Summer, the union of Earth and Sun. We honor the harvest, the Earth Mother. This day is a reflex point, a kind of pause for earth, as she prepares to head further into the deepening harvest. As the sun soon rises in the East, we will begin this day, and we honor the harvest time, the time of gathering the abundance of the earth, and the fruits of our labors, real and symbolic.

"We begin this ritual with sacred smudge – *Artemisia*, or mugwort. I'll pass the shell around, and each shall bless and cleanse the next. You may either silently or aloud voice your prayers for this day, and this season.

Sophia found this very intriguing, how each person in turn would take the bowl of smoking herbs, and mimic the gestures of "bathing" the next one in the smoke. Jeremy had done this before, she knew, so she followed his lead as the bowl came around to her. She found herself really enjoying the sweet smell of the smoke; it wasn't acrid like tobacco smoke, which she often smelled outside school during lunch. And it didn't make her alarmed, like the smell of marijuana. Sophia reasoned it couldn't hurt to join in with a silent prayer, too, since no one would hear it. She took a breath, and thought of her family. She loved her family, and felt so close to each of them. Somehow it seemed like they would be close forever, and always there for each other, and then she got afraid that when she got older, maybe things would change, and she was worried that they wouldn't be as close. Would she go away to college, or maybe her parents would grow older and get sick? She decided to say a prayer for her whole family that everyone would be OK, and everyone would stay close to each other. That seemed like a good thing. Mouthing

"Thank you" she passed the bowl along to the next person, and felt somehow satisfied.

Once the smoldering bowl had passed around the circle – Jim picked up his drum and began a slow, steady beat.

Jim spoke to the group, "Shamanic practices have been found all over the planet. My own heritage with the Celts recognized the passing of the seasons, and later with the building of Stonehenge, and the Grange tunnel, humans worked to ritualize the seasonal shifts. The use of the drum provides a heartbeat for these ceremonies, like the heart of mother earth. At every point in the earth's turning, we can tune in to listen to what the earth is saying to us, She is speaking to us all the time, and we use this time to listen especially to her message. Let the beating of the drums take you to that place where you can hear the message that mother earth has for you as the sun rises in the east, and the light of the new day washes over you. As you sit and close your eyes, allow your heart to be your guide revealing your truth to you."

Sophia closed her eyes and was taken in with the sensory experience of the smell of the smoke, and gentle drumming, and the bird calls and chirping that had begun as the light came up. It was all strange, exciting, and mysterious. Jim began to sing or chant something from another language, and she found that intriguing. She found her head nodding slightly to the rhythm of the beat, slow but steady, and insistent. A little faster than a heartbeat, but like a heartbeat that just keeps going.

With her eyes closed, and the rhythm of the drum beat, and the gently rocking motion of her body, Sophia was taken by a sense of riding on Lightning, and galloping through the woods on a forest trail. She could see the dappled sunlight coming through the leaves and branches, and could feel the thrumming of the hoofbeats on the earth as Lightning easily moved along the trail. She recognized that movement of the horse underneath her, she could feel his strong body as he powerfully charged ahead. She could sense that way they connected almost as one in this rhythm of rider and horse. Sophia opened her eyes momentarily, feeling slightly dizzy, so she could get her bearings. All around her the people in the circle were also sitting with eyes closed, or gazing slightly downward, nodding their heads or swaying through their torsos to the beat of the drum.

Closing her eyes again, Sophia dove back into the vision and sensations of racing her beloved horse through fields and forests, and coming to the edge of a great river, by a giant oak tree. She sensed the Connecticut River, and she could feel the expanse and power of the river before her. She felt that it had almost called her here. In her mind, looking down the riverbank, she saw other horses also along the riverbank, too. There was a magical feeling to this dream-like image. A word came to her -- *beshert*. She had heard it from her Jewish friends at school. *Meant to Be.* She knew it often meant for a couple finding each other, but really, this image was feeling like it spoke to what was meant to be, for her.

As the drum continued to beat, Sophia relaxed into the space, and allowed the dream-like sequence to continue. She knew she was awake, since she could feel the damp grass under her, and she could hear the drumbeat, but still it seemed that somehow she was in a dream. She smiled as in her mind she felt Lightning under her again, his strong and substantial body turning against her legs and moving. She felt his undulating movement as he began to trot and then canter along the wooded path. Sunlight flickered across her vision, as though speckled through trees, and she was moving with the horse through the woodland. They burst through the trees and into the full sunlight of a field of tall grasses. The grass was thigh-high and a beautiful lime green, the seed heads full to bursting. Sophia could feel the warmth of the sun on her back as she moved along the dirt track. Ahead she could see a farmhouse and barn, and she knew it was the farm she was moving Lightning to.

The rhythm of the drumming changed. Four sharp loud beats of the drum sounded then, repeated by four more, then again, then again. More rapid drumming continued and Sophia found her mind now back in the present. As the drumbeats ended she opened her eyes, and saw that Jeremy had a grin on his face. They made eye contact and he nodded his head.

Old Jim sat for a few minutes in quiet, then he said a few words about holding your vision internally for a brief while to let it marinate inside of you, allow it to reach its fullness as the grain had reached its fullness at this time. He said a short prayer, thanked the land, and the Native People, and his teachers; gave thanks for the visions, then rang a bell, signaling the ritual was over.

He came over to where Jeremy and Sophia were standing.

Sophia was looking out into the distance. Jeremy stepped next to her and she instinctively leaned into him, dropping her head onto his shoulder.

"It's so weird," she began. "Like, how does that happen like that? I am sitting here and close my eyes, and all of the sudden I am dreaming, or imagining, this whole scene I am making up. Like, it's in my own mind, but it seems so real! I could feel just like I was riding Lightning, my horse, through a farm field and into the woods, and it was actually happening. "

She turned to Old Jim. "And it was happening at this farm where Jeremy works. So it hasn't happened in real life, but then I think I am just wishing it would happen. Like hoping it will happen. What is this?"

Jim smiled gently, giving a kind of shrug, with eyebrows raised. "Well, I am glad you had that vision," he replied kindly. "It's always what you -- I -- hope is going to happen. But you don't know.

"Shamanism is called the world's oldest religion. I don't know if that's true, but supposedly it cropped up all over the world, in many different indigenous cultures, and it has these simple practices like drumming and journeying. I have been drumming like this for a long time, and there are people, like you, who have these -- let's call them visions -- that could be dreams. Or imaginings. Or it doesn't matter what you call them. And you can decide what they mean, or if they mean anything. Some folks find them reassuring; some find these images disconcerting. I feel like I provide this opportunity to try something and see what comes of it. Do you have an idea what it means for you?"

Jim's non-answer was somehow reassuring, strangely. It was for Sophia to decide what it meant for her.

Sophia inhaled deeply. Exhaled. "OK. It feels to me like it is meant to reassure me that moving Lightning to the new barn is the right thing to do."

"That's so cool," Jeremy nodded his assent. "I felt like the vision I had the last time when I was here was also somehow a sign that something was happening, or supposed to happen. You know," he paused, "This new gig I am doing, working on Stengel's Farm, is really something. I can't describe it, exactly, but it feels like I am into something that is way more than just, like, a summer job. Like I was meant to do this now. I love music and everything, but I really enjoy the work on the farm. And Doug, too. And that vision I had last time was an affirmation for that."

Old Jim nodded to them, placed one hand momentarily on each of their shoulders, and smiled. "You two are really good people. Stay open to the signs and signals the universe sends you." He then turned and walked back to his small altar in the center of the circle, engaging others who had attended the ceremony.

Sophia was still wavering between the dream she had experienced and being present in the circle as the rising sun illuminated the group. She felt the sun warming her back, and looked down to see the dew glistening on her shoes. There was a growing joy inside her as she opened to an appreciation for this day.

As Jeremy moved to help Old Jim with his various accoutrements, his cell phone rang.

Looking at the screen, he saw it was his Dad.

"Hey Dad! What's up? Jeremy turned to walk away from the others still milling around.

"Hey Jeremy! OK to talk?"

"Sure, what's up?"

"Well, I didn't get to talk with you about a letter from Oberlin addressed to you on the side table in the living room."

"Yeah, it came yesterday." Jeremy had opened the letter, now wishing he had taken it to his room, instead of dropping it on the table.

"So, since it was opened and lying there, I picked it up. Apparently you were supposed to complete your acceptance paperwork and this letter indicates you missed the deadline. What's going on?" His dad sounded concerned, maybe a bit upset.

"Uh, I don't know. I guess I forgot that I had to complete the paperwork already."

Ben was silent for a moment. Then he responded, "What's going on, Jer? How did you miss the deadline? Did you just forget, or what?"

Jeremy walked around a large circle, then looped back. "Well, I guess I got confused. And maybe I could wait for another year. Like I was looking forward to going to Oberlin and everything, and then I wasn't sure. I got all twisted up in my head about it, and I guess I missed the deadline. And now I don't know what to do."

Jeremy's father's tone was softer. "Is this something you want to talk about?"

"I guess so."

"OK. Do you want to talk now? Or should we talk at home?"

"Maybe at home. I'll be back in about 45 minutes."

"OK, great. I'll see you at home, Jeremy."

"OK."

"I love you, son."

"Love you too, Dad."

Jeremy breathed a sigh, and turned to see his sister saying good-byes to some other folks.

Old Jim was toting a plastic bin to his truck, and hoisting it over the side of the truck bed.

"Hey," Old Jim called to him. "I was thinking maybe I should come out to this farm you two are talking about and check it out. You know, pick up the vibe of the place."

Jeremy felt another moment of relief. "Yeah, that would actually be great. It's like this land has a way of reaching out to you, and it would be awesome to see what you think. I'd need to ask Mr. Stengel about that, of course."

"Very good, then! You talk to Mr. Stengel and let's make a plan."

As they drove home, Jeremy mentioned to Sophia about the conversation their father wanted to have with him when they got there.

"Is he mad at you?" Sophia said, worried.

"I don't think so. But he didn't sound all happy either."

Sophia considered, then said, "Are you unsure about Oberlin? Do you not want to go?"

"No, I want to go, but it's just all weird. Like, I was totally going to major in music and develop my ability to compose. I was thinking that my background in rock and some international music would naturally morph into some interesting jazz stuff. Anyway, then I got this job and I'm really stoked about going to the farm and working! I want to see how the plants keep growing through the end of the season and then how the fall harvest goes. It's like everyday is a new day, and things like sun and rain and cold and heat affects everything. And it's so cool! But, like, it's so hard, too. I see how hard it is for Doug, and how hard he works, and I can't believe it. So I am really intrigued."

Sophia nodded. "I can see that. Has this thing with Old Jim complicated going to college?"

"Yeah," Jeremy rubbed his chin as he drove. "In my visions I keep seeing the fields and plants and feeling this connection to the land that seems really strong. So I want to honor that too. Even though it's weird." Jeremy snorted. "It's like this shamanism has gotten into my head."

Sophia agreed. "Pretty strange, for sure. My vision -- or whatever -- was really strong too, if that's the right word. I mean, what the hell! I was seriously riding Lightning, and I could feel him right here" -- she gestured between her knees -- "just like I was riding him. So, yeah, I think it's cool. So do you want to stay home? Not go to college?"

Jeremy glanced over at her. "I don't know! I can't make up my mind. I think Mom and Dad would freak out if I said I wasn't going to school, but I feel like there is this opportunity in front of me right here, and I should see what it's all about. Maybe go later."

"So, could you put off going to school until the winter or something? Like after it's snowing?"

Jeremy considered that. "That is a VERY cool idea. I think that could work. Best of both worlds. I could still apply for a deferment. I'll try that with Dad."

When they got home, they saw both parents' cars were in the driveway. Jeremy and Sophia got out of the car and went inside.

Ben and Alice were standing in the kitchen, coffee cups in hand. They turned as the kids came in the back door into the mudroom.

"Hey, kiddos! How was the ceremony, or ritual, or whatever it is?" Alice was smiling and gave them each a warm hug hello. She leaned back and looked into her son's eyes. "OK, so tell me what this is all about! You aren't going to college?"

Jeremy squirmed out of her grasp. "No, Mom! I am just really confused right now. I don't know what's going on. I DO want to go to college! I've been looking at Oberlin for years! I definitely want to go, but now that I've been working on the farm, I really dig it --"

"So to speak," said Sophia, cocking her head.

Jeremy shot an annoyed look at his sister. "--And so I was thinking I wanted to stay on and maybe work here for a full season. Maybe go to college in the second term, or next year…"

Ben launched in. "And when were you planning to talk to us about this? We hadn't heard anything about this plan! We've already put down the down payment. Oberlin is a highly prestigious academic institution. They are expecting your matriculation paperwork!"

Ben's voice was rising as he spoke.

Alice intervened, "Dear, calm down! We are just talking about this, so we can all be calm and reasonable."

Ben took a deep breath, exhaled, and continued. "We now will have late fees to pay -- look at the letter" he waved the single page letter in his hand, partially crumpled. "It's very clear that the matriculation paperwork was due two weeks ago!"

"Look Dad, I'm sorry! I 've been conflicted," Jeremy was shrugging his shoulders. "I didn't know how good working on the farm was going to feel…"

"So, what, now you think you want to become a farmer? Are you kidding me?" Ben seemed incredulous. "Do you know what kind of life farmers have? Do you know how hard farming is? You can't make money doing that!"

Alice interjected. "BEN! Calm down! What's got into you? Jeremy is saying he wants to check this out. He's not saying he wants to be a farmer for his whole life! Besides, who are you to talk? You've been schmoozing with Doug Stengel to try to get him to preserve his farm in perpetuity! This has taken months -- even years -- of discussions! What kind of pompous crap is this about your own son becoming a farmer?"

Alice put her arm protectively around Jeremy's shoulders. "I'm sorry honey. You do sound conflicted. Dad's not helping." Sophia saw her shoot Ben a warning look behind Jeremy's back.

Ben took another deep breath. He turned around and poured another cup of coffee. He faced the bay window over the sink looking into the back yard. Early autumn leaves framed the scene. The dogs were nosing around the woodpile in search of chipmunks.

He turned back around. "OK. Sorry. I've been doing somersaults on this farm deal. Jeremy, I apologize. I was just so looking forward to you going off to college. So proud of you. Now I'm -- confused myself." He walked over and gathered Jeremy in a bear hug. Jeremy was still at first, then tentatively put his hands around his dad's back. They held each other a moment.

Ben took a step back and looked at Jeremy with his hands on the young man's shoulders. "So let's talk about the plan, eh?"

Alice put her arm around Sophia. "We all want you to be happy, Jeremy. We just want to know what is happening. Not get blindsided."

Sophia nodded. "Love you, bro. We're all here for you, no matter what." She reached out one arm and gathered her father in. "Love you too, Dad."

Alice looked at the three of them, then moved in herself. A four person cocoon.

CHAPTER 31

For Beth it was harrowing. Horrible. Two women came into her house, followed by another couple, as she sat in her upholstered chair in the living room, now bare except for this chair, and a side table. She didn't understand who all these people were. She thought she might know them, but the vibe they were giving off was of frustration and resentment, and their faces were set with a determined look. She trembled inside, afraid of what they might do to her. One of the women she was pretty sure was her daughter, Marion, who looked tired and worn out. She thought she also recognized the woman with her. The third woman she also recognized, with her long blonde hair turning gray, and her olive green fleece jacket zipped up to her throat, a long paisley print skirt dusting the tops of her brown boots. That woman just looked mean, and haughty. This wasn't anyone she was going to like, anyway, whether or not she knew her. Beth gripped the arms of the chair as they approached her. The first two bent down next to her to get on eye level, and one of them spoke.

The one woman -- her daughter? -- had just mentioned to her that it was about time to head out to the car. She stood at Beth's side now, smiling but also tears crept down her cheeks. What the hell?

"Beth, it's me, Brodi," the other one said in a soothing voice. "You know me, right? I am your daughter-in-law. And this is your son, Danny. And his wife, Jessica. We're here to help move you to your new home, our home. The moving truck's all loaded up, we just need this chair, and you are riding with us in our car to our house. That will be your new home."

She sounded polite and sincere, but Beth didn't trust her, or any of them. Her memories of these people flitted through her mind, making her more confused. And she had no idea what this woman meant, moving to a new home. She lived here! She had lived here with her husband for over 50 years, and she was fine living here. They had taken her furniture piece by piece this morning, moving out all the boxes as she had just sat here, drinking coffee and watching silently. Yesterday the woman and the man had been here and alot of her things were taken out of the house by all these other people! Beth had no idea who they were, but clearly her things were being given away to just anybody.

"Mom," the first woman said, "Please let's get up now and let's head out into the car to drive home. We're all exhausted from packing up and we've got a long road ahead of us." Her eyes were filled with tears and her lower lip trembled a bit. ""C'mon Mom."

The four of them watched her as Beth looked from one to the other. Her face slowly setting into a fierce look of determination.

The man and one woman looked at each other, and then moved each to her side. She could sense them bending down, and each one had gently gripped her upper arm.

"Let's get up now, Beth."

"Let's go, Mom."

Beth wrenched her arms from both of them. "I'm not going anywhere! This is my home and I'm staying here. Get out!" She blistered them with venom. For a small, older woman she had surprising strength. She made to kick them though they both jumped aside pretty quickly.

"Marion, do something!" Danny pleaded.

Marion's resolve strengthened. "Mom," she stated evenly. "Don't do this! We are here to help."

"Oh, for Christ's sake," said the third woman who had been standing aside. "Just pick her up!" Her tone was clear; she'd had enough of this.

Beth felt like a caged animal and tried to get up on her own, but that had been difficult for her for years now, and the overstuffed chair made it nearly impossible. She squirmed and twisted trying to inch herself more toward the front of the chair, as the two attempted to re-grasp her arms. She twisted and turned furiously, and nearly fell onto the floor.

"Catch her, Brodi! She's falling!" Marion lurched forward to catch Beth as she slid from the chair, and between the three of them they did manage to keep Beth from landing on the floor, although it was very painful for Beth. She continued to squirm for a minute in their arms, but it was clear that she was overpowered, and she went limp with exhaustion.

"I hate you!" was her defiant taunt.

"Let's just get her to the car," said Danny. "Ready? One, two, three." And they together heaved up, so she was forced to stand on her own feet.

They lifted and steered her across the room, and Marion held the front door as they maneuvered her through the doorframe and onto the front steps. Marion hurried around the three of them to stand before Beth as they started down the three steps. "Careful," she said.

Beth was walking in a slow, resigned fashion, as though asleep or heavily drugged. She wasn't really participating in this movement, and made herself very heavy. She was frightened.

"Where are you taking me?" she asked in a plaintive voice. "Leave me alone! I want to stay home. Please! Let me stay in my home!" Now she was crying inconsolably. They assisted her into the back seat of a Honda Accord. Marion leaned across her and buckled the seat belt, which felt like a restraining device to Beth. She immediately grabbed it and tugged, but it was immobilized. She was panicking. She screamed. She began thrashing back and forth.

"Oh God, she's going to hurt herself!" Marion cried again, distraught. "Mom! Please settle down! You are going to be alright! Mom!"

"At least she's restrained," said the other woman. Beth hated her.

Brodi said, "Marion, do you want to ride in the back with Beth, or shall I? We'll have to keep her from hurting herself."

Beth realized it was hopeless, again. She felt the seatbelt tightly wrapped around her body, and she was pinned to the seat. Her squirming had only caused the belt to remain tightened and further immobilized her. A small groan escaped her lips. She was breathing heavily, almost panting. She peered out the window of the car, now dotted with raindrops. Beth noticed how the drops reversed the view she was seeing; the top of the drops clinging to the window reflected the grass and driveway, while the bottom of the drops reflected the gray sky above. The pattern of colors and round shapes of the droplets were almost perfectly dispersed across the window. For some reason, this comforted her. Beth breathed a deep sigh.

The four people were now standing alongside the car, glancing in at her as they talked. She realized they were talking about *her*.

"This isn't good, Marion," the one named Danny said. "She's completely out of it."

"It's been a huge strain on her, Danny. We're forcing her out of the home she's lived in for 50 years, for God's sake. Of course she's upset. You've got to be understanding about that."

"I always knew she was crazy," said Jessica, the blonde. "She's completely wacko now. Her craziness has been coming on for years, more and more. Glad she's not coming to live with us."

"Oh, shut up, Jessica! Don't talk like that. She's not crazy, she's just confused."

"And you can talk to me," Beth interjected. "I am not crazy and I can talk for myself."

"Oh, Mom, are you OK?" Marion turned around and approached the car, leaning into the now-opened window. "You scared me so much." She went to the backseat.

"So what, now you are going to act like that was just a game?" Jessica sneered.

"Jessica, leave it alone," Danny finally intervened with his wife.

Danny turned back to his mother. "Mom, are you OK? I'm sorry we had to be so rough back there."

"No help from you!" Beth said. "What am I doing in the car? Where are we going?"

Marion realized Beth had no idea what had just transpired. She looked directly at her mother. "Mom, you are coming down to our house in Amherst now."

"The hell I am! I live here!" Beth reached down and deftly unbuckled her seatbelt, opened the door and swung her legs from the car. Grabbing the doorframe she heaved herself up to her feet.

Brodi stepped in front of her, effectively blocking her way. She said, calmly and firmly, "Beth, please get back in the car. We know this is hard, but we have been talking about this for months now. Marion and I are looking forward to you coming to live with us. And now it is time."

Marion had come around the back of the car, and gently but firmly put her arm around her mother. Having an intuition, she said, "Mom, do you want to say goodbye to the house?"

"Yes. Yes, I do." Beth, seeming calmed, turned to the house, wiping away a tear running down her cheek. "Good bye," she whispered. She took a few steps toward the house, putting her hand over her heart. Her gray hair blew in the slight breeze, and tears dropped freely down her cheeks. Her old house. She was leaving her old house. She couldn't believe it.

Beth turned, moving between Marion and Brodi and climbed back into the car. She buckled her seatbelt and sat there staring straight ahead. Brodi climbed into the driver's seat, and Marion went around and climbed in the passenger's side of the back seat. She looked at her mom, but didn't say anything.

As they pulled away from the house, Marion reached over and gently took Beth's hand.

Beth looked out the window of the car, away from Marion. "I don't understand why you are all doing this to me. I was doing fine by myself, in my own home. I had all my memories there, all those years. And you just swooped in and took them away. Took *me* away. Because you could, because I'm an old lady and not strong enough to defend myself."

Marion held Beth's hand. "Mom, I know it's scary and confusing, but you will come to enjoy being with Brodi and me. We will create new memories in our home, which will be your home too."

Marion and Brodi made eye contact in the rear-view mirror.

Beth spoke again, "I hate that other woman. Who is she? She's horrible."

Marion smiled slightly, trying to hide it. "Mom, that's Jessica, your daughter-in-law. She's Danny's wife. They live out in Adams. They've been married for 20 years now."

Beth turned to look at Marion. "I don't care who she's married to. She's a bitch."

"You've got that right," mouthed Brodi, smiling slightly.

They arrived at Marion and Brodi's home about an hour later. Marion exited the vehicle and helped her mom get out. Beth squinted up at the house. "I haven't been down here in awhile."

"That's true," said Marion. "And now this is going to be your home, too. Let's go in and see your room."

They walked up the front steps, and Marion opened the front door. "Your room is here on the right. We remade the guest room for you, and closed off the bathroom."

Marion stood aside and let Beth enter the room first. They had moved her bed down and placed it with a view out the window. A tall Eastern white pine swayed gently in the breeze in view in the yard. Marion had cut and hemmed the sheer white curtains from Beth's front room, and one bookcase held family pictures, and some precious knick-knacks from Beth's home.

Beth moved to the bookcase, and she touched the pictures one by one. "This one's of you kids at Hampton Beach", "This one's of your father and I on our honeymoon in Hawaii," "Here's your father on his boat -- he was a handsome man!"

"Yes he was, mom," Marion smiled, "Mom, can I get you anything? Tea, or maybe a glass of water?"

"I'd love a cup of tea, dear," Beth sighed.

Brodi moved over to her side, picking up a case from the desk.

"I had this new watch made for you, Beth. You remember the one we tried out a few weeks ago? This one's even better. It'll help with the transition to moving down here." She opened the case and showed Beth the watch.

It gleamed nicely in the light from the lamp. Beth reached for it, "It's nice. I like the sleek black look." Brodi relaxed a bit.

"So, it works like a watch -- it tells date and time. And it does some other things, too. Do you want to try it on?"

Beth stretched out her wrist, and Brodi carefully strapped it on. Fortunately she had her wrist size matched so it fit perfectly.

"So, when you bring the watch up to look at it, the date and time come right on. The face is touch sensitive, so you can tap it gently" -- she demonstrated -- "and it will tell you when your next pills need to be taken."

"Oh! I like that! I am always forgetting about those damn pills. Seems like Dr. Stone is giving me more and more every time." Brodi showed her the features of what the pills looked like, and when they were taken. She demonstrated how the alarm was set with a gentle reminder tone for the pills.

"Oh, that is very good," Beth was very intrigued with the device. Brodi asked if she wanted to learn more, and she said yes. She showed her the identification features, the reminder features, and then said, "And, it's a phone!"

Beth looked at Brodi like she was crazy. "What? A phone?"

"Yep. You can make simple calls from this watch -- it can hold up to 10 stored numbers, and you can talk for up to 10 minutes at a time." She showed her how to activate the phone, find the stored numbers, and then said, "Let's call Marion." They dialed Marion who picked up as she walked back into the room.

"Hello!"

"Hi Marion, it's Mom!" She was practically yelling, but this broke whatever tension remained as they wondered, oo'd and ah'd over the device.

Marion set the tea pot and cups down on the desk, and handed Beth a cup.

"What do you think, Mom? Is this going to be OK?"

"We'll see how it goes," replied Beth. "Seems OK for now. I will be down here with you two. And Edna," at that moment the beagle wandered into the room, sniffing around, then jumped onto Beth's bed.

"Make yourself at home!" Beth smiled.

After some brief conversation, Beth admitted to being tired and asked if she could lie down.

"Of course, Mom. This is your home, so you can do whatever you like. We'll scoot out now and leave you to it." She hugged her mother deeply, and looked sideways at the dog. "You coming?"

The dog showed no interest in vacating the bed, so they exited, closing the door as Beth pulled back the covers and climbed in next to the dog.

Marion and Brodi wandered into the kitchen. "Coffee? Tea?" asked Brodi.

"Scotch?" replied Marion. Brodi gave a start, then observed the wry smile on Marion's face.

"Really. Oh my God!" Brodi came over and wrapped Marion in a bear hug.

Marion sobbed briefly, then pushed away and wiped away her tears.

"That was not unexpected. We should have been ready for something like that. People who are experiencing early dementia will have those moments. She was scared, caught off-balance, and so she naturally tried to lash out." Marion bustled to brewing tea. She glanced briefly outside and noticed for the first time some red-tinged leaves on the maple in the yard.

"No thanks to Jessica and Danny." Brodi shook her head in wonderment.

"They are just out of their depth on this. Danny was always uncomfortable around any kind of disability or illness. When Dad was dying -- you remember -- Danny could barely force himself to go visit. And Jessica is just used to medicating herself around anything uncomfortable. She was probably high this morning. Did you see those dark circles around her eyes? Pathetic." Marion was back to her in-charge self.

"I was so glad that Beth was receptive to the new watch! " Brodi said, with a hint of pride.

"Yes, honey! That is going to make such a difference for her, and for us," Marion agreed. "Can we get that synched up to our phones?"

"Already done," Brodi nodded. She walked over and picked up Marion's phone.

She touched the screen, located the app. "Look," she stood beside Marion, tilting the phone in her direction. "Here's the app, click here, here's Beth's info. Meds taken, time, her location. This icon will let you call or text her. And here's her location!"

Marion glanced down, squinted, then she shook her head. "Technology! What the heck!" She kissed Brodi's cheek. "You are a wizard!"

Brodi smiled. "Not to mention this device is going to make us some cash. Just sayin'!"

Marion took her tea, handed a cup to Brodi, and went to sit on the sun porch. Facing south, it was full of lovely early afternoon sun.

"What a week!" Marion exhaled. "And her complete fugue state at home was scary."

"Makes running the nursing workforce at the hospital seem a piece of cake, eh?" Brodi sat next to her, careful not to spill tea.

"You're funny! I can't believe that we finally got Mom all moved down here! And I never thought I could take a week off to get it all done, but here we are."

Brodi half turned to Marion, "You are amazing! You can re-prioritize on a minute's notice, and help Beth, and I know you'll be able to refocus on your real job when you need to. That's your skill."

"Thanks," Marion said, smiling again, and tearing up again. She leaned fully against Brodi then, allowing her support to fill her with peace.

After a moment, she sat up, wiped her eyes, and said, "So, what's next?"

CHAPTER 32

Old Jim steered his batted pick-up onto the dirt drive in front of the farmhouse. Jeremy emerged from the barn at just that moment, wiping his hands on an old oil-stained rag, which he then shoved into the back pocket of his faded and stained jeans. Old Jim climbed out of the cab of the truck, looking around at the farm and the land.

Jeremy walked across the drive. "Hey, Jim, thanks for coming out here. Really appreciate it!"

Old Jim nodded, "'Course! This is a real pretty property here. The river over there?"

"Sure is. Want to walk around and get a feel for the place? I talked to Doug. He said it was fine, and he'd like to meet you if it works out. He's off getting parts for the hayer anyway."

"Sure. That's why I came out. See what we could see." Jim stopped, thoughtful for a minute, and turned back to his pick-up. Opening the aluminum tool bin in the back, he pulls out a satchel that Jeremy has seen before, containing some of Jim's ritual materials – sage, rattles, and some other esoteric-looking things.

They turned and walked side by side. Jeremy began, a bit hesitant, to tell him about working on the farm. He described how he had started working in the summer, and had found himself trying to get out here everyday now, even coming for a few hours after school. It was hard farm work, and he was showing the effects of spending so much time at work in the outdoors; looking fit and healthy. Jeremy carried himself more upright and walked with a confidence that hadn't been there even six months previously.

As he spoke, he warmed to his topic. He described tilling fields for the wheat harvest, and weeding the potatoes and beets. His knowledge of the farming ways had grown impressively in a relatively short time. Jim listened to the young man, nodding in understanding and appreciation.

They walked the farm road between two fields, the potatoes to the left and the beets to the right. A slight breeze carrying the smell of soil and early fall wafted past them. The sun was rising in the eastern sky and the warmth of the day rose alongside it. Jim's senses took this all in as he walked.

"You know, Jeremy," he started, "I've spent my years working to stay connected to the land, to the sky, and to the turning of the seasons. I can sink into the *beingness* of a place, the way this moment is evolving through time in this place. Here we are, just at the Autumnal Equinox, and I can feel the whole earth making the turn toward shorter days, less light, colder nights, and the harvest coming. I can feel the way the sun and the rain have been absorbed in these crops, and the way that nature is expressing herself in these plants, these fruits."

Jeremy smiled, "That's really cool! I hope to learn that, too."

Jim continued, "And your story is tied somehow to this land, to being in this place. I can feel how your presence is infused in this land and these crops now. I know your people did not come from this land, but somehow the land is speaking to you, and talking to you in special ways as well. You are part of this landscape, and your story is now woven here."

As they passed through a narrow band of trees and undergrowth that was wild and unkempt, the trees swaying above their heads, Jeremy noticed birds darting among the undergrowth. The birds' chirping and cheeping were sweet melodies as they walked. Jeremy took a cue from Old Jim, and listened to the wind and birds. He took a deep breath as they moved along, and spent a moment trying to identify individual birds. Chickadees for sure, some finches, maybe a robin. It was a beautiful chorus of sounds and lilting songs. And the way the birds flickered in and out of the sunlight and shade, a real choreography of movement was unfolding. It was a moment of clarity and sublime grace for Jeremy as he unfolded his story to Old Jim. Old Jim asked a question here and there for clarity, or inquiry, and Jeremy felt his story revealed for himself as well, almost as though he were listening to someone he didn't know, and to a voice he didn't recognize. Jeremy had a sense of awakening he didn't know resided in himself. He felt the truth and the power of his narrative of the deep past, and of the future. He marveled at his own words, and his own thoughts and his own reflections. He found he went back in time, in his own life, and began speaking of his life from the very moment of his birth, born to African-American parents whom he had never met. He imagined their struggle to live and survive, inner city blacks in a surprisingly racist city here in New England. He spoke of the story he did know, of how Alice and Ben had adopted him when they thought they could have no children of their own, and had loved him and cherished him. He described feeling a part of a marvelous community here in Amherst, part of a tribe of broad thinking and respectful people, for whom color was but one attribute among many that need not define who you were, but perhaps explained some of the ways you thought, or felt. He told Old Jim about his love of music and especially rhythm, and the deep sounds he could make with his instrument. He spoke of his joy at making music with others, with his friends. How this music making transported him to other times, and other places.

As he talked, Jim continued to nod and smile. "You know, Jeremy, I could feel this inside of you. It's *sonder*. I could feel this deep connection to music and rhythm. This is why I invited you to drum the rhythm at our equinox and solstice gatherings these couple of times. I could feel the power of rhythm within you, and not because you are black, but because this sense of timing, rhythm, and steady beat comes from somewhere deep within you. It is yours."

Jeremy felt an excitement he had not experienced before. He flicked a glance to his right at Old Jim, and saw an old man with a long, white, flowing ponytail, the deep creases in Old Jim's face, and the crow's feet of age and wisdom.

They continued to walk along through the field, now through corn growing high on either side of the dirt road. The sky above was blue, with a few scattered clouds drifting past. Old Jim was still listening and his eyes shifted right and left as he walked.

"And this place," Jim said, "This place is something special too. I can feel how deep the roots go through this soil, into the earth. And it's not just the roots of the trees, or even these crops. It's the roots of people, people like you."

Jeremy's glanced sideways. "What do you mean, people like me? You mean black people? You mean slaves? What?"

"No, not slaves. And not black people *per se*. Though we are seeing a resurgence of black farmers in this country, which is a wonderful thing. But I do mean people like you who find the land calling to them. I do mean folks like Doug who have a non-rational connection to land or to a place that ties them to it. That's what I mean."

Jeremy relaxed a bit. He appreciated Jim's kookiness, and the way Jim thought about things. It was different to talk about being connected to the land, or connected to a place. Jeremy did feel that there was something that you couldn't point to, something you couldn't identify, that was like roots; that was like a cord that ties you to a place. Jeremy thought of his Granddad's nephew, who had a son who went back to a Farm Camp year after year. Even after he went off to a prestigious college in New York, he still felt connected to that camp, and to the kids who came to that camp. It was like a calling for him.

As they walked through the second windrow of trees and brush, Jeremy noted the stone wall that ran through the undergrowth, a straight line of built stones from centuries ago, marking the edge of a field where a team of horses once dragged a plow. Squirrels and chipmunks darted among the stones with acorns and other goodies to plant and hide for the upcoming winter. The wind ruffling the leaves in the trees added a level of background to the symphony of sounds. There was a moment of magic involved here. They were walking in the shade of the tall oaks, and the tall trees tossed gently in the wind, and the wind formed a kind of container all around them, a protection. They then emerged into a field of tall grasses – rye, Jeremy knew – and they kept walking. Through the trees ahead they could see the shimmer of the river itself.

Jeremy knew the Connecticut River really was at the heart of this story. It had been designated as the first American Blueway in the United States, in recognition of its iconic status. As the two progressed across this field heading toward the river's edge, Jeremy dropped into a reverie about the landscape and the history here. As he looked about him, from this vantage point, he couldn't see any human habitation or indeed, any other people.

Just as they neared the trees before them, a fox darted out from the undergrowth, a blur of beautiful burnt red with a bright white plume for the tip of the tail. It glanced briefly at them as it trotted away along the edge of the field. When it was 50 yards away, it stopped and turned, actually sitting down for a moment, watching them. Assessing them. Jim chuckled. "Wily old fox, seeing if we are going to pursue. We are not, dear friend. Go along your own way."

With that the fox turned and leaped into the bushes and undergrowth, out of sight.

Old Jim turned to Jeremy. "Fox has come to you today! He is reminding you of your strength and your ability to be strong and persevere. That is a good omen for you. It is not everyday that we see Fox, or that Fox shows itself to us. Take that energy into yourself, and feel the power of Fox in you."

Jeremy wasn't actually certain how he felt about all that, but he did think it was pretty cool to see a fox when he was out here on the farm. The tamed and the untamed.

They walked down to the water's edge, and noticed a motor boat offshore, about halfway across the river, and there were four men in the boat. The men were looking at the shoreline where they stood, and were gesturing and one was taking photos. The boat was gently gliding downstream with the current, then it turned and moved back upstream at about the same speed. The men continued to stare at the shore, and talk together, clearly interested in exactly where they stood.

Jeremy looked out. "What the…" he started, his voice trailing off.

Old Jim pursed his lips, slowly nodding to himself.

"If I'm correct, those are the developers who wanna buy this property. They are clearly taking in the optics of the site from the river. I hear they want to build a tall residential and office tower. They are checking out how it's going to look from the river view. Looks like they are also maybe thinking of a little marina, so the folks who live here can moor their boats for a spin on the river."

"Those bastards!" exclaimed Jeremy. "Acting like the land is theirs already. Doug hasn't even thought through what he's going to do at this point. He told me so. He's still going back and forth. He loves this land, and he wants to protect it forever. But he needs the money so he can retire in comfort. He's got some medical thing going on that he is worried will cost lots of money for treatment. He's caught between a rock and a hard place, he says. Those fuckers…"

Old Jim turned to Jeremy, his one eyebrow raised.

Jeremy looked down. "Sorry for the language. It's just that I feel for the old guy. He's crotchety, and kind of rough around the edges. But it's partly because he cares…Whereas those guys – they don't care! They only care about money, making money. It's bullshit."

Old Jim nodded, and then walked over to a tall oak. This tree spread wide above the bank and the river, and its trunk was broad enough that Jeremy and Jim could not have encircled it with their outstretched arms. Jim placed his hands against the trunk and leaned into them, eyes closed. He took a deep breath and smiled.

Turning back to Jeremy he said, "This old oak says not to worry, young man. It's been here for more than 100 years, and it will be here for 100 more."

CHAPTER 33

The pick-up truck towing the horse trailer rolled up to the barn and slowed to a stop. Sophia hopped out of the passenger's seat, and slammed the door. She paused and looked into the sliding windows and said something to the horse in the back. A Honda Accord turned into the drive just then, coming to a stop just a few feet from where Sophia stood, and Marion climbed out from the driver's seat, while Alice and Audrey climbed out of the back seat. Marion helped Beth from the passenger seat. Alice had invited Marion and Brodi to come along and bring Beth, to give Beth something to do in her new life here.

Jeremy dropped down from the driver's side of the pick-up and they all gathered at the rear of the horse trailer.

Sophia looked at all of them. "I can't believe this is happening! I am so excited that Lightning will be out here with all this land and the river close by. He's going to love it!"

Alice hugged her daughter. "This is the right thing for you both! I'll be sad that you are so far away from home; it used to be that going riding was 5 minutes over to Muddy Bottom Farm. This is 25 minutes away! But it's so good!" Her eyes welled up.

Sophia quickly hugged her mom, then turned. "I'm going to make sure the stable is ready. Jeremy, just keep Lightning calm." She ran off behind the barn.

Jeremy and Sophia had spent the last few weeks getting the stall and paddock ready. They had mucked out the stall, and spread new hay. Outside they had replaced a few posts, and had solidified the cross bars. Jeremy had actually replaced the hinges on the gate, which Doug had taught him with power drill, new iron hinges, and a level to make sure it hung level and true.

He unfastened the back gate on the horse trailer, and gently lowered the tailgate to the ground, forming a gentle slope. Lightning turned his head to see what was going on back there, but was closely tethered to the tiebar in the front of the trailer, so his actual movement was restricted. His giant muscled backside and black tail were in their faces.

Jeremy spoke soothingly to the horse. "Good boy, Lightning. We're at your new home."

Audrey walked over to the farmhouse, and called in through the open screen door.

"Hey, Dad! You in there?" A muffled voice from deep inside the house responded.

Audrey turned back to the assembled group in the drive. "He'll be out shortly."

She walked over behind the barn, too, to check out the paddock. At one time, in the long-distant past, she had two horses here, and had been the one to keep them up, grooming and riding for hours on end across the fields and trails through the local woods. As fall was upon them, she could sense that turning toward harvest and the shorter days. It was a feeling of tempered heat, and bluer sunlight, the leaves on the trees slowly moving away from the bright and deep greens of summer, and toward the subtle golden and crimson hues of autumn, the earth and dryness upon them. And her memory took her back to a time when she was the one cantering along the forest paths, jumping over fallen logs and branches on her horse, and feeling the warm sun dappling through the leaves, and the light splashing on the river. The smell of fall was an anchor for those memories.

How many seasons had turned in this place during her lifetime? How many summers had turned to fall, with shortening days, and the light coming more in a slant across the fields and through the trees. How many dry winds had whispered the coming chill, and taken the heat off the days? She was 50, so 50 summers. And she thought about her dad, now 82. 82 summers turning to fall. And then she imagined her grandparents, and great-grandparents who had also lived and worked on this farm. All those previous generations living and working through the growing seasons and feeling the hope and the bittersweet coming of the harvest. Dozens, perhaps hundreds of those summers and harvests, sun and wind and rain, heat and cold, drought and flooding, all of it coming in cycles and stretching back to when the first plows cut the first furrows on the first fields in the valley. She could imagine the forests which blanketed the valley floor when the Native people -- Nonotuck and Nipmuk and Pocumtuk -- were here. Trails and footpaths through hardwood and softwood stands, leading toward the great Connecticut River, and canoes moved through the waters. Fishing with nets and spears. Then as white people moved into the area there was clearing the trees, opening up farmland, displacing the Native population. Time swirled.

This was the kind of speculating that Audrey missed about the farm. She didn't miss too much else, really, and she knew that had to do with her Dad, who could be stern and cruel, and losing her Mom, who had been a very strong woman, and the ghost of her older brother. She had loved it, but had moved on.

Sophia ran back to the truck, and with Jeremy gently led Lightning out the back, talking to him over and over. Then she led him to a paddock next to the horse barn. She opened the gate and let the black horse loose to roam the enclosed space. It was a large oval with two other horses inside. Lightning was a pretty social creature, Sophia knew, so she wasn't concerned with how her horse would behave, but pecking orders sometimes needed to be respected, and the other two horses approached Lightning cautiously. There was some swishing of their long tails, and some neighing, some sudden jostling, but soon they all went back to munching on the hay that had been generously sprinkled along the fences of the paddock.

Doug appeared on the porch and waved to everyone. He showed no concern about the horses. He had been moving, riding and boarding horses since he was a kid. These three horses would figure out how to get along.

Doug gave his daughter a hug, and then went over to shake Beth's hand. It was a deliberate movement, even deferential, recognizing an elder peer. They smiled and talked in hushed tones together, and the others turned to the horses.

Marion stood next to Sophia, watching the horses. "Looks like they are going to get along."

"So far," Sophia responded. "Sometimes horses have some dominance/submission relationship to work out over time. It is hard to tell right off the bat, though they do look like they will be easy with one another."

Marion smiled. "You're relieved to see it."

Sophia shrugged. "To be honest, the other stable had kind of gone downhill, especially after the pandemic. It seemed like the folks running the stable kind of lost their way, somehow, and it felt neglected. I started to feel like Lightning was lonely, too. He needed some socialization, and this place feels very alive."

Marion gave a quizzical look. "Socialization? Like having friends?"

"Exactly! And that's the vibe I was getting from Lightning. He was lonely. You have to talk with the horse. You have to listen to what they are saying, too."

Alice overheard this conversation, and smiled. "And you could tell what Lightning was saying?"

Sophia nodded her head. "I know him, Mom. We're connected. He lets me know what's going on. He's happier here. He wanted to get out of there."

Alice smiled. "Of course he did! You are like your grandmother -- she could talk with the animals too. She would often talk to her tropical fish, her cats, her chicken and goats. She said they talked back to her, too. I believed her -- all her animals lived long and healthy lives."

Doug grunted. "My wife had that, too. Always made the horses less anxious. She could walk up to any new horse and within a minute or two just climb up and ride -- without a saddle! Said it was all about speaking with the horse with respect, and not making it do anything it didn't want to. I believed her."

Beth walked a little way away, and looked out over the corn fields toward the distant peaks of the mountains. "It's so peaceful here, and so beautiful. I can see why the horses like it. I feel like I could live here!"

Marion watched her mother. She was slightly in shock at the rapid de-escalation from a few days ago, when they were bringing her down to Amherst. The woman who was practically feral that day was standing here feeling the breeze on her face and appreciating normal conversation. Or as normal as a conversation about talking to horses and fish could be.

She walked over and put her arm around Beth again. "Mom, I am so glad you came along with us today! These people are all part of our lives."

Beth slipped her arm around Marion's waist. "Oh honey, you just can't know. This takes me back to my own early days in Dalton. Lots of kids had horses, or farms. This feels very natural."

Beth turned to Doug. "It's gorgeous farmland that should be protected! Farmland Forever, correct?" She looked around at the others. Doug looked down at his dirty work boots.

Alice smiled, "Well, Beth, that is certainly how we all feel! Heck, my kids are just now invested in this farm–Sophia's just brought her horse out here, and Jeremy's got a regular job."

Jeremy added, "And speaking of which, I got to get back to work!" And he trotted off to the barn.

Doug looked at Jeremy's retreating back and said, "You know, I am just trying to figure out what the plan is, for when I retire. I'm old– almost 83–and it's too much for me, special as it is. Only a couple of choices, so if any of you have an idea on what to do, you let me know."

Marion turned to Beth, and gently took her arm, "Mom, let's go over and see the horses," and walked Beth a little ways away closer to where the horses stood together.

Alice looked at Doug, "So, Doug. What about that Agricultural Preservation Restriction that Ben's been mentioning? Doesn't that help?"

Doug smiled. "Guess there's shop talk around the dinner table at home, eh? Well, yes, that'll help if I decide to work with the Valley Land Trust folks, yes. But there's real money on the other side."

Alice said, "Look, it's none of my business! Money talks and people walk as they say. But this farm is gorgeous and you feel how special it is."

"Damn it, I can! But you just don't walk away from $5 million without taking a second look!"

"$5 million! Oh my God, Dad! That's what they are offer- ing?" Audrey was shocked. "That's unbelievable!" Audrey walked away from the others, almost stumbling in shock.

Alice asked, "I am sorry, I had no idea. Is the land worth THAT much to develop?"

"I guess it is to them," Doug shrugged.

"I can't believe it. No wonder you're not sure which is the right way to go," Alice agreed.

Doug stood slowly shaking his head. His lips pursed. Audrey had seen that expression before. Her dad, normally taciturn, had said more than he planned to.

"Dad. Let's you and I talk for a minute."

Alice took the cue and turned on her heel to join Marion and Beth some ways away.

Audrey nodded, half to herself, and steered her dad along the dirt track past the barn. "Dad, I love you, even when you are a mean bastard. And you can do whatever you want with this farm. I want you to be happy. What do you want to do?" She said, putting her hand on his arm.

"Oh, I don't know," Doug replied, patting her hand on his fore-arm. "Some days it's the land, some days it's the cash. To be honest, I get mad at you and Ryan for not wanting to continue with farming. Then I'm mad at myself for driving you both away. You were neither of you farmers. It's hard work. And thankless most of the time."

Audrey sighed deeply. "No, we are not farmers. We had different paths to tread."

Doug nodded, "Hell, yeah. And your mom and I raised you to be smart, independent thinkers. We encouraged you to get the most out of school, and to follow your dreams." He laughed. "I guess you both did just that! So I can't really blame you."

Audrey said, "Well, thanks for saying that now. At the time it seemed like you blamed us for not toeing the line here."

Doug nodded. ""Yep. I know it felt that way. But after your mom passed I wasn't much good for anything for awhile. I knew you and Ryan needed something else, but I had no idea how to get that for you. So I got hard and stubborn."

Audrey agreed. "Yes you did. And now here you are facing your own next stage." They walked a moment in silence. "So, what's your thinking?"

Doug shrugged. "Dunno. I go back and forth. Money -- the land. To be honest, I was hoping someone could help me make a decision. What do you think?"

"I'm not sure. I can't believe they offered that much money for this place! It's upsetting somehow. I'm in shock!"

Doug turned to glance at Audrey, "I didn't want to burden you with the details, but yes, they have offered almost $5 million for the farm. It's such an outrageous sum that I couldn't believe it at first. And I do wish you and Ryan were in this with me!"

"Dad! I love this place! I love all the energy you put into this land, and how hard you and Mom worked everyday, and took care of us! But we left and I support you in WHATEVER you want to do!"

The rain that had been threatening all morning now started to fall. Big drops at first, immediately moistening the soil. It quickly moved into a steady downfall, and they turned to run for the barn. Marion, Beth and Alice moved quickly into the shelter of the indoors.

As they all shook off the raindrops, Audrey moved her dad again a little ways away from the others.

"Dad, this is a big decision, but we will back you up. We want what's best for you."

Doug nodded. "And I have to consider this land, too. Our family has been here for 7 generations. That is a long stretch to be here with your roots in the dirt. I feel a responsibility for this land. I know things change, that we can't be holding on to the past --" here his voice wavered, "But I just wish *something* had stayed permanent."

Audrey stepped right next to her dad. "I miss Mom, too, Dad. I think about her all the time. I feel her presence on this farm. Like she's still here with you."

Doug added, "And your older brother. I mean Mike was a kind of question mark. I don't know if he would have decided to become a farmer, take over the farm, but I feel like he would have. It's left me adrift in many ways. Heck, I didn't expect to be here now having buried those two before me." Doug's face showed the grief and the pain. Audrey gave her father a big hug, then looked into his eyes.

After a moment, they walked to re-joined the others. "That rain was threatening all morning," Doug observed. "Glad you all got it to shake down."

"It's a good late summer rain," Beth observed. "Obviously the ground's ready to soak it up."

Sophia had walked Lightning back into the barn, and was wiping the horse down. The horse was frisky from the cool rain, and danced away from her as she rubbed his coat. They could hear her laughing and talking with the horse. She finished and tied the horse in his stall, talking with him as she freshened his water and got some oats to put in the feed tray. She stayed beside the stall and talked to him in low tones as he settled in to eat.

"Guess he's feeling pretty at home," Marion observed.

Doug nodded. "Horses have a sense when things are OK."

"Guess you know horses pretty well," Alice added.

"Been around them my whole life," Doug agreed. "You get to know 'em. Besides, they let you know when something's not right. They are very clear."

Beth stepped over to Doug, gently touching his arm. "Sometimes the animals have something to teach us, do they not?"

Doug tipped back his cap, scratched his head, and replaced the cap. "You ladies, I guess, are here to keep me focused on this whole thing. That's what my wife would have done, too. She'd have kept at me to make up my mind. 'Make up your mind, Doug,' she'd have said. 'It doesn't help to dither around. You just look in your heart and decide.' Then she'd go about her business."

The women looked at one another, eyebrows raised.

"I guess that's our cue. Sophia, are you staying out here and riding home with your brother, or do you want to come home with us?" Alice called out to her daughter.

CHAPTER 34

The three businessmen from Georgia were once again scoping out the farm with clipboards and architectural drawings unfurled across the hood of the black Cadillac Escalade.

Doug Stengel exited the farmhouse, dressed in a collared shirt and slacks this morning, although the dirt and oil on his hands belied the hours of work he had already put in since sunrise. He was accompanied by another man with a briefcase, an attorney in pressed slacks and crisp white shirt. His expensive Salvatore Ferragamo tasseled moccasins bespoke his status more clearly than anything. The two of them walked across the drive to the awaiting Georgians, handshakes all around.

There were pleasantries, followed by some minor, then bolder joking. At one point the three Georgians were all laughing hard, while the two local men smiled and nodded. Perhaps the out-of-towners, in the shared moment of humor and camaraderie, failed to notice the lack of full engagement with this male bonding ritual being enacted. Perhaps, being from the major metropolis of Atlanta, they, once again, misjudged the two men from this rural Massachusetts farming community. It became clear to the tallest of the group after some moments that it was time to shift energies, to set them all on the same page.

"Doug," John Engle said, "We're real happy to be here to discuss our offer and our plan for the transfer of the property. Yesterday we went to the town offices and began the process of submitting our applications for permits and the staging of construction, of course contingent on your willingness to sell. We are very excited to come to you with what we consider to be a generous offer. Are we ready to discuss terms at this point?"

Doug smiled broadly and nodded his head. "Well, I guess we can all agree that this is a big discussion. You know I'm a farmer, so I don't necessarily move fast like you guys from the big city. You have talked about your offer, and have hinted that you really want to buy this property. When you say, 'Discuss terms,' I think you mean, am I ready to sell?"

John looked at the other two for agreement, "Well, yes. Aren't we on the same page with that? Is there something we missed? " John seemed genuinely confused. The others glanced between themselves.

Doug smiled a not-really-friendly smile. "Well, you see, I know you have offered me $5 million for this property. And I have looked over your plans for the property – the landscaping, the buildings, the mixed-use development, marina and café. It's very impressive…"

"Doug, let's face it. The $5 million is so much more than you could ever hope to get for this property from any other developer. No one else has the vision of scope, nor do they have the resources to bring to bear on this kind of development. We hired a local architectural firm, we are in discussion with local building contractors, and we have approached the local town government to begin the permitting process. We are on top of this whole enterprise. We have made numerous trips up here to keep you in the loop personally especially since Wayne Thibodeaux passed away. I think we have been very transparent."

"That is very true," Doug said, nodding in agreement. "Transparent. You've been crystal clear in what you want to do with this property." He paused for a moment.

"The thing is," he started back in, "When Wayne and I were talking together, it seemed more personal. He may have had the same vision as you," here he waved his hand over the architectural drawings, "But he gave me the feeling that he actually cared about what had come before."

The Georgians seemed momentarily taken aback. John again jumped in, "Well, I can assure you that Wayne and I had numerous consultations back in the office in Atlanta to discuss this operation, and the progress of his conversations with you, Doug. While he is no longer with us, I can tell you I feel I know what his intentions were."

"Do you?" Doug looked mildly skeptical.

"Well, to the best I could." John countered. "We have attempted to pick up where Wayne had left off; carry on despite his being gone."

"Yup. I could see that," Doug said. "I could see there wasn't much love lost between you two."

John looked down and scratched his forehead. Pursed his lips. "We were business partners, Doug, not family."

"No, I could see that. " Doug tilted his head to one side. "I could see that this was a financial deal to you all, while I had been getting the feeling that Wayne had a bit more soul in it. He could feel a connection to this land that he was trying to understand.

"I'll bet you maybe didn't know that Wayne came from farming?" Doug watched the surprise register on John's face. "Yep. His grandfather was a farmer in some small Georgia farm town – Senoia, I think. When we walked this land he would reminisce about going to his granddad's land when he was a boy, and how rich that farmland was. Red dirt. They were still raising cotton there, tho' it wasn't with slaves anymore, and they raised corn, peanuts and some cattle, too. I could see the memories slipping back in for Wayne. I got interested in what this land was doing, working on him as he spent time here. That was why I kept our conversations going. I don't know what he relayed back to you, but I hadn't made any promises. A lot of 'un-huh,' and 'that sounds interesting.' I made no commitment to him at all."

John responded seemingly frustrated. "Oh, of course I knew that, Doug. But Wayne was always the dreamer in the office partnership. It wasn't like this was the first deal he had some hair-brained idea about. But he was up here so often I was pretty sure he had given you a fair outline of our plans, and also let you know how much we were willing to offer. You won't see anything else like this coming along."

Doug shrugged. "Nope, I guess I won't. And I don't mean to be hasty, because that amount of money is really something to ponder. I never in a million years thought we'd realize that kind of capital from selling this land. Never."

"So what's the hesitation, Doug?" John pushed for an advantage.

"Well, son," Doug looked at him. "I don't know exactly. Maybe my own ties to this land don't feel quite finished yet. I'm just not quite ready to sign on the dotted line, if you know what I mean. There is just something tickling the back of my mind and I don't think I've fully determined what it is yet."

"Doug, I can see you have your lawyer here. Let's do this. We can hand over to your team our offer," here he turned to Mick, his second-in-command, reaching for a folder containing documents which were handed over from a briefcase. "And you and your team, your lawyer, can look these over and see what we are offering. It's legitimate. You can have the full amount in your bank account within 6-9 months. We would take over all the permitting, the land testing, and ownership accountability. It's an outstanding deal."

John extended the folder to Doug, who looked at it, looked up at John, and then took it, immediately handing it back to the lawyer.

"Fair enough." Doug said. They shook hands.

"We'll expect to hear from you," John said as they turned to go.

With brief nods to the others, the Georgians got back into the giant black behemoth, the driver climbed into the car, they turned and left the driveway, picking up speed as they headed down the road.

Doug turned to his lawyer, "No rush."

He walked away then, a man inside himself, some inner question wrestling with him. He was a man possessed in this moment, possessed by a choice, possessed by a dilemma, possessed with two worlds opening before him. And this choice, this need to make a decision felt large. Monumental. He could feel the gestational weight of a decision coming, pushing, forcing him before it, with two futures opening up.

Doug felt his age, and felt his tiredness. He felt the decades of farm work claiming his body and his mind. He could feel the earth pulling him down, gravity claiming what was rightfully its own, what he had spent his entire life working toward. As he turned and began to walk toward the river, he could feel his body moving through the air, through the slight breeze blowing, and through time. He could feel the closeness of his Fran, now 20 years gone, and the specters of his children, alive and dead, walking by his side. He had to decide, he knew that, but the truth was that he hadn't decided yet. No one knew that, no one knew what was inside his mind, or his heart. The truth was he was an independent thinker, and a very quiet man. Fran had known him best, because she had studied him, up close, for 40 years. She had watched him, and stood by his side. And were she here with him, now, in this moment, walking through this early fall afternoon heat and light, sun glistening off the river through the row of trees, a bright spot seen through the darkened hedgerow, she would have known his mind was troubled, just by watching the furrow on his brow, and the way his hands trembled by his side. He was unsettled.

As he walked, deep in his reverie, he glanced up to see Jeremy astride the tractor in the field up ahead. Jeremy, a young man entering the prime of his life, rode the tractor with an air of confidence and self-assuredness that hadn't been there just months before. Jeremy was carefully harvesting the corn in the field, and the tall golden rows were falling before the steady march of the combine harvester. Doug looked at the young man, and he simultaneously saw himself at that age. He saw himself as that young man, astride the combine, and mowing down a similar track of corn rows, decades in the past, in a similar heat, in a similar sun, sweat glistening his brow, his shirt sticking *just so* to his back, and his eyes squinting into the bright.

The overlay of now and then, present and past, gave Doug a glimpse of something glimmering, like the river through the darkened trees before him. His mind was clouded with worry, with angst, but there was something out there, ahead of him, that was clarity, that was definitive. It tickled his mind like a good Bob Dylan song lyric, catching his attention and not letting it go. He wanted to know the *right* decision. He wanted his children to want what he had wanted, or maybe to feel the sense of obligation he had felt to his own father. To his grandparents. And their grandparents. Keep the family line going. But that wasn't Ryan, and that wasn't Audrey. So different, so independent, both with a streak of stubbornness they got from him, and a streak of the dreamer they inherited from Fran. And they both seemed to be living full and enriched lives. So why was it important to him that they be the ones to carry on the farm? Why was blood necessary? It wasn't like actual blood was used to water the soil. But we pretended that actual blood was what tied us together, didn't we? *Blood is thicker than water,* we'd say. *Blood runs deep. Family is family.*

"So what?" Doug wondered aloud. The sound of his own voice startled him.

He looked ahead and saw Jeremy mowing down the rows of golden corn, slowly and steadily making his way across the field, not allowing the heat of the day, or the brightness of the sun distract him from doing a perfect job that Doug's father would have been proud to see. That young man is letting his roots sink into this soil even now, thought Doug.

At that moment, Doug caught a movement in the trees down by the river, and Sophia appeared riding Lightning, emerging from the darkened woods onto the trail. The movement also drew Jeremy's eye, and he looked up and waved to his sister. The beautiful black horse was trotting, muscles rippling under its coat, and then it slowed to a walk as Sophia tugged on the reins. The girl waved back at her brother, then brought the horse to a standstill. Jeremy cut the engine on the combine, and grabbing a water bottle he hopped off and trotted himself to where the girl and horse stood. He stopped next to the horse, taking a pull on the water bottle while his sister animatedly talked to him, gesturing with her riding crop along the river.

Doug couldn't hear what they were saying from this distance. In his slight reverie, he was captured by the tableau of sister, brother, and horse. He wished for a moment that he was a painter, or even a photographer, and could capture the moment he was witnessing. There was a poignancy there. These two siblings, siblings by choice, by their parents' choices, by love, were laughing together, and smiling. Bonds of family, not of blood. At one moment Sophia looked up toward Doug, shielding her eyes from the sun, and then waved to him. Jeremy also looked over and waved. Doug smiled and waved back, then decided to walk over.

"Morning, you two," he said smiling. "How was the ride, Sophia?" He patted the horse along its strong neck, feeling the muscles and strength in the animal.

"So beautiful!" she exclaimed. "We went down to the river and rode along the footpath heading north. I love the woodland you have preserved back there. We stopped to talk to that old oak tree there. It was just glorious, and we were the only ones out there."

"Don't think a lot of people know about that path anymore," said Doug. "When there were more farms along the river, there was more traffic. It's been a long time now, though. Fewer and fewer folks. Even less traffic on the river itself, surprisingly."

Doug turned to Jeremy. "Doing a fine job on the harvest, son. "

Jeremy smiled, and looked proud of himself. "Well, I want to be careful. It seems like it'll be a good crop this year, and it's already getting on to early fall harvest time. It needs to be harvested now."

"My brother, the farmer!" Sophia laughed. "I never in a million years would have thought that."

Jeremy looked down at his boots and scuffed the dirt. "I guess I like it. It's – satisfying. You can definitely see what you've done. Like you can mark it off."

Doug nodded. "Yep. I think that's right. There's satisfaction at the end of the day when you can look and see what you've done."

They stood looking out across the field in the sun, the light green of the corn standing tall against the brown rows of cut-off stalks where Jeremy had already passed. The sky was crystal blue, the morning fog having burned off and the sun was heating things up. A slight breeze blew and kept a freshness in the air. They could smell the cut corn. The wind died down, and the chirping of the birds in the trees came to them across the field. The gestalt was overwhelming in its beauty and in its simplicity. They all felt it. Even Lightning seemed to share it, and turned its head as if to look across the fields as well.

* * *

When she approached the barn, Sophia saw Audrey and some guy walking around the side of the barn, stopping when they saw her.

"Hey Sophia!" Audrey said. "How is it going?"

"Fantastic!" Sophia replied. "It's real pretty down by the river. "

"That's so true! This is Ryan, my brother, up from New York. Ryan, this is Sophia."

"Nice to meet you, Sophia." Ryan said. "What's your horse's name?"

"Good to meet you too. His name's Lightning," Sophia said. "Did you live here too when you were little?"

"Oh yeah," Ryan said. "Audrey's my big sister. We grew up right here, and Audrey used to ride horses just like you. I had to get out of this cow-town and get off to the big city, though. Bright lights! Big city!" He waved his glad hands side to side in a funny way.

Sophia laughed at the gesture. "So are you just back to visit, or what?"

Ryan shook his head. "You know, Sophia, I don't really know. I came back to see my big sister here. And now here I am back home again. It's kind of spooky, and it's kind of cool."

"It's totally cool! I love riding my horse here, and he loves riding here, in the woods near the river." She looked around, the breeze gently blowing her own chestnut hair behind her.

"Sophia, you look like you were meant to be here," Audrey remarked. "Seeing you on that horse and looking out at the distant trees reminds me of riding here as a girl. I felt so special, and like the whole world was mine."

Sophia looked at Audrey, her brow knitted together. "Yeah! That is totally it! I can't believe how right it feels. And you two, back together as brother and sister, it's like something out of a fantasy."

Ryan smiled and cleared his throat. "Uh, yeah. Well, I am back after 15 years, and in that way it's kind of a fantasy, but really? It's spooky, too."

Audrey looked at her brother, and protectively slung her arm around his shoulders. "Little bro', I am thrilled you came back! You can't believe how much we've missed you, and how you coming back makes everything fit together somehow. It's like a piece of the puzzle has been found. A piece I now realize was missing."

Sophia was bent over at the waist, leaning on the pommel of the saddle and looking at them. "Brother and sister. Like Jeremy and me. We're really different, but we're also tied together by some invisible bond. You know, he's not actually my brother by blood." She said this with eyes wide and with no irony.

Audrey looked back wide-eyed and slowly nodded her head. "Really? You two look so much alike!"

Sophia made a grimace. "You know what I mean!" She shook her head in mock disbelief.

Ryan seemed confused, and looked back and forth between them. "Am I missing something?"

Audrey smiled. "Never mind."

At that moment the tractor came into view around the end of the row of trees and headed toward them on the farm road. The drone of the tractor motor got louder as it approached, the driver bouncing up and down as he drove over the ruts and potholes in the road. As he got closer, Jeremy could be seen smiling and looking happy. His shirt was damp with sweat and he looked tired in the afternoon sun, but his smile was broad and warm.

He cut the motor as he pulled up a short distance away.

As he jumped down he said, "Hey Audrey! What are you doing out here?"

Audrey smiled back, "Hi Jeremy! Thought I'd drop by and see how things were going. This is Ryan."

"Hi Ryan!" Jeremy approached wiping his hands on a rag that was hanging out of the back pocket of his jeans. "I'm Jeremy. Work for your -- dad, I guess."

Momentarily taken aback, Ryan proffered his hand and shook Jeremy's. "Nice to meet you." He looked back and forth between Sophia and Jeremy. "Brother and sister?"

"Yeah, notice the family resemblance?" Jeremy smiled and tilted his head toward Sophia, who tilted her head back, smiling.

Ryan laughed. "OK, whatever. So you work on the farm here?"

Jeremy nodded. "Yep. I like Doug, uh, your dad. He's totally cool. Did you work on the farm when you were a kid?"

Ryan laughed. "Yes I did, and you are welcome to it! I hated the farm work. I hated always being dirty, and having to get up early every morning to do chores. I hated that the work was never done! And then there was dear old dad. Never a warm fuzzy dad at the best of times."

He looked around. "It is a gorgeous place, but I am still glad I don't live here anymore!"

Jeremy looked around thoughtfully. "And I don't want to leave."

"You know Jer," Sophia pursed her lips, "Even when we were kids, you liked helping Mom in the garden. You loved watching the tomatoes getting redder and redder through the summer. So this thing you have for this farm, and this land, maybe it makes some sense." With that being said, she turned and led the horse to the barn.

Jeremy smiled broadly, and shook his head slowly. "I hadn't thought of that. But she's right. I did love helping Mom in the garden, and it always seemed a bit miraculous the way the plants sprouted, and then grew, leafed out, and then bam! Fruit would appear! I loved that."

Ryan looked at Jeremy. "Sometimes our sisters know us better than we know ourselves." He then glanced over to Audrey.

"C'mon bro, let's go find Dad. I think I know where he might be." She tilted her head in the direction of the river, along the dirt farm road. They turned together and started walking in that direction.

Jeremy watched them walk off, then he turned back to the barn. As he went from the bright sun into the relative darkness of the barn, he paused while his eyes adjusted to the dimness.

"Hey," Sophia said. She was standing next to Lightning, brushing his sleek coat while he ate some hay from a pile by his front hooves. The horse looked over at Jeremy at that moment, as though assessing the likelihood of Jeremy's interrupting this quiet tableau.

"Hey," Jeremy walked over to the fridge and pulled out his lunch in a brown paper bag. He turned and sat on the picnic table tucked into the corner, sitting on the table top with his feet on the seat, facing Sophia.

"So it was a good move coming here?" He began rummaging in the lunch bag.

"Lovely. Really lovely. I wish I could come out and ride every day."

"You can if you want to. Doug wouldn't mind."

"Oh I know," Sophia said wistfully. "But I can't drive just yet, and I need to work after school to make money, so I have that stupid job. It's too far to come on my own, so I need transportation. But riding makes me feel so happy!"

Jeremy was digging into a sandwich, and obviously relishing the experience. "Well, maybe you could come out here to work too. Maybe Doug would take you on as another farm hand, like me, and then you could ride when your work day is done. Plus, Jake is here…"

Sophia cocked her head to think about it. "Maybe…I am not sure that working on a farm is what I want to do with my life, though. And let's leave Jake out of this discussion!"

"And working for Dunkin' Donuts...?"

"I'm not going to work there forever! I just needed a job and they hire anybody. Besides, it's 5 minutes from our house. I can bike there."

"You could drive out here with me, so that wouldn't be a problem. Doug's got me working almost every day now."

"Yeah, I guess so. It looks like really hard work though. You always come home dirty and sweaty. And sometimes you fall asleep before dinner after working all day."

"That's only on the really hot days when I've been in the sun all day. That really tires me out. Besides, you couldn't do some of the work I do. You're not strong enough."

Sophia bristled at that. "Screw you! I am plenty strong enough and you know it!"

Jeremy was fishing in the bag for a bag of chips, and found an apple. Sophia made sure there was water in a bucket near the horse, and went to get her lunch from the fridge. Fetching a cloth lunch bag, she climbed onto the picnic table too.

"Sorry," Jeremy mumbled. "It's just really hard work and I haven't seen you ever do really hard stuff like this. It's hard even for me. I'm sure you could do it, if you tried."

They continued to eat in silence for a few minutes.

Sophia said, "You know, you can be a real shit sometimes. I feel like I could be really something, and working with horses might be it. I can ride, and I've taken enough lessons so I could teach riding too. I want to be useful, and I want to be self-supporting. I want to do good in the world, and working with animals and people seems like a good way to do that. Screw it! I can work hard."

"All I mean is you have to stick with it, is all," Jeremy responded, contrite.

CHAPTER 35

There is that undefined yet unmistakable moment in the afternoon, when it was clear it had turned to late afternoon, and the sun was more rapidly setting, headed toward the horizon, signaling the end of another day. Three people walked and crested a small rise, and Doug came into view. He was standing with his hands shoved into the back pockets of his worn jeans, looking away from them. The sun was behind the tall oaks and maples at their backs. Doug was in shadow; his profile was outlined against the brightly illuminated trees across the river. The river was bathed in golden sunlight as well, and the sun's rays glistened off the rolling waves in the river.

The three approached Doug, who seemed caught in reverie. When they got closer, Christy Brown called out, "Hello Mr. Stengel!"

Somewhat startled, Doug swiveled around and seeing them, smiled.

"Hello Christy! Ben! Brodi!" His broad smile was matched with the big hand extended to them, clearly glad to see them. "Nice surprise!"

Shaking hands all around, Doug half turned back to the river. "Isn't it glorious this time of day!"

"Truly lovely," murmured Christy. "You know, I had a hunch to come out here today to see you, and I called Ben and invited him along. He doesn't actually know I didn't call ahead."

Doug smiled a reply, "Well, turns out I'm glad to see you."

Ben felt a wave of relief. He hated socially uncomfortable situations. Christy Brown was the President of Valley Conservation Land Trust, well-known and respected throughout the Pioneer Valley.

"So, how are you doing, Mr. Stengel? I haven't seen you in awhile, and I hear all kinds of things from Ben, here." Christy was turning on the charm.

"Well, not too much is going on, as it turns out. Just trying to move the farm towards the harvest, and not get killed in the process. How are your folks?" Doug and Christy's father had known each other forever as old Hadley farm families.

"Oh they are good. Getting on, you know. Dad said to say "Hi" when I told him I might see you. So are things going OK? I met your farmhand back there – Jeremy – Ben's son. He's a good worker?"

"He's great! Works hard! Wish my other two were half as motivated."

"Wish I could get him to be as enthusiastic about chores at home!" Ben added in.

Doug winked at Christy. To Ben: "I think if you paid him, you'd unearth that enthusiasm."

They all chuckled.

"True enough."

Brodi interceded, "So how is the harvest going, Doug?"

Doug nodded as he spoke, "Well, to be honest, may be the best crop in many a year. You know, for once it seems the weather pattern was perfect. We'd get hot sun, dry everything out, then clouds and rain for a few days to soak the soil just right, then out come the sun again and the pattern would repeat. Craziest thing. That's why we got two full crops of hay and two full crops of corn this year. "

"And the help?" Christy pressed. Doug turned to look at her directly, now, appraisingly. Her head was slightly tilted to one side, a lock of auburn hair fell across her face, which she deftly tucked behind her ear.

Doug had always appreciated Christy's easy-going, nature woman vibe. She was always a little tan, accentuating her freckles, and wore clothes that spoke to her outdoorsy orientation. Heading up the local land trust was something she seemed to do with ease. What Doug was also appreciating in this moment, was the keen and incisive mind he sensed in this line of inquiry. Under the guise of interest in him, she was assessing the farm as well.

He smiled. "You know, I've had two local Hadley boys out here for a few seasons. They're good workers and come by farming honestly. Both their families have farmed, so it's in the blood, so to speak. I think Matt and Jake are both gonna get married and settle down here, raise a family. Maybe farm….

"But I'll tell you one thing, and it's not because you're here, Ben. " He turned a strong eye to Ben, then flicked his glance to Brodi. "And I know you know Jeremy as well, Brodi.""

"He's like family to me as well," Brodi chimed in.

"So, I could kind of feel it in my gut when I met him. He's drawn to this land; it's speaking to him. And he understands that, and he talks right back. That young man is having a conversation with the land it-self. It's responding. It's responding to someone who knows what he means. His love of this land and this work; it's in his soul. It's really special. Most farmers don't talk about it; it seems kind of silly and a bit crazy, but that sense of belonging doesn't come to everyone."

"So what are you saying Doug?" Christy's eyebrow furrowed in a question.

"It's not completely clear in my mind yet," Doug said. "I was thinking I wanted you to come out here and walk with me for a bit. And here you are! Help me formulate what this all means."

He turned to face the river. The Connecticut flowed by, ever in motion, ever shifting as the great waters flowed by. A fisherman in a rowboat sat anchored across the water, his fishing pole extended over the bow. The big oak stood nearby, standing sentinel to the passage of time of generations. The four of them looked out over this scene, reminded perhaps of so many days and years that this same scene had been re-played on this river. The landscape here had been undeniably altered dramatically by farming, and agriculture. But that had been for well over 300 years. Standing here, Doug could almost imagine the endless forests that had covered this landscape before that time, but still this view was what most people had known for centuries. Thomas Cole had painted this view in the mid-1800's as *The Oxbow*, one of the most iconic Hud-son River School paintings of that time. Those paintings had defined the vision of this area, and that to the west, for that century. And Doug felt the weight, the responsibility of this in his bones. He had no inkling 70 years ago that he would hold one of the keys to the future of this valley in his hands. Not that it was his alone, of course, but clearly some of the responsibility to decide fate and future lay with him. He didn't take this lightly.

He turned at this moment to Ben. "If it was your land, what would you do?"

Ben looked for a long moment into Doug's eyes. He said, "This is the story of countless farmers and children of farmers every-where. The farming lifestyle is hard work, with no real guarantees for success, and no assurances that if things went well this year, that you could count on things going well next year. It's a tough call, Doug."

Ben sighed, brushed back his close-cropped gray hair, "Doug, I don't know what you are thinking relative to the decision you face on selling this land. I can't imagine what it would mean to have my life and the lives of my family changed, altered forever, through the decision of handing the land over to someone, and leaving the future to them. I think those developers are presenting an excellent case for their vision of this property. Homes, condos, commercial development, a marina. It all sounds pretty wonderful. I'm sure the plans and drawings they have created give a visual look at what they are proposing. Drawings are useful, and you can visualize the transformation of how this property could go forward. And lots of cash for you…"

Doug smiled at that. "Yep. More money than I could ever have dreamed about in my lifetime or my kids' lives." He scratched his brow, making a confused face.

Ben continued. "And, Doug, I find myself in a strange position now. I never in a million years would have predicted that my kids would now be wrapped in this discussion. Who knew?"

Doug smiled appreciatively. And chuckled. "You're right there. And I love seeing 'em around here. They are like grandkids to me. They seem to love this land. Those other two young men work hard, and they don't goof around. But it's really just a job for them. But your kids…it's something else for them. Can't completely explain it."

Doug cocked his head to one side. "Let's walk back," he said and they climbed back up the embankment and into the warm sun. Ben and Brodi looked at one another, and fell behind Christy and Doug who walked ahead.

Ben said in a lowered voice, "What do you think's going on here?"

Brodi turned slightly toward Ben, "Sounds like he's thinking about the legacy of the land. How to harvest that legacy. He's thinking about the way this land will be held going forward. I'm not hearing that the money's the real thing for him."

"No, I don't think so," Ben agreed.

As they walked back on the dirt road, they saw the red fox trot out from the trees on the right, pausing in the sunshine momentarily to look their way. Although it was some ways off, they could see the lush orange-red fur in the sunlight, and the white flashes in its muzzle. Then it turned and abruptly disappeared into the corn on the far side of the road, out of sight.

"Oh, so pretty," Christy remarked. "I never get tired of seeing those wild creatures hereabouts.

"And those foxes are not generally very social. They keep to themselves mostly, and do their hunting by night," she added. "We see them coming through our back yard occasionally, but mostly I see them on my way home at night, crossing in front of the car."

Doug nodded slowly. "I always liked the fox. The fox is careful, and plans ahead. Relies on its intuition, but is fierce and protective of its young. You can't really surprise a fox, because their sense is so well-tuned into its environment. They have excellent hearing, and keen eyesight. And they are great with camouflage; they can seem to disappear, just like that fellow up there. Foxes are skilled at appearing and disappearing like that. A fox will protect the den to death, which is unusual in the animal kingdom. A fox is loyal, and very connected to its homeland."

Christy turned to Doug, "So does all that give you any ideas, or what?"

Doug smiled and gently shook his head. "Me? No! Or at least, I don't think so. I mean who knows what's going on with a fox? Could be he's just out hunting supper for himself and his brood."

"Well, you were just talking about Jeremy and Sophia practically being like family."

Doug nodded, "I was, wasn't I?" He asked the question, really, of himself.

Ben and Brodi looked again at one another. Ben raised one eyebrow in a questioning face.

Doug caught the movement out of the corner of his eye. He chuckled.

"Old man going crazy?"

Ben turned bright red. "Sorry Doug, " he stammered. "I am just a bit confused here. I thought you were certainly heading for selling your farm to the big developers, but now I have no idea what you are planning, or why we're here."

Doug nodded. "Well, that's just about right. You see, Ben, I like you folks, and I can certainly see your point in wanting me to sell my land to you and your organization. You make all the good arguments for preservation, conservation. And Christy is an excellent steward of this valley and all its resources. And I trust her, ever since she was a kid she had a righteous streak."

He gave a one shouldered shrug. "But you're not offering much money!" Here he laughed out loud.

"And those guys," he waved generally off into the distance, "They're offering me almost five million! Five million dollars! "

He turned and continued walking toward the farmstead. The three of them fell into pace alongside Doug.

Christy spoke, "That's a lot of cash Doug. There is no way we can come anywhere near that amount. Not in five million years! Doug, what we have to offer is that this farm, this land, this valley will remain in this condition forever. In perpetuity is the phrase. And as the Executive Director of the Valley Conservation Land Trust I can tell you this is a powerful thing. In partnering with the state of Massachusetts with their Agricultural Preservation Restriction you can stay living here, we'll help you with the legal documents, and we'll work to transition the running of the farm to whomever is next. "

She turned to Ben and raised an eyebrow.

Ben nodded. "As we have said, Doug, the Valley Conservation Land Trust has preserved 100's of properties in this valley. This property is beautiful, and so pristine. You have stewarded it well. That development would inevitably pollute the river with construction runoff, and then the groundwater would be affected too."

Ben glanced at Brodi. Brodi took up the cue.

"Doug, I am not obviously a main part of this, except that Ben's my best friend, and I love those kids like they were my own." She nodded in the direction of the farm house. "This property is iconic in a way, the farm fields along the river, your sustainable woodlands, the red barn and wooden fencing. Oh my God! It is so lovely it brings tears to my eyes. And to think you have the ability to preserve this for posterity. What a gift! That has to stand for something!"

Doug came to a stand still. He looked back and forth from Ben to Brodi. "You two are a tag team!" He looked at Ben. "You are over here with the moral argument." Then turning to Brodi, "And you are the voice of beauty!" Doug shook his head. "Perilous waters here!"

Turning to Christy he said, "I can see you brought your A Team!" She smiled.

He began to trudge along to the barn again. Up ahead the red barn came into view, the afternoon sun glinting off the sides of the crimson building. They could see Jeremy doing something with the tractor, and Sophia walking Lightning and putting the horse into the horse pen alongside the barn. Jake was walking with her.

As they walked closer Audrey and Ryan came into view as well. They had been sitting on the picnic table in the shade, their butts on the table itself, and their feet propped on the seats, obviously in an intense discussion about something. Ryan was gesticulating with his forearms and hands as he spoke, and Audrey sat with her arms folded across her chest. At one point she raised an index finger and made a point. They looked up when the foursome caught their attention. Audrey made a final point, then got up, brushing the dust off the seat of her pants. She squinted into the sun toward the approaching adults.

"Hey! You look pretty serious! Make any big decisions out there?"

"You'd be surprised!" Doug responded. "Or maybe not!"

Doug motioned Jeremy and Sophia over. "You two come over here a minute."

The two teens glanced at one another, but slowly walked over to the awaiting adults.

Doug looked squarely at Ryan. "Hello, son," He began. "How you doing?"

"I'm OK Dad," Ryan replied cautiously. "How are you? "

"I'm good, I'm good," Doug smiled. "You know I never told you that I had read your last book. Pretty good. 'Course I didn't understand the city talk too much, but it seemed pretty realistic. I liked the characters."

Ryan seemed taken aback. "Uh, thanks, Dad. Didn't know you had read any of my books."

"Yep," Doug nodded. "Read 'em all. Liked the second one the best, I have to say."

The others smiled while listening to the exchange, knowing bits and pieces, and maybe filling in the blanks.

"I guess my point is," Doug looked more directly at Ryan, "I guess I realized finally that you have found your life and your passion in your writing and illustrating. It's clearly your way. This," and here he swung his arm wide to encompass the farm, "Was never your path."

"Nope," Ryan agreed, nodding his head in agreement. "You are right there. I tried and I tried when I was young, but I...hated this life."

Doug held up his hands in a gesture of surrender. "I know." Then he turned to Audrey. "And your gift is teaching, and dancing. I also read that article about you in the *Gazette* last spring about your tutoring work with the kids who have learning problems. Sounds like you know how to reach them," he smiled. "Probably could have used someone like you when I was a little tike in grade school. Never did like math and numbers."

Jeremy and Sophia were listening to this exchange and glancing back and forth.

Doug then turned to Jeremy. "Now you, young man," he smiled, "You can't get enough of getting the dirt under your fingernails, or riding that tractor. You show up here bright and early and don't seem tired at the end of a long farm day."

"No Sir, I'm not." Jeremy nodded. "I love watching things grow, and helping them along. And tinkering with the tractor or the combine is real fun."

"And you have a knack with growing things. There's no question. That's your passion," Doug added. "What do you think of this place?"

"Oh gosh, I love this farm." Jeremy said. "I never thought I'd love it this much, but it's amazing."

"And what about you, young lady?" Doug turned to Sophia. She reddened with the sudden attention.

"Me?" She stammered. "Why, I love riding here. It's perfect. And I can feel that others have ridden here before now. Oddly."

Doug smiled. "I am an old farmer, but I know exactly what you mean there, young lady. There are gentle spirits alive in these woods, and they welcome you. I know they do."

Doug nodded at Jeremy and Sophia. "You know, you two have brought this place alive again in a way that it hasn't been. I've been coasting along here for a while. Getting by, but I'd kind of lost my way. Especially after my wife and my oldest boy passed away, it was like the real life of this place had died too. Things were routine, but not enjoyable, or even really interesting. Having you two around has been a big boost to me and this place."

Doug then looked over to Ryan and Audrey, "And I love you kids," here he choked up a bit, "So much, and it kind of broke my heart when it was clear this wasn't the life for you. I'm sure I rode you two a little too hard, trying to force the farming life into you. But neither one of you took to it. Then you resented me, and left angry. I wondered if you'd come back at some point. But you have your own lives to live!"

"So now," Doug looked at Christy and Ben, "You two have got to help me out. I need to keep this place going as a working farm, with Jeremy staying on here, and a place for Sophia to board her horse as long as she wants, and maybe open up the barn to board other horses here too. But we have to figure out a way to do that."

"Plus you have to get me some additional capital! I mean," Here he gestured arms upraised, "Something more than 10% of what the big boys from Georgia are offering, please!"

Christy laughed. "So, if we can find the cash, we have a deal?"

Doug laughed as well. "I would think that's a big "if", but yes. So, how do we make sure about Jeremy, and Sophia, and the horses?"

Here Ben chimed in. "First of all we use the APR so it's permanently protected., which also raises the offer with the state monies. We could write covenants into the purchase agreement, pretty simple. We could write the sale for now, and you could continue to live here and farm, or we could write the sale for the future…The Board will have to see about the offer of purchase, though."

Christy turned to Ben. "Let's you and I talk for a moment, " and they walked away toward the cars parked in the driveway.

Brodi looked at the young people, "I think you two have helped Doug make his decision about what to do with his farm. Am I right, Doug?"

"Absolutely," Doug replied. "You two sparked my sense of responsibility and pride in this land. Like I said, I'd lost my way for a while. But this past summer has been like a breath of life for me. Energy is infectious. Interest is infectious. You two have brought both!"

Sophia and Jeremy looked at one another and smiled. Audrey walked over to them, and she hugged the two teens.

Christy and Ben had started back over to them.

Christy spoke, "Doug I think we have an offer you wouldn't be able to refuse."

Doug smiled. "I don't think you came up with that phrase."

Christy laughed. "You're right about that. And we'll need your lawyer anyway, since there will be paperwork."

So the decision was made that day. A decision seemingly made in a split second, just like that, but really the culmination of many seconds leading up to that moment. Moments like individual breaths. Each individual breath is only a simple in and out, a rising and falling of air entering the body, and leaving the body, beginning with a breathing in and ending with a breathing out. And yet, that one breath was connected to the breath before it, and the breath after it, that is all the way from the beginning, right up until the end. For Doug, this moment of decision had been like that. At some point in the past, at some moment, the inkling of the idea had started, and then the idea developed, and grew, and shaped, and formed. It had changed, and evolved. And then a decision was needed, and the moment to make that decision approached, and then it was here. In the end it all seemed so simple. It was the simplicity of making the right decision. It was preserving what was right, and true.

And with that ending came a new beginning.

Gratitude and Acknowledgements

First of all, this is a work of fiction based on my understanding of the complex process of farm succession. I am dramatizing some of the dynamics at play in such a transition; an actual farm succession transition is complex and unique in each instance. Any inaccuracies as to the actual process are in the author's understanding.

Thanks to Rebecca for supporting and encouraging my writing and publishing of this book, patiently and lovingly watching this process unfold over 10 years. You read the first draft and gave me tremendous editing feedback to support the next drafts. This would not be manifesting now if not for you.

My mother-in-law, Martha Nelson, and good friend, Rich Lapan, both published authors and writers, gave me encouragement and sound, well-considered advice to the unfolding writing process.

I want to thank my first editor, Amber Hatch, who dove into the third draft of this immense undertaking and helped craft the book you now hold in your hands. Amber's practiced eye brought this story to life.

Thanks to Carl Vigeland and Combray House Publishing for editing help, and getting the manuscript into this form so you, the reader, can read it.

As with many authors I have had a chorus of well-wishers and supporters standing beside me, eager to see the final product, and often expressing amazement that anyone would undertake such a venture. Special thanks to Daniel Pope and Ken LaBlond, who sat in circle with me discussing this work. So valuable! I send out a big thank you to my sisters Jean, Linda, and Liz, and brothers-in-law Bill, Tom and David. And my dear, dear friends Peter McSherry, Bob Jenne, and Rich Laffin also deserve credit for standing beside me through a long tunnel of verbal updates on the manuscript, editing, and publishing.

Thanks to the Kestrel Land Trust (kestreltrust.org) for giving me the opportunity to volunteer as a Land Steward in our beautiful Pioneer Valley, as well as to organize the Revive Outside Program, taking kids and families into the woods to explore wild nature. Kestrel Trust serves as a model of land stewardship, connecting people and the places they love. Our valley is the beautiful place it is in large part to Kestrel's work.

I want to acknowledge Land for Good (landforgood.org) a New

England-based organization, for allowing me to sit in on one succession planning webinar for farmers who are in the exact position that Doug Stengel finds himself. This is a real challenge facing so many farmers today, thinking how to help the farm continue into the future. Land for Good provides technical support, education and referral to help older farmers move toward retirement.

Thanks to Denise Barstow Manz of Barstow's Longview Farms in Hadley, Massachusetts in helping me see the farm transition process from the younger generation's perspective. And thanks to Susan Roitman, a volunteer with the Kestrel Trust, who kindly shared reminiscences of growing up on a local Massachusetts farm to bring some additional reality to this writing.

Of course, a shoutout to all the farmers who provide us with food on our tables! Your work with the land has inspired this writing. We wouldn't be here without you!

I acknowledge that some of the experiences in this book were informed by learning and praying with various teachers and healers with whom I have had the distinct honor of working. Many of these experiences were deep in the past, and so what is presented in this book is an inventive collage of those times. Deep gratitude to Michael Harner, Sandra Ingerman, Leslie Gray, Marilyn Youngbird, Richard Deertrack, the Coastal Ohlone native people of California, and others.

Made in United States
North Haven, CT
07 October 2025

80537256R00183